## About the Author

Long before embarking on romantic adventures of her own, **Julia Justiss** read about them, transporting herself to such favourite venues as ancient Egypt, World War II submarine patrols, the Old South and, of course, Regency England. Soon she was keeping notebooks for jotting down story ideas. When not writing or travelling, she enjoys watching movies, reading and puttering about in the garden trying to kill off more weeds than flowers.

# Regency Rogues

# Regency Rogues:

## Stolen Sins

JULIA JUSTISS

MILLS & BOON

First Published in Great Britain 2020
By Mills & Boon, an imprint of HarperCollins*Publishers*
1 London Bridge Street, London, SE1 9GF

REGENCY ROGUES: STOLEN SINS © 2020 Harlequin Books S.A.

*Forbidden Nights with the Viscount* © 2016 Janet Justiss
*Stolen Encounters with the Duchess* © 2016 Janet Justiss

ISBN: 978-0-263-27949-8

0120

**MIX**
Paper from
responsible sources
**FSC™ C007454**

This book is produced from independently certified FSC™ paper to ensure responsible forest management.

For more information visit: www.harpercollins.co.uk/green

Printed and bound in Spain
by CPI, Barcelona

# FORBIDDEN NIGHTS
# WITH THE
# VISCOUNT

To the Beau Monde group of RWA,
without whose historical expertise and
graciousness in sharing it, this book could
not have been written.

# *Prologue*

*London—late April, 1831*

'So your half-brother is getting married.'

At his best friend's comment, Giles Hadley, ostensible Viscount Lyndlington and Member of Parliament for Danford, looked up from the reports he was studying in the small private room of the Quill and Gavel, a public house near the Houses of Parliament. 'George?' Giles asked, not sure he'd heard correctly.

David Tanner Smith, Member from the Borough of Hazelwick, gave Giles a patient smile. 'Yes, George. Have you another half-brother?'

Stifling his first sharp reply—that he didn't care who or whether his irritating half-brother married—he said instead, 'What makes you think George is getting leg-shackled?'

'It all but says so in the *Morning Post*. "Lady M., daughter of the Marquess of W.," David read, "has been seen frequently of late in the company of the Earl of T.'s younger son, the Honourable G.H. The lady has wealth and impeccable connections, the gentleman aspirations to high office, even if he is not to inherit. Might this be a match made in political heaven?"'

'Lady Margaret, daughter of the Marquess of Witlow— if I'm correctly filling in the newspaper's discreet blanks— certainly possesses the credentials to make an ideal wife for any man wanting to dominate Tory circles,' Giles admitted. 'No wonder George is interested.'

'Indeed. With the marquess's wife in delicate health, Lady Margaret has played hostess for her father for years, ever since she lost her husband—Lord Roberts. Died in a carriage accident, tragically soon after their marriage.'

'Five or six years ago, wasn't it?' Giles asked, scanning through memory.

'Yes. Besides that, her brother doesn't care for politics. Which means the man who marries Lady Margaret will not only gain a wife with extensive political expertise, but also inherit all the power and influence the marquess would otherwise have expended on behalf of his son.'

'A shame she supports the wrong party,' Giles said. 'Not that *I've* any interest in marriage, of course.'

'A greater shame, if reports I've heard about the lady's charm and wit are true, to waste even someone from the wrong party on George.'

Just then, the door slammed open and two men hurried in. With a wave of his hand towards the stacks of paper on the table, the first, Christopher Lattimar, MP for Derbyshire, cried, 'Forget the committee reports, Giles! The session's going to be dissolved!'

'Truly, Christopher?' David interposed. Looking up at the last arrival, Benedict Tawny, MP for Launton, he asked, 'Is it certain, Ben?'

'For once, Christopher isn't joking,' Ben replied, his handsome face lit with excitement. 'Grey's tired of the Tories making endless delays. He's going to take the issue to the people. Which means a new election!'

'That's great news!' Giles cried. 'Sweep the Tories

out, and the Reform Bill will be sure to pass! Equal representation for every district, a vote for every freeholder, an end to domination by the landed class—everything we've dreamed of since Oxford!'

'An end to rotten boroughs, for sure,' David said. 'I doubt we'll get the rest—yet. Though I'm not sure why, as a future earl, the rest is so important to you, Giles. To any of you, really. I'm the only one here not of the "landed class".'

'You're the son of a farmer—which makes you "landed" by occupation,' Christopher said with a grin.

'My late father's occupation, not mine,' David replied. 'I'd be lucky to tell a beet seed from a turnip.'

'Whether we get the reforms all at once or by stages, it's still a landmark day—which calls for a toast!' Ben said. Stepping to the door, he called out, 'Mr Ransen, a round of ale for the group, if you please.'

'Did you truly believe, when we sat around in that dingy little tavern in Oxford recasting the future, that we would ever see this day?' David asked, shaking his head with the wonder of it. 'Our views certainly weren't very popular then.'

'Neither were we, except with the inn's doxies. What a mismatched set!' Christopher laughed. 'Me, ostensibly the son of a baron, but really the offspring of one of Mother's lovers, as the snide were ever fond of remarking. Giles, ostensibly heir to an earldom, but estranged from his father, with the favoured half-brother dogging his heels, practically panting with eagerness to step into his shoes.'

'And making it clear to our classmates that, should he attain that earldom, he'd not forgive or forget anyone who befriended me,' Giles added, suppressing the bitterness that always simmered beneath the surface.

'Then there was me, illegitimate son of a lowly governess,' Ben chimed in. 'The snide never tired of recalling that fact, either.'

'But all still gentry born,' Davie said. 'Unlike this true commoner. It's selfish, I know, but I'm glad you three never quite fit in with your peers. I can't imagine how lonely Oxford would have been otherwise.'

'You wouldn't have been lonely,' Christopher replied. 'You're too clever. You always knew the answers, no matter the subject or the don. Who else could have coached us so well?'

Before his friend could reply, the innkeeper walked in with their ale. Claiming glasses, the four friends raised their mugs.

'To Giles, our impatient leader; to Davie, our philosophical guide; to our rabble-rouser, Ben; and to the final accomplishment of our dreams,' Christopher said. 'To the Hellions!'

'To the Hellions!' the others repeated, and clinked their mugs.

While the others drank, Davie turned to Giles. 'A new election means new strategy. Will you campaign?'

'I'll make a run through the district,' Giles said, 'but my seat's secure. I'll probably go canvass in some of the boroughs we're still contesting. Maybe we can pry more of them out of the hands of the local landowners.' He grinned. 'Maybe we can even steal some away from the father of the oh-so-accomplished Lady Margaret.'

Davie laughed. 'I hear his seats are pretty secure. But by all means, give it a try.'

Giles downed the last of his ale. 'I just might.'

## Chapter One

A month later, from her seat in the open carriage in front of the hustings in the market town of Chellingham, Lady Margaret Roberts smiled out at the crowd. 'You will all turn out for the election tomorrow, won't you? I'd be most grateful if you'd vote for my cousin, Mr Armsburn! I assure you, he will do his very best to serve your interests in Parliament.'

'If he promises to send you back every time he needs a vote, it's his!' one of the men next to the carriage declared.

'Aye, and mine, too, for such a pretty smile,' the man beside him shouted.

'Thank you, gentleman,' she replied, blowing each of them a kiss. The crowd's roar of approval made her laugh and blow another.

Ah, how she loved this! The excitement of the milling crowds, the rising anticipation on election day as the votes were given, knowing that the winner would take his place in Parliament and help forge the destiny of the nation. The thought that she might in some small way have a part in the making of history was a thrill that never faded.

Since the bitter pain of losing her husband Robbie, resuming the role of her father's hostess and political assistant had been her chief pleasure in life, the only pursuit that distracted her from grief.

The love of her life might be gone, but there was still important work to do. Or at least, she told herself so in the loneliness of her solitary bed.

Pulling herself from her reverie, she looked up—and met a gaze so arresting she instinctively sucked in a breath. Deep-blue eyes—like lapis sparkling in moonlight, she thought disjointedly—held her mesmerised, the pull so strong she felt as if she were being drawn physically closer to him.

And then she realised they *were* closer. The owner of those magnificent eyes was making his way through the crowd towards her carriage. At the realisation, her heartbeat accelerated and a shock of anticipation sizzled along her nerves.

Those fascinating eyes, she noted as he slowly approached, were set in a strong, lean face with a purposeful nose, sharp chin and wide brow over which curled a luxuriant thatch of blue-black hair. The gentleman was tall enough that his broad shoulders, clad in a jacket of Melton green, remained visible as he forced his way through the crowd.

Just as he drew near enough for her to note the sensual fullness of his lips, he gave her a knowing smile, sending a shiver of sensation over her skin.

How could he make her feel so naked while she was still fully clothed?

And then he was before her, smiling still as he extended his hand.

'How could I not wish to shake the hand of so lovely a lady?' he asked, his deep voice vibrating in her ears like a caress. And though she normally drew back from physical contact when there were so many pressing close, she found herself offering her hand.

His grip was as strong and assured as she'd known it would be. Waves of sensation danced up her arm as he clasped her fingers, and for a moment, she could hardly breathe. If she were given to melodrama, she might have swooned.

Taking a deep breath, she shook her head, trying to recover her equilibrium. 'I hope you will be equally amicable about according your vote to Mr Armsburn?' she asked, pleased her voice held a calm she was far from feeling.

His smile faded. 'I hate to disoblige a lady, but I'm afraid I'm here to support Mr Reynolds.'

'The radical Mr Reynolds? Oh, dear!' she exclaimed, her disappointment greater than it should have been. 'I fear our politics will not be in agreement, then, Mr—'

Before the gentleman could answer, a tide of men washed out of the tavern across the street. 'Free beer, free men, free vote!' they chanted, pushing into the square. From the corner, a group of men wearing the green armbands of her cousin's supporters surged forward. 'Tories for justice!' they cried, shoving against the free-vote supporters. Several of the tussling men fell back against her horse, causing the gelding to rear up and fight the traces. Alarmed, she tugged on the reins, but the panicked animal fought the bit.

The gentleman jumped forward to seize the bridle, settling the nervous horse back on his feet. 'You should get away in case this turns ugly,' he advised. Making liberal use of his cane to clear a path, he led the horse and carriage through the throng and on to a side street.

'There's a quiet inn down Farmer's Lane,' he told her

when they'd turned the corner. 'I'll see you safely there, then locate your cousin.'

She opened her lips to assure him she'd be fine on her own, but in truth, the sudden rancour of the crowd, the shouts and sounds of scuffling still reaching them from the square, disturbed her more than she wished to admit. 'I would appreciate that,' she said instead.

Within a few moments, they reached the inn, the gentlemen sent the horse and carriage off with an ostler and offered her his arm into the establishment. 'A private parlour for Lady Margaret, and some cheese and ale,' he told the innkeeper who hurried to greet them.

'At once, sir, my lady!' the proprietor said, ushering them to a small room off the busy taproom.

Once she was inside, shielded from the view of the curious, the gentleman bowed. 'It is Lady Margaret, isn't it?'

'Yes. But I don't believe we have been introduced, have we? I'm sure I would have remembered you.' No woman under ninety with eyes in her head and any sense of appreciation for the male of the species could have met this man and forgotten him.

'We've not been formally presented—a lapse I am delighted to rectify. But the Borough of Chellingham has long been in the pocket of the Marquess of Witlow, so what other lovely lady could be canvassing for his candidate than his daughter, the celebrated Lady Margaret?'

'Oh, dear! That makes me sound rather…notorious.'

He shook his head. 'Admired and respected—even by your opponents. I don't believe the squabbles outside will escalate into actual violence, but with "free beer" and elections, one can't be sure. Promise me you'll remain here until your cousin can fetch you. Though I cannot help but feel a man lucky to have so lovely a canvasser working on his behalf should take better care of her.'

'How can I thank you for your kindness—and to a supporter of your opponent?' she asked. 'Won't you at least allow me to offer you a glass of ale? I hate to admit it, but I would feel easier if I had some company while I…calm my nerves.'

That might have been overstating the case—but for once, Maggie didn't mind imposing on the gentleman's obvious sense of chivalry, if it meant she could command his company for a bit longer.

And discover more about the most arresting man she'd met in a very long time.

He smiled then—setting those sapphire eyes sparkling, and once again sending shivers over her skin. 'I wouldn't want to leave you…unsettled.'

Oh, the rogue! She bit back a laugh, halfway tempted to rebuke him. Those knowing eyes said he knew exactly how he 'unsettled her' and didn't regret it a bit.

With that handsome figure, fascinating eyes and seductive smile, he'd probably unsettled quite a few ladies, her sense of self-preservation argued. It would be prudent to send him on his way before he tempted her to join their number.

After all, she'd had a lengthy page from that book, and wanted never to pen another.

But despite the voice of reason, she didn't want to let him go.

The landlord hurried in with her victuals on a tray, offering her a perfect excuse to delay. 'You will allow the innkeeper to bring you a tankard of his excellent home brewed? Mr Carlson, isn't it?' she asked, turning to the proprietor. 'My cousin, Mr Armsburn, told me you have the best ale in Chellingford. I know he's drunk many a pint when coming through to campaign.'

'That he has, Lady Margaret, and bought rounds for

the taproom, too,' Carlson replied. 'I'm happy to stand a mug to any of his supporters.' After giving them a quick bow, he hurried back out.

'Now, that is largesse you cannot refuse,' she told her rescuer.

'Even if I'm accepting it under false pretences?'

'We needn't upset Mr Carlson by telling him that. He's been a Tory voter for many years.'

'No wonder you charm the electorate—if you know even the names of the local innkeepers.'

She raised an eyebrow. 'Of course I know them. One cannot represent the best interests of the district unless one knows the people who live there, and their needs. But you have the advantage; you know who I am, but have not yet given me your name. All I know is that you're misguided enough to support a Radical.'

He laughed, as she'd meant he should, and made her an exaggerated bow. 'Giles Hadley, ma'am, at your service.'

The note of challenge in his tone puzzled her for the few seconds it took for the name to register. 'Giles Hadley!' she repeated with a gasp. 'The leader of the Hellions, the infamous Viscount Lyndlington—although you do not use the title, do you? Should I be expecting a whiff of fire and brimstone?'

He laughed again. 'Rumours of our exploits have been highly exaggerated! I doubt we were any more given to frequenting taverns and consorting with the, um, gentle ladies who worked there than most undergraduates. We just patronised a humbler class of establishment, and consulted, rather than patronised, the patrons.'

'So what was this about being hell-bound?'

He shrugged. 'One of the dons who was a clergyman heard that, if we ever had the power, we would eliminate churchmen's seats in the Lords. The sacrilege of wanting to upset the established order, along with our "dissolute" activities, led him to denounce us all as the Devil's minions. As for my title as a viscount, it's only a courtesy accorded to the son of an earl. I prefer to be known for what *I've* accomplished.'

'Which is quite a bit, I understand! I've heard so much about you!'

'If you heard it from my half-brother George, no wonder you've been imagining me with wings and a forked tail,' he said drily.

She shook her head. 'Most of what I know comes from my father and his associates—who see you as a rising star in the Whigs. My father, who does not praise lightly, has several times lamented that Lord Newville managed to snag you for the Reform cause before he could persuade you to join the Tories. I am honoured to make the acquaintance of a man so esteemed by my father!'

And she was—awed enough at meeting the man even his opponents spoke of as likely one day to become Prime Minister that for an instant, she forgot his physical allure.

But only for an instant. With her next breath, the shock of learning his identity was once again subsumed in awareness of the powerful attraction he generated.

What a combination! she thought dazedly. That intense masculine appeal embodied in a man pursuing a career she admired above all others. And despite what he'd said, there was something of the wicked about him.

Rather than preening a bit at her obvious admiration, though, as most men world, he seemed somewhat discomforted—an unexpected display of modesty that only enhanced his charm.

She barely suppressed a sigh, immobilised by eyes that seemed to look deep into her soul.

'Thank you for the compliments, though I'm sure I

do not deserve them,' he said after a moment, as if only then realising that they'd spent the last several minutes just gazing at each other. 'And forgive me for speaking slightingly of George. From the article I read recently in the *Morning Post*, it appears I should wish you happy?'

'Wish me happy?' she echoed. As his meaning grew clear, irritation flashed through her. 'Certainly not! As a member of my father's Tory caucus, I see Mr Hadley quite often, but there's no understanding between us. Newspapers!' She shook her head impatiently. 'The gossips have been pairing me off ever since I came out of mourning.'

'So you are not about to bestow your hand on my half-brother?' At her negative shake of the head, he smiled again—that brilliant smile that made her stomach do little flips and curled her toes in her half-boots. 'I have to admit, I am glad to hear it.'

No female he smiled at like that would ever look at his half-brother. Dazzled, she said without thinking, 'George Hadley isn't looking for a wife, but someone to reflect his glory, and I make a very poor mirror.'

Not until those honest but appallingly indiscreet words exited her lips did she realise how much Giles Hadley had unsettled her. She seldom voiced unflattering assessments of her acquaintances, and never to a stranger.

Flushing with mortification, she said, 'Pray, excuse me! That was most unkind, and I should never have said it.'

'Even if you know it to be true?'

'Whether or not it is true is irrelevant,' she shot back, flustered. 'I am not generally so critical. Or at least, I seldom utter such criticisms aloud,' she amended more truthfully.

'Then I am all the more honoured by your honesty.

And relieved, I must say. Women usually find George charming.'

'Truly?' She frowned, replaying in her mind's eye a typical exchange with the man. 'Perhaps with ladies he *wishes* to charm. When we converse, he always seems to be looking towards my father, as if he's much more interested in Papa's approval than in mine.' She made a wry grimace. 'Makes me feel rather like a prize pullet he's bartering to install in his hen house. And I should not have said that, either.'

Hadley laughed. 'If that's true, he's even more a fool than I thought—and *I* should not have said *that*! But there's bad blood between us, as I imagine you know.

'So I understand. I always find it sad when there is a dissension within a family.'

A bit more than dissension—there'd been a scandal of rather large proportions, she knew, although she'd heard none of the particulars. Hardly to her surprise, he did not attempt to enlighten her.

Before she could introduce some safer topic, her cousin's aide, John Proctor, rushed into the room. 'Lady Margaret, are you all right?' he cried. 'Armsburn and I have been looking everywhere for you! When I heard about the ruckus on the square, and then couldn't find you...' He exhaled a shuddering breath. 'I knew Michael would have my head for leaving you on your own, had you been harmed or even frightened! Please, forgive me!'

'Nothing to forgive,' she replied. Except his arrival, which would doubtless mean an end to her interlude with this fascinating gentleman. 'Mr Hadley took good care of me.'

The two men exchanged bows. 'Hadley, we are much in your debt for safeguarding Lady Margaret,' Proctor said.

'It was my pleasure,' Hadley replied. 'I'd advise you to take better care of your lovely canvasser in future, though. If I find her wandering unattended again, I might just keep her.'

His words, and the beguiling smile he directed at her as he said them, sent a little zing of pleasure through her. Empty gallantry, she told herself, trying to fight the effect.

Before she could try to determine how genuine the compliment might be, Proctor took her arm and all but tugged her out of her chair. 'Can I escort you back now, Lady Margaret? Your cousin is most anxious.'

'I wouldn't wish to worry Michael, of course.' With regret, she turned to her rescuer. 'I very much enjoyed our conversation, Mr Hadley. Despite holding opposing views, I hope we may continue it at some time in future.'

'You could not desire it more fervently than I! Good day, Lady Margaret,' Hadley said, and bowed over her hand.

As his fingers clasped hers, her heart fluttered and a flush of heat went through her. It took her a moment to remember to pull free from his grasp.

'Good day to you, Mr Hadley,' she said faintly, acutely conscious of his gaze on her as she walked out.

She *would* like to meet him again, she thought as her cousin's aide escorted her through the taproom. Though it would be better if she did not. She cringed inwardly as she recalled the unguarded words she'd let slip about his half-brother. A man mesmerising enough to cause her to suspend all of her breeding and most of her common sense was best avoided.

But oh, how he stirred her mind and excited her senses!

'I hope you weren't too friendly with Hadley,' Proctor said after he'd helped her into the carriage.

'Since when do I become "friendly" with men I hardly know, John?' she replied sharply.

Proctor held up a restraining hand. 'Please don't be offended, Lady Margaret! I know it's not my place to question your behaviour. But Michael—and your father—trust me to watch out for you. I'd have you steer clear of Hadley. He's a dangerous man.'

'Dangerous—how? Surely you don't believe all that nonsense about the Hellions! My father told me he admires him.'

'His own half-brother refuses to associate with him, and he's completely estranged from his father. His views are extreme, even for a Radical: he'd give the vote to every man in England, from the highest lord down to a common stew from the London slums. I've heard he even favours abolishing the House of Lords entirely!'

'Shocking, certainly,' she allowed, unsettled to have the radical nature of his positions confirmed—if what Proctor said was true. 'But Papa has always favoured an open exchange of views, even if the two parties cannot ultimately agree. I doubt I could be endangered just by talking with him.'

'Perhaps. But a man with such extreme political views might have equally radical social ideas—advocating Free Love and the abolishment of marriage, perhaps. I wouldn't trust a lady in his company, certainly not alone in a private room.'

Did Hadley believe in Free Love? No wonder he seemed wicked! The naughty idea sent a spark through her still-simmering senses. Oh, she could readily imagine making free with him!

She shook her head to rid her mind of the lusty—and pointless—thought. She had nothing more erotic in mind for her future than directing Papa's dinners—and perhaps throwing a kiss to a voter.

Turning back to Proctor, she said, 'At a busy inn, with the door to the taproom standing open? Hardly a convenient site to lure someone into impropriety. Although I wouldn't mind debating Free Love and the abolishment of marriage with him,' she added, watching Proctor's face.

At his look of horror, she laughed. 'Relax, John, I'm teasing! Though it serves you right, trying to lecture a woman of my age about her behaviour. How did the canvassing go? Does Michael think he'll hold against Reynolds?'

It took only that bit of encouragement to launch Proctor into a detailed explanation of how the campaign had fared in the rest of the town.

Normally, Maggie would have listened with rapt attention. Today, however, her mind kept drifting back to a certain gentleman with vivid blue eyes and a seductive smile that had made her feel more like a desirable woman than she had since…since the debacle with Sir Francis.

That memory ought to apply a fast brake to this runaway carriage of attraction. Recalling Hadley's flowery last words, she frowned.

Of course it had been gallantry. What else could it have been? They'd barely met, after all. And handsome as he was, he surely was accomplished in the fine art of flattery, and of persuading women who should know better that he found them more desirable than he did.

She sighed. It seemed she was a slow learner.

And yet… She had not imagined the spark that flared before them. She might have little experience, but she could still remember that enchanted time, when love for her childhood companion Robbie had transformed into something more, a layer of desire enveloping the friendship and tenderness. Ah, the mesmerising beauty of touch, the thrill of surrendering to passion, the ecstasy of possession.

How she ached for its loss!

No, she was not imagining the physical response she'd felt. But did Hadley truly find her desirable? Since an affair was too dangerous to contemplate, was there any point in pursuing this further?

Common sense warned to avoid a man who might prove such a temptation. But surely life was meant to be *experienced*, not hemmed in by caution. Such pleasures as it presented should be grasped greedily, before they were snatched away—losing Robbie had taught her that, too.

She was seven-and-twenty, a widow unwilling to risk her heart by marrying again, and she might not have many more opportunities to be tempted.

His seductive person aside, Hadley was a fascinating man, with views and values she would be interested to debate. From the not-so-flattering words his half-brother had dropped about him, she'd expected he might be something of a wild man, and he did have an untamed essence about him. An aura of purpose, too, with a trace of impatience, as if he were in a great hurry to do important things. And there was more than a trace of anger smouldering under the surface, particularly when he mentioned his half-brother.

Or was that just the passion that seemed to simmer in him? Recalling it sent a response swirling through her, and suddenly the carriage seemed too hot.

Yes, she would see more of him, she decided. He addressed the Commons frequently, her father said. Popular as he was, there was no question that he would be re-elected to the next Parliament. If she visited the Ladies'

Gallery after the sessions began again in June, she would surely hear him speak.

Before she heard more of his politics, though, she ought to learn more about the man. If he truly were dangerous, it would be best to know beforehand just how much of a risk he might pose.

But who to ask? Papa, who abhorred gossip, would be unlikely to tell her more than the bare minimum about Hadley's background.

Then she recalled just the person who would happily spill every detail she might want to know. As soon as she returned to London, she decided, she would pay a call on her great-aunt Lilly.

Lounging in his chair, Giles took his time finishing the home brew, which was as excellent as advertised. So he'd met the renowned Lady Margaret—and found her as witty and even more attractive than Davie had pronounced her.

He had to admit, he'd hoped to see her. When the four friends had drawn up that list of the boroughs to canvass, he'd chosen this one because it was known to be controlled by her father—and she was known to often canvass on behalf of his candidates. After the discussion of the possibility that she might marry George, and Davie's description of her, he'd been curious to meet the woman.

As he'd approached her carriage, he'd been impressed by her engaging smile and the ease with which she mingled with the crowd, by her obvious enjoyment of bantering with them and their enthusiastic response to her.

And then he'd caught her eye.

He shook his head, bemused. Some curious sort of energy had flashed between them, literally stopping him short. Despite the press of people, the babble of voices, the stamping of hoofs and rattle of passing carriages, he'd had the ridiculous feeling that nothing existed in the world but the two of them.

He didn't remember walking closer, but suddenly he was beside her, unable to keep himself from smiling, compelled to touch her—even if all that was permissible was for him to shake her hand.

He hardly recalled what he'd said to her during their interlude at the inn, and could only hope it hadn't been utter nonsense. He remembered only two salient points from their conversation: her father approved of him and she wasn't going to marry George.

The relief he felt about the latter was surely excessive.

He couldn't recall ever feeling such a powerful and immediate connection to a lady—and had no explanation to account for it. She wasn't a beauty in the traditional sense. Her hair was chestnut, not gold, her figure rather taller than average, her face longer than oval, with a generous mouth and pert nose decorated with freckles. But something in those vivid green eyes had sparked a physical attraction that went straight to his loins and drew him to her like a thirsty man to a cool, clear stream.

Though he was too bitterly conscious of his mother's fate ever to become a rake, he was hardly inexperienced, having enjoyed his share of discreet liaisons, always careful to take precautions to protect the lady. He wasn't some green lad just out of university, susceptible to being bowled over by an attractive woman.

In sum, he couldn't figure out what it was about Lady Margaret that had struck him so profoundly.

He did know he would seek her out again, if only to see if his unprecedented reaction would recur a second time. Or whether upon further acquaintance her attractions would seem no more remarkable than those of any other pretty, intelligent lady.

He paused a moment, frowning. Although Lady Margaret had emphatically disclaimed a relationship, if the newspapers had been puffing off a possible match between her and George, they must have been given some encouragement for the notion—very possibly from his half-brother. Marrying into an important political family would be just the sort of thing George would see as a prudent step towards the career as a government leader he coveted.

*The prize pullet he's bartering to install in his hen house.* Giles recalled her words with a chuckle. She certainly deserved better than that.

If associating with a woman George might have marked as his own caused problems with his half-brother, so be it. Pursuing this fascinating lady would depend on his—and her—inclinations alone.

## Chapter Two

A week later, the butler ushered Lady Margaret into the front parlour of the Grosvenor Square town house of her great-aunt, the Dowager Countess of Sayleford. 'I've ordered a full pot of tea and a plate of biscuits to sustain us,' her great-aunt declared after receiving her kiss on the cheek. 'Make yourself comfortable, and tell me all about the campaign in Chellingham.'

As her great-aunt knew well, her preferred topic of conversation would normally be the elections. Though Maggie was fairly bursting with curiosity about Giles Hadley, she didn't want to open herself to the questions— to which she didn't have answers—Aunt Lilly would certainly fire at her if she delayed discussing politics to make enquiries about a gentleman.

So, though she had shockingly little interest in conveying the results in Chellingham, she dutifully gave a brief recitation of what had happened in the campaign.

'Glad to hear Armsburn held the seat,' her great-aunt said. 'My sources with an ear to Parliament tell me that one of the Grey's government's primary aims will be to eliminate boroughs like Chellingham that are controlled by the local landowner.'

'Yes, and I'm afraid it's virtually certain a bill to that effect will pass. I found the county full of inflammatory rhetoric! Even in normally placid Chellingham, there was alarming…disruption.'

'Disruption?' her great-aunt repeated, frowning. 'What do you mean? Surely you weren't endangered!'

'No, not really. Oh, there was a scuffle in the street next to my carriage between two rival parties, some of whom had imbibed more ale than was good for them,' she admitted. 'In any event, I was quickly rescued by a most charming gentleman.'

Her great-aunt's frown deepened. 'Where were Michael and Proctor? I would have expected them to rescue you, if rescuing were needful.'

'They were at another gathering place when the incident happened.'

'Your father will not be happy to hear that.'

'No, but there was no harm done, so you mustn't tell him.'

Her great-aunt eyed her for a long moment before finally nodding. 'Very well, it that's what you wish. So, who was this "charming gentleman" who protected you when your kin failed in their duty?'

'Another Member of Parliament—from the opposition, actually.' Trying to keep her tone as neutral as possible, she said, 'Mr Giles Hadley.'

Her great-aunt's eyes widened. 'Giles Hadley—you mean Viscount Lyndlington?'

At her nod of assent, her great-aunt continued, 'Oh, my! Charming, you say? To hear some of the rabid Tories tell it, he's the devil incarnate!'

'His half-brother often paints him in that light. But Papa admires him, and I give far more credit to his opinion. It did make me curious, though—the difference between Papa's view of him and his brother's, and I do wonder what happened to create such a breach in the family. I'm sure Papa knows, but I didn't think he would tell me much.' She grinned at her great-aunt. 'Whereas, I knew *you* would tell me everything!'

'What did you think of Hadley?' came the unexpected response.

Caught off guard, to her irritation, she found herself flushing. 'I suppose it's obvious I found him attractive.'

Her great-aunt raised her eyebrows, a mischievous twinkle in her eye. 'Since I cannot remember you ever enquiring about any other gentleman, I'd already assumed as much. Excellent! It *has* been six years since you lost Robbie. More than time enough for you to be moving on.'

'Don't be thinking that, Aunt Lilly!' she protested, raising a hand. 'I'm not angling for another husband!'

'Why not? You're still young, and attractive, and it's more than time enough for you to be over your disappointment about Sir Francis. And your grief.'

Once, she'd hoped Sir Francis might help her bury the grief—and look how disastrously *that* had ended. Both episodes being still too painful for her to discuss, she ignored the question, saying instead, 'I found Giles Hadley… fascinating, that's all. Those compelling blue eyes seem to look deep within you. There's a restless energy about him, a sense of anger lurking beneath the surface, to say nothing of what I understand are quite radical political views. He's certainly different from any other gentleman I've known! And yes, he does…attract me. But I'm not about to do anything foolish.'

Her great-aunt looked at her speculatively. 'You are a widow now. I don't advocate foolishness, but with discretion, you can do what you want—marriage, or not.'

'All I want right now is to know more about his circumstances. It's rather obvious that his half-brother hates him. Not that I've discussed him with George, but whenever the opposition is brought up, he never loses the opportunity to get in a dig about his half-sibling. I suspect much of his spleen stems from knowing the viscount will inherit, even though George is the brother favoured by their father. But why, Aunt Lilly? What happened to fracture the family?'

'It's an old and quite interesting scandal.'

'About which, I am sure, you know all the details.'

'Naturally.' Her great-aunt smiled. 'What other benefit is there in having lived so long in the midst of society?'

'So—what happened?'

'It began many years ago, just after the current earl inherited. He and his best friend courted the same woman—Giles Hadley's mother. She loved the friend, not the young earl, but the friend was a younger son with no title or income, and Randall Hadley, already Lord Telbridge, would have both. The friend intended to go to India and make his fortune, but the girl's family, which was in dire financial straits, wouldn't let her wait on the possibility that he might one day return a nabob. Understandable, really; he might just as well die of a fever, or be killed in one of the native wars. They pressured her into agreeing to marry Telbridge, which she did ten days after the friend left for India.'

'Poor lady,' Maggie said, thinking of how awful it would have been if family duty had forced her to marry someone other than Robbie. 'And then?'

'All was well until several years after the wedding, when Telbridge somehow learned that his wife and the friend had stayed alone together at a hunting cottage the night before he left for India. Pressed by the earl, his wife would not deny that they had been lovers—and that she could not therefore assure the earl with perfect certitude that the son she bore him nine months after the wedding was in fact his. Wild with jealousy and anger, he sent them both away. Deaf to any pleas of reason, he divorced her and cut off all support—funds, lodging, even schooling for the boy. He remarried soon after the divorce bill was passed by the Lords, and has since devoted all his wealth and affection to the son of his second wife. As far as I know, Telbridge has not set eyes on the viscount in years. But all the rancour in the world will not alter the fact that since Giles Hadley was born after Telbridge married his mother, and was acknowledged for several years as the earl's son, under law, he will inherit, for all that Telbridge now shuns him.'

Maggie shook her head. 'Poor boy! No wonder he refuses to use his courtesy title. But from what you say, he grew up with no resources at all. I would expect him to be a simpleton or a savage, but he seems quite cultured. Did his mother's family step in to help?'

The dowager smiled thinly. 'Though admittedly, the scandal of the divorce placed them in an awkward position, I've always held that blood should care for blood. The girl's parents, however—doubtless with a glance over their shoulder at the financial boon the earl had provided them upon the marriage—disowned her. The boy might have grown up a savage, but for the intervention some years later by his aunt who, once she married, persuaded her husband to sponsor the boy and raise him as befitted his station.'

'Lord Newville?' she asked. 'Papa told me he had taken Mr Hadley under his wing.'

'Quite. The Newvilles took care of mother and son, financed Hadley's schooling, and sponsored his candidacy into Parliament. After what he suffered at his father's hands, it's not surprising he turned into a Radical, committed to limiting the power of the aristocracy.'

'What happened to the lady?'

'By all accounts, she was content, living in rural isolation with her son. I expect she hoped that one day the man she loved would return for her. But as it turned out, her family was right about that, if little else. He died in India several years after her divorce, and she did not long outlive him.'

'Now that his eldest son has made such a name for himself, and knowing he will one day inherit, isn't it time for Telbridge to make peace with his heir?'

The dowager shook her head. 'Randall Hadley was always a proud, unyielding man. I think it was more the satisfaction of winning the woman away from his friend, rather than affection for the lady, that led the earl to wed her in the first place, and he couldn't tolerate the idea that his wife had been touched by another. It's only thanks to the good sense of Hadley's aunt that the successor to the earldom won't be a complete Hottentot.'

'So there isn't much chance of father and son reconciling?'

'I wouldn't wager on it,' the dowager said. 'The earl is too stubborn; his second son, from what I hear, is so jealous and resentful of the heir he takes every opportunity to speak ill of him to his father. As for the viscount, he will inherit whether they reconcile or not. I would expect he has little desire to approach a man who left him and his mother destitute. Certainly, Telbridge has done nothing in the years since to prompt his son—if the viscount *is* his son—to seek a reconciliation.'

'Perhaps,' Maggie said with a sigh. 'But it is still sad.'

'Family squabbles are as old as time. Read your Bible,' the dowager advised.

'That doesn't make them less regrettable.'

'Indeed. However, if you do intend to…pursue an acquaintance with Giles Hadley, I would do so cautiously.'

'Why do you say that? Surely you don't think he's "dangerous", as John Proctor warned! Even if he should subscribe to Godwin's theories on abolishing marriage, I cannot see him forcibly seducing a woman.' She laughed ruefully. 'He wouldn't need to.'

'I've heard nothing of that—rather the opposite, actually. His *amours* have been few, and the ladies involved were treated with great courtesy. No, it's just that I'd not like to see a lovers' triangle descend to the second generation.'

'Lovers' triangle?' Her puzzlement gave way to irritation as she made the connection. 'That *Morning Post* article again! Surely you don't give any credence to newspaper gossip. I have no interest in wedding George Hadley, no matter how much he sidles up to Papa!'

'Though the writers do expend an inordinate amount of ink speculating about their betters, there is always some thread of truth in the reports. Perhaps George Hadley thinks he's "sidled up" to your father successfully enough that he's in a fair way to winning your hand. It would be an excellent match for him.'

'Well, it wouldn't be an excellent one for me,' Maggie retorted with some heat. 'I don't like the man, and I'm not so committed to the Tories that I would marry someone for their political advantage. Nor would Papa try to persuade me, no matter how much George Hadley tries to turn him up sweet.'

'Yes, but that's not the problem,' the countess continued patiently. 'Don't you see? There is no love lost between the brothers. Isn't it possible that, having read the newspaper reports as the rest of us have, Giles Hadley might seek you out, just to put a spoke in the wheel of his half-brother's plans? Now, I'm not saying Hadley turned up in Armsburn's borough with that in mind. Most likely he was in Chellingham for political reasons of his own, met you by chance, and admires you sincerely—why ever should he not? Given the history between the two, though, I would be cautious.'

For a moment, the thought that Giles Hadley might have approached her with the intent of beguiling her so he could crow to his brother about his conquest made her feel sick. That scenario was too reminiscent of the debacle with Sir Francis.

But an instant later, a deep conviction rose up to refute that scenario. Regardless of his reasons for coming to Chellingham, the attraction between them had been genuine—she was sure of that. Whether or not he would pursue the connection because of his brother's interest in her, or in spite of it, she didn't know, but the spark lit between them had not been the product of her imagination.

What she chose to do about it, now that she knew his full background, was still up to her. She was no more interested in becoming the bone of contention snapped over by two pugnacious half-brothers than she was in becoming George Hadley's prize pullet.

And she definitely didn't intend to risk falling in love.

'I will be cautious,' she promised the dowager as she finished her tea and set the cup back on the tray. 'That's why I came to talk to you, Aunt Lilly. You always give such excellent advice.'

'Advice is about all one has to give at my age,' her great-aunt said tartly. 'I'll let you go with one last bit: don't let anyone worry you into marrying again, unless you truly wish it. I had several offers after Creighton died, but none could hold a candle to him, and I wouldn't settle for a lesser man.'

'That's how I feel about my Robbie,' Maggie said, her eyes sheening.

'Not that I didn't amuse myself from time to time,' her great-aunt added.

'Aunt Lilly!' Margaret laughed. 'You'll make me blush.'

'As if I could, with all you must overhear, spending so much time around gentlemen! But I worry about you, child. You were inconsolable after losing your husband, and then when it seemed you'd found happiness again, the affair with Sir Francis ended so badly. I would so like to see you passionate about life again.'

'I enjoy my work with Papa.'

'I'd have you not just "enjoy" life, but be truly thrilled by it—illumined from within! You know what I mean— I can see it in your eyes. If Giles Hadley offers you the possibility of tasting such joy again, don't let the dull voice of prudence prevent you from furthering the acquaintance. After all, you cannot find what you won't risk looking for. Just keep in mind the possible complications.

'And I intend to end this homily with a recommendation about marriage, and you may as well not protest,' her great-aunt continued, holding up a hand to forestall any objection. 'Much as I would oppose you being pushed into marriage, neither would I like you to miss out on the blessing of children. A thought to consider, while you're still young enough to have them.'

Maggie worked hard not to flinch. That was a fact of which she was too bitterly aware.

Masking her discomfort from her perceptive great-aunt by rising, she said, 'I must get back. I've not been home yet, and Papa has a large party coming for dinner tomorrow night for which I haven't even begun to prepare. He'll want a complete account of the Chellingham elections, too. Thank you for tea—and your counsel, Aunt Lilly.'

'You are always welcome to both.'

As Maggie bent to kiss the dowager's cheek, her great-aunt reached out to pat hers. 'I pray for your happiness, child.'

Maggie felt the burn of tears and blinked them away. 'Thank you, Aunt Lilly. If something exciting should happen, you'll be the first to know.'

Her great-aunt chuckled. 'With my contacts, I certainly will—whether you tell me yourself or not!'

During the drive from her great-aunt's town house back to her father's in Cavendish Square, Maggie replayed their interview over and over. After hearing Giles Hadley's story, she was more fascinated by the man than ever. How had he reconciled the rural isolation of his early years with rejoining the world of the *ton* when his aunt had come to rescue him? Did he remember anything of the days he'd lived at his father's grand estate in Hampshire?

Despite his education and upbringing, if he knew nothing of that estate or its people, how could he become a good landlord to his tenants and a proper steward of the land entrusted to him, once he inherited? Or would he remain in London, furthering his career in Parliament, content to let some estate agent or secretary manage his acres and tend its people? What a tragedy for them that would be!

She would love to ask him about his plans, but their acquaintance was nowhere close enough for her to broach such personal matters.

Then there was the problem of the possible rivalry between him and his brother over George's supposed pretensions to her hand. Though she was certain there was a genuine attraction between herself and Giles Hadley, she'd already proven rather miserable at discerning whether a man's attentions stemmed from her charms, or the charms of her lineage, wealth and connections. Would Mr Hadley indulge her curiosity and encourage her interest because he found her as intriguing as she found him? Or if she followed through on her desires, might she be leading herself into another painful disappointment?

Yet, as even Aunt Lilly had implied, youth wouldn't last for ever. In the years since Robbie's death, she'd met many gentlemen, without feeling anything like the strong and immediate attraction she'd felt for Giles Hadley. If she let caution dissuade her from at least discovering where it might lead, she might never have another chance.

After all, she was wiser now, more suspicious of attention and flattery than she'd been before the episode with Sir Francis. As long as she kept her head, the worst that could happen by furthering the relationship would be the disappointment of discovering Giles Hadley was not as fascinating—or as fascinated by her—as she'd thought. She felt certain Giles Hadley would never endanger her, or compel her to go where she didn't wish to follow.

There'd be no question of 'compelling', though. Just thinking of the mesmerising blue gaze and the heated feeling in the pit of her stomach when he smiled at her set her pulses throbbing. But surely she was prudent enough to resist the most dangerous of all temptations, and restrict herself to friendship.

She really did wish to know him better...as a friend and companion, she told herself.

*As a lover, if you could imagine a safe way to manage it*, the voice of honesty answered back.

But only as long as she could invest herself just so far, without any possibility of committing her heart.

The short drive to the Witlow town house ended before she came to a definite decision. So much for thinking herself level-headed! Exasperated with such dithering, she decided as she descended from the carriage that she would attend some debates after the new Parliament convened. If an opportunity presented itself to speak further with Mr Hadley—or he sought her out—she would take it as a sign to proceed.

Because in the end, in that sphere beyond words or logic, the pull she felt to him was irresistible.

## Chapter Three

Two evenings later, Giles arrived back in London and headed for the room at the Quill and Gavel, eager to compare notes with his friends about the election results. He found them all present as he walked in, Davie offering him a mug of ale, Ben Tawney urging him to a seat.

'What happened in Chellingham?' Christopher asked. 'Did Reynolds manage to snatch the seat from Witlow's man?'

'I'm afraid not,' he confessed, to the groans of his listeners. 'Michael Armsburn did so well in the verbal tally, we didn't bother asking for a formal vote. Riding around with Reynolds, one could tell it was hopeless. Even the unemployed former soldiers one would expect to rally to the Reform cause told us they intended to vote for Witlow's man. Said his lordship had watched out for their families while they were off fighting in the wars. How did all of you fare?'

'A win in Sussex!' Ben announced. 'We'll own the county now.'

'Wins in Merton and Warrenton as well,' Christopher added. 'The Whigs should return an overwhelming majority.'

'That calls for another round, don't you think?' David asked. After walking to the door to beckon the innkeeper to bring more ale, he said, 'Ben and Christopher, why don't you make a tally of the projected gains, district by district? I expect we'll be recalled to committee as soon as Parliament reconvenes.'

Once the two friends settled at the table, Davie raised his mug to Giles. 'So,' he said in a quiet voice pitched for their ears alone, 'what did you think of Lady Margaret?'

Surprised, Giles felt his face flush. 'How did you know I'd met Lady Margaret?'

Davie shrugged. 'You'd said you'd try to help the Radicals win one of Witlow's seats—yet you chose to canvass for one that we knew at the outset was very unlikely to be turned. A seat that just happens to be held by a cousin of Lady Margaret's, for whom she has often campaigned. And that, after hearing your brother might have matrimonial designs upon the lady. So, what did you think of her?'

'Sure the Home Office shouldn't employ your talents to keep track of dissidents?' Giles asked, disgruntled that his motives had been so transparent. 'Very well, I was quite impressed. She's a natural campaigner—the crowds love her. She seems passionate about politics and the welfare of the people in her father's boroughs.'

'A shame she's passionate for the wrong party,' David said, his perceptive friend watching him entirely too closely for Giles's comfort. 'Did you talk with her?'

'Yes. Her person is as appealing as her politics are not. I have to admit, I was quite…strongly attracted. By the way, she denied any interest in marrying George.'

'Did she? I don't know that her lack of interest would weigh much with your half-brother, compared to the advantages of the match. One can only hope her father has a care for her preferences, rather than for giving a leg up to a rising member of his party. Do you intend to pursue the connection?'

'Yes, I do.' *At least long enough to see if the extraordinary attraction he'd felt lasted beyond that first meeting.*

'And what of George?'

Giles shrugged. 'Having never in my life consulted George's preferences before doing something, I'm not likely to start now.'

Davie nodded. 'Very well. Just make sure the lady doesn't get caught in the crossfire, if there is any.'

Giles grinned. 'One thing you can count on: I will always protect a lady.'

Before they could join their friends at the table, a liveried messenger appeared at the doorway. 'A note for Mr Hadley.'

After Giles raised his hand, the man gave him the missive and walked out. Scanning it quickly, Giles frowned. 'It's from Lord Grey. He wants me to join a dinner meeting he's about to begin with some of his committee chiefs.'

Ben whistled, and David raised his eyebrows. 'Congratulations on having the party leader call for you!' Christopher said. 'Maybe there's a cabinet post in your future?'

'I doubt that. I'll have to go, though, unfortunately, it's at Brooks's Club—which is probably why Grey didn't invite all of us. He knows I never grace the halls of Brooks's unless I'm summoned.'

'Maybe you should go there more often,' Davie advised. 'Many of the senior party leaders are members; let them get to know you better.'

'I'd rather meet here, with all of you.' Giles smiled.

'Planning strategy and dreaming dreams of change, as we have since that grimy little inn at Oxford.'

'Being a Hellion was all well and good,' David allowed. 'But challenging the prevailing view has served its purpose. Now that the goals we dreamed about are going to be realised, shouldn't we turn our efforts into getting a hand in determining how they are implemented?'

'Very true,' Christopher said. 'Why not take advantage of whatever benefits membership at Brooks's can offer?'

'You could even pass them along to us,' David added with a grin. 'It's the only way *I'll* ever gain access to them, after all. Their politics might be liberal, but never in this lifetime are high-born Whigs going to allow the orphaned son of farmer into their club, regardless of how highly placed his sponsor might be.'

'Or the illegitimate son of a governess,' Ben added.

'A gently born governess, whose father is now a viscount and acknowledges him,' Giles reminded Ben. 'If you asked, your father would likely sponsor you at Brooks's.'

'So the members could mutter under their breath about my mother as I walk by, like the boys did at Oxford? I think not.'

'As for me,' Christopher said with a grin, 'being in the unusual position of being considered my legal father's son even though I'm not, I *could* be put up for membership. Except that dear legal Papa is a Tory who frequents White's.'

'I doubt they would have voted me in, had Lord Newville not been insistent,' Giles said. 'I can only imagine how much arm-twisting was involved.'

'Your nomination did place the members in an awkward position,' David said. 'Many of them are friends of your father, and there's the sticky matter of George. If anything happens to you, George gets the title; like our Oxford classmates, few there would want to befriend you and offend him, in case some day he attains real power.'

'We'll just have to see that he doesn't,' Giles retorted.

'Faith and the devil, that reminds me!' Christopher exclaimed. 'Wychwood told me that George lost his seat!'

'In Hampshire, my father's county?' Giles asked, astounded.

'Yes. Despite how strongly the voice vote went in favour of the Reform candidate, Wychwood said George insisted on a formal counted vote. And lost it decisively.'

The other three whistled as the significance of that registered. 'Pity his poor servants—and any other unfortunate who crosses his path in the next few days,' Christopher said. 'He'll be as quick to lash out as a temperamental stallion with an abscessed hoof.'

'He'll surely look for some way to transfer the blame to you,' David warned.

'And whine to his father about it,' Christopher added.

'I'd avoid him,' Ben advised.

'I always do,' Giles replied. 'But now, I'd better get to that meeting. With any luck, I'll be back to drink another mug before midnight.'

'Take good notes, so you can give us a full report,' Christopher said as Giles shrugged on his coat and headed for the door.

As he walked out, Davie followed him, then stayed him with a hand on his arm. 'This might not be the best of times to provoke a quarrel over a lady,' he said quietly.

'I don't intend to quarrel,' Giles replied. 'If he tries to start one, I'll ignore it, as I always do.' *No matter how much I'd like to plant a facer in the middle of that smug face,* he added silently.

'Just…watch your step. I've always thought George

like a coiled snake, ready to strike if cornered. Don't give him any more reason.'

'I shall be the soul of diplomacy.'

'Giles, the most hot-headed member of our group?' David retorted. 'Just remember that resolution, if you encounter George when I'm not there to restrain you. It would be…undignified for a rising Member of Parliament to mill down a former Member in public.'

'Besides which, George would be sure to haul me up on assault charges. Temper or no, I promise to be on my best behaviour.'

And he would be, Giles promised himself as he walked out to hail a hackney.

Several hours later, dinner and consultation with Lord Grey and two of his ministers complete and a sheaf of notes in hand, Giles had just left the small private dining room when an unwelcome voice assailed his ears.

Hearing his name called again, he turned towards the card room, girding himself for the always unwelcome encounter with his half-brother.

'It is you, then,' George said, and walked towards him.

At least he'd won that small satisfaction, Giles thought as he waited for his half-brother to approach: George had finally learned that Giles would not come running to him when his half-brother beckoned, like the lackey George wanted him to be.

As the man proceeded closer with his measured, self-important tread, Giles noted he was splendidly dressed, as usual, in a dark coat featuring the newly popular cinched-in waist, an elaborately tied cravat of fine linen with a large diamond winking out from the knot, and long trousers. A walking advertisement for his tailor, and for being a man who spared no expense on his person.

George stopped beside him, looking him in the eyes for a moment without speaking. His half-brother was of a height, but had the fairer hair and hazel eyes of their father and a pleasant face that, when it wore a congenial look Giles seldom saw, was accounted handsome, or so numerous society ladies seemed to think.

Apparently Lady Margaret wasn't of their number. That recollection pleased him more than it should.

When Giles refused to rise to the bait of asking his brother to tell him what he wanted, at length George broke the silence. 'Didn't believe at first you'd actually entered a gentleman's club, instead of hobnobbing with the lowborn sorts you usually associate with. Devil's teeth, to think how much blunt Lord Newville must have dropped, bribing the members to get you accepted here! But in this instance, I suppose I should thank him for sparing me having to track you down in that dive you frequent.'

Drawing in a deep breath through his gritted teeth to stem the rising anger, Giles made no immediate response. He'd long ago figured out the best way to deal with his half-brother's demeaning remarks was to ignore them, no matter how infuriating—thereby depriving George of the satisfaction of provoking him.

'Do you having anything of substance to say, or did you just want to tender the usual insults?' he said in a tone as bored as he could manage. 'If the latter, I'll bid you goodnight.' With a nod of dismissal, he turned to go.

'Wait! I do have something else to say.' George stayed him.

Much as Giles would love to snub him and walk out, if his half-brother truly wanted to speak with him, leaving now would only delay the confrontation. Tenacious as a bulldog, George would simply run him down somewhere else.

Wondering what his brother could possibly wish to discuss with him—unless he'd already figured out a way to blame Giles for his electoral defeat—he raised an eyebrow. 'Perhaps you might wish to do so somewhere more private than Brooks's entry hall?' With a gesture, he indicated a small anteroom.

After George followed him in, Giles said, 'I've still got work to do tonight, so I'd appreciate your keeping this short.' With what he considered true nobility, he refrained from adding that it involved important business for the new Parliament—the one in which George would not be serving. After closing the door, he said, 'Shall we dispense with the charade of exchanging pleasantries? Just say what you must.'

'I will be brief. I'm warning you to leave Lady Margaret Roberts alone. She's a gentlewoman from a distinguished family, her father a nobleman highly regarded by his peers. Neither need be embarrassed by it becoming known that she associated with *you*. And at a common inn, no less.'

Baffled, Giles stared at George—until his mind made the connection. 'You mean, in Chellingham?'

'As far as I know, that's the only time she's displayed such a lapse of judgement. Although I understand there was some disturbance that necessitated her removal, and that at the time she let you make off with her, she was not aware of who you were.'

'It being more acceptable for the lady to leave with a stranger than to leave with me?' Giles inserted.

'Well, of course she shouldn't be leaving with a stranger! Armsburn and Proctor were highly negligent in leaving her alone to begin with. Although it would have been better still if she'd not put herself forward, campaigning for her cousin.'

Although admittedly Giles was not conversant with who belonged to which circle of friendship among the Tory membership, he was not aware that Lady Margaret's cousin and his half-brother were close. And if they were not…

'How did you know what happened to Lady Margaret in Chellingham?' When his half-brother stuttered for an answer, Giles voiced the unbelievable, but only logical, conclusion. 'You weren't having someone *spy* on her, were you, George?'

'Someone should keep tabs on her, since it's obvious neither her cousin nor his aide were doing such a good job of it,' his half-brother replied defensively.

There could be but one reason for George to go to the trouble of having the lady watched: he *must* be set on marrying her. Even so, the behaviour was unsettling, and definitely raised his hackles on Lady Margaret's behalf.

'Is Lord Witlow aware of your…protective oversight?' He knew Lady Margaret couldn't be—and was reasonably sure what that lady's response would be if she found out.

'Lord Witlow would be gratified that I concern myself with the welfare of his dearest daughter,' George replied loftily.

So her father wasn't aware of the scrutiny either. Which made the behaviour even more disturbing. 'He might also not appreciate having someone wholly unrelated keeping his daughter under observation.'

George gave an impatient wave. 'My motives are of the purest. Besides, I cherish hopes that we will not long remain "unrelated".'

So George did intend to press his suit. 'You've spoken with his lordship on this matter?'

'He's doubtless aware of my regard,' George evaded.

'And the lady?'

'I haven't as yet formally declared myself,' George admitted. 'But on a matter as important as family alliances, she will follow her father's guidance, and he will certainly approve. Now that I have revealed my honourable intentions, I expect even someone like you to respect them, and not sully the lady with associations that could only be to her detriment.'

Keeping a tight hold on the simmering anger he didn't seem able to completely suppress, Giles said evenly, 'I would do the lady the honour of allowing *her* to choose with whom she wishes to associate.'

George stared at him a moment. 'Meaning, you *do* intend to pester her with your attentions?'

'I have never "pestered" a woman,' Giles retorted. 'If a lady indicates she is uninterested in my company, I am not so boorish as to inflict it upon her.' That shot flying entirely over his brother's head, he added, 'As I said, it is the lady's choice.'

'Excellent!' George said, a self-satisfied look replacing the hostility of his expression. 'I may be easy, then. Her father would never allow an association so detrimental to her good name and the regard in which she is universally held. That being all I wished to ascertain, I will bid you goodnight.'

Avoiding, as he always did, using either Giles's last name or honorary title, George nodded and walked back towards the card room.

Leaving Giles staring after him incredulously.

He should be happy, he told himself as he gathered up his papers again, that his half-brother's incredible arrogance spared him the necessity of wrangling with George over his intention to seek out Lady Margaret. Apparently, his half-brother thought the lady a puppet who moved at her father's command. And he was certain the marquess would command her to stay away from Giles, and marry George.

Fortunately, Giles already knew the first assumption was unlikely—Lady Margaret had told him plainly that her father respected him.

As for the latter, Lady Margaret seemed sincerely attached to her father, and probably would not willingly displease him. However, Giles doubted the independent lady he'd seen joking with voters on the hustings would let her father compel her into a marriage she did not want.

That conclusion cheered him almost as much as avoiding an ugly confrontation with his half-brother.

Nothing George had told him altered his intention to seek out the lady, at least until George or—he frowned at the thought—his watching minions discovered Giles had seen her again. By then, he should have confirmed whether or not his attraction to her—and hers to him—was strong enough for him to justify navigating the tricky course around his half-brother's presumptions.

He had no clear idea what sort of relationship he envisioned. Not marriage, certainly—his tenuous position and his past were too chequered to inflict that association on any woman. But the lady was a widow, and perfectly able to indulge in a discreet dalliance, if their respective desires led that way…

Tantalised by the thought, Giles set off for the hackney stand, eager to report back to his friends at the Quill and Gavel. As he climbed into the vehicle, it suddenly occurred to him that he had another pressing reason to seek out Lady Margaret, whether or not the powerful connection between them recurred.

Giles felt the lady ought to know that his half-brother was keeping her under surveillance.

At Lady Margaret's probable reaction to that news, he had to smile.

## Chapter Four

Shortly after the opening of Parliament two weeks later, Lady Margaret climbed the stairs to the Ladies' Gallery in the upper storey of St Stephen's Chapel. The odd arrangement in that chamber—a round bench surrounding a wooden lantern at the centre of the room, whose eight small openings allowed a limited view down into the House of Commons below—would make watching the debates difficult, though she would be able to hear all the speeches.

And she'd *heard* that Giles Hadley was to give an address on behalf of the Reform Bill today.

She claimed a place, thinking with longing of the unobstructed view that, seated right on a bench beside the members, she enjoyed when she attended the Lords to listen to her father. The best she could hope for in this room, if she were lucky and the gentleman stood in the right place, was to catch a glimpse of Mr Hadley's head. Remembering that gentleman's magnificent eyes and commanding figure, seeing no more than the top of his head was going to be a great loss.

Would his voice alone affect her? Her stomach fluttered and a shiver prickled her nerves, just as it had each time she'd thought of the man since their meeting several weeks ago. And she'd thought of him often.

Doubtless far too often, for a man she'd met only once, who did not appear at any of the *ton*'s balls or parties—where she'd looked for him in vain—and who did not frequent the same political gatherings she attended.

But oh, how even the *thought* of him still stirred her!

She would certainly try to meet him today. After spending the last several weeks finding herself continually distracted by recalling their encounter, sorting through possible explanations for the magic of it, and wondering whether it might happen again, she was tired of acting like a silly schoolgirl suffering her first infatuation. She wanted her calm, reasonable self back. For even if he did seem as compelling upon second meeting as he had upon the first, at her age, she should be wise enough not to lose her head over him.

Besides, seeing him again in the prosaic light of a Parliamentary anteroom, it was far more likely that he would cease being the stuff of dreams and turn into just another normal, attractive man.

Soon the session was called to order and a succession of speakers rose to address the group, met by silence or shouted comments from the opposing bench, depending on how controversial the subject being addressed. After several hours, stiff from sitting on the hard bench, Maggie was about to concede defeat and make her way out when the voice that had whispered through her dreams tickled her ears.

Shock vibrating through her, she craned her head towards the nearest opening, hoping for a glimpse of him.

The light dancing on the wavy, blue-black curls sent another little shock through her. Nerves tingling and breathing quickened, she bent down, positioning herself to catch even the smallest glimpse as he paced below her.

His voice held her rapt—oh, what a voice! Her father was right—Giles Hadley was a born orator, his full, rich tones resonating through the chamber. As he continued to press his points, even the disdainful comments of the opposition grew fewer, and finally died away altogether.

When the rising volume and increasingly urgent tone indicated the approaching climax of the speech, Maggie found herself leaning even further forward, anxious to take in every word.

'For too long,' he exhorted, 'we have allowed the excesses of Revolutionary France to stifle the very discussion of altering the way our representatives are chosen. But this is England, not France. Are we a nation of cowards?'

After pausing to accommodate the chorus of 'no's he continued, 'Then let nothing prevent us in this session from doing what all rational men know should be done: eliminate these pocket boroughs that give undue influence to a few voters or the wealthy neighbour who can sway them, and restore to our government a more balanced system of representation, a fair system, a just system, one that works in the harmony our noble forebears intended!'

As his voice died away, he came to a stop right below her, his head bowed as he acknowledged the cheers and clapping from the Whigs, the mutter of dissent from the Tories. Then, as if some invisible force had telegraphed her presence, he looked up through the opening, and their eyes met.

The energy that pulsed between them in that instant raised the tiny hairs at the back of her neck. Then an arm appeared in her narrow view, pulling him away, and he was lost to her sight.

Straightening, Maggie found herself trembling. Thrilled by the power of his oratory, she remained seated, too shaken to move.

Papa had said everyone expected great things of him, and she now understood why. How could Lord Grey resist adding so compelling a Reformer to his staff? Even the Tories had fallen silent under the power of his rhetoric.

When he spoke with such passionate conviction, she suspected that he'd be able to persuade her to almost anything.

An alarming thought, and one that ought to make her rethink her intention to meet him again.

She was debating the wisdom of going downstairs and seeking him out, when suddenly the air around her seemed charged with energy. Startled, she looked up— into the blue, blue eyes of Giles Hadley.

Her mouth went dry and her stomach did a little flip.

'Lady Margaret!' he said, bowing. 'What an unexpected pleasure to see you again.'

She rose to make him a curtsy. 'And to see you, Mr Hadley. That was a very fine speech.'

He waved a hand. 'The plain truth, merely.'

'Perhaps, but the plain truth elegantly arranged and convincingly presented. It's no wonder the full chamber attended to hear you speak.'

He smiled, his eyes roaming her face with an ardency that made her pulse kick up a notch. 'I'd rather flatter myself that *you* came to hear me speak.'

'Then you may certainly do so. I did indeed come with the hope of hearing you, and was richly rewarded.'

His eyes brightened further, sending another flutter of sensation through her. 'Considering the many excellent speakers you've doubtless heard in both chambers, it's very kind of you to say so. Surely I ought to offer you some tea in gratitude? Normally, we could take it in the committee room, but with the session just begun, everything is rather disordered. Might I persuade you to accompany me to Gunter's?'

'I would like that very much.'

He offered his arm. After a slight hesitation, she gave him her hand, savouring the shock of connection that rippled up her arm.

She did have the answer to one of the questions that had bedevilled her since their last meeting, she thought as he walked her down the stairs. The effect he had on her was definitely not a product of election excitement or the danger of that skirmish in Chellingham. Leaving caution behind in this chamber of debate, she intended to enjoy every second of it.

'So,' he said after they'd settled into a hackney on the way to Gunter's. 'Did my speech convince you that the time is right for reform?'

'Your arguments are very persuasive,' she admitted.

'I hope your father and the Tories in the Lords agree. With so many Whigs returning to the Commons, passage of the bill in the lower house is certain. Though many in the Lords resist change, even the most hidebound cannot defend the ridiculousness of a pocket borough with a handful of voters having two representatives, when the great cities of the north have none.'

'True. But Members are not elected to represent only their particular district, but the interests of the nation as a whole,' she pointed out.

'Another excuse to oppose change that the Tories have trotted out for years!' he said with a laugh. 'Let's be rational. When a borough contains only a handful of voters who must cast their vote in public, they usually elect the candidate favoured by the greatest landholder in the area.'

'Who, since he does own the property, should look out for its best interests and those of the people who work it and make it profitable,' she countered. 'Which is why giving every man a vote, as I've heard you approve, could be dangerous. A man who owns nothing may have no interest at all in the *common* good. With nothing to lose, he can be swayed by whatever popular wind is blowing.'

'Just because a man owns property doesn't mean he tends it well, or cares for those who work it. Oh, I know, the best of them, like your father, do. But wealth and power can beguile a man into believing he can do whatever he wishes, regardless of the well-being of anyone else.'

*As his father had?* Maggie wondered. 'Perhaps,' she allowed. 'But what about boroughs where the voters sold their support to the highest bidder? Virtue isn't a product of birth. Noble or commoner, a man's character will determine his actions.'

'With that, I certainly agree.' He shook his head admiringly. 'You're a persuasive speaker yourself, Lady Margaret. A shame that women do not stand for Parliament. Though since you favour the Tories, I expect I should be grateful they do not!'

At that point, the hackney arrived at Gunter's, and for the next few moments, conversation ceased while Hadley helped her from the carriage and they were seated within the establishment. As Hadley ordered the tea she requested in lieu of the famed ices, Maggie simply watched him.

She'd been intensely aware of him, seated beside her

in the hackney during the transit. But she'd been almost equally stirred by his conversation.

Most gentlemen felt ladies were either uninterested in, or incapable of understanding, the intricacies of politics. Only her father had ever done her the courtesy of discussing them with her. Even her cousin Michael Armsburn, and the several other candidates for whom she had canvassed, valued her just as a pretty face to charm the voters.

None of the men she'd supported had ever invited her to discuss their policy or its philosophical roots. Giles Hadley excited her mind as much as he stirred her senses.

Or almost as much, she amended. He mesmerised her when he talked, not just the thrilling words, but watching those mobile lips, wondering how they'd feel, pressed against hers. She exulted in the tantalising magic of sitting beside him, the energy and passion he exuded arousing a flood of sensation in her, the heat and scent of him and the wondrous words he uttered a sea she could drown in.

Oh, to be with a man who burned with ardent purpose, who inspired one with a desire to be with him, not just in bed, but out of it as well!

Tea arrived shortly thereafter. Maggie forced herself to cease covertly studying the excellence of Giles Hadley's physique, the breadth of his shoulders and the tapered elegance of his fingers, and concentrate on filling his cup.

After they had each sipped the steaming brew, Hadley set down his cup with an apologetic look. 'I'm afraid I must confess to not being completely truthful about my reasons for inviting you here.'

Her great-aunt's warning returned in a rush, dousing her heated euphoria with the ice water of wariness. 'Not truthful? In what way?'

'Much as I am enjoying our excursion to Gunter's, we could have taken tea in the committee room. Except there is a matter I feel I must discuss with you that demanded a greater degree of privacy than would have been afforded in a Parliamentary chamber.'

Foreboding souring her gut, she said, 'Then by all means, let us discuss it.'

'I spoke with my brother not long ago. As you know, we…are not close, and he generally does not seek me out unless he wishes to dispute with me about something. The matter he wished to dispute about this time…was you.'

So she *was* to be a bone of contention? Not if she could help it! But perhaps she should hear him out before rushing to conclusions. 'What was the nature of that dispute?'

Hadley shrugged. 'You've read the journal reports—and so has George. Apparently my half-brother thinks you favour him—or he believes your father approves of him, and would favour his suit. He warned me to stay away from you.'

Some of the anger, hurt and despair of the episode with Sir Francis rose up, nearly choking her. 'And so you sought my company to spite him?' she spit out at last. 'Do you think to beguile me, and then boast to him about it?'

He straightened, frowning. 'Not at all! How could you imagine such a thing? Besides, if I were trying to charm you and boast of my conquest, would I have told you about our disagreement?'

'Do you think you *could* charm me?'

His irritated expression smoothed, a roguish smile replaced it, and he smiled at her, that smile that made her knees weak. 'Do *you* think I could?'

'If you did, and we were compromised, we might be forced to wed. Then you'd be stuck with me for life—

a fate which ought to give you pause,' she said tartly, mollified.

His smile faded. 'I would never do you the harm of marrying you.'

Before she could figure out that odd comment, he continued, his expression serious, 'But that's not what I meant to talk about. Did you speak with my half-brother about our meeting in Chellingham?'

It was her turn to be puzzled. 'No, I've not seen him since I returned to London. Why do you ask?'

'As far as you know, George is not a friend of your cousin Mr Armsburn?'

'They are acquainted, certainly, but not close.'

'The only place we've met, before today, was Chellingham. My brother specifically mentioned how detrimental to your reputation it would be if others discovered you'd been alone with me at the inn there. If you did not relate our encounter to George, and your cousin or his aide, Mr Proctor, didn't inform him, how could he have known about it?'

Maggie paused a moment, thinking. She'd spoken with Aunt Lilly, but that lady would never divulge, even to her friends, confidential information about her niece, particularly if it involved a gentleman and would therefore make her the subject of gossip and conjecture. She was quite certain she'd not mentioned their meeting to anyone else.

'I don't know,' she confessed.

'Then it seems my suspicions were justified. Outlandish as it sounds, in order for my half-brother to have known that you'd accompanied me to that inn in Chellingham, he must have been keeping you under surveillance.'

She shook her head a little, not sure she could have

heard him correctly. 'Are you trying to tell me that your brother has someone…*spying* on me?'

'You weren't aware of it?'

'Absolutely not!'

He nodded, looking grim again. 'Your father wouldn't have asked him to do such a thing, would he?'

'Why would he? I had my cousin and Proctor to watch over me. If Papa *had* thought I needed additional protection, he would have chosen someone I know better than your brother to provide it. And I am sure he would not have done so without informing me and explaining the need for it. No, I don't think Papa authorised this. Shall I ask him?'

'Perhaps you should. I wouldn't want to accuse my half-brother unjustly.'

The enormity of what he'd just told her registered. 'Why in the world would your half-brother want to have me watched?'

'He told me he intends to ask for your hand. Perhaps, with the turmoil over the Reform Bill and rumours flying of possible electoral violence, he wanted to make sure the woman he wants to marry didn't come to any harm.'

'Or he wished to make sure the woman he plans to marry did not behave in a manner of which he doesn't approve!' she retorted, more and more indignant as the implications registered. 'The effrontery! How dare he have someone tail me as if I were a…a petty thief he was trying to prove guilty of larceny!'

Giles's lips twitched. 'I didn't think you'd find the idea very appealing. May I assume from this that you are now even less likely to consider an offer from my half-brother?'

'If he has indeed so grievously imposed on my privacy, you may assume the chances of my accepting an offer from him to be non-existent!'

He smiled at that. 'Then I am almost glad of his arrogance. But…there is one thing more I feel I must say, before we drop the unpleasant matter of my brother.' He paused, his smile fading. 'I do hope you won't feel I'm telling you this just because the two of us do not get along.'

'I think I can count on your honesty.' She hesitated, unsure how much she could or should say, given how brief their acquaintance was. 'Even though I understand that you have not been…kindly treated, either by your father or your half-brother.'

He grimaced. 'We are estranged, that is certain.'

She respected his reticence, and admired his restraint in not pouring out the complaints her comment invited—complaints, according to what Aunt Lilly had told her, he would be well justified in making. 'So, what else did you wish to tell me?'

'Would your father compel you to wed a man of his choice, even if you had no particular desire to do so?'

'I cannot imagine he would. Besides, should he try to, I am of age, and have property and assets of my own over which he has no control. There would be no way he could force me to marry against my wishes.'

Giles nodded. 'So I thought. However, George has been…much indulged by his father.' Maggie noted he did not say 'our' father. 'He is quite used to getting whatever he wants. And it seems he wants to marry you. He believes your father would favour his suit, and that you would follow your father's guidance in the matter of the choice of a husband.'

She gave a short laugh. 'No wonder he seems so little

interested in charming me, and so much more interested in beguiling Papa.'

'George can be quite…unpleasant, when he is prevented from obtaining what he desires. If he does in fact make you an offer, and you refuse him, just…be careful.'

She'd been about to take another sip of her tea, but at that, she looked up to stare at him. 'You don't mean he would try to…force me! Or harm me, for refusing him!'

'No, no, probably not that. He would be more likely to start some malicious gossip in an attempt to blacken your name. So if you do refuse him, you might wish to be on your best behaviour.' He winked at her. 'No trysts at secluded inns in small market towns.'

She laughed. 'I will keep that in mind, Mr Hadley.'

'Very well. Now, much as I hate to bring this tryst at a very public place in the huge metropolis to an end, I fear I am due at a meeting in half an hour. Can I escort you home first?'

'No, I have some errands to complete.' Even more reluctant than he to have their time together come to an end, she added on impulse, 'Father is hosting a dinner tomorrow night for some friends, not a policy meeting, but a wide-ranging discussion of political ideas. The guests will be quite varied in background and opinion. Would you like to attend?'

'Are you sure your father would want me?'

'Papa enjoys a free exchange of opinions. I know he would be interested in hearing more of yours. And let me assure you in advance, your half-brother will not be invited.'

'Will you be acting as hostess?'

'For the dinner. I shall probably leave the gentlemen to their discussions afterward.'

'Then I should be delighted…' He paused, frowning. 'I

*should* be delighted, but I was not exaggerating George's malevolence. I didn't note anyone tailing us to Gunter's, so he may not discover that you accompanied me here, but my presence at your father's dinner will surely excite enough comment to reach his ears. Probably, the knowledge will merely increase his enmity towards me, which is a matter of no import—the fact that I breathe daily increases his enmity. He might, however, seek you out for an explanation. I would not have you harassed.'

His concern that she *not* be drawn into a squabble between brothers dissipated the last of the caution generated by Aunt Lilly's warning. 'I refuse to allow your half-brother to dictate whom I may or may not invite to my home. If he tries to take me to task for it, I assure you, I am quite capable of putting him in his place.'

'That I would like to see!' Hadley declared, then paused, still looking troubled. 'You are sure? The last thing I want is to introduce any unpleasantness into your life.' His frown dissipating, he gave her an intimate smile, his voice lowering to a seductive murmur. 'I would rather introduce you to pleasure.'

She looked up at him, her gaze caught and held by the power of his. Feeling a little breathless, she had to force herself to look away.

That comment made his amorous intent plain enough, she thought, thrown back into uncertainty by the realisation. She could put any potential affair to a stop right now…if she wanted. But did she want to?

Just because she was certain he would be amenable to dalliance, didn't mean she had to make a decision about it right now. Besides, there could be pleasure in less: conversing, flirting—even a simple kiss.

'My father and I would be honoured if you would

come to dinner tomorrow night,' she found herself replying.

His smile broadened and his eyes lit, as if she'd just
given him a treasured gift. 'Then I will certainly be
there.'

'Until tomorrow night,' she said, a little giddy. What
was she getting herself into?

He escorted her out and summoned a hackney. 'You
are sure you'll be all right? You don't even have a maid
or a footman to carry parcels.'

'I never bring my maid if I'm visiting Parliament—
she'd be bored to death, poor thing, and it would unnec-
essarily delay her work. Since I'm ordering supplies for
dinner, they will be delivered later anyway, so no need
of a footman to carry parcels.'

'What, no gowns or slippers or feminine fripperies?'

She laughed. 'At the risk of having you find me totally
unwomanly, I confess I don't spend much time on gowns
and slippers and fripperies.'

'I could never find you anything but delightful.'

At that, she looked back up at him, into eyes that
once again seemed to see deep within her. Enchanted,
mesmerised, she didn't *want* to look away. Every nerve
quivering with awareness, had they not been standing on
a public street, she might have gone into Hadley's arms.

A pedlar with his handcart pushed past them, breaking the spell, and Maggie stepped away. 'You'd better
summon a hackney yourself, else you'll be late to your
meeting.'

'Thank you again for accompanying me for tea.'

'And to you, for tea…and your warning.'

He turned as if to go, then paused, looking back at
her over his shoulder. 'Do you really think I could beguile you?'

'All too easily,' she answered, before realising it would have been more prudent to turn that question aside.

He reached over to take her hand. Little eddies of delight swirled through her as he raised it and brushed his mouth against the thin kidskin sheathing her fingers. 'Then I'm very encouraged. Send me the invitation. I'll definitely come…exchange views with your father.'

With a bow, he handed her up into the carriage, waved his cane in farewell, and walked away.

Hand tingling, even more enchanted than she'd been after their interlude in Chellingham, Maggie watched him until the departing carriage set off, robbing her of the sight.

## Chapter Five

That evening, Maggie waited up for her father, who had attended a dinner with some of his political cronies at Brooks's. Although she was certain the marquess would not object to including Giles Hadley in their gathering—the purpose of the entertainment being, as she'd told that gentleman, to explore a wide range of ideas—she also knew he would be surprised by her invitation, and curious.

Best to meet that curiosity head-on. Unfortunately, she wasn't sure she could do a very good job of explaining it to her father when she didn't fully understand it herself. She just knew she wanted to see more of Giles Hadley, and since he didn't attend society functions and was unlikely to turn up at Tory gatherings, luring him to her father's home was probably the only way she was going to manage it.

She really didn't want to tell her father that.

But since the invitation had been tendered, the gentleman had accepted, and she had no intention of revoking it—the need to see him again being greater than her reluctance to discuss the reasons for it with her sire—she'd have to tell Papa—something.

She was dozing over her book in the library when at last she heard her father's distinctive step in the hallway.

'Papa, could I have a word with you?' she called out as he passed the library door.

At the sound of her voice, he stopped short and peered into the room. 'Is that you, Puss? What are you doing still up?'

'There's something I wanted to inform you about. Nothing of importance, but I know you will be tied up in committee meetings all morning, and was afraid I might miss you. It will only take a moment.'

Her father came over to place a kiss on her forehead. 'I always have time for you, sweeting. Shall I pour you some wine?'

'No, this really won't take very long.'

'I think I will rest these old bones while we talk,' he said with a smile as he seated himself. 'So, what's amiss?'

'Nothing! It's just that I invited someone else to join us for dinner tomorrow night, and wanted to let you know beforehand.'

'I thought we'd included everyone we thought could contribute to the conversation. Who did we forget?'

'Well, it's not someone we normally include, but he does have quite interesting views. You've even told me you admire him, though you disagree on almost every particular. It's Mr Hadley—Mr *Giles* Hadley.'

He looked perplexed for a moment before the name registered. 'Viscount Lyndlington, you mean! Unusual that he insists on spurning the title, but I suppose, given the situation between him and Telbridge, understandable. Of course he's welcome, Puss—but how did you come to invite him? I wasn't aware that you were acquainted.'

'Oh, yes! I met him in Chellingham—you remember, I was canvassing for Michael, and he was there to rally support for Mr Reynolds. We spoke briefly, and I found him quite interesting. Then today, we spoke again when he came up to the Ladies' Gallery after he'd given a speech at the Commons.'

'An eloquent plea for passage of the Reform Bill, I understand.'

'Yes, he's quite an excellent speaker. If it is inevitable that the bill will pass the Commons, and he is certain it will, then it might be useful to have a thorough discussion before it comes before you in the Lords.'

'You must have found him persuasive.'

'I did. Not that I agree with all his views, of course. It's true, though, that there was quite a lot of reform talk even in Chellingham, and that borough is as conservative as conservative comes.'

'I will look forward to debating his views.'

'Very good, Papa. That's all, so I'll bid you goodnight.'

When she came over to give him a kiss, he caught her hand, staying her. 'Had I forgotten you telling me you'd met Mr Hadley in Chellingham?'

Maggie felt her face redden, and hoped in the dim candlelight, it wouldn't be apparent. 'I don't believe I mentioned it, specifically. Since at the time, I wasn't sure whether or not I would ever see him again, I didn't think it important.'

'Nor can I remember you visiting the Ladies' Gallery any time recently to hear the speeches.'

'I'd been remiss in not visiting sooner.'

'This young man must have made quite an impression on you.'

So much for thinking she'd got through their little chat without having to explain her interest in Giles Hadley. 'Yes, Papa, he did,' she admitted.

'I thought your favour might lie with a different Mr Hadley.'

'George?' She shuddered, and for a moment, debated telling her father it was almost certain *that* Mr Hadley had been spying on her. But asking Papa whether he'd authorised such a thing, especially when she was nearly certain he had not, might force her to disclose she'd seen a bit more of Giles Hadley than she'd thus far admitted. Deciding to say nothing, she continued, 'He may be a good Tory, but I cannot like him, Papa. He's too…calculating. And completely self-absorbed.'

Her father nodded. 'With the wealth and affection Telbridge lavished on the boy, small wonder he thinks of little beyond his own interests. It's probably just as well he lost his seat. In my estimation, his ambitions rather exceed his abilities.'

'That was my impression,' Maggie said drily. 'Unless the measure of a man is the inventiveness of his tailor.'

'Should I be asking Giles Hadley what his intentions are?'

'Good heavens no, Papa!' she protested, embarrassed by the very idea. 'Promise me you will do nothing of the sort. Yes, I find Mr Giles Hadley…attractive. An excellent and persuasive orator with unique ideas I would like to hear more about. But that's all!'

Her father retained her hand, rubbing the fingers. 'Would it be so bad a thing if you were interested in… more? I know losing Robbie broke your heart, and whatever happened with Sir Francis hurt you deeply. But it hurts *my* heart that you are wearing out your youth playing hostess for an old man, instead of enjoying a husband and setting up your nursery.'

Tears stung her eyes at the mention of those old wounds. 'I like being your hostess!' she protested. 'If you're tired of having me preside over your table, I can always retreat back to my house in Upper Brook Street, or visit Mama at Huntsford.'

'You know I love having you here! Though your mama would, of course, appreciate a visit.' He sighed. 'Sometimes I do feel…selfish, however, for not doing more to urge you to go on with your life.'

'I have gone on with my life.'

'Have you, Puss? Or are you just treading water, holding your place against the current, refusing to allow yourself to be swept into something new?'

'Papa, how poetic!' *And unfortunately, how true.* But how could she allow herself to be swept away when she no longer trusted any man to tell her the truth? And even if she could, when she no longer believed a mere marriage of convenience would wash away the lingering ache of loneliness and loss?

The possibility of opening herself to more—to anything that might cause the sort of devastation she'd experienced after Robbie's death—was unthinkable.

*A flirtation with Giles Hadley might make you forget it for a while,* a little voice in her head whispered.

Ignoring it, she said, 'For now, enlivening conversation at dinner by adding an articulate, dissenting voice is as "swept away" as I care to be. Will that suffice?'

'It's a start,' he said, patting her cheek. 'But don't keep holding your place in that stream for too long. I still have aspirations of bouncing your children on my knee before I'm too decrepit to lift them.'

*Her children.* She swallowed hard. 'I'll try not to disappoint you. But please, let's not be tasking Mr Hadley to help me provide you with them just yet.'

He laughed. 'Very well, Puss. We'll have him to dine a few times first. An excellent young man, by the way.

Many an individual who suffered the setbacks he endured in his youth would have railed at his fate and become a bitter or frivolous wastrel, marking time until he inherited. Giles Hadley confronted his situation with courage, and with quiet determination and considerable effort, earned himself a place in the governing of this nation. I admire him for that.'

'So do I, Papa. And now I will bid you goodnight.'

After exchanging a kiss, they both walked upstairs to their bedchambers. But after blowing out her candle and settling back on her pillow, Maggie found she was no longer sleepy.

What had she really intended to accomplish with her impulsive invitation? To see if Giles Hadley could fit into her world—or she into his?

Did she want *him* to 'sweep her away'? She *wanted* him. That was certain. Every feminine part of her came to aching, needy life when he was near. The strength of that physical attraction made her only too acutely aware of how much she missed 'enjoying a husband'.

But it was a great leap from that to a more serious relationship, one she was nowhere close to being ready to take. Although, she suddenly realised, unlike every other man of her acquaintance, she probably didn't need to fear that *this* Mr Hadley would feed her sweet lies to win her favour—or her hand.

She had no idea what his current income was, but when he inherited the earldom, he would be a very rich man, with no need of her wealth. Though his half-brother George might prize her for her political ties, her Tory associations would be of no assistance whatsoever to the Reformist Giles; indeed, they would be a detriment.

Wedding her would offer him no real advantage, her only usable attributes—her lineage and breeding—being possessed by numerous other single females. Perhaps she could, cautiously, trust Mr Hadley when he told her how he felt about her.

And then she had to laugh. Had he not just told her quite plainly he had no interest in marriage? In fact, he'd made that odd comment about not 'harming' her by marrying her. As if she were a Tory candidate who would suffer for allying herself with a Reformer.

She considered the remark for a few minutes before dismissing it, unable to puzzle out the enigma. With neither of them interested in anything serious, perhaps she *could* let down her guard, feel free to be herself and simply enjoy his stimulating conversation and electrifying presence.

As for the physical attraction… He had all but invited her to a discreet affair, amicably conducted, no strings attached.

The very thought of it sent a spiral of warmth and longing through her. Even Aunt Lilly had admitted to 'amusing herself' after she'd been widowed. Oh, if only there were a truly safe way to do so!

But it was way too early in their acquaintance to worry about that. Before one directed a horse towards the highest fence, one must first saddle and bridle him, and get to know his paces. So for now, as she'd told her father, she would stick to the simple enjoyment of listening to his views…and the exquisite, tantalising pleasure of having him near.

In the late afternoon of the following day, Giles poured a glass of wine for Davie in the sitting room of their suite at Albany. 'You don't intend to accompany Ben and Christopher to dine with the committee members?' Davie asked.

Not wishing to reveal any more information than he had to, Giles simply shook his head as he handed Davie his glass.

'I promised Lady Greaves I'd come to Moulton Street tonight. It's their son Dickon's birthday. You'd certainly be welcome, if you'd like to join me.'

'I don't want to intrude on a family dinner.'

'You wouldn't be intruding. Sir Edward and Lady Greaves would love to see you.' Davie raised an eyebrow at him. 'You can't avoid polite society for ever, you know. Eventually, you will be an earl.'

Giles took a sip of wine, delaying the need to respond. How could he explain to Davie his continuing ambivalence about his eventual inheritance? As Davie knew all too well, he'd been angry and resentful as a young man, once he'd grown old enough to fully understand what his father had done to him and his mother. From the time his aunt pulled him from poverty and sent him to school, he'd been driven to prove he could become successful without any assistance from the earl. He'd thought, as time went on and he built his reputation, his achievements towards that goal would make it easier for him to reconcile himself to the future that must be his.

So far, it had not, nor had he been able to make himself act on any of Davie's increasingly frequent reminders that he ought to begin easing himself into his father's world.

'The current earl is, I understand, quite vigorous,' he said at last. 'Who knows, we may have abolished the aristocracy before he cocks up his toes. And since by then, you will most likely be Prime Minister, you will outrank me.'

'The farmer's whelp lording it over the lord?' David chuckled. 'Unlikely. Seriously, you really should become at least a little involved in the Season. Sir Edward and

Lord Englemere would be delighted to have you come to any of their entertainments, and once the *ton* discovered you would actually accept invitations, you'd have a flood of them.'

'What, subject myself to evenings of boring balls or tedious musicales with some dreadful soprano screeching away, or some equally dreadful young miss trying to display her limited prowess at the keyboard? If I want to waste time, I can take a nap.'

'What are you doing this evening? Not staying here napping, I hope.'

*Tread cautiously*, Giles told himself. 'Actually, I have a prior commitment. With, I should point out, a well-respected member of society. I'm invited to dine at the Marquess of Witlow's.'

Davie's hand froze with his glass halfway to his lips. 'At the Marquess of Witlow's?' he echoed, his eyes widening in surprise. 'With Lady Margaret as your hostess?'

'I expect so, since I understand she usually plays hostess for her father.'

'Did Lord Grey ask you to talk with Witlow? Try to negotiate to find some common ground before the bill comes to the floor that might persuade the Lords to pass it?'

'No, he didn't.'

'Then how—?'

Giles had hoped Davie, the most discreet of his friends, wouldn't press him, but it appeared that wish was not going to be fulfilled. 'I happened upon Lady Margaret after my speech at the Commons yesterday,' he reluctantly explained.

He had no intention of adding that he'd hoped she might come, had castigated himself as an idiot for thinking he sensed her presence while he was speaking, and then had been thrilled to glance up into the Ladies' Gallery and discover she was in fact in attendance. He'd found himself trotting up the stairs to the Gallery before he realised what he was doing.

And, ah, the strength of the desire that pulsed through him as she raised those lovely green eyes to meet his gaze... He'd felt an overwhelming compulsion to persuade her to remain with him—and the need to warn her about George had not, at first, even crossed his mind.

'I spoke with her afterwards...' At Davie's lifted eyebrow, he admitted, 'Very well, we took tea together. Before I sent her on her way, she invited me to dinner. Since I haven't heard from her today, I assume the marquess didn't tell her to rescind the invitation.'

Davie let out a low whistle. 'The lady must have cast quite a spell for you to voluntarily venture into the enemy's lair.'

Giles grinned. 'I don't expect they'll have me for dessert. And, yes, I find Lady Margaret intriguing; we had quite an interesting chat about politics during tea. But don't go picking out names for my firstborn.'

'None of us is ready for that!' Davie said with a laugh. 'But I admit, I am surprised. Though perhaps I shouldn't be. You've been alone for some time now, and you've never been interested in Beauties with more hair than wit.'

'Lady Margaret is certainly not that.' Now that he'd been forced to open up about the lady, Giles found it was...a relief, to be able to talk about the object of his inexplicable attraction with a perceptive friend. Davie would give advice if he thought it fitting, and unlike Ben and Christopher, do so without roasting Giles mercilessly about the connection.

'I was attracted to her from the outset, even more so

after talking with her after the session. She delivered a rather eloquent philosophical defence of conservatism, but at the same time, was willing to admit there are valid reasons for reform, as well as significant public support for it. I suppose I expected that, as a Tory, she'd be dogmatic and dismissive in her views, and was surprised to find her so open-minded. And so well spoken about politics.'

'She has been her father's hostess for years. One would have expected her to pick up some information about the process.'

'Perhaps, but you've observed many of the political hostesses. They create a congenial atmosphere to encourage dinner conversation, support their husband or relative's position ardently and campaign with enthusiasm. But most have neither interest in nor understanding of the intricacies of policy. I can't recall any who could articulate a position with as much eloquence as Lady Margaret. It was…energising to debate what I love with so knowledgeable and passionate a lady.'

'And she's so much more pleasing to the eye than most of your Reformist orators,' David agreed with a laugh. 'But—what of George? If you dine with the marquess, he's sure to hear of it. One can well imagine his reaction—especially now that he's lost his seat. Even though you said when you met him at Brooks's the other night, he didn't seem disturbed about it.'

Possibly because he was more disturbed about Lady Margaret—a concern Giles *hadn't* divulged to Davie. 'Perhaps he thinks the earl can countermand the election, as he has fixed every other setback George has experienced. In any event, I broached the problem to Lady Margaret. She was quite adamant that she wasn't going to allow George to dictate whom she entertained.'

'All very well, but she doesn't know him as you do. Can you feel easy, setting her up for his possible enmity?'

Giles shifted uncomfortably. He'd had second thoughts about attending for that very reason, despite his strong desire to further his relationship with the lady. 'I considered bowing out,' he admitted. 'But dammit, I don't want to allow George to once again try to dictate my life! In any event, he's more likely to direct his ire at me, rather than at the lady, and I'm used to dealing with it. If he should be unpleasant to Lady Margaret…he'll answer to me. Nor do I think the marquess would take very well to having his daughter harassed, and he has more power even than the earl. I'm confident I can proceed without causing difficulties for her.'

'If you are satisfied, that's good enough for me. Enjoy your dinner, then! I'll be most interested to hear what topics are discussed.'

'I intend to enjoy it—and hope to escape that Tory den with most of my hide intact.'

'I shall be back later to commiserate, if you need to return and lick your wounds.'

'I shall hold you to it.'

While Davie put down his glass and went off to change for dinner, Giles remained in the sitting room, sipping his wine. He was relieved to find his faith in his friend justified; after ascertaining the basic facts about Giles's relationship with Lady Margaret, Davie had neither pried for more nor quizzed him about it.

So, what did he hope to accomplish tonight?

There was the political aspect, of course. Lord Grey might not have sent him to the dinner, but the invitation did provide a sterling opportunity to sound out one of the leaders of the Lords about his position on the upcoming reform legislation. If he could discover from Lord Witlow what areas of compromise there might be, the bill could be tailored to accommodate that before it left committee. Anything which improved the chances for getting the bill approved as quickly as possible in this session would be a great advantage.

He would need to be on his guard, though. He didn't know who the other guests might be, but it was reasonable to expect some would be hidebound conservatives. He'd better prepare himself to be attacked.

Still, if he'd managed to survive the verbal and physical assaults mounted against him at Eton, before Christopher and then Ben had arrived to befriend him, he wasn't too worried about the venom of politicians. Especially as he came as an invited dinner guest. He doubted his host would allow anyone present to hurl at him the sort of vicious epithets about his mother that had resulted in so many bloody-knuckled exchanges during his schoolboy years.

The larger looming question was, of course, the lady: what did he intend to do about Lady Margaret?

As impressed with her—and attracted to her—as he was, he was not at all interested in marriage. As Davie noted, he and the other Hellions were still junior enough not to need a wife's connections to advance their political careers. And for reasons he'd never bothered to fully analyse, the very idea of marriage aroused some deep, nameless aversion.

Perhaps it was the disastrous aftermath of his parents' union, or the lingering guilt he couldn't shake at having inadvertently been the cause of that failure. Given his political aims and affiliations, as he'd informed her today, a union with him could do Lady Margaret no good whatsoever. And if anything happened to him before the current earl's demise, his unfortunate wife would inherit only the enmity of a half-brother more than ready to step into his shoes.

Fortunately, one of the few benefits of being estranged from the earl was it allowed him to avoid the society in which Telbridge and his half-brother moved. If there were any scheming, marriage-minded females who took the long view, figuring that enticing into marriage a man of modest means now would pay off later when said husband inherited a wealthy earldom, they could hardly weave any webs to trap him when he never appeared at any of their social events.

He intended to enjoy his ambivalent position in his single, solitary state for a good deal longer. Although, he did chuckle to imagine the consternation it might create in Reform circles were he to turn up with a wife who had as strong a Tory pedigree as Lady Margaret.

He *was* powerfully attracted to the lady, and was reasonably certain she returned the compliment. A widow with her own property who was not dependent upon some relative for her support—and therefore not under their control—was exactly the sort of female he'd looked to in the past for the few affairs in which he'd indulged.

And Davie was right—it had been a long time since his last liaison, which had ended amicably when the lady in question decided she wanted to pursue remarriage. He'd kept busy with work since, and when the need for intimacy could no longer be denied, had a friendly arrangement with a discreet lady of the trade, who accommodated his desires with expertise and enthusiasm.

Might Lady Margaret be amenable to an affair?

Desire dried his mouth and tightened his body.

How he'd love to bury his fingers in her thicket of auburn hair, pulling the pins free until the heavy mass billowed down around her shoulders! Watch those green eyes darken with passion as he slowly disrobed her, fanning her desire higher and higher as he kissed and caressed the flesh as he bared it. He could imagine the feel of her breasts, heavy in his hands, the nipples tightening under his tongue. Then to proceed lower, over the silk of her belly, into the valley between her thighs, to the hidden centre of her desires…

He was throbbingly erect, just contemplating it. But he'd better douse those amorous thoughts before dinner. He'd hardly be able to hold his own against the enquiries that were likely to be fired at him by the Conservative diners with the velocity of volleys from a British square, if he spent the meal in a glassy-eyed haze of lust.

Besides, though he had no doubt Lady Margaret was attracted to him as well, being attracted and inviting him to an affair were rather large steps apart. For the time being—or until she sent him unmistakable verbal or non-verbal cues indicating such a leap interested her—he had better just focus on enjoying the lady's conversation.

Taking a deep breath, he told himself to banish dreams of trysting and concentrate on politics.

To his surprise, it required an unusually strong application of will to do so, as his normally all-consuming passion suddenly seemed not so all-consuming.

But even with lust banished to simmer beneath the surface, his whole body still tingled with anticipation at meeting Lady Margaret again soon.

## Chapter Six

Several hours later, Giles entered Lord Witlow's town house in Russell Square. So this was where Lady Margaret had been raised, he thought, noting the Adamesque decor in muted tones, augmented here and there with Greek statuary and Oriental vases. Tasteful, classic and understated, like the lady.

He took the stairs with alacrity, telling himself the excitement coursing through him stemmed partly from anticipation of the spirited political debate he expected at dinner—and not just because of his strong desire to see his hostess again.

He found the anteroom occupied by a dozen or so guests, gathered in clusters, and already so absorbed in their discussions that they scarcely looked up as the butler intoned his name. He did not at first see Lady Margaret, though the simmering undercurrent of energy heightening his senses indicated that she must be present.

And then he spied her, walking over with her father to greet him, beautifully dressed in a gown of deep green that set off her eyes. Though he lamented the demise of the fashion for very low-cut dinner gowns, Giles noted, running an appreciative gaze over her figure, that the new lower-waisted style emphasised her slender form and accentuated the swell of that far-too-well-concealed bosom. As he raised his eyes to her face, she extended her hand.

He bowed over it, feeling a tremor vibrate through her fingers as he raised them to his lips. He had to fight to keep himself from letting his lips linger over the soft kidskin, while his nostrils filled with scent of violets. Concentrate on politics, he warned the senses that urged him to cut her from the group and whisk her away somewhere they might be private.

'Father, I'm sure you remember Viscount Lyndlington— or Mr Hadley, as he prefers to be addressed. I was so impressed by his speech to the Commons, I took the liberty of adding him to our gathering.'

'I heard from several sources about the eloquence of that address,' the marquess said. 'Let's see if you can be equally eloquent in persuading some of my colleagues to your views tonight.'

'I hope in turn to become better acquainted with your objections to it,' Giles replied. 'Knowledge and openness to altering opinions will be the only way compromise can happen.'

'I shall look forward to the exchange,' the marquess replied. 'I believe you know most of the gentlemen?' He waved a hand towards the rest of the room.

Giles forced himself to take his eyes from Lady Margaret, who was shyly smiling at him, and gaze around him. He'd been expecting a gathering of Tory lords, but the group was in fact much more varied. Beside several of the marquess's associates from the Lords stood his good friend Lord Bathhurst and the irascible Baron Coopley, one of the most rigid Tories. But also present were the railroad man and inventor George Stephenson, several Tory MPs, and one of the Committee of Four whom Lord Grey had charged with drafting the Reform Bill, Sir James Graham.

This grouping should indeed provide for some interesting discussion, he thought, hopeful that prospect would make it easier to concentrate on politics—and ignore the allure of Lady Margaret, to whom his gaze kept returning, like a child's toy pulled by a string.

Another guest was announced, and host and hostess moved on to welcome him. Giles watched Lady Margaret's graceful sway of a walk as long as he thought he could get away with it without the raptness of his attention becoming notable, then made his way to the group which included Sir James.

'Hadley!' the Whig leader said in surprise as Giles joined them. 'I didn't know you were acquainted with the marquess. I'll look forward to having a friend in my corner during the debate tonight. Though you'll hear the variety of views Lord Witlow enjoys, I fear we shall still be outnumbered.'

Avoiding any comment about his connection to the marquess, Giles said, 'How does Lord Grey think the lines will be drawn, once the bill comes out of committee?'

As he expected, it required only that question to launch Sir James and the two MPs standing with him into a spirited debate about how the legislation would progress, a discussion Giles would normally have followed avidly. Tonight, he listened with half an ear, surreptitiously trying to keep Lady Margaret in sight.

She was a good hostess, greeting each newcomer, sometimes allowing her father to direct the conversation, sometimes, with gentlemen who were obviously old family friends, giving the newcomer a hug or a kiss on the cheek.

Giles never thought he'd be jealous of venerable gentlemen from the older generation. At least, he told the impatient little voice within that clamoured to be near her, she wasn't gifting her kisses to any man who looked virile enough to be his rival as a lover.

Startled to realise his interest in Lady Margaret had somehow progressed from admiration to evaluating other men as competition, he followed Sir James's group in as the butler called them to table.

To his disappointment, he wasn't seated near his hostess—the elderly Marquess of Berkley and Lord Coopley had that honour, as was proper for the two highest-ranking guests. He *was* surprised that he'd been seated adjacent to his host, a place that would normally have been reserved for a gentleman of higher status. Unless, he realised with a rueful grimace, one took into account his position as a courtesy viscount.

At first, conversation was general, with comments on the food and wine and an exchange of pleasantries and social news among the gentleman. Having nothing of interest to contribute, Giles listened politely, his glance straying to Lady Margaret at the other end of the table.

She was smiling at Lord Coopley—and what a lovely smile it was, he thought, those generous lips upturned and her eyes brightening. He liked what she'd done with her hair tonight, thick coils of auburn fire pinned atop her head, with little tendrils curling down to kiss her brow and earlobes—as he would love to. That luscious mouth, too.

'…do you not think so, Hadley?'

Startled by the sound of his name, he jerked his head back to find the marquess regarding him, a slight smile on his face. Realising he'd not only been rudely inattentive to the host who'd done him the honour of seating him beside him, he'd also been caught staring at the man's daughter, he gave himself a sharp mental rebuke, feeling his face heat.

If he were a parent worth the name, Lady Margaret's father must already be curious about the link between them. The last thing he needed was to give the marquess a distaste of him by exhibiting the sort of ill-bred behaviour his half-brother always accused him of—or worse still, have Witlow suspect the strength of his amorous interest in Lady Margaret.

That subject concerned the two of them alone.

'I'm sorry, my lord, I didn't quite hear. Could you repeat the question?'

'Certainly.' A little twitch to his lips, as if he didn't believe Giles's excuse for an instant, but didn't mean to call him on it, Witlow complied. This time, Giles listened closely, telling himself sternly for the remainder of the dinner to concentrate on his *host*.

Once the diners ventured into political matters, the conversation became stimulating enough to hold Giles's attention, despite the ever-beckoning temptation of Lady Margaret seated at the other end of the table. Giles deferred to Sir James, letting the senior Member shoulder the burden of defending the Reform cause, adding a comment only when called upon. Not that he was afraid of speaking out, but it would be presumptuous for a junior member to put himself forward when Grey's aide was present, an experienced man better known to this group than he.

Some time later, he heard Lord Coopley call his name. 'So, Hadley,' the baronet said in his gravelly voice, 'your half-brother tells me you carry a torch for the Friends of the People?'

'In a way,' Giles replied. 'Since Lord Grey himself formed the group, all of us who call ourselves Reformers are happy to carry on his ideals. Who could disagree with the notion that talent and virtue should be the chief requirements for a Member of Parliament?'

Apparently able to disagree, Lord Coopley sniffed. 'Every male eighteen and older to have a vote? Parliaments to be elected annually? One member of Parliament for each twenty thousand citizens? Bah! How could the nation's business be done, with Parliament forming and breaking up every season, and any Tom, Dick and Harry who could stagger to the polls after drinking a quart of election gin able to cast a vote? In private, no less, so one would never know where he stood! I suppose you sympathise with the Spencean Philanthropists, too, who would confiscate all our land and parcel it out, a few acres to every man, woman and child in the land?'

'Did my half-brother tell you that, as well?' Giles asked, irritated. Trust George to make him sound like the most rabid radical imaginable.

'He did. You're not going to call the Earl of Telbridge's son a liar, are you?'

Much as he would like to, he knew it wouldn't be prudent. 'Certainly not. Though it's true we agree on very little,' he replied, trying to walk a cautious line between dismissing the charge as nonsense and agreeing he supported a position he didn't.

Coopley uttered a bark of a laugh. 'Distributing land to everyone! I'd like to see what a tailor or a baker or a bricklayer would do with ten acres of prime farmland!'

'Or a Parliamentarian or lawyer?' Giles replied with a smile. 'I think we are all better off staying within our spheres of expertise. I'm sure Mr Stephenson would not like to have me conducting experiments on steam power, lest I blow him sky-high.'

As he'd hoped, the gentlemen laughed, easing the tension.

'Lord Coopley, could I beg your assistance?' Lady Margaret interposed, touching that gentleman's arm. 'Was it the Warrington Exetors who returned a Tory candidate for the last Parliament, or the Covington Exetors? Your memory for names is keen as a huntsman's knife, and you know everyone who is anybody.'

'Covington, my dear, Covington,' Coopley said, patting her hand. 'The family have been Tories since Peel's administration.' Either forgetting Giles or losing interest in baiting him, the older man launched into a detailed description of each administration in which an Exetor had served.

Giles risked catching Lady Margaret's eye to give her a quick nod of thanks, to which she replied with a slight smile and a lift of her brows before turning back to her dinner partner.

A short time later, the footmen cleared the table, and Lady Margaret stood up. 'Gentlemen, I'll leave you to begin your more...*lively* debates. Thank you all for coming, and I'll bid you goodnight. Papa, I'll be reading in the library; come see me later, if the vigorous discourse you're sure to enjoy after my departure doesn't totally exhaust you.'

Giles watched her walk out with appreciative eyes. Initially disappointed that she did not even glance in his direction before she left the room, he brightened when he recalled her parting comment about repairing to the library.

Had that been aimed solely at her father...or could he flatter himself that she'd meant it partly for him, too?

At the idea of having her to himself for a few moments, excitement flared, and he immediately began scheming how he might politely get away without exciting comment.

Sir James was watching her, too. 'She certainly rescued you deftly!' the baronet murmured to Giles after she disappeared from view. 'What a consummate hostess! I wish I had the like!'

'Lady Graham is a very gracious hostess,' Giles replied.

'My Fanny does her best, but she doesn't truly enjoy it,' Sir James replied. 'You need only look at Lady Margaret to see she thrives on discussion and debate. An excellent campaigner, too, which my Fanny most decidedly is not! The travelling, the dust, the crowds all exhaust her. There was talk a while back that Sir Francis Mowbrey might lure Lady Margaret away from her father to work her magic on his behalf, but in the end, it came to nothing.'

'Sir Francis Mowbrey, the Tory MP from Suffolk?' Giles asked, hoping he sounded like a politely interested guest—rather than like a man completely obsessed by the lady.

'Yes, he wooed her some years ago, not long after she came out of mourning. Sir Francis was making a name for himself in Tory circles and had all the right qualifications: old landed family, educated at Eton and Cambridge, related to many of the peers in the Lords, not to mention the ladies found him charming. They were engaged, but just before they were to wed, Lady Margaret cried off. Sir Francis was quite public about his displeasure over the break; understandable, I suppose—it was a better match for him than for the lady, as he would gain access to her considerable fortune, as well as her Tory contacts and political expertise.'

Surprised, Giles said, 'I wouldn't have expected Lady Margaret to be a jilt. Or capriciously change her mind at the last minute.'

'Well, let's just say Sir Francis was better at wooing than he was at fidelity. He liked the ladies as much as they liked him, and though he was discreet about it, apparently continued his little *amours* even after the engagement. The *on dit* was that Lady Margaret got wind of it, and decided she didn't want to become a wife who had to look the other way. Fair enough, I suppose.'

The man sounded like an arrogant jackass, Giles thought, though he made himself utter something appropriately banal. Better not to express his disgust, and risk alerting the baronet to the intensity of his interest in the lady.

But if Sir Francis had been foolish enough to lose the esteem of a woman of Lady Margaret's stature by trysting with other females, he didn't deserve her.

And if he'd led her on with declarations of love that turned out to be hollow, that might explain, Giles suddenly realised, why an eminently eligible female like Lady Margaret had chosen not to remarry.

Their attention was recalled by the marquess, who invited each guest to give his opinion on what would be the most important matter to be brought before Parliament in the current session. Mentally filing away what he'd just learned from Sir James, Giles returned his attention to matters political, biding his time until he could take his departure.

Finally, after an hour of intense debate came the lull that enabled him to make his escape. Pleading an early day working on committee reports, he expressed his appreciation to his host and took his leave. After enquiring of a footman where he might find the library, so he could bid his hostess goodnight, Giles walked in the direction indicated and towards the encounter he'd been anticipating all night.

The door to the library stood ajar. Intending to announce himself, he paused on the threshold, taking in the scene within.

Lady Margaret sat on a sofa near the fire, a full brace of candles on the table beside her, a slight smile on her face as she gazed down at the book she held. Light from the blazing hearth played in a teasing dance on her auburn hair, setting the burnished locks aglow and illumining her pale face with a blush of amber.

The sight of her, looking so solitary and yet so serene, struck his chest like a blow. In a rush of memory, he recalled how, after being put to bed, he'd sneak back to the small parlour in the little cottage he'd occupied with his mother, wanting another story or a goodnight kiss. He'd slip in to find her alone and reading, and think how beautiful she was. Long before he'd learned that they were poor, that they'd been cast off by his father, that she was living in exiled disgrace, he'd felt such a deep sense of peace and safety when she welcomed him with a hug before carrying him off to bed again.

Lady Margaret cast so similar an aura, for a moment he had the ridiculous feeling that he was coming home.

Before he could shake it off, as if that special energy that sizzled between them had alerted her to his presence, she looked up. 'Mr Hadley!' she exclaimed. 'Is the group breaking up so soon?'

'No, the rest of the gentlemen are still avidly engaged. I believe they'll be there until the brandy gives out.'

She laughed softly, a musical sound that made him want to smile. 'Since the supply is virtually inexhaustible, they should be there until dawn. But you need to leave?'

'Well…' He gave her a rueful grin. 'To be honest, I must admit I made my excuses early…hoping to have a private word with you.'

Her smile widened. 'And I was hoping you might slip away. Won't you come in?'

A body blow from a skilled pugilist couldn't have kept him from advancing towards her. 'With pleasure.'

# *Chapter Seven*

Looking up to find Mr Hadley standing on threshold, so discretion-meltingly handsome with his broad-shouldered form outlined by the darkness beyond and his face illumined by candlelight, she at first thought she'd longed for him so fiercely, she was only imagining his presence. Then he smiled, confirming he was no illusion, and her foolish heart leapt in gladness.

'I'm so pleased you took my hint that I'd be in the library,' she said, trying to slow her pulse as she waved him to a seat on the sofa beside her.

'I'm so pleased you gave me the hint.'

Now that she'd got what she'd hoped for, she felt unaccountably shy. 'Did you enjoy the discussions?' she asked, feeling even more foolish for falling back on the prosaic, when she really wanted to ask him all about himself—his youth, his schooling, how he'd developed an interest in politics, what he wanted to achieve…whether he would reconcile with his father. Oh, she wanted to know *everything* about him!

He laughed. 'The exchange did indeed become more "lively" after your departure! With Sir James to buttress my position, I flatter myself that I gave as good as I got, and managed to rattle a few firmly held opinions. Enough that I thought it prudent to depart and leave them to enjoy their brandy in peace.'

'I thought you held your own admirably during dinner—and with great diplomacy. Especially with Lord Coopley.' She sighed. 'I'm afraid he can be quite dogmatic, but he's been Papa's mentor since he entered the Lords. He'd be so hurt if he learned Papa had hosted one of his "discussion evenings" and we had not invited him.'

'I did rather feel like a Christian in the arena after the tigers were released. Thank you again for the rescue, by the way. Browbeating aside, I found it useful to hear all the arguments the Tories may summon; it will help my committee prepare the best responses to counter them. Because the Lords *must* pass the bill this session.'

'Must?' she echoed, puzzled. 'Why "must" this time, when they've already failed several times before?'

'Surely you observed the mood of the country when you went out to Chellingham! There's even more agitation in the counties, especially in the northern industrial districts around Manchester, Liverpool and Leeds. Memories of the St Peter's Field Massacre are still vivid. By failing to vote for reasonable change, the Lords could foment the very rioting and civil discord they think to avoid.'

Alarmed, she was going to ask him to elaborate when he held up a hand. 'But enough politics for one evening! First, let me compliment you on a delicious dinner. After the bachelor fare I usually settle for, it was quite sumptuous! You really are, as Sir James asserted, the perfect hostess, providing for the needs of your guests, making sure everyone is included in the conversation, inserting a soothing comment here and there if the discussion gets heated—without the overheated gentleman ever noticing he'd been deflected. Quite masterful!'

'Thank you,' she said, flushing with pleasure at his praise. 'I do enjoy it, especially "discussion evenings" such as this one, where there are a range of views exchanged. Alas, despite the best pamphleteering efforts of Anna Wheeler and William Thompson, I fear women will not get the vote soon. This gives me some way to contribute.'

'Your lady mother does not enjoy playing hostess?'

'Mama's health is…delicate. She lost two babes in London in the early days when Papa first sat in the Lords; the experience left her with a permanent distaste for the city and, I'm afraid, for politics. Much as she and Papa dislike being apart, she now remains year-round in the country, while Papa resides here when Parliament is in session.'

'But your brother does not? As active in politics as your father is, I would have thought he would urge his son to stand for one of the seats in his county—or in one of the boroughs he controls.'

'I'm afraid Julian has no interest at all in politics—much to Papa's disappointment.' She laughed ruefully. 'I was the child who inherited that passion. After Mama took us into the country, it was always me, not Julian, who pestered Papa to tell us all about what had happened during the session after he came home to Huntsford. When I spent my Season with my great-aunt Lilly, I persuaded Papa to let me play hostess for a few of his political dinners—and loved it! And so, after…after I was w-widowed,' she said, not able even after all this time to speak of losing Robbie without a tremor in her voice, 'I took it up again.'

'Your brother stays in the country, as well? I don't re-call ever hearing of him in town.'

'Yes, he watches out for Mama, to whom he is devoted, and manages the estate. After all, he will inherit it, and such a vast enterprise requires careful supervision. Papa began to train him for it when he was quite young, and Julian loves working the land.'

'While you prefer the city?'

'Oh, no, I love being at Huntsford! My husband's es-tate is in the same county, and had things…not worked out otherwise, I would have been content to live out my life there. Afterward, I…needed to get away. Fortunately, Papa was willing to take me on again as his hostess.' She gestured around her. 'So here I am, back in the bosom of my family, though I do return almost daily to my own house in Upper Brook Street. Father, Mama, Julian were everything to me when…when I lost my husband. I really don't know how I would have survived without them. Ex-cuse me, I know I probably shouldn't say anything, but that is what I find so tragic about your situation—that you are estranged from your own father, and from the land and people it will one day be your responsibility to manage and look after.'

He seemed to recoil, and worried she'd trespassed on to forbidden ground, she said, 'It's none of my business, I know. I hope I haven't offended you.'

He'd clenched his jaw, but after a moment, he relaxed it. 'You're quite brave. Most of my acquaintance don't dare mention the earl.'

She gave him a rueful smile. 'Foolhardy, rather than brave. It just…makes my heart ache to hear about a fam-ily estranged from one another. After losing two siblings and…and my best friend and dearest love, those few I have left are so precious to me. One never knows how much time one will have with them. Another reason I enjoy playing hostess to Papa.'

He nodded. 'That's true enough. With the thoughtlessness of youth, I never imagined I would lose my mother so early.'

'She must have been wonderfully brave. To endure being isolated, with even her own family abandoning her.'

He laughed shortly. 'A child accepts what he knows as "normal". It never occurred to me while I was growing up in that little cottage on the wilds of the Hampshire downs that we were isolated or alone. Of course, like most boys, I wished I had brothers to play with, but Mama made the humble place we occupied a haven, full of joy and comfort. By the time I'd been away long enough to understand what had happened, why we lived as we did, it was too late. Too late to tell her how much I appreciated the love and care she gave, and the tremendous strength and courage she displayed in creating a happy home for her child, despite her own sorrow.' He shook his head. 'When my aunt came to take me away to school, I pleaded not to have to leave. I was certain I would be content to spend my whole life there, in that little cottage.'

Emboldened by having him answer her other questions, knowing she was pushing the bounds of the permissible, but unable to stop herself she said, 'So you don't think you would ever be able to forgive your father—the earl?'

His face shuttered. Alarmed, she feared he'd either say nothing at all, or give her the set-down she deserved for asking so personal a question. But after a moment, he said, 'Mama could have lied, you know. Denied that she and Richard had been lovers. My aunt told me that the earl had assured her he'd always known she loved Richard, and only wanted the truth. And then he punished her for giving it to him, in the most humiliating fashion possible. Disgraced. Divorced. Repudiated by her own family. How can I forgive him that?'

The anguish in his tone broke her heart, and she wanted to reach out to him—the isolated child whose adored mother had been mistreated and scorned.

'I don't know,' she said honestly. 'But I do know that anger eats away at the soul, creating a wound that festers. One cannot heal until one lets it go.' Advice she would do well to heed herself, she thought ruefully.

'Would that I could follow such wise counsel,' he said. 'Perhaps some day, I will.'

'It was presumptuous of me to offer it,' she admitted.

'Caring,' he corrected. 'You do offer it out of… compassion, don't you?'

Oh, it wasn't wise for her heart to ache for his pain—but it did. 'Yes,' she whispered.

With a sigh, he picked up her hand and placed a kiss on it. At his touch, their discussions of politics, her family, his past—all the words in her brain disintegrated, leaving her conscious only of sensation, as the simmering connection between them flamed up, powerful and resurgent. She caught her breath, her fingers trembling in his, fighting the urge to lean closer and caress his cheek.

Then he was bending towards her, his grip on her hand tightening as he drew her against him. She closed her eyes and angled her face up, offering her lips, filled with urgency for his kiss.

He brushed her mouth gently, as if seeking permission. She gave it with a moan and a hand to the back of his neck, pulling him closer. Groaning, he dropped her hand to wrap his arms around her, pressing her against his chest while he deepened the kiss.

At his urging, she opened her mouth to him. He sought her tongue and tangled his with it, sending ripples of pleasure radiating throughout her body. She rubbed her aching breasts against his chest, wanting to be closer, impatient with the layers of cloth that kept them from feeling flesh upon flesh.

Time, place, everything fell away. She was consumed by him, devouring him, afire with ravening need that raged stronger with every stroke of his tongue.

Lost in mindless abandon, she wasn't sure how much further she would have gone, had he not suddenly broken the kiss, pushed her away, and jumped up to stumble to the hearth.

'Voices!' he rasped, his tone breathless and uneven. 'Coming this way.'

She heard them then, the shock of cold air against her heated cheeks as he abandoned her slamming her back to the present even as she recognised her father's tones and Lord Coopley's growling bass.

'Th-thank you,' she stuttered, raising shaking hands to straighten her bodice and smooth her disordered curls.

Seconds later, the two men entered the library, stopping short when they saw she wasn't alone. 'Hello, Papa, my lord. Is the group breaking up?' she managed.

'Yes, the others have gone,' her father said, looking curiously between her and Hadley. 'Coopley and I were going to have one last brandy.'

'As you can see, Mr Hadley lingered to thank me for dinner, and I'm afraid I waylaid him with some further conversation, even though he'd informed me he needed to get away to prepare for a meeting tomorrow. But I shall let him go now.'

Whatever her father might be thinking about finding the two of them alone together, he made no comment. 'We will wish you goodnight, then, Mr Hadley. Thank you for attending our little gathering, and I hope we will have the pleasure of your company again soon.'

'The pleasure was certainly mine,' Hadley replied. 'Lady Margaret, Lord Witlow, Lord Coopley.' He bowed, and before she could more than nod, he strode from the room.

'Will you join us, Puss?' her father asked.

The last thing she needed now, with her body in an uproar and her mind in disarray, was to face her father's all-too-perceptive scrutiny. 'No, you'll wish to finish whatever discussion was ongoing, and I don't want to prevent you. I am rather sleepy, so I'll take myself to bed.'

She rose and walked over to give each man a kiss, hoping her father wouldn't notice her breathing was still uneven and her hands were trembling.

At a pace she hoped looked decorous rather than panicked, she exited the library.


The following morning, after tossing and turning for hours, Maggie got up at first light. Too restless, and irritated by her restlessness, to attempt to return to sleep, she decided to go for an early morning gallop. The rush of cold air and exhilaration of a hard ride would settle her, clear her muddled mind, and help her decide what she must do.

She rang for her maid, donned her habit, and as the first grey light broke over city, gathered her horse and a sleepy groom and set out for Hyde Park.

She knew what frustrated desire felt like—she'd experienced it often enough, after friendship with Robbie turned to passion, and before they could be wed. Tiring her body with a strenuous ride would dissipate it. If only it might also dissipate the confusion in her brain, and resolve the tug and pull between the compulsion to pursue a relationship with Hadley, and the caution that warned she had far too little self-control where he was concerned, and ought to avoid him.

Sending her groom home after she made it safely to the park, since the sun would be well up by the time she was ready to return, she urged her mare to gallop. For the next hour, she alternated between riding hard and resting her mount, until her hands ached and her legs were trembling.

But the clamour of her body for more of Hadley's touch had not abated. Not was her mind any clearer than when she'd set out.

Irritated at herself for this unusual inability to make up her mind, she was walking her lathered mare along the path when, rounding a corner, she came upon the cause of her dilemma, trotting on a high-stepping chestnut gelding.

His horse, obviously fresh, reared up, giving Maggie a few seconds to calm the sudden racing of her heart at seeing Giles Hadley again.

He dismounted and walked towards her, his face alight in a smile. 'Lady Margaret! How delightful to see you. Though it is rather early for a ride.'

Oh, how she could lose herself in that smile! It took all her increasingly feeble strength of will to keep herself from running to him and throwing herself in his arms. 'I don't like to waste the morning in bed. At least, not alone.'

Horrified she'd actually said that aloud, her cheeks flamed as, after a shocked moment, he threw back his head and laughed. 'Now, that's a sentiment with which I can heartily concur.'

He fell in step beside her—just a hand's breadth away.

The air between them fairly sparkled with sensual tension. Oh, she wanted…how she *wanted*.

She hadn't felt this powerful an attraction, this irresistible a need, since the early days of her marriage with Robbie. Love might be out of the question…but it was only the matter of the ever-ticking clock before the possibility of passion was lost, too. Could she pass up this chance to feel again its heat and power and fulfilment?

A pied piper to lead her wherever he wished, he looked down at her as he took her hand and kissed it. 'My very dear Lady Margaret.'

Her world narrowed to the wonder of his blue-eyed gaze, the force of the need flowing from her to him, from him to her, in that simple clasp of fingers.

Before prudence had a chance to try to wrestle will back under control, she blurted, 'I'm about to be very unladylike. But as I discovered some years ago, one cannot depend on the future; if one sees something one wants, one should seize it while one can.'

His eyes searched her face. 'And you see something you want?' he asked softly.

'You,' she whispered. And then sucked in a panicked breath, terrified, once the word had been spoken and couldn't be taken back, that her brazenness would shock or offend him, that he would utter some blighting word and walk away. Would he be gentleman enough not to make her a laughingstock at his clubs? she wondered, light-headed at the risk she'd just taken.

Never taking his eyes from hers, he shook his head a little. 'Excuse me, Lady Margaret. Did you just suggest what I think you did?'

'Yes,' she said tartly, her face burning now with heat of another sort, 'and I do wish you would answer, instead of staring at me in that confounding way. If you intend to refuse, please do so, and let me bid you good day and quit the park before I expire of mortification.'

'You must know I'm not about to refuse!' With a laugh, he lifted the hand she'd almost forgotten he still held and brought it to his lips. 'You must excuse my shock; I've never been offered *carte blanche* by a lady before. But now that I've recovered, I have only two questions: Where? When?'

She better do this immediately, before she lost her nerve. 'My house—Upper Brook Street, Number Four. Now. The elderly cousin who lives with me for form's sake is very deaf, and never rises before noon. Come by way of the mews. I'll tell the grooms to admit you.'

He nodded, and without waiting for anything more— she was now so agitated, she couldn't have stood still a moment longer in any event—Maggie tugged on the reins and led her horse away.

Giles stared after the retreating form of Lady Margaret, still not sure he'd heard her correctly. Rapidly he replayed the conversation in his mind: yes, it had not been just wishful imagining. She really had invited him to become her lover.

Now.

Hell and damnation, what was he doing just standing here?

With a joyful laugh, he tugged on the reins to bring his horse close, then threw himself into the saddle. After one reckless, whooping delight of a gallop around the deserted Rotten Row, startling milkmaids and scattering cows, he pulled up, laughing.

He still couldn't believe it. After the suspicion in the eyes of her father when he caught them in library last night—after kissing her with wanton abandon on the sofa in her father's library, the door open, a roomful of guests only a few doors away, any one of whom could have walked in and discovered them, he'd thought he'd be lucky if she even spoke to him again.

He'd come to the park to ride before his meetings this morning, to clear from his mind the fog of last night's brandy and to work out how best to apologise. He couldn't explain it to himself—how he couldn't be near her without wanting to touch her, couldn't touch her without wanting the feel of her body pressed against his, his mouth on hers...

Instead of being forced to grovel for forgiveness for his effrontery, after three short meetings, she was inviting him into her arms. He shook his head, marvelling. The progression towards that invitation was like no path of seduction he'd ever trod before. There'd been virtually no flirting, no exchange of remarks laden with suggestive *double entendres*, no meaningful glances, no surreptitious touches in public, heightening desire by inciting it when it could not be sated.

Just a great deal of conversation centred on politics, sensual tension ever humming between them, and one sanity-robbing, blazing inferno of a kiss.

Lord bless a lady who knew her own mind! The connection must be as powerful for her as was for him.

He took another circuit around the park, letting the gelding walk off the heat of the gallop, until he judged the lady would have had enough time to return home and prepare herself. The thought of her removing her habit, brushing out her hair, waiting for him, naked under her dressing gown, tightened his chest and hardened other things until, almost dizzy with desire, he could scarcely breathe.

His mouth dry, his member throbbing, he imagined

that first touch. He'd worship her with hands and mouth before the first possession. Giddy with delight, on fire with need.

As for the committee meeting to begin soon, he dismissed it without a second thought. The Whigs had been trying to pummel through a Reform Bill for almost ten years; this one could wait a few hours for his attention.

He—and Lady Margaret—could not.

Grinning, he turned his mount towards Upper Brook Street.

## Chapter Eight

By the time Maggie reached her town house, the heat of the ride had evaporated, leaving second thoughts to ambush her with the ferocity of a Reform zealot decrying a rotten borough. As she turned her horse over to the groom, she opened her mouth to tell him a gentleman would be coming for whom he must unlock the gate… but the words died on her lips.

She took the stairs to her bedchamber, directing a passing housemaid to go for hot water and another to help her out of habit and into a morning gown. Although she did keep clothing in both locations, since she was to spend several days at her father's town house, her lady's maid would be awaiting her there. Polly would think her mad when she turned up later, saying she'd inexplicably changed her mind and decided to go to her own home after her ride to bathe and change.

Not as mad as Mr Hadley would think her, when he arrived shortly to discover she'd changed her mind about an affair.

Oh, why could she not have reined in her raging desire before she blurted out that ill-judged invitation? She'd rather walk through the House of Lords in her shift than suffer through the interview she was about to have with her erstwhile lover.

He was almost certain to be angry, and with good cause. At best, he would think her a featherhead who didn't know her own mind; at worst, he'd accuse her of being a tease—or a wanton. It made her sick to think of forfeiting his respect and friendship.

She took a deep breath to settle the nausea. There were worse things. She could weather this loss.

Yet another loss.

Steeling herself for the uncomfortable interview to come, she walked down to the parlour to await Giles Hadley.

She was pacing restlessly when he arrived, some fifteen minutes later. After a knock at the door, a puzzled footman showed him in, and he came over to take her hand and kiss it. 'I'm afraid the groom forgot to leave the gate unlocked,' he said, squeezing her fingers. 'I had to bang and shout before I attracted attention, and he let me in and took my horse. I hope I didn't keep you waiting too long.'

He looked down at her face as he said that, and his smile faded. 'What's wrong?' he asked, his eyes narrowing in concern. 'What happened?'

She pulled her hand free, the nausea returning with her nervousness. 'Nothing—except I'm an idiot. I'm very sorry, Mr Hadley—'

'Giles. I think it's past time for you to call me Giles, don't you?'

Ignoring that, she began again. 'I'm very sorry, and I know I'm acting like a perfect ninny, but…but I'm going to have to rescind my offer. I…I can't do this.'

'I see.' He took a step back, studying her face. 'You… no longer want me?'

'No, that's not it at all! Surely you know how much I want you—I promise you, I've never before in my life propositioned a gentleman! It was entirely the unprecedented strength of the attraction between us that drove me to it. That, and the bitter knowledge that the intimacy that brings such joy is precious, and often fleeting, meant to be seized and appreciated while we can. But I can't risk it.'

Too agitated to remain still, she took to pacing the room, looking back at him as she spoke. 'I'll be indelicately blunt. Unlike most matrons who indulge in a tryst, I don't have a husband who could cover up any…unfortunate consequences. I couldn't bear to shame my father, and it would kill me to bear a child that I had to give up and could never acknowledge. And before you say anything, neither would I want to drag you into "doing the honourable thing"—forcing us into a marriage neither of us is prepared for.'

Sighing, she came back to stand beside him and looked up to meet his sombre gaze. 'Yes, I still *want*—more than you can imagine. But for so many compelling reasons, I cannot *have*. I am so sorry.' She swallowed hard, fighting back the humiliation of tears. 'I…hope you will not think too badly of me.'

She tried to look away, but he took her chin and tilted it back to face him. To her surprise, his expression seemed…tender, rather than aggrieved. 'I don't think badly of you at all. Rather the opposite! After what my mother suffered, I understand only too well the penalty imposed upon a woman for a dalliance that a man enjoys with no risk of retribution. To deny what one so strongly desires, in order to not shame family or harm innocents, is an honourable act. But a *carte blanche* doesn't have to be completely blank. One can write a few rules upon it.'

She shook her head. 'I don't understand.'

'Do you not?' At her puzzled look, he laughed softly. 'As I'm sure you know, there are many delightful ways to pleasure other than the…consummation that could put you at risk.'

She thought of how, after a long time apart, Robbie had been able to bring her to her peak with just a kiss, while he stroked and fondled. How at any time, his mouth and fingers could tease her closer and closer to that summit, close enough that she might have reached completion, even had he not claimed her.

But what of *his* pleasure? 'Do you mean you could be satisfied with…less than full possession?'

In answer, he bent down and captured her mouth. Her lips acutely sensitive after her hasty journey from arousal to frustration to excitement to disappointment, Maggie moaned, his lips coaxing her immediately to response.

'You see,' he murmured, breaking the kiss. 'So many delightful roads to pleasure. If a sensible caution is all that holds you back, you need resist no longer.'

'But what if I…want more?' she asked, by no means sure that, under the mind-numbing drug of passion, she'd have the will to restrain herself.

He chuckled again. 'I'll just have to refuse you. For protection's sake, I shall retain the most essential part of my clothing. But do not worry, my sweet. I shall very much enjoy removing all of yours.'

It was a dangerous, outrageous suggestion—but she so wanted to believe it possible. The consequences for failure, however, would be dire.

Her conflict must have been written on her face, for he said, 'Shall we try?' Dropping her hand, he went to the hearth and plucked a poker from the fireplace. 'If I should forget my resolve, use this.'

'What if I forget?'

'When you are satisfied, there will be nothing to forget.'

A tremor went through her at the thought. 'And what of your…satisfaction?'

His eyes lit, the smouldering blue light irresistible. 'I can show you the ways. Shall I? Now?'

He bent and kissed her again, unabashedly seductive, his tongue insinuating itself into her mouth, stroking, teasing, advancing and withdrawing. Dizzy, she clung to him, pressing against him, taking the kiss deeper, until they were both panting for breath.

She would burn to a cinder if she didn't have this. 'Now,' she said. Knocking the poker aside, she took his hand and led him to her bedchamber.

Once inside the room, she pulled him to her. Angling her head up, she wrapped her his arms around neck and brought her lips to his for another sweet, drugging kiss meant to banish every possibility of misgivings or regret. But as they stumbled towards the bed, she realised muzzily that she wasn't sure what should happen next, if the usual progression from kissing to completion was to be avoided.

Uncertain, she halted, and broke the kiss. His breathing ragged, he looked down at her, ran a finger gently over her cheek. 'What is it? More doubts?'

'Just…I'm not sure what to do…now.' She waved towards the bed. 'Perhaps better not to go there?'

'How about here?' He urged her to the end of the bed, sat her down and took a step back. 'Now, you tell me what you want.'

'What I want?' she repeated stupidly.

'Yes. How do I pleasure you best, my sweet lady?'

At the idea of boldly stating aloud how she wanted him to make love to her, she flushed scarlet. 'I d-don't know if I can,' she stuttered, need warring with embarrassment. 'I've…never done this before.'

He must have sensed she was on the brink of another panicked retreat, for he said quickly, 'Let me imagine, then. If I do something you don't want, just stop me.'

Before she could stutter out a reply, he sat beside her, wrapped his arms around her and leaned her back against him. Acutely sensitive to his touch, she jumped with surprise when, instead of the more intimate caress she anticipated, he began to massage her shoulders.

It felt heavenly, though, so good it quieted, for the moment, the shrill voice of passion that wanted more. After a moment, with a sigh, she relaxed against him, leaning back into the soothing ministration of his hands.

'Yes, relax, my sweet,' he murmured against her ear. 'This is for you, only for you. At your pace, according to your desires. Only yours.'

Like water dripping off a roof after rain, she felt doubt and tension slide away, one small drip at a time, until at last she was emptied of all worry. As those turbulent emotions exited, need moved in to fill the space, until her whole body was smouldering in slow, sweet arousal.

As if sensing she was ready for more, he bent down to nuzzle her neck, then sucked and nipped his way towards her ear. She shuddered as he reached the sensitive spot below the lobe, then licked and suckled the edge. 'Do you like that?' his whisper rasped in her ear.

'Yes,' she breathed, squirming to turn so she might meet his lips.

But gently, holding her in place, he massaged from her

shoulder down her arms and under, stroking along her ribs. With a whimper, she arched her back, straining to bring his caressing fingers up to her breasts.

Seeming to understand, he halted, lifting his hands up to cup her breasts. A long shuddering sigh escaped her as he rubbed his thumbs over each peaked nipple.

'Do you want this?' he whispered.

'Yes!'

'Tell me,' he urged. 'Tell me what you want.'

'I want you to…to caress my breasts,' she got out, finding it easier this time to voice the need.

She felt his hardness surge against her, and she realised, in a little flash of awe and gratification, that it aroused him to hear her say the words aloud. Emboldened by the knowledge, she said, 'I want to feel your hands on my naked breasts.'

Ah, once again she felt that delicious hardness press more firmly against her as he bent to place a long, nibbling kiss on the nape of her neck. 'Gladly.'

The drum of her heart accelerated as he moved away a bit, and she felt his hands unfastening the tapes at the back of her gown. 'Hurry!' she urged, increasingly impatient, now that she'd envisioned it, to feel that intimate touch.

He worked the bodice free, and she helped him shrug it off, but the skirt still held shift and stays in place. 'Females,' he said, kissing the bit more of her back bared by the removal of the bodice, 'wear entirely too many garments.'

Murmuring agreement, she wriggled on the bed, expecting him to unlace and remove the restricting skirt. Instead, he reached up to grab a pillow, dragged it down and leaned her back against it.

As she lay back, the stays beneath her breasts pulled

the fine linen of her shift tight across her nipples. Before she could think what he was doing, Giles took nipple, fabric and all into his mouth and suckled.

The heat and wetness of his mouth, the friction of the fabric created a sensation both similar, and entirely different, from anything she'd experienced before, when loving had begun only after she'd been completely undressed. The friction sparked a tremor that seemed to go straight to her core, sparking there a similar reaction of warmth, wetness, and tightening the spiral of desire.

His mouth moved to her other breast, bringing the magic of moisture and friction to that nipple while his thumb circled over and rubbed the wet fabric. Tension coiled tighter as the fire within built and built, until she was straining towards the peak.

Her skin flushed with heat, she tossed her head restlessly, tilting her hips, instinctively trying to move in the familiar, rhythmic pattern. As she writhed beside him, he moved his mouth to claim hers, his lips demanding entry, his tongue sweeping in to lave and dominate. At the same time, he swept an arm down under her skirts.

She kissed him back just as fiercely, seeking out his tongue, darting with hers to explore and lave each corner of his mouth. Then gasped, as his hand beneath her skirts caressed and squeezed in a slow ascent…his whole hand surrounding her ankle…two fingers tracing the delicate skin behind her knee…a single finger tracing the top edge of her stocking, sliding under and out, under and out. And finally, finally, while she whimpered her need, he moved the hand up and cupped her.

She wiggled beneath it, wanting him to go further, but for a maddening few moments, he simply rubbed that mound with his whole hand. Finally, when she thought she would shatter if he delayed any longer, he slid two fingers down to caress the tiny bud at her centre.

After so many years of abstinence, it took only this single touch to send her spiralling into the abyss. Crying out, she tensed as pleasure ignited, sending sweet fulfilment rushing outward in waves from her centre through her body to the very tips of her fingers, her toes, her earlobes.

A few mindless moments later, as the tremors faded, she sagged back, replete. In the vastness of the ocean of contentment, one small worry floated forth as, finally conscious of his rapid breaths and the still-hard member pressed against her, she realised he had not yet had his satisfaction.

Before she had recovered enough for speech, he bent to kiss her again, this time light and tender. Murmuring, she opened her mouth to him. But after a minute of gentle caresses, his tongue grew bolder, laving hers, teasing the tip. A spark of arousal flamed up out of the ashes of fulfilment.

Within a few moments, her heartbeat accelerated and she felt the pulse begin to pound in her ears again. And then, he moved his fingers from her little nub and nudged them at the entrance to her passage.

She gasped, arousal building in one giant leap, and pushed against him, wanting the exquisite caress of those fingers to slide deeper, to the very core of her.

But he took his time, progressing deeper ever so slowly, each minute a new bit of flesh igniting as he touched it. When at least he'd penetrated to the depths of her and began a slow advance and withdrawal, advance and withdrawal, she was sobbing with arousal.

But he would not be hurried. Only gradually did he increase the rhythm, and when his thrusting fingers finally reached a rapid tempo, she shattered in a climax so intense, she lost all sense of who and where she was.

When the earth had settled, the stars realigned, and the ability to breathe and speak returned, Maggie gazed up to see Giles watching her, a slight smile on his lips.

She smiled back, tried to lift a finger to trace his lips, and couldn't quite manage it. He caught her hand and kissed it.

'That was—glorious,' she told him. 'Thank you.'

His smile widened and he made her a little bow. 'Your humble servant is pleased to serve.'

She shook her head at him. 'But it's not right.'

His smile vanished. 'What do you mean?'

'That was the most erotic experience of my life—and you are still completely clothed.'

He grinned again. 'What would you have me remove?'

'Nothing! Not yet. But if you will pour me some restorative wine—there should be a decanter on the table over there—I will endeavour to do the removing.'

'I like the sound of that. But remember—the breeches stay on.'

She gave him a long, slow smile. 'So did my shift.'

She saw him catch her meaning in the widening of his eyes and sharp intake of breath. Bounding up, he soon located decanter and glass, poured a generous amount, and offered it to her.

She sat up and took a long swallow, then handed him the glass. She could see the erection straining against his trouser flap as he carried the glass back to the table, and another spiral of anticipation and delight whirled through her.

She stood, unhooking her skirt, stepping out of it and tossing it away; she didn't want its clinging length to get in the way of what she planned. When he came back to the bed, she motioned to the place she'd been seated and said, 'Sit, please.'

He promptly complied, then looked up at her. She could see the rapid pulse beating at his temples and smiled, pleased at this evidence of his heightened desire.

She stood before him and began untying his cravat, slowly unwinding and removing the broad band of linen, then folding it neatly. He wasn't the only one who knew how to heighten anticipation with delay. After flicking back the edges of his shirt, she moved her hands to massage his shoulders and bent to kiss his bared throat.

He sighed when her lips contacted the rough skin, then groaned as she licked her way to the hollow where the pulse beat strongly. Massaging still, she kissed up his throat to nibble his jaw, evading his mouth when he tried to meet her lips, and continuing to lick and nip from the jawline up to his ears, his cheekbones, across his closed eyes, to his brow and into the hairline.

Reaching down, she lifted his arms and pulled the shirt over his head. She stepped back a moment to admire him, all muscled shoulder and strong arms and broad chest, where the flat nipples puckered.

He hissed between his teeth as she slowly ran a fingernail over each one.

Lifting her skirts, she bared herself to the waist, watching his face as he watched her. He opened his lips, an inarticulate mumble, and she placed a finger over his mouth to forestall any protest. Then she sat down on his lap and straddled him, her naked torso pressed against his trousers.

She felt his member leap as she wound her legs around his back and rocked her hot, moist, naked centre against his fettered erection. With a gasp, he cupped her bare bottom and pulled her closer. Wrapping her arms around him, she kissed him hard, rubbing her breasts against his bare chest while he picked up the rhythm, thrusting against her.

He must have been as ready as she had been, for after half-a-dozen such thrusts, he turned rigid in her arms, gasping into her mouth as his completion swept over him. Kissing him still, she followed him down as he collapsed back on to the bed, his chest drenched in sweat, his breathing ragged.

Rolling over to cuddle beside him, she pushed the moist hair off his brow and stroked it, waiting for his breathing to steady and slow, aglow with more peace and contentment than she'd felt since… She pushed her mind back from the thought. This moment was for enjoying now, without tarnishing it with sadness from the past.

At length, with a groan, he pushed himself up on his elbows. 'Thank you, my sweet. Although if we hadn't made this…unusual bargain, I should have to apologise for…reaching the finish line so quickly.'

'No matter. Shall we rub down the horse and prepare him to race again?'

His eyes lit. 'Absolutely. Although for safety's sake, I should do the "rubbing".'

'Absolutely not. When I serve, my service is complete.'

She walked over to the dressing table, poured water in the washbasin and returned with it and a soft rag. He stayed her hands when she attempted to unbutton the trouser flat.

'It will be all right,' she told him, going down before him. 'I promise, my knees shall not leave the floor.'

'If you're certain.'

'I am.' Pushing his hands aside, she plucked open the buttons and pulled the flap free, exposing his spent member. Gently and carefully she washed it with the rag, then the upper part of his legs and his belly. Once he'd been cleansed, she began pulling the rag slowly over the exposed skin. She bent down and blew a breath over the dampness, watching as he shivered, the little hairs on his stomach standing on end.

Pleased, she moved the damp cloth back to his now-stirring member. Up and down she stroked, alternating the soft caress of the rag with a long exhale over the tightening skin, bending closer each time, until her lips were almost but not quite touching him.

She looked up, into blue eyes locked upon her. 'Does this please you?' she whispered.

'Yes.'

'Tell me. Tell me what you like.'

He smiled slightly, picking up the game. 'I like having you stroke me. I like feeling your warm breath on my cock.'

At the words, she felt her own nipples tighten and the moist heat build between her legs. She bent and licked the hard velvet tip, which jerked under her ministrations. He gasped, his hands clutching the bedclothes, his arms rigid.

'Do you like that?'

'Yes. I love having your tongue on my cock.'

'Good.' She bent forward again and grasped him with one hand, holding him steady as she took him in her mouth, slid him in and back out.

'Do you like that?'

'Devil's breath, yes! I could live for ever inside your mouth.'

She leaned forward to suckle him again. Oh, what a wonder he was, all hardness and sinew, silky tip and satin shaft. She loved the taste and feel of him, loved the groans she elicited as she licked and suckled, laved and stroked. After a few moments, he dropped the bed-clothes and clutched her shoulders, thrusting with her as she took him to completion.

As he fell back on to the bed, limp, she returned the basin and refreshed the wine glass. She was sitting beside him, sipping from it, marvelling at the power and beauty of sensual pleasure, when he stirred and opened those incredible blue eyes.

And smiled at her.

Her foolish heart expanded and she smiled back, a smile of pure joy and contentment. Oh, how easily she could become accustomed to this loving—and this man!

'That was beyond words glorious,' he told her, sitting up to accept the wine glass and take a long sip. 'But it wasn't right.'

'No?' she said with a chuckle. 'You didn't seem to complain at the time.'

'Ah, but that's because I knew I would insist on having my turn.'

Her simmering senses sparked as the meaning of those words penetrated. Before she could respond, though, he continued. 'I believe a little more undressing is called for, once we finish this wine.'

'If you wish.'

He gave her a long, slow, heated scrutiny. Her skin prickled as his gaze passed over it, as if she could literally feel his touch as his eyes inspected her. 'Oh, I wish—to touch *everything*.'

They shared the glass, then Hadley returned it to the table and came back to the bed. She looked up at him, little eddies of excitement swirling in her stomach, and all her nerves once again primed for his touch.

'First, this.' he said, and began raking the pins from

her hair, until the heavy mass fell to her shoulders and down her back.

'If you only knew how often I dreamed of doing this,' he murmured as he continued to comb his fingers through her hair until he'd winnowed out all the pins. Then he arranged the waves over her shoulders, down her back, and around her breasts. Hands on her shoulders, he took a step back, once again studying her.

'Glorious,' he pronounced, and kissed her.

She murmured in protest when he broke the kiss, and he chuckled. 'Do not fret, my sweet. There will be more of that, soon enough.' Urging her to stand, he unlaced her underskirt, pulled it down, and helped her step out of it. He stood up and drew her close, kissing her again, light and gentle, then deeper and penetrating. While he drugged her with his mouth, he slowly raised the hem of her shift, until he could reach her garters. After unhooking her stocking, he urged her to sit.

He knelt before her, slowly rolling down the stocking, and kissing the skin of her leg as he bared it: inner thigh, knee and the soft skin behind it, along the shin, around the fullness of calf, across the smooth arch of the foot, until he pulled it free from her foot and suckled each toe in turn.

Glad she was seated, for she would have been too dizzy to stand, she braced herself on the bed as he started on the remaining garter and leg. Once he had her barelegged, he stood her up, unlaced and tossed away her stays, then pulled the shift over her head.

She stood before him completely naked now, but so sensitised by his touch that she felt no embarrassment. Only an exuberant confidence, from seeing the need blazing in his gaze, that he found her desirable, and anticipation for what he would do next.

In answer, he eased her on to the bed and against the pillows. 'Close your eyes, my sweet, and just *feel*,' he murmured.

And so she did. He began at her temples, kissing and stroking lightly, over her cheeks and lips, her ears and chin. He fisted his hands in her hair, then brushed the silky strands against her shoulders, her arms before he nibbled and kissed them. Slowly he progressed lower, teasing with the satin brush of her hair, tantalising with the soft pressure of his mouth and the wetness of his tongue.

She was breathing hard again, feeling the climax building, by the time he reached her waist, her hipbones, the round of belly. But to her dismay, he bypassed her aching centre, instead moving down her legs, her knees, her ankles and toes.

She pulled at his hands, trying to urge him higher, but he would not be hurried. Gently detaching himself, he returned to his slow transit up and around her legs, setting off delicious vibrations in nerves she didn't know she possessed.

And then, finally, his mouth moved to the tender skin of her inner thighs. At his urging, she let her legs fall open, giving him full access to the most intimate part of her. When she thought she could stand the wait no longer, he at last moved his mouth to her.

He parted the nether lips and licked delicately at the little bud within. Frantic, she twisted her head from side to side, lifting her hips to bring him closer. Then, with tongue and fingers, he traced the path into her slick passage.

So near to the precipice was she that only a few strokes would have been enough to send her spinning into the free fall of climax. But this time, she wanted them to reach that pinnacle together. Rolling away from him, she sat up, then pulled him to lie down beside her, his head towards the bottom of the bed, then lay back down with her own head on the pillow.

Understanding her intent, he eagerly returned to tasting her, while she slid her hand under the waistband of his breeches to clasp the erection now within her reach. Stroking him while he laved her, the two of them mingled their cries as they reached the summit together.

For a long, sweet time, they lay panting, spent. Recovering more quickly than Maggie, Giles crawled up to lay on the pillow, then repositioned her with her head resting on his shoulder, her arm across his bare chest, and her leg wrapped around his. After tossing the rumpled blanket over her nakedness, he kissed the tip of her nose and promptly fell asleep.

Lying in his arms watching him, content, replete, Maggie realised she was feeling…happy. Something she hadn't experienced in so long, she'd almost forgotten what it was like.

That realisation should have terrified her, and maybe it would, later. But for this glorious moment, in the wondrous present, she would simply enjoy it as a gift.

All too soon, Giles stirred. She held her breath as his sleepy eyes opened—would he shatter this magic by tossing back the covers, throwing on his clothes and bidding her a cheery goodbye as he hustled out to his meetings?

She saw that moment recognition of time, place—and his companion—register in those bright blue eyes. Which then widened, as a smile warmed a face alight with what she didn't dare call tenderness.

'My sweet lady,' he murmured. 'My very dear Lady Margaret.'

Despite her efforts to restrain it, her own heart swelled

with an answering emotion. 'After this morning, I think it should be "Maggie", don't you?'

'My very dear Maggie,' he repeated, and pulled her head down for a kiss—gentle, caressing almost—cherishing. As he released her, he said, 'I wish we'd awakened in the Outer Hebrides.'

Puzzled, she angled her head at him. 'You have a fondness for cold Scottish islands?'

He chuckled. 'No, my love! But if we were in the Hebrides, I could resume the delightful business that has occupied us this morning. Since we are unfortunately in London, I suppose I must finally bow to my responsibilities and get back to work. I can only hope Davie hasn't already sent out a search party, certain he's going to discover my cold, dead body in some dark alley somewhere.'

'You seldom miss meetings?' she guessed.

'I'm normally the first to arrive and the last to leave. But this morning I had a more pressing engagement. Although, to make up, I probably will be the last to leave.'

Reluctantly, she slid away and off the bed. Now that the loving was over, she should feel awkward, standing completely naked before a man she knew so slightly.

But he had loved her so well and so tenderly, all she felt was warmth and gratitude.

Tracking down his shirt, she brought it over to the bed, while he moved to sit up and lifted his arms for her to slip it back over his head. 'The cravat is probably hopeless,' he advised as she brought that over. 'I'll have to stop by my rooms to change out of riding gear anyway, before I go to Parliament. Though I heartily approve of my valet's current uniform,' he said, leaning forward to press a quick kiss on each bare nipple. 'Can I help you, or would you rather call your maid?'

'I'd appreciate the help. I'm sure the staff already has

an accurate notion of how we spent the morning, but I'd rather be dressed when I face them. My lady's maid, who's been with me for years, would probably freeze any gossip, were she here, but unfortunately she's at my father's house. And incidentally, since I left to ride at dawn, *she's* probably wondering if she should send out a search party to look for my cold, dead body.'

As she talked, she tossed on her shift, gathered up stays and stockings, and went to the clothes press to extract her habit, and Giles stepped closer to help her into them. He made an excellent lady's maid; Maggie refused to let herself speculate how he'd become so skilled.

Once she was dressed, he took one hand and kissed it. '*Will* the servants gossip?'

'I don't think so. They've all of them been with me a long time, and I like to think they are fond of me. Besides, if it comes to it, I'm a woman of age with my own household. I'm not accountable to anyone for my conduct.'

'I'd prefer there weren't any salacious talk, though.'

'No, I wouldn't imagine that titterings about a tryst with a woman from the wrong party would help the image of—'

'I don't care about me!' he interrupted. 'But I should definitely take exception if anyone were to malign *your* reputation.'

'Thank you, that is kind.' The euphoria was slipping away, and much as she didn't want it to end, she had to ask. 'Will I…be seeing you again?'

His expression turned incredulous. 'Did you truly think one time would be enough?'

His reassurance delighted her much more than it should. 'I didn't know. As I told you, I've never done this before. I didn't know whether, once the…novelty was over, you would want to…continue.'

He shook his head disbelievingly. 'I cannot wait to touch you again. When can I return?'

She laughed. 'I don't know. I'll have to check my schedule, as I imagine you will need to consult yours. Truly, I didn't plan for this to happen today.'

'I heartily approve of your spontaneous idea.'

'Not totally spontaneous. Following through on the desire was, perhaps. But I'd been thinking about it for a long time—probably from the first moment I met you. I tried to talk myself into being prudent and responsible, but every time I see you, prudence and responsibility seem to fly out the window—and in flies this great, fierce bird of need that grips me in its claws and won't let go.'

He leaned over to kiss her again. 'Here's to great, fierce birds. I hope you keep a whole flock of them.'

She shook her head. 'You must think me absurd.'

He cupped her face in his hands. 'I think you delightful. Whimsical. Fascinating. The most glorious lover who has ever touched me. But now I must go. Do check your schedule and send me a note. Number Six, Albany. And make it *soon*.'

'Number Six, Albany,' she repeated.

He pulled her to him and gave her one last kiss, deep, cherishing, possessive, powerful. 'Oh, yes—soon!' she said, and let him go.

# *Chapter Nine*

Maggie stood in the doorframe, watching Giles as he descended the stairs, then walked back into the bedchamber to pour herself another glass of wine.

Goodness, two glasses of wine before luncheon! But then, the occasion deserved it. She'd just propositioned a man she knew very little, had him come to her house in broad daylight, and spent the morning making love to him while the staff went about their duties and her cousin snored, blissfully unaware, in a nearby bedchamber.

What had come over her?

She'd known Robbie all her life, the transition from best friends to lovers as natural and gradual as growing older. She'd known Sir Francis for several years, been engaged for several months, and even then, only succumbed to his urgings when the protection of a wedding ring loomed. Now, she'd just taken to her bed, if not to ultimate surrender, a man she'd met…three times?

Maggie shuddered. By the world's measure, she'd be judged a woman of easy virtue, even a harlot. And yet… and yet.

It was more than just the powerful physical connection. Something about him, his passionate support of the causes he found important, and his willingness to devote his life to them, seemed to mesh so well with her ideals of sacrifice and service, making him seem like a friend of long acquaintance, rather than a man she'd barely met. It felt right and natural to sit across the table from him and debate politics; to lie in his arms and thrill to his caresses; to pleasure him and bring him to bliss.

She wanted to do all those things again and again.

A little chill of foreboding cooled the euphoria of satiation. This could end very badly. There was no question Giles Hadley saw this as a pleasant but temporary, short-term liaison. It would be all too easy for her to want much more.

She didn't dare let herself want more.

What was it that sailors had once said about voyaging towards the edge of the known world—'beyond here be dragons'? Having dared to venture into something she'd never experienced, behaving in a way she wouldn't previously have considered possible, she might well learn the bitter truth of that maxim.

But having had just one taste of Giles Hadley, she was not about to stop now.

An hour later, properly garbed in her habit, Maggie rode back to her father's town house, trying out, during the transit, various explanations for her very tardy return.

A wasted effort, as it turned out. Her maid sat in her bedchamber, bent over some needlework, but before she could utter a syllable, Polly looked up and exclaimed, 'Lord and stars, missy, what do you think you're doing?'

Damning the guilty flush heating her face, Maggie gazed at the maid who'd been with her since she was a child at Huntsford and Polly a junior nursemaid. No point trying to deny what the maid already knew, not that she had intended to waste any effort trying to conceal an affair that was probably already the focus of speculation below stairs at Upper Brook Street. 'I didn't imagine I could hide anything from you,' she said with a rueful laugh. 'But I didn't expect you'd find out this soon. Who told you?'

The maid raised her eyebrows. 'You leave at dawn for a ride that normally takes you an hour, and are gone four. Don't you think I sent that worthless groom back to look for you, and with a flea in his ear for leaving you alone? When he didn't find you, he stopped by Upper Brook Street—doubtless to delay having to return and report you missing! They told him you were…entertaining a gentleman. Now, you needn't be worrying the news will get out anywhere but this room and Number Four! We've all of us seen you go through more heartache than one body should have to bear, and we'd none of us add to it by tarnishing your name. But gracious, child, what are you thinking?'

'I suppose you want me to tell you I *wasn't* thinking, but that's not exactly true.'

With her own mother ill for much of Maggie's life, confiding in Polly had become a childhood habit she'd never outgrown; the wise but sharp-tongued woman had been her supporter and comforter from the days of scraped knees to times of devastating loss. As Maggie trusted she would be now, whether or not she approved of her rash actions.

'Oh, Polly, I've missed Robbie for so long and so keenly. In some ways, Mr Hadley couldn't be more different than the quiet country gentleman I meant to spend my life with. But he does make me…*feel* again! The same sort of excitement and delight in life that Robbie did. And the passion. I don't expect to find again a love like ours, but can't I enjoy myself a little, before I dwindle into an old widow?'

'I've no objection to you finding pleasure—who deserves it more? But there's no reason you couldn't "enjoy yourself" by choosing another fine gentleman to marry—' She held up a hand, forestalling Maggie's protest. 'I know, I know. But even if the husband wasn't the equal of your Robbie, he could provide you with the passion you seek—*safely*. How can you even think of risking—?'

'I'm not! I'm hardly likely to forget what the consequences would be for conceiving a child out of wedlock, and I have no more desire to disappoint Papa and tarnish my name than you would have to see it. I *was* intimate with Mr Hadley, but in a…controlled way. We'll not do anything that will risk my becoming with child.'

The maid shook her head. 'I've heard of them "French letters", or whatever it is the apothecaries call what decent people ought not to use, but nothing will truly stop a babe. I don't doubt this Mr Hadley is as charming as the devil himself, but it's still not worth the risk, child.'

'We're not using a "French letter". We are…limiting our intimacy to include only what will avoid any chance of conception,' Maggie explained, her face flaming, unable to describe it any more plainly even to a woman who knew every mishap she'd ever suffered and every mistake she'd ever made.

It took a minute for Polly to puzzle it out. 'You mean you're not letting him—'

'No. As long as I avoid the ultimate act, why shouldn't I take some pleasure, when, after so long alone, I've discovered a man who intrigues me, whom I intrigue in turn?'

'I don't like it, Miss Maggie,' Polly said, shaking her

head. 'He might be a fine gentleman, and if you like him this much, I'm sure he must be. And he might tell you now that what-all you're doing is enough for him. But a man's a man, and sooner or later, he'll want more, you take my word on it. And then what?'

'Actually, I think it's more likely I will want more,' Maggie admitted. 'But knowing the consequences, I think I can manage to be at least that prudent—although you would say,' she continued, watching the expression on Polly's face, 'that I am not being prudent at all.'

'Ah, child, you know I only want what's best for you. To see you happy and well loved and settled in your own home again, as you were with your Robbie. But you'll not be finding that if you're giving away your favours to "intriguing" gentlemen, without benefit of your wedding lines.'

That cut a bit too close to the bone, even coming from Polly. 'I don't *want* any wedding lines!' she snapped back. 'Much better to enjoy passion and part when passion cools, than to be yoked for life to a man who no longer interests me.' *Or love again and risk a loss that might drive me to madness.*

Though she didn't imagine the fire of attraction she felt for Giles Hadley would be banked for a long time. Nor, unfortunately, could she honestly claim that she believed she would find life with him tedious, once satiation had honed the sharp edge off appetite.

It was far more likely she'd find living with him very much to her taste.

But it was too late to back away now, nor did she want to. Like a troublesome filly who'd got the bit between her teeth, she would run as far and fast as she could—probably until Giles Hadley tired of the arrangement. She'd just have to restrain her enthusiasm by remembering Hadley expected a short, idyllic interlude, remind herself that was what she wanted, too, and be prepared to send him away at the first sign that he was ready to end it.

If she had any regrets afterward, she would deal with them.

She would certainly never regret the passion.

She came back to herself to discover Polly shaking her head, her expression concerned. 'Lost as a maid gazing at the moon, dreaming of her lover. Don't look to me like you're about to lose interest in this gentleman.'

Probably true. But she wasn't going to spoil the days ahead worrying about that. 'What I'm interested in at the moment is changing my gown. I've got the household accounts to review, and I'm afraid today is an at-home afternoon.'

And while she was reviewing accounts, she could also review her calendar…and figure out how soon she could see Giles Hadley again.

A short drive away, Giles strode into the entrance to Parliament, a spring in his step. Whistling a merry tune, he headed towards the committee rooms, absently nodding a greeting to the men he passed.

A dawn gallop in the fresh air—and then one of the most sensual experiences of his life. Had any man ever had a more glorious morning?

He'd known from his first glimpse of her that Lady Margaret attracted him. From the first discussion at the inn in Chellingham, her understanding of Parliament and political theory had intrigued him. But never in his fondest imaginings had he anticipated what a skilled, sensual and inventive lover she would be.

Though she was a paradox, he thought with a chuckle.

Initially tentative and uncertain, shy as a fawn in a meadow and as ready to bolt. Unable at first to voice what she wanted without blushing...then later, when he put himself literally into her hands, pleasuring him with boldness and skill.

He couldn't remember being this relaxed, refreshed and...*happy* for a long time—if ever. If this was bewitchment, he wanted more of it!

It had all happened too fast; his senses and mind were still too stunned in the brilliant, lingering afterglow for him to understand yet the full significance of what they'd done. Or how they would navigate the tricky waters of an intimate relationship and avoid compromising her reputation.

Somehow, they would. Where exactly they might be going, he wasn't sure. All he did know was he had to have her, and they *must* go forward.

Secure in that conclusion, he entered the committee room, still humming. Looking up from a stack of papers, Davie exclaimed, 'Giles, at last! I was beginning to think you'd been abducted.'

'No, just some...unexpected business I had to take care of.' Oh, how lustily he had cared for it, he thought with a private smile.

Ben looked him up and down. 'Business, eh? Humming a tune, smile on his face and a spring in his step? Looks to me like a man who's been well satisfied. What do you think, Christopher?'

Glancing up from the document he was drafting, Christopher's eyes widened and he grinned. 'My, my, my. Madame Seraphene must have been unusually skilled last night! About time! With all the impediments keeping the bill from passage last session, you've been as grumpy as a hen who'd lost her last chick.'

'Have you ever!' Ben said with a laugh. 'So, Giles, *did* she try something new? The intimate details, please!'

'Find a lady of your own, and make your own details,' Giles threw back, irritated that the source of his well-being had been so transparent. Though he was confident his friends would cease bantering and be as discreet as nuns were he to reveal the truth, they'd also want to know—since he never trifled with ladies—exactly what his intentions were.

Giles had as yet no answer to that question.

'Maybe your luscious Madame Seraphene has a recommendation?' Christopher said.

'Do your own committee work,' he shot back. 'Or ask Ben to advise you. He's familiar with every bordello in London.'

As Giles had hoped, that was enough to set the two friends off trading good-natured insults over their relative familiarity with the pleasure houses of the capital. Relieved to be free of their scrutiny, he sat down at the table—to face Davie's curious gaze.

'You do seem unusually—blithe,' his friend remarked, studying Giles. 'Nor do you usually visit Madame when there is another woman in your sights.'

The last thing he needed was a grilling by the most perceptive member of their group. 'Later,' he told Davie, and opened the dossier of papers.

The rest of the day passed in a blur, Giles unable to recall by nightfall either what he'd read of the bill or any of the notes he'd scrawled in the margins. His friends swept him off to dinner, their animated chatter covering his unusual reticence, with only Davie—of course, Davie—occasionally glancing over with a look that said he *had* noticed it.

He'd have to tell Davie something, eventually. Fortunately, Davie would wait for him to speak in his own time, rather than hound him for immediate answers.

Returning to their rooms after dinner, he'd gone through the correspondence with eagerness—to find no missive from Lady Margaret. Disappointed, he tried to tell himself that she would have been late returning to her father's, probably had many duties to attend to, and wouldn't have had time to consult her schedule.

Surely she would bid him visit her again soon.

The book he chose did not engage, nor, when he gave up in disgust and sought his bed, did he find oblivion in sleep. He tossed and turned before giving up to indulge himself, now that he was alone, in reviewing every detail of that wondrous morning.

After falling asleep late, he awoke in the faint predawn light, impatient and dissatisfied—until it occurred to him to wonder whether Lady Margaret rode every morning. His rueful smile at having fallen into intimacy with a woman about whom he knew so little, not even her usual routine, was lost in excitement as a new possibility occurred.

If he were to go to Hyde Park now, might she turn up?

Once the idea was envisioned, there could be no return to sleep. Despite the few hours of rest he'd obtained, Giles scrambled up, pulled on his riding gear, and sent for his horse.

A short time later, he trotted his mount into Hyde Park. A low fog veiled the landscape, obscuring everything at a distance, blurring into hazy outlines the objects nearby. Restless, eager, Giles signalled his horse to a trot, hoping that around this bend or the next, Lady Margaret might materialise out of the mist.

He'd rounded the last curve and was regretfully directing his horse towards the exit gates when he suddenly came upon the slender figure of Lady Margaret mounted on her grey mare, a ray of just-emerging sun burnishing her auburn hair to flame. Excitement and pure gladness swelled his chest.

A moment later, she saw him and pulled up, the groom following her halting as well. Startled to see the servant, Giles was forced to abandon the greeting he'd intended, scrambling instead to come up with a form of address appropriate for a lady who was merely an acquaintance.

'How nice to see you, Lady Margaret.' *So much for your vaunted eloquence, Hadley,* he thought with disgust.

'And you, Mr Hadley. Peters,' she said, addressing the groom, 'I shall stop at Upper Brook Street before I return to the Square. I'm sure I can trust Mr Hadley to escort me there safely, so you may go. Oh—and tell Polly she need not worry, I will be fine.'

Grinning, the groom bowed. 'I'll be sure to tell her, your ladyship. Right tore a strip off me yesterday, she did, for coming home without you!'

'Your hide will be safe today,' Lady Margaret promised. At her nod of dismissal, the groom trotted off.

Once the man was out of earshot, Giles said, 'My very dear Lady Margaret, I am enchanted to see you! Though I must say, I hoped to have had a note from you earlier.'

'Oh, that.' She coloured a little. 'It's just...when I sat down to write one, I didn't know what to say. And then to have to ask a footman, or my maid, to carry it to Albany for me...' Her blush deepened. 'In any event, I wasn't sure you'd want to...return so soon.'

'Not return? Last night would have been better—or yesterday afternoon. I was useless at the committee meeting; all I could think about was you, and our morning together.'

'Then, you'd like to go there with me…now?'

His heart—and other things—leapt. 'More than anything. Shall I give you a few moments to ride there first?'

She laughed ruefully. 'Since my whole staff knows what's going on—indeed, my maid has already taken me to task for it—I suppose we could arrive together and boldly enter the front door! But on the chance that not all of London yet knows about us…yes, give me a few moments.'

Concerned, he rode over to catch at her reins. 'Your maid has taken you to task! Devil's teeth, what effrontery! Would you rather I not visit you? I don't want to make life…uncomfortable for you!' *Though it would kill me to stay away.*

'No, I want you to come! Surely you know how much,' she replied, looking up at him, the banked passion in her green eyes immediately raising the level of his desire. 'Polly's looked after me all my life. She just doesn't want me to do something foolish that might get me hurt.'

'I wouldn't want to do anything that would hurt you, either.'

In the flash of an instant, her troubled expression turned provocative. 'What you do to me definitely doesn't hurt. I've lain awake most of the night, impatient for you to do it again.'

'Then let us go now, while we still have most of the morning! How late does your cousin sleep?'

'Until noon. But don't worry. Timid little thing, she is so grateful to have food, lodging, and the leisure to pursue her own interests, I could probably ride naked down

St James's, like Lady Godiva, and she'd not reprove my behaviour.'

'I would. I insist that all naked riding be done with me.'

Her smile heated and she licked her lips. 'I look forward to it.'

'Not half so much as I do.' With that promise, he slapped the mare on her rump and set horse and rider off towards the park gates.

One slow circuit of the park, and he would head after her. He spent that transit in glorious anticipation, recalling the taste of her mouth, the pebbled softness of her nipples under his tongue, the satin of the skin beneath her ears, behind her knees, the responses he drew from her as he laved her passage and the tight bud hidden above it. And what she did to him…

He recalled Ben's comment about inventiveness, and his chest tightened, until it was difficult to breathe.

Would she have some new clever technique to pleasure him? He couldn't wait to find out.

## Chapter Ten

Maggie returned from Upper Brook Street to her father's house the following morning in a glow of satiated satisfaction. Having the previous day agreed with Giles that they would meet every morning, unless one or the other had a commitment that precluded it, she could look forward to each new day with an anticipation she hadn't felt in years.

Ah, what a new day! Her well-pleasured body tingled at the memory.

She felt reasonably sure she was proceeding with sufficient discretion. Papa was used to her coming and going between their two dwellings, and would be unlikely to question her; most of the *ton* was abed until afternoon, so the chance of anyone discovering their crack-of-dawn assignations was slim, and she felt secure about the discretion of servants who had watched over her since childhood. In addition to which, she had no doubt that Polly had warned all the staff that if the merest whisper escaped either dwelling, the offender would be turned off without a character.

The only concern that might trouble her happiness—and she refused to spoil the idyll of the present with worry—was the possibility of Giles Hadley deciding he was ready to end the arrangement.

If that happened, so be it. In the interim, she intended to suck from the liaison every possible morsel of joy—an emotion she'd had experienced too seldom these last few years.

As she walked in, the butler came over to meet her. 'Lady Margaret, I thought you'd wish to know that Mr Hadley—Mr *George* Hadley,' he clarified, not looking her in the eye, 'has called upon your papa. They are in his study.'

That announcement was enough to dissipate her cloud of euphoria. Remembering what Giles had told her about how vindictive his half-brother could be when denied what he wished, Maggie felt a niggle of foreboding.

'Thank you, Rains. After I change, I'll be in the morning room, if Papa wants me to join them.'

Had George come to ask her father for her hand, as Giles had told her he intended? Maggie wondered as she went up to her bedchamber. If he were rushing his fences with a proposal, she was going to have to reject him—and deal with what might be unpleasant consequences.

If she must, she would, she told herself philosophically. Were a proposal in the offing, she'd just as soon get it—and any unpleasant consequences—over with, so that possibility wouldn't cloud a future now brilliant with the promised pleasures of her association with George's much more compelling brother.

She walked in to find Polly with needle in hand and her morning gown draped across the bed.

The older woman looked up to study her face. Maggie tried, unsuccessfully, not to blush. 'What lovely needlework,' she observed, gesturing towards the tambour frame the maid had set aside.

Predictably ignoring Maggie's attempt to divert her, Polly said, 'You don't look so over the moon this morning. Having second thoughts already?'

'No,' Maggie snapped, irritated at having another bucket of cold water dumped on the lingering warmth of her morning tryst. 'I shall probably ride and then stop at Upper Brook Street every morning for the foreseeable future. I will notify you when that changes.'

Rather than being chastened by the rebuke, Polly merely chuckled as she helped Maggie out of her habit. 'You should know by now that toplofty tone won't discourage me from speaking my mind, if it's something I think you need to hear.'

'Please, do not let me hear anything! Rains already told me Mr George Hadley has called on Papa, which is dispiriting enough for one morning. Help me into that gown, please, in case Papa needs me to join them.'

'At least that's a gentleman who might do the proper thing, and ask for your hand,' Polly observed as she settled the garment around Maggie.

Maggie repressed a shudder. 'If you knew the gentleman better, you'd find the idea of a proposal from him more appalling than appealing. George Hadley is interested only in George Hadley, and what a wife can do for *him*. Specifically, a wife with the correct political connections and a handsome portion.'

'Isn't that what all gentlemen want?'

'Which is why I haven't married again,' Maggie retorted. Turning so the maid could finish the ties at the back, she said, 'If you want to do me a good turn, pray that this Mr Hadley did *not* come to ask Papa for my hand.'

A short time later, Maggie descended to the small back parlour. In truth, she *was* curious why George Hadley was closeted with her father. Since he would not be serving in the next Parliament—unless his father had found him another pocket borough to represent—he wouldn't be part of Papa's caucus. Perhaps he intended to get himself returned for the following session, and wanted to tap her father's expertise in planning his strategy.

She only hoped his reasons were political. In any event, if she were not summoned to join them, Papa would doubtless tell her later what they had discussed.

Her thoughts had drifted back to the delightful interlude with Giles when a current of cool air alerted her that the parlour door had been opened. But instead of her father, the man striding into the room with the familiarity of a family member was George Hadley.

Before she could wonder what had happened to the servant who should have announced the guest, Hadley swept her a bow. 'My dear Lady Margaret! I'm so pleased to find you alone.'

Not at all pleased, she said, 'Mr Hadley, what a surprise! I thought you had called upon my father.' She looked pointedly towards the door. 'He did not accompany you?'

'No, he knew I had a matter of some…delicacy to discuss with you.'

Was it the proposal she'd dreaded? Drat Papa for not warning him off! Although the man was so self-absorbed, he was probably oblivious to hints, even active discouragement. Incapable of believing she'd refuse him, unless the rejection came from her own lips.

Well, it was going to—unless she could head him off. 'I cannot imagine a matter so delicate you would not wish to discuss it with Papa present. As political friends and allies, we've spent many an evening talking over policy.'

'A modest observation,' he noted with an approval that

made her grit her teeth. 'Quite proper that a lady not be so forward as to anticipate more—though you cannot be totally unaware of my admiration for you.'

*Your admiration for Papa's power and my money, you mean.* 'As I admire all those who dedicate themselves to serving their country. We share that esteem; anything *more* would be out of the question. I am quite content in my position as hostess and companion to my father, and have no wish to be anything else.'

She could hardly make it plainer. But as she feared, he was not to be deterred.

'Ah, but you could be so much more! A wife and mother, a helpmate to a man of rising prominence and power who could secure your position well into the future. Which, you must allow, a man of your father's advancing years cannot. My dear Lady Margaret, becoming my wife would bring us both such advantages!'

So after reminding her of her father's eventual demise, and without any declaration of tender emotion—not that she would welcome or believe one—she was to accept his hand?

'Sir, I pray you will not continue in this manner!' she cried, exasperated. Catching him by the arm before he could go down on one knee, she said, 'There is no need to say more. Though fully aware of the honour of the offer you were about to make, I cannot accept.'

He patted her hand before she snatched it away. 'Your father warned me you might have some missish reservations about a change in your position. But only consider the benefits! You would be allying yourself, not with a mere baron, but with the scion of a noble family of impeccable lineage, whom you could assist in continuing the important political work so cherished by your esteemed sire. Allying yourself to a man of youth and vigour, who can give you the children so necessary to the happiness of any woman. A man of means, who would maintain you in the style appropriate to your station. Nor do I have any objections to your continuing to call yourself "Lady Margaret."

She wagered he would not, since the title indicated he'd snagged a wife of higher birth than his own. And he might be a 'man of means' now, but when his father died and Giles inherited, gaining control over the income from the estate currently being lavished on the second son, he'd be using *her* funds to buy his hunters, pay his tailor, and maintain the household.

Though she would like to tear him limb from limb for referring to her darling Robbie as 'merely a baron', she made herself say in a civil tone, 'Benefits indeed, had I a desire to remarry. But I have not.'

When that statement finally penetrated, he stared at her. 'Not remarry? How could you not wish to? Even with a woman's limited wit, you must realise how imperative it is for a lady of your…mature years to get herself settled while it is still possible.'

'My "wit" is not so limited that I do not know my own mind,' she snapped, struggling to keep her temper under control. 'Beyond politics, we have little in common, Mr Hadley. I am convinced we would not suit, and I would appreciate it if you cease importuning me and accept my decision.'

He finally seemed to understand what she was saying, for his smile faded. 'You truly mean to refuse me—you, who have been on the shelf for six years? You may be a marquess's daughter, but at your advanced age, you are unlikely to receive a better offer. Unless…'

His eyes narrowed and his expression turned hostile. 'You cannot believe that my *half-brother* would propose to you? I'm sorry to disillusion you, but I must warn you that though he *trifles* with widows, he doesn't marry them. I heard about your little *tête-à-tête* in Chellingham! I would have thought your father would forbid your associating with a jumped-up soldier's bastard, who has neither the training nor the breeding to assume a more elevated role!'

'If he has not the training, that is more the fault of his father, the earl, than it is his,' she flung back.

'His father, the *earl*?' he scoffed. 'So he *has* drawn you in! I would urge you to stay away from him! Giles Hadley spoils and destroys everything he touches, and has from the moment of his birth. You must have heard how he ruined his mother's life, turning her into an outcast shunned by all good society.'

'*He* ruined her?' Maggie shook her head, hardly able to believe she was hearing him correctly. 'That's ridiculous! He was only a babe, hardly responsible for the behaviour of the adults involved!'

'Indeed?' he said with a sneer. 'I would have credited you with more wit than to accept his Banbury tales!'

*The wit you have already disparaged?* she thought, incensed. 'Enough! I will not be drawn into the quarrel between you and your half-brother. Since I have refused your most obliging offer, there is nothing left to say. Good day, Mr Hadley.'

'You think to dismiss me like some…*lackey*?' he cried, his handsome face distorting with anger. 'I will not be treated thus by a mere female! You would do well to remember that what I want, I obtain, and woe to those who stand in my way! If you choose to ally yourself with Giles Hadley, you thrust yourself into more danger than you could possibly imagine.'

'Put myself in danger?' she echoed, her hands shaking from the effort to refrain from slapping him. 'Surely you are not trying to *threaten* me?'

'Warn, only,' he temporised, and then summoned a smile. 'Any danger would be swiftly dissipated, once you were sensible enough to accept my hand. What an outstanding team we would make!'

Flabbergasted that he had the audacity to berate her in one breath and renew his suit in the next, she said, 'I believe I have already made clear there is no chance of that. Now, once again, Mr Hadley, I must insist that you leave.'

'A command that I second,' came her father's voice from the doorway. 'Did my daughter not just order you to go?' The marquess crossed the room to stand protectively beside her. 'Then get you gone, sirrah—or do I need to summon a footman to assist you?'

His expression transitioning rapidly from surprise, to incredulity, to the petulant frown of a child denied a treat he expects as his due, Hadley bowed stiffly. 'As you wish, my lord, Lady Margaret.' Straightening his shoulders, with an air of injured dignity, he walked out.

Once the door closed behind him, her father gave her a quick hug. 'Are you all right?'

'Quite fine—if a little out of temper.'

'As well you might be!' The marquess shook his head. 'I could scarcely believe it, when Rains came to tell me Hadley was closeted with you.'

'I do wish you had not inflicted him on me,' she said ruefully.

'I certainly did not intend to! You'd already made your feelings clear, so when he broached the reason for his visit, I told him quite plainly that you would not consider accepting his offer. I suppose I can't blame an ardent suitor for wanting to confirm that disappointing news with the object of his affection, but from what I overheard just now, it appeared he did not want to accept the truth from you, either. You had to ask him more than once to leave? I only wish I had come down sooner!'

She considered telling her father he'd also threatened her, but Papa was angry enough already. 'Thank you, but I had the situation in hand.'

'I have no doubt!' her father said with a laugh as he ushered her to the sofa. 'I am disappointed in Hadley, though. I knew he'd been much indulged, but I still expected him to be a gentleman.'

'Hardly a gentleman! More like a spoiled child.'

Her father gave her a penetrating look. 'Are you sure knowing Giles Hadley is worth it?'

Startled, she looked at him, trying to keep her expression bland. Just how much did he know about her relationship with the fascinating Giles? Not that he had any say in her behaviour—but she wouldn't want to disappoint her father.

'What has that to do with George Hadley's offer?'

'He gave me quite a harangue about making sure you were protected from his half-brother's "evil influences"— at least until he could wed you and assume the vigil. I imagine he would be even more incensed if he were to hear that after thwarting his hopes, you continued to associate with his detested brother.'

'Surely you're not suggesting that I terminate my friendship with Giles Hadley,' she said, choosing her words carefully, 'because he has the misfortune to be related to a man who acts like a wilful child? Besides, would not my cutting his half-brother just encourage a bully?'

'Perhaps, but it's my daughter he's bullying.'

'Don't worry, Papa,' she told him, giving his arm a

squeeze. 'Remember, you taught me how to aim at vermin and shoot straight.'

Her father laughed. 'True, but I never intended you to have to use that skill on vermin the size of the Honourable George Hadley.'

'Who turned out to be not so honourable,' she said with a sigh.

'Indeed. I shall write to his father, and ask that he be summoned home—as a favour to me. That should be enough to remind the earl that since his precious second son is not a peer and no longer sits in Parliament, he *can* be arrested. I won't have him harassing my daughter.'

'Thank you, Papa. But it's late, and if I don't consult with Cook soon, we'll have no supper tonight.'

'Goodness, can't have you dwindle away to nothing, my sweet. Don't worry your pretty head about any more unpleasantness with George Hadley. A word to his father, and we'll table that bill before it leaves committee.'

'I would appreciate that!' Relieved to be able to transfer the problem of George Hadley to her father, she gave him a kiss and stood up. 'Now, to order your dinner!'

'Make it a good one! I'm going to study some notes Bathhurst made about the Reform Bill that's nearly certain to pass. I'll need something to cheer me.'

'Cheering it is,' she said, and walked out. She felt cheered herself, knowing that George Hadley would disturb her no more.

Now, she could concentrate on the much more enjoyable prospect of her mornings with his half-brother.

## Chapter Eleven

Later that afternoon, Giles had returned to his rooms at Albany to pick up some documents when he heard a knock at the door. Opening it, he found the porter on his doorstep.

'There's a gentleman to see you, Mr Hadley,' the man said. 'A Mr Angleton, from Romesly. He said you wouldn't know him, but he's from the county your half-brother used to represent in Parliament.'

Wondering why the gentleman would seek him out at his lodgings, rather than at Parliament, Giles said, 'Tell him I cannot spare much time, as I'm already overdue at committee, but I will see him.'

Curious why someone from Hampshire would want to consult him, Giles waited impatiently until the porter escorted in a short, spare man dressed in the plain but well-made attire of a prosperous merchant or tradesman.

The man made him a bow. 'Thank you for seeing me uninvited, Lord Lyndlington. As I told your man, I'm James Angleton, of Romesly—a village within Abbots-weal, your father, Lord Telbridge's, estate.'

'Good to meet you, Mr Angleton,' Giles replied, swiftly deciding it would be too much trouble to object to the use of his courtesy title by this man who'd probably never heard him called anything else. 'What can I do for you?'

'I—and the other electors in the county—need your help.'

'I shall help if I can,' Giles said, motioning the visitor to a seat. 'But if this concerns Abbotsweal, you should rather address yourself to Lord Telbridge. As you must know if you live near the estate, I have no power there, and no influence whatsoever in the running of it.'

'Aye, that's true—for now. But as the heir, you will have both, one day.'

Resistant as always to even thinking of a life beyond his duties in the Commons, Giles said, 'Although the earl and I are estranged, I bear him no ill will.' Which was not exactly true, but he didn't intend to air his dirty laundry before a stranger. 'I have every expectation that he will continue to direct Abbotsweal for many years to come.'

'We, too, hope he continues in health and vigour. But in the interim, Lord Lyndlington, the electors in the county have a problem. As you doubtless have heard, we chose not to return your half-brother to Parliament. He…has never had much interest in the common folk, and displayed little knowledge of the needs of either tradesmen or farmers. I imagine the fact that we elected another man, rather than the earl's son, came as an unpleasant shock. I very much doubt Mr Hadley will forget or forgive the slight, nor, I expect, is the earl very happy about it.'

'Probably not,' Giles replied. 'But my acquaintance with the earl is slight—' *more like non-existent* '—so my opinion about his reaction is no more informed than yours.'

'Though you've not resided on the estate since you were a child, knowing you would one day inherit, we in

Romesly have followed your career with great interest. We're impressed and encouraged by your ideals, and your dedication in working to implement them. So, with the prospect of reform upon us, we decided to take a great risk, and throw in our lot with you.'

'Throw in your lot with me?' Giles repeated. 'I'm sorry, but I don't understand. I represent Danford. What can I do that affects you?'

'You represent Danford now, but when you inherit, you will represent *us*. In rejecting Telbridge's son, we've effectively burned our bridges with the earl. There will probably be retribution, although it's too early to tell yet what form that will take. The other electors nominated me to call on you and beg you not to wait until you inherit to come to Abbotsweal and get to know the district and its people. We are most anxious to introduce you around the area, so you can become familiar with it, and with us and our needs. If Lord Telbridge knows you are active on our behalf, it might blunt whatever retribution he might be contemplating against us.'

'Would not having me tromping about the village and the surrounding countryside incense the earl even more? It might appear to him that you—and I—are anticipating his demise.'

'Perhaps,' Mr Angleton allowed. 'But in the end, we agreed the benefit of having you up to snuff about the estate from the moment you receive your inheritance outweighed the possibility of further offending the earl. Besides, since you *are* going to inherit, there is nothing unreasonable about you visiting the village and freeholders thereabouts. Were you and your father not estranged, you would have been doing so since you came out of short pants.'

'Probably,' Giles admitted. 'However, it doesn't seem

proper for me to be poking about Abbotsweal without having been invited by the earl, or at least informing him of my intent.'

'You can certainly inform the earl if you wish, though we don't consider it necessary. Lord Telbridge may own the land, but he doesn't own *us*. Every farmer and merchant and tenant has the right to look out for his own interests, and to invite whomever he chooses into his home or shop. If we choose to invite *you*, that's none of the earl's business. I won't press you now, Lord Lyndlington. But won't you at least consider it?'

Troubled, Giles got up and paced the room. With everything in him, he resisted the very idea of reaching out to the earl, and despite the townsman's assertion, he didn't see how he could visit the estate without at least informing Telbridge of his intent. He turned back to Mr Angleton, intending to give him a regretful but firm refusal, and met a glance of such hopeful entreaty the words withered on his lips.

Even the idea of 'Abbotsweal' burned in his gut like acid. But, sent by his anxious neighbours, the man had come all the way to London to see him. He could at least let them down more gently.

Though let them down he would. Never while the earl still breathed would he set foot on the land from which Telbridge had cast out his mother.

Maybe not even then.

'Very well, Mr Angleton. I make no promises, but I will consider it.'

The man broke into a relieved smile. 'Thank you, Lord Lydley! I have other business in London that should me take a week or so. May I call upon you before I leave for your answer?'

'Yes. Send me a note here to arrange a time.'

'Good day, then, my lord. And may I add, I do hope we will see you at Romesly in the near future!'

*A vain hope, that*, Giles thought as he ushered the man out. But he needn't consider the disturbing matter any more right now—he had an important piece of legislation to draft. Putting the earl and his visitor out of mind, he packed up his papers and set off for the committee room.

The following morning, too filled with anticipation to sleep any longer, Giles Hadley rose before dawn and called for his horse. Tiptoeing through the common area of the rooms he shared with Davie, he sent a rueful glance towards the chamber where his friend dozed peacefully. Although Giles often rode early, normally he returned to breakfast with Davie and discuss the work they'd be engaged upon that day. Though his friend had as yet said nothing to him, it would take a man far less perceptive than Davie not to notice Giles's continuing absence at breakfast and his repeated late arrivals in the committee room.

Although Davie would bide his time, waiting for Giles to speak when he was ready, Ben and Christopher had surely noticed his tardiness, too. Sooner rather than later, they would take him to task for it. He really needed to figure out what to tell them.

But he wasn't going to waste a particle of energy this morning worrying about that, he told himself as he strode down the steps and back towards the mews. Not with the glorious prospect ahead of a hard ride, and then a sweet session with his delightful, sensual Maggie.

He'd felt a niggle of unease when he impulsively proposed their bargain, worried that he'd grow frustrated with less than a full possession. And though he certainly would prefer to make Maggie completely his, so sensitive was he to her touch, and so inventive the ways and places she came up with to touch him, that he now had no doubt he'd be intrigued by the arrangement for the indefinite future.

Which was even more exceptional, when he considered that they were meeting daily, something he'd seldom done with his previous amours, when the press of political obligations often occupied him far into the night. Perhaps it was the happy circumstance of trysting first thing in the morning, before he became caught up in business...but he didn't think so.

Nor could he remember being this excited, this energised, this...*happy* in any previous arrangement. Perhaps not since the end of his carefree childhood in that little cottage with his mother.

But enough analysing, he thought as he took the reins from the groom and threw himself up on his mount. Maggie would be racing her mare in the park, awaiting him. He meant to speed to her side and treasure every moment of their precious morning together.

A heavy, swirling mist veiled the park as Giles rode in, impatient to see Maggie again and frustrated at having to proceed slowly in the limited visibility. He turned his mount into Rotten Row, straining his ears over the sound of his own horse's hoofbeats, listening for the muffled trot of another rider.

Several rode past before he saw Maggie, emerging ghost-like out of the fog in a dark habit on her grey mare. Delight bubbled up like champagne uncorked, fizzing over into anticipation that tingled in all his nerves.

Mindful that in the cloaking fog, there might be unseen listeners, he called out a prosaic 'Good morning, Lady Margaret. Not so auspicious a day for riding.'

'Yes, I'm thinking a short ride would be desirable this morning. Won't you walk your horse beside mine?'

She'd never before asked to *ride* with him before setting off for their morning interlude, he thought with a stab of alarm. Surely she couldn't have developed misgivings, and want to end this?

A panicked feeling he didn't want to examine too closely flashed through him at the thought. Squelching it, he said, 'What is your pleasure, my lady?'

'You will find that out soon enough,' she replied, pitching her voice to reach him alone.

Relief coursed through him along with a thrill of expectation. 'I cannot wait.'

'But you will, for a bit. I thought you would want to know that I received a most…interesting call yesterday. From your half-brother.'

Nothing like the mention of that name to cast a fog-damp blanket over his enthusiasm. 'From George? What did he want?'

'He first sought out my father to ask for my hand. Since you'd warned me he might do so, I'd already spoken with Papa and let him know I would never countenance such a match. Which he informed your brother. Apparently unable to take Papa's word for it, George then sought me out, first trying to point out the advantages of a speedy marriage for a—' she gave a rueful chuckle '—woman of my "advanced age" who'd been six years on the shelf and might not receive another such attractive offer.'

'The devil he did!' Giles exclaimed. 'I knew he was maladroit, but that beggars belief!'

'Belief was an article in short supply,' she agreed. 'Particularly after, with what I thought was saintly restraint, I replied in quite a civil tone that though cognisant of the honour of his offer, I could not accept it. He tried to convince me to change my mind, and when I wouldn't, he warned me about you.'

'I can only imagine what he said on that front,' Giles muttered, angry and irritated that Maggie had been subjected to his brother's ill humour—on his behalf.

'He said—well, let's simply say he was not complimentary. In fact, I am glad you warned me how... unpleasant he can become when he is thwarted, else I might have been ill prepared for what happened next. I'd just asked him to leave a second time when, having no idea that he had not left the house after their interview, my father was informed of his presence and came to rescue me. Though your half-brother wasn't ready to follow my orders, he acquiesced readily enough to Papa's command that he leave.'

'I am certain he did. Damnation!' Giles swore, swatting into the air with his riding crop. 'Excuse my language, but I am so sorry that you had to suffer through that. George knew you were seeing me?'

'He knew about Chellingham. I don't think he knows about...this.'

'There's no guarantee he won't find out,' Giles said grimly. 'And if he does...he could be even more unpleasant. It makes no difference to me—our encounters are always bitter. But I'd not for the world cause you any further difficulties.' Hardly able to get his mouth to form the words, he forced himself to add, 'If...if you think it wise, we could...discontinue our meetings.'

'What, allow your spoiled child of a half-brother to dictate our actions? Certainly not! I thought we'd agreed on that point before.'

Relieved, Giles still felt it necessary to offer her one more chance to reconsider. 'You *are* sure?'

'I am. I only told you about the episode so you would

be on your guard, and not be caught unaware if your brother seeks you out to complain about my rejection, or hold you accountable for it.'

'Thank you for the warning! He might well try to take me to task, but that's nothing out of the ordinary. I learned long ago how to handle George.'

'The thing is,' she said, her voice tentative, 'I don't want to make a bad situation worse. Knowing he will probably hold you responsible for the disappointment, are you sure *you* want to continue the relationship?'

'There is nothing I desire more! I told you before we began, I want never to cause you any anxiety. Only to bring you pleasure.'

She smiled at him, her eyes lighting with a heat that fanned the banked flames of his desire. 'Then why are we still riding in the park?'

'I'll see you soon,' he promised, his excitement and anticipation rekindling as she kicked her mare to a trot and disappeared into the mist.

The shock of learning of George's harassment and its threat to disrupt their arrangement must have added an extra edge to his impatience, for the time necessary to complete a full transit of the still-foggy park seemed an eternity to Giles. He was itching with impatience and breathless with desire by the time he was finally able to bound up the stairs to Maggie's bedchamber.

He entered upon his knock, to find her still fully clothed in her habit, and smiled. He never knew how he would find her—fully dressed, in her shift, and once, delectably, completely nude beneath a gentleman's banyan.

'So, are we to have a slow undressing?' he asked, striding over to give her a kiss.

Which she ducked to avoid. 'No. I was thinking of what might happen, if I were never to see you here again.'

His eyes widened in alarm and panic tightened his gut. 'I thought we'd agreed—'

'Oh, we did. But then I thought how it might be, if we had decided it would be wiser to terminate our arrangement. What might happen, if we were to meet later, by chance, perhaps at the house of a mutual friend. How, despite our best efforts, we could not keep from succumbing to a taste of the forbidden.'

'I like the sound of that,' he said, reaching for the buttons of her jacket.

'No, you mustn't!' she warned, batting his hand away. 'You cannot remove any of my garments, nor can I remove any of yours.'

He shook his head, mystified. 'Then—what? Are we to have only conversation? If so, I shall do my best... though with you so near, I can't vouch for how coherent I will be.'

'Conversation...of a sort,' she replied with a wicked little smile that stiffened his flagging hopes. 'Sit here.' She gestured towards the foot of the bed. 'Talk if you like, but you may not touch me.'

That sounded more promising, as he couldn't imagine a conversation with Maggie taking place on a bed that wouldn't lead to some sort of thrilling consummation.

'Let's pretend,' she murmured, sitting beside him, 'that we've just encountered each other at Sir James Graham's salon. Our host has invited us to walk in the garden, while he speaks with other guests. We find a bench—secluded, but still near the house. We chat for a while, until...I cannot resist doing this.'

He sucked in a breath as she leaned over to trace her tongue along his neck, just above the starched cravat, from beneath his ear to the base of his throat. His hands tightening into fists, he leaned his head back to give her fuller access, and with an approving murmur, she licked and sucked at the skin beneath his chin.

His breathing was already erratic when she abandoned that to nibble and nuzzle his earlobe, then lick inside the shell of his ear while she combed her fingernails through his hair, massaging the scalp in rhythm with her stroking tongue.

Suddenly she pushed him away and sat back up. 'Someone is coming along the pathway,' she whispered. 'We turn and smile and greet them, and after speaking with us, they walk back towards the house. We are alone again—for the moment.'

This time she ran just the very tips of her fingers over his face, caressing his forehead, his brow, his nose, his cheekbones with the lightest of touches. She ended by outlining his lips with a fingertip.

He opened his mouth and sucked the finger in greedily, laving it with his tongue until she pulled it free and traced his lips again with the wetness.

Every nerve of his body vibrated with tension and anticipation. Incredibly, after so little contact, he felt himself begin to spiral towards his peak, and instinctively reached for her. She held him off, hissing a warning. 'Someone else is walking this way. We rise, and smile, and chat with them. Ah, now they are returning to the house, and the bench is ours again. For the moment.'

She lifted his hand to her lips and began to nibble and lick each finger in turn. He heard his heartbeat thundering in his ears, and felt almost dizzy, trying to sit upright. A groan tore itself from his throat when she took his thumb in her mouth and sucked on it, then bit down on the tender pad.

'Night is falling,' she whispered. 'Now, with darkness our ally, we can dare to do more.'

With that, she kissed him, pulling his hand to her breast while she slid her other one beneath the waistband of his trousers, where his erection throbbed. She whimpered when he insinuated his fingers beneath the jacket of her habit, pushing aside the bodice so he could caress a nipple, rigid beneath her shift.

The kiss went deeper, wilder, a clash of tongues and teeth, ardent, impassioned, striving for the peak. She clasped her hand around his swollen length, stroking him, rubbing her wetted thumb against the sensitive tip, until he felt the convulsions carry him away to bliss.

He was lying flat on the bed when he came to himself again, still panting and dizzy. 'I think I just fell off the bench.'

Laughing, she leaned down to kiss him. 'It is my aim to make you fall off benches—often.'

'A laudable aim. First, however...' he pulled her down in an embrace and slowly began pushing up her skirts '...it's my turn to make *you* fall off.'

# *Chapter Twelve*

Later, after Giles had pleasured her fully dressed and then both of them again, not so fully dressed, they reclined on the sofa sipping wine, languid and satisfied.

'I suppose you must leave soon,' Maggie said regretfully, giving him a lingering wine-flavoured kiss.

'As I'm sure you must as well. Sometimes I wish there were no world beyond the doors of this chamber.'

A little thrill of surprise and pleasure ran through her to hear him express what she'd been feeling. 'So do I.'

'I hope at least this made up for the unpleasantness with George.'

At his mention of George, something disturbing about that interview recurred to her. She opened her lips to ask him about it, then shut them. Their intimacy was increasing daily, but he might not appreciate her enquiring into a matter as sensitive as his mother.

'What is it?' When she hesitated again, he said, 'Go ahead, say it! Surely you trust enough in our friendship, that you can speak your mind to me.'

Yes, *friendship*. She reminded herself she wanted to share that, and passion, and nothing more. 'Very well. Your brother told me something rather strange when he was railing against you—that you'd destroyed your mother. It sounded like an oft-repeated taunt, even though the very idea is ridiculous.'

Seeing something like a shadow pass over his eyes, she said, 'Surely *you* don't believe that?'

For a moment, he gazed into the distance, and Maggie sensed his thoughts were far away. Then he looked back at her, a slight smile on his face. 'My earliest memory of her was of standing in what must have been her bed-chamber, watching as someone—her maid, probably—fixed a diamond necklace around her neck. Her black hair was an intricate mass of curls, and she wore a silky gown of bright blue—the colour of her eyes.'

*Like yours*, Maggie thought.

'From a child's perspective, the room was incredibly large, with long blue hangings at the windows, gilded furniture, an impossibly high poster bed. Mama sat upon a stool covered in white satin. She looked like a princess— I thought she *was* a princess. But in the cottage where I grew up, she wore her hair in a simple chignon, dressed in plain kerseymere, and lived in a few bare rooms with scuffed wooden furniture, eating off earthenware instead of china and drinking from a wooden cup instead of a crystal goblet. Because of me.'

Maggie's heart contracted with a sympathetic pain at the sorrow on Giles's face. 'Surely *she* never reproached you for it!'

'No, never! There was always a sadness about her, though she did all in her power to see that I felt loved and happy. For years I thought the memory of her dressed in silk was only a dream. I didn't find out what had happened until much later, after my aunt—my mother's sister— took me away to school.' His face hardened. 'It was at Eton that I first met George. He quickly made sure that I knew every detail of my mother's disgrace—and that the other boys knew that, despite my reputed title, I was in truth a bastard.'

'He's been trying to make your life miserable for that long?'

He nodded. 'Growing up wild on the Hampshire downs, milling about with the local children, made me a better fighter than George. He had to get someone else to hold me off when he taunted me. Or when one of his toadies maligned my mother.' He laughed shortly. 'Since I wasn't afraid to take on even the biggest of them, it's a good thing that Christopher Lattimar turned up to watch my back.'

'Did you not go back to see your mother on school holidays?'

'By the time I was allowed to leave on holiday, she wasn't there to go back to. By then, I knew why there had always been an air of melancholy about her, and a sense of…patient expectation. Much as I know she loved me, I think she *was* waiting—for Major Richard Kensworthy, the man she loved, to return from India and claim her. While I was away at school, she got a letter informing her that he'd been killed in a skirmish. Apparently distraught, she took a walk over the downs in the midst of a storm. Our maid-of-all-work told my aunt that she came back soaked to the skin and shaking with chills. She developed an inflammation of the lungs, and before they could fetch me from school, she died.'

Maggie could hardly imagine how awful it must have been—torn from his beloved mother, bullied and taunted at school and forced to endure hearing her maligned as an adulteress, then losing her without even the chance to say goodbye. 'I'm so sorry,' she whispered, laying a hand on his cheek.

He took and kissed it. 'Thank you. It's a very old wound, and mostly healed.'

'*Mostly,*' she noted.

'I told myself that later, when…I came into enough funds, I would buy the cottage where I'd been so happy. When I made enquiries about it recently, I was told it was part of a large estate, and the owner had no wish to sell. Perhaps he will, some day; I will certainly continue to pursue it. Her grave is there.'

Once again, his eyes went unfocused, and she could almost feel him being pulled into the past. Then he shook his head and looked back at her. 'But I'm not the only one to have suffered a loss. Despite my half-brother's ridiculous words about your "advanced years", I've no doubt you could have remarried any time you wished, which makes me believe you did not wish to. Because your first husband was so compelling, you didn't believe anyone else would ever compare?'

So he remembered that she'd told him Robbie had been the love of her life. 'Compelling, definitely!' she said with a smile. 'Robbie and I grew up together—his estate, an ancient barony even older than my father's titles, borders ours. He and my brother Julian and I roamed the countryside, and of course, I wanted to do whatever they did. As you may remember, my mother lost two babes, and never truly recovered her health. After I'd scared off my third governess, overseeing me was turned over to a junior housemaid—Polly—who became maid, friend, and confidante, and who was not nearly as strict as Mama would have been about confining me to proper maidenly activities. If I hadn't been so mad about politics and desperate to have Papa's ear on his visits home, I might have grown up an untutored savage.'

'Instead, you studied philosophy and literature,' he guessed.

'Languages, too. I cajoled Julian into letting me share

his tutor. Boys are always taught so many more interesting subjects than girls! With Mama ill much of the time, I did learn to run a household, though I'm hopeless at needlework or sketching. Robbie didn't care about things like that. He thought it splendid that I could climb trees and shoot straight and catch more fish than he did.' Her smile softened at the memory. 'When he came back from university, so handsome and serious and yet still so dear a friend, I'd put up my hair and let down my skirts. Falling in love came as naturally as breathing. Despite my interest in politics, after the Season my great-aunt Lilly insisted I have, I expected to marry him and spend the rest of my life at Raven's Cliff, only a few miles from where I was born. But then came the carriage accident.'

'His death devastated you.'

Even after so many years, her throat closed and tears threatened. 'Yes,' she whispered, unable to say more. He wrapped his arms around her and pulled her against his chest, hugging her close in wordless sympathy.

Releasing her a moment later, he said, 'Then I'm mistaken in thinking I'd heard you'd been engaged again, several years ago?'

Sir Francis Mowbrey was a topic almost as unpleasant as Robbie's death, and one, despite their growing friendship, she had no intention of discussing. 'Yes, briefly. We decided we should not suit. Have you never been back to your father's estate since you left with your mother as a child?'

'No, nor have I any wish to see my father. If he is my father. The way my half-brother tells it, I'm the brat of a younger son who died obscurely in a battle half a world away.'

'But you were born within the confines of marriage, which makes you the earl's heir, regardless of the feelings between you. Knowing you will eventually inherit, surely at some point he will summon you and begin to acquaint you with the duties you will one day have to take over.'

Giles shrugged, his gaze hardening again. 'I make no such assumption.'

'Does your father manage Abbotsweal himself? Or does he use an agent?'

'As I haven't been there since I was too young to notice such a thing, I have no idea.'

She probably shouldn't press the point, but she felt so strongly, she couldn't help herself. 'But you need to have an idea—more than an idea. You need to *know* the land and the people who work it, intimately! Your Radicals talk about reforming government, giving every man his say. Perhaps you will go as far as the French, confiscate the land people like my father have managed for centuries and parcel it out to tenants, or anyone greedy enough to hold out their hand. But for now, the health of the land and the well-being of those who live on it depend on the man who owns it—the man who bears the title. He likely serves as magistrate for the county, director of the parish poor house, and supports the livings of the pastors who minister to its people. Directs which fields will be planted with what crops, provides updated tools to farm the land, keeps his tenants' cottages in repair, sees to the care of their elderly and to those who are sick or in need. Would you know which curate to give which living on your father's land? Who to appoint as judge? Who to sit on the poorhouse committee?'

'Of course not,' he replied, impatience and irritation clearly written on his face.

Since he was already angry, she might as well finish. 'I know it's not my place to harangue you about this, but only think, Giles! When your father—when the earl—

dies, and Parliament sends you the writ of summons to the Lords, you can ignore it. Refuse to serve. Never visit the estate. But then the people there will have no voice. You are responsible for them, even more so than for the people who voted you to represent them in the Commons. *They* can elect someone else, should they be unhappy with your service. The villagers and tenants and farmers and householders of Abbotsweal cannot. Would you leave them at the mercy of some hireling, or even worse, with no oversight at all?'

Making no answer, he pushed away and sat glaring at her, arms folded.

'Very well, I'm done. I imagine you are now quite impatient to get on your way,' she added ruefully.

Still silent, he stood, adjusted his clothing, and turned to stride out. At the doorway, he halted. 'You really are brave, you know. Few of my friends dare speak of my mother, and none of them—no one—has the audacity to take me to task about fulfilling my "duty".'

'It needed to be said, little as you wished to hear it.' She gave him a gallows grin. 'And I didn't think you'd strike a lady. In truth, though, you *should* get to know the people and the land. Do not make all those who depend upon Abbotsweal suffer for the enmity between yourself and the earl. Please, Giles, at least consider it.'

He stared at her for a long moment, his face grim and shuttered. And then, most unexpectedly, he threw back his head and laughed. 'You don't happen to know a tradesman named "Angleton" from the town of Romesley, do you?'

Relieved that he no longer seemed so angry, she said, 'I don't believe so. Should I?'

'If I didn't know better, I would swear you coached him up and sent him to my rooms yesterday. Apparently delegated by the town and county that chose not to re-elect George, he called on me to urge that I visit Abbotsweal and become acquainted with its people. As you have just done.'

'How wonderful that they are eager to meet you!' she cried. Then, reminding herself that *he* was the one who had to become convinced such a visit represented a priceless opportunity, she damped down her enthusiasm. 'Will you?' she asked quietly.

To her dismay, his expression hardened again. 'I don't know. As I told him, I will…*consider* it.'

With that, he walked out the door.

With a sigh, Maggie watched him go. Would he come back again, or had her plain speaking alienated him for good? Something twisted in her chest at the idea that he might never visit her at Upper Brook Street again, should the pleasures of intimacy not be sufficient to overcome the anger she'd aroused by badgering him about his duty.

But if there could not be an honest exchange of opinion between them, nothing more than a temporary lust would be possible anyway.

She drew herself up short at the direction that thought was headed. There wasn't *supposed* to be anything more between them beyond a temporary lust—and, if she were wise and lucky, a lasting friendship.

Still, what kind of friend would she be, if, without a word of caution, she let him continue down a path that seemed so clearly to her to be one of disaster for him and those who would depend on him?

Not her father's daughter, who'd been raised to love and care for the land and its people.

Sighing again, Maggie straightened her habit and prepared to return to Cavendish Square. Though the very thought of not seeing Giles again sliced like a knife to the bone, she couldn't regret forcing him to listen to her views. She only hoped he would honour his word, and consider them.

A disgruntled Giles returned to his rooms at Albany to change and ready himself for Parliament, glad that Davie had already departed for the committee rooms. He couldn't believe, after opening himself up to discuss his memories of his mother—something he did very rarely— Maggie had blindsided him with her insistence that he think more carefully about his eventual inheritance.

After avoiding, as a rule, thinking about the earldom at all, to be harangued about it twice in the space of two days seemed incredible.

He could still remember the confusion he'd felt, when a woman he'd never met invaded their cottage to demand that his mother let her take him away to school. The hurt and sense of betrayal when his mother, instead of laughing in the woman's face, had *thanked* her—and turned him over without even a token protest. The shock and disbelief of learning during their travel to Eton that, not only did he have a father he didn't remember, the man was still living and was wealthier and more prominent than he could imagine. The soul-deep anger that smouldered still over how that father had spurned and humiliated his wife and abandoned his son.

The vastness of his shame and guilt at discovering he'd been responsible for his mother's banishment and anguish.

He felt an almost violent aversion to accepting anything that came from the earl, who had chosen to do nothing to assist him or his mother during the poverty of his childhood, or at any time since as he grew to manhood. Somehow, it seemed a travesty to be forced to accept a largesse that would never be offered, if the law didn't require it.

And so, all these years, he'd put the succession and what it would mean for him out of mind. Distancing himself from the society in which his father moved, despite his uncle's and Davie's increasingly frequent hints that he needed to become familiar with the world and the duties that would eventually be his. Stubbornly holding himself apart from his heritage, ignorant of the scope and range of responsibilities that would fall to him sooner or later, when the earl died.

As they both grew older, that hour would come sooner rather than later.

Much as he hated to admit it, Maggie was right; it probably *was* time for him face up to the future he could not avoid.

Mr Angleton's invitation provided an excellent opportunity to begin.

As he shrugged on his coat, Giles thought ruefully that, much as he'd castigated George for being spoiled and self-absorbed, on this matter, he'd been just as immature. He'd excused himself for ignoring the problem, citing the important national issues in Parliament that demanded his immediate attention, while this 'other matter' was distant enough to be put off. But in reality, he'd been metaphorically sucking his thumb in the corner like a resentful child, refusing to prepare for his future out of spite for the father who'd rejected him.

The realisation was sobering, and he didn't much like the picture it painted of him.

Then he smiled, recalling Maggie's passionate conviction as she championed the cause of the tenants and villagers. Ignoring every warning sign that normally silenced Davie or anyone else who dared to mention forbidden topics, she'd forged ahead in the teeth of his angry resistance. So convinced that he must recognise the truth of what she said, and so sure that he would do what was right, once he did.

*Do not make all those who depend upon Abbotsweal suffer for the enmity between yourself and the earl.* If he did not take up the invitation from the Romesly electors and intervene to ally himself with these people, would he be doing just that?

*You are responsible for them…* But that wasn't quite fair. He hadn't asked the Romesly voters not to support George. Though, he admitted with a sigh, given an alternative, how could anyone of sense *not* have voted George out of office? Still, it had taken courage for the electors to reject the choice of the most powerful man in the county.

Encouraged by the principles he'd avowed over his years in Parliament, the electors had counted on him to stand by them when they did so. How could he let them down?

How could he force himself to return to the land from which he and his mother had been evicted all those years ago? Where the father he wouldn't even recognise still lived?

Conflicted, and irritated by his indecision, he threw on his greatcoat and prepared to join his friends in the committee room. Mr Angleton had told him he'd be in London for some time; Giles didn't need to make a final decision now.

But the spectre of becoming Earl of Telbridge seemed to loom much closer.

Early that evening, throwing down his pen in disgust, Giles rose from the table in the committee room. He'd had difficulty concentrating all day, the questions about the future raised by Maggie and the elector from Romesly affecting his ability to hammer out policy in the present.

'I've had enough for today,' he told Davie, who'd gazed over at him as he stood up, a question in his eyes. 'Let's begin again tomorrow.'

'Early tomorrow?' Ben asked, giving him a pointed look.

To his annoyance, Giles felt his face redden. 'Early enough.'

'Shall I save a place for you at the Quill and Gavel?' Davie asked.

'Yes, I've some matters to attend to, but I'll meet you there later for supper.'

'Perhaps I can help you work out that point of law.'

Giles knew Davie meant far more than the minutiae of the language for the Reform Bill. Maybe it was time to confide in his friend. 'Perhaps. I'll see you later.'

Having considered and rejected and reconsidered the idea several times over the course of the afternoon, Giles ordered a hackney and set out for Cavendish Square. His friends knew all about Parliament, crafting laws and getting out the vote. But none of them knew anything about managing an estate.

He knew only one person who did. And if he intended to begin preparing for the responsibilities that would inevitably become his, he at least needed to know what to look for when he accepted Mr Angleton's offer to visit Romesly.

Which, he realised, some time over the course of the day, he'd decided to do.

Fortunately, since he wasn't exactly sure how he would have explained the reason for his call to Lord Witlow, the butler informed him that Lady Margaret was at home. Leading Giles into another elegantly appointed room done in the Adams style, all classical pilasters and pale plaster, the butler went off to commune with his mistress.

Giles found himself pacing impatiently, though had little doubt that, once informed of the identity of the caller, curiosity alone would prompt Maggie to receive him.

As he expected, after only a brief wait, the butler ushered her in. Just the sight of her, her auburn hair glowing in the candlelight above a green gown that accented her eyes and flattered her slender figure, warmed his heart and smoothed the hard edges off his urgency.

'Mr Hadley, what a pleasant surprise!' she said, giving him her hand. 'Will you take some refreshment?'

'That would be much appreciated.'

'Please, do be seated, and tell me how I may assist you. Rains, will you bring wine?'

As soon as the butler exited, he gave her hand a lingering kiss. 'How lovely you look tonight! I find myself wishing we were at Upper Brook Street.'

'You look quite delicious yourself,' she replied, smiling at him before giving her lips a naughty lick that made him want to consign his serious errand to perdition and carry her off where they might indulge in activities not prudent to perform in Cavendish Square.

'But alas,' she continued, putting a halt to his lascivious imagining, 'I know you wouldn't come to Cavendish Square with trysting in mind.' The sparkle faded from her eyes and a look of distress creased her brow. 'Particularly if you are still so angry about my outspokenness this morning that you intend to…terminate our arrangement.'

'Terminate it!' he cried, astounded that she might imagine that to be the reason for his visit here. 'Of course not! How could you even think that?'

'You were quite angry when you left. I did insist on meddling in what is none of my business.'

He'd spent so much of the day pondering what to do, he'd completely forgotten that he had, in fact, initially been irritated by her persistence. 'I'm not angry any more. Although what we were discussing *is* the reason for my visit tonight.'

Understanding immediately what he meant, she said, 'You've come to a decision, then. Are you going to accept Mr Angleton's offer?'

'I think I must. As you pointed out so persuasively, whether I like it or not, the earldom will one day be mine, and with it, the responsibility for managing the land and caring for its people. The responsibility is vast, and so is my ignorance. I cannot afford too long a visit to Abbotsweal now, when I need to help prepare the bill for its first reading, but even a short trip could begin to chip away at that mountain of ignorance.'

'I'm so pleased!' she exclaimed, her enthusiasm making him feel even better about the decision. 'I knew, if you could just be brought to think rationally about it, you would embrace the task. You need only the proper training to become an effective guardian and advocate for Abbotsweal.'

'I certainly need that. In fact, I was hoping that you and your father might offer me some suggestions about what to look for and ask about when I visit Romesly, so I might take the fullest advantage of the trip.'

'I'm sure Papa would be happy to! Let me have Rains see if he can join us.'

After sending the butler off in pursuit of her father, she looked at him thoughtfully. 'We can both make suggestions for what you might explore during your visit. But if you'd like my opinion...'

'On a matter about which you feel so strongly,' he

said with a grin, 'I expect I shall have it, whether I want it or not.'

'How very unhandsome—if, alas, also true!' she replied with a laugh. 'It occurred to me that, although you *should* visit the village and speak with the farmers, those enquiries alone will not give you an accurate picture of an earl's job, which is the co-ordination and management of a rather vast enterprise. The only way to learn about that task is to watch someone performing it. Do you think you could spare a few days to visit Huntsford? My brother Julian is an excellent manager, trained since childhood for the task. I know he would be happy to take you around the estate and show you the duties involved in running it.'

'Would you escort me to Huntsford?' he asked, surprising himself with the question.

Initially looking startled, she quickly recovered. 'If you wish me to.'

The prospect of spending unhurried time with her, seeing the world that had moulded her into the fascinating creature she'd become, the world he must one day inhabit, sent a thrill of anticipation through him.

There might even be a few discreet opportunities for intimacy.

'I can think of nothing that would give me more pleasure. Well, I can think of a few things, but not anything we dare do in your father's front parlour.'

To his delight, she was blushing when the door opened.

'Good evening, Mr Hadley,' the marquess said as he strode in. 'Now, what's this mysterious purpose Rains tells me my daughter has summoned me to consult with you about?'

'Really, Papa, it was hardly a summons!' Lady Margaret protested as she walked over to give him a kiss. 'I'll let Mr Hadley tell you about it himself.'

Giles gave her a rueful smile. 'If I'm about to embark on this endeavour, I suppose I ought to call myself "Lyndlington".'

Lord Witlow raised an eyebrow. 'Your father has invited you to Abbotsweal to begin learning about the estate?'

'No, not Telbridge. Surprisingly, a request was made by some of Abbotsweal's merchants and farmers for me to visit Romesly, one of the villages on the estate, and the surrounding area.'

Witlow gave a huff of impatience. 'That business with your mother happened over twenty years ago. It's long past time for the earl to have got over his injured dignity and look to the future of his heritage, by training his heir to manage it. Well, visiting Romesly is a start.'

'Yes, but it won't show him what is actually involved in managing an estate,' Lady Margaret said. 'I thought perhaps I could take him to Huntsford and let him go about with Julian for a few days.'

'An excellent idea!' the marquess replied, and then chortled. 'If it gets back to Telbridge, which doubtless it will, perhaps it will shame him into finally doing *his* duty.'

'I thought you would approve,' Lady Margaret said.

'Otherwise you'd not have invited my opinion, eh, Puss?' he teased, tweaking one of her auburn curls.

'You know I value your advice—even when it conflicts with my desires,' she replied, giving him a hug.

Giles watched them, startled at first by their open display of affection. Suddenly his mind was filled with a vision of himself as a youngster, returning to the cottage after fishing with some of the boys from the neighbouring farm. Mama had met him on the porch with a kiss, and invited the boys to linger for a mug of water and a slice of bread. While they ate, she stood behind him, her arms draped loosely about his shoulders, listening attentively as he nattered on about every small detail of his fishing expedition.

A profound sense of sadness struck him, part grief at his mother's passing, part longing for the joyous intimacy that Lady Margaret shared with her father, the warmth and comfort of close family he had not experienced since childhood.

Thankfully, he had his friends, who were almost as good as family.

Almost.

'You shall have to watch out for my "managing" daughter, Lyndlington,' the marquess said, recalling him. 'She'll have you out riding the acreage and tending crops and calling on tenants before you know what's happening.'

'Those all sound like things I need to learn to do,' Giles replied.

'Indeed. If I do say so myself, Esterbrook makes an excellent estate manager—which is my only solace for having a son so uninterested in politics. I wish I could accompany you, but with your forces marshalling against us, I must be here to prepare for the assault.'

'As one who will be assisting with the marshalling, I won't be able to stay long at Huntsford, but I appreciate your lending me your son's expertise. And your knowledgeable daughter's assistance as well.'

'The latter I shall surely miss, so mind you don't linger at Huntsford too long, Puss. I shall write Julian tonight, Lyndlington. We may have opposing views, but I admire the vigour of your intellect and the passion of your opinions.' The marquess chuckled. 'I shall look forward to the day you take your place in the Lords! But for now, I must return to work.'

'Shall I have Cook prepare a tray for you, Papa, or will we dine as usual?'

'I'd like to see your smiling face at the table—after which I shall have to repair to Brooks's for a tiresome meeting.'

'I must be off to dinner and some tiresome meetings as well,' Giles said. 'Lady Margaret, please send me a note when you're ready for the excursion to Huntsford. I'll delay my visit to Romesly until afterwards—when hopefully I'll have a better notion of what I should be looking for.'

'Send you a…note?' she repeated, raising an eyebrow in query.

Did she fear that, now that they would be seen associating openly, he might cease his clandestine visits?

Did she really think he could stay away?

'Yes, a note. In the interim, I shall follow my usual routine. *All* of my usual routine.'

'Very good,' she said, looking relieved. 'I expect it should take about a week to arrange—if that will be agreeable?'

'I am at your disposal,' he replied with a wink. Turning to the marquess, he said, 'Thank you again, my lord, for your advice and your invitation. I shall look forward to meeting your son.'

The two men bowed, and Lady Margaret walked them to the door. 'Papa, I'll see you later. I shall look forward to showing you Huntsford, Mr Hadley.'

'I shall look forward to seeing it with you,' he replied, letting a glance convey what he could not say out loud in her father's presence: how much he hoped that during their journey, she'd be sharing with him more than just her ancestral home.

Feeling as if he'd had a burden lifted, Giles walked out to hail a hackney. It wasn't until he was seated in the vehicle, bowling along towards dinner with his friends at the Quill and Gavel, that it struck him how easy and natural it had seemed to consult Maggie.

Normally, he hated asking for help, working twice as hard as he might otherwise have to in order to sort out problems on his own. The lingering effects, he supposed, of having to stand alone against the world during his early days at Eton.

Even more ironic, he was actually *anticipating,* rather than dreading, his upcoming journey into a life he'd never wanted.

Because Lady Margaret would accompany him, easing the transition, as she eased the tension in his body and carried him to delight?

Better not study too closely the implications of that fact. And simply focus, for now, on the satisfaction of having taken the first step towards accepting his destiny.

## *Chapter Thirteen*

The next afternoon, Maggie was attending to the myriad of details that would keep her father's household running smoothly during her absence when Rains appeared in the small back parlour she used as her office. 'The Dowager Countess of Sayleford to see you, Lady Margaret.'

'How lovely,' Maggie said, feeling guilty for not having made time to see her elderly great-aunt since her initial call, when she'd gone trolling for information. 'You've shown her into the Blue Salon?'

'Yes, ma'am. Lady Sayleford has already ordered refreshments,' he added.

Trust Aunt Lilly to have no compunction about issuing commands in her nephew's house. 'What are we having?'

'Tea and cakes, Lady Margaret,' the butler replied, trying to hide his smile.

Maggie chuckled. 'Tell her I'll join her directly.'

After washing the ink off her hands and tidying her gown, Maggie hurried to the salon, wondering what might have prompted her great-aunt to seek her out, rather than issuing a summons for her to call at Grosvenor Square. Some delicious piece of gossip she couldn't wait to share?

A moment later, she walked into the Blue Salon and gave her visitor a kiss. 'Aunt Lilly, what a delightful surprise!'

'If my great-niece saw fit to call upon her old great-aunt occasionally, it wouldn't be such a surprise,' that lady returned tartly.

Trust Aunt Lilly to go straight to the point, without wasting any time on the social niceties. 'You are quite right, Aunt, and I should apologise. With Parliament convening again and the hubbub over the efforts to push through the Reform Bill, Papa has been busier than ever with his political dinners, which means I have, too. But that's no excuse for neglecting you.'

'It certainly is not,' the dowager agreed. 'I have heard you've been exceptionally busy. Particularly after your early morning ride.'

Maggie froze, shocked into silence. Could her great-aunt know about her morning rendezvous—and if so, how had she found out?

By the time she'd gathered enough wit to search for a reply, she realised her obvious chagrin at the pronouncement would make it rather difficult to fob it off. Before she could give it a try, her great-aunt shook a finger at her.

'No point trying to tell me you have no idea what I mean, missy. Guilt is painted all over your face! Besides, you could never tell a convincing lie, and you know it. But I didn't come to take you to task, though I probably should.'

'You didn't?' Maggie said, still trying to wrap her mind around the horrifying news that her great-aunt knew she'd been trysting with Giles Hadley.

'No.' Her great-aunt chuckled. 'That would be rather hypocritical, after I'd practically urged you to take a lover. And if I were angling for one myself, Giles Hadley would certainly catch my eye!'

'Indeed,' Maggie said faintly.

'Thank heavens that monster Napoleon no longer terrorises Europe! I've not been abroad for ages, and a nice long sojourn on the coast of Italy during a chilly English winter and spring would be just the tonic. So I wanted to tell you that I stand ready to assist if any little…consequences develop.'

Maggie felt her cheeks flame, while sickness at the very thought of such a catastrophe made her stomach churn. 'We've…arranged things to make sure nothing like that ever happens.' She shook her head, still a little stunned. 'I can't believe I'm talking to you about this.'

'I would have hoped you'd have your mama to talk with about whatever most concerns you. Sadly, Ophelia hasn't been strong enough to fill that role for years. I want you to know in your present…circumstances, you'd have someone sensible to protect you, if protection should be needed.'

'Protection rather than chiding?'

Her great-aunt reached over to take her hand. 'How could I chide you for doing something that makes you happy, child? It broke my heart to see how devastated you were after you lost your Robbie. You've been simply *existing* for too long! How could I not rejoice to see the bloom back in your cheeks, that long-absent sparkle in your smile, the bounce back in your step? I noticed the difference in you the moment you entered the room! All I ask is that you be as prudent as you can—and relish every moment of joy. One never knows when there will be another.'

'Of that, I'm well aware,' Maggie said.

'You don't envision anything…longer term?'

'Probably not. I don't think so—oh, I don't know! Since *I* effectively propositioned *him*, there has been no discussion of his expectations.'

'You propositioned him? Bravo!' her great-aunt said, with an approving nod. 'I wouldn't have thought you'd have the gumption.'

'Or the foolhardiness,' Maggie said.

'Why, are you already regretting it?'

'Oh, no! It's been…wonderful. I'd forgotten just how wonderful it can be between a man and a maid. I shall be grateful to him for ever, just to have once again tasted that sublime pleasure.'

Her great-aunt raised an eyebrow at her tone, which was perhaps too enthusiastic. 'Are you sure you're not beginning to want something more?'

Maggie snuffed out the flicker of hope before it could catch fire. 'I can't, Aunt Lilly. I don't think I could bear loving like that again. I admit, this is the first time since Robbie that any man has interested me enough for the thought to enter my mind. But we didn't begin the affair with any intention of it being more than a mutually enjoyable interlude. I intend to continue considering it only that.'

'Probably wise for you to tread carefully, my sweet. One broken heart is enough for a lifetime.'

'With that, I can certainly agree. But—Aunt Lilly, how did you find out?' The idea that, even as they sat here drinking tea, the tantalising *on dit* about aloof Lady Margaret dallying with a lover might be blazing through the *ton* like wildfire across dry grass, made her feel ill.

'Don't worry, my dear, I haven't heard a whisper of gossip—yet. It probably will get out sooner than later, by the way, a fact for which you should prepare yourself. In the meantime, I have my sources,' she ended, looking smug.

'Your sources? But if there's not gossip, you must mean…from within my own *household*?' Maggie cried.

'Don't get your feathers ruffled,' her great-aunt said, patting her hand. 'After your mama was so ill for so long, and your father off at Parliament, how else was I to learn how you were getting on? I needed to have some way of knowing if anything were amiss, in case you required someone to step in and assist. And with your mother unable to fill the role, *you* needed someone who could be a companion.'

It took only a moment for Maggie to piece it all together. *'Polly?'* she gasped.

'How else would a junior housemaid suddenly get herself advanced to being the maid and companion of the daughter of the house? I'd had my eye on her for some time, and when I was sure she might be the one, broached the possibility to her. She was quite enthusiastic, and it was the trick of a moment to get your father to agree.'

'I can hardly believe it. Polly, *spying* on me all these years?'

'I'd hardly call it "spying"!' the dowager objected. 'Has she not always been a friend, confidante and supporter when you needed one? Looked out for your welfare, rejoiced with you in your happiness, sustained you in your sorrow?'

'Yes,' Maggie admitted.

'Well, then. Heavens, child, it wasn't as if I'd been paying her to report back to me! All I did was obtain her the position, and tell her to call on me if circumstances developed she thought you might not be able to manage alone.'

'Like the repercussions of taking a lover,' Maggie muttered.

'Very true. Polly might sympathise, but she hasn't the resources to assist you, should assistance of that sort become necessary. So, of course, she told me about it.'

'I still can't believe it.'

'You might rather thank me for being such a good judge of character. I think she has served you well.'

Aunt Lilly was right; it was silly to cling to her outrage over having a loving relative place a concerned individual to guard her, with instructions to call for assistance if the need arose. 'She has served me well,' Maggie admitted. 'But I do wish you'd told me about the arrangement sooner.'

'Well, now I have. I understand you are taking Hadley to Huntsford?'

'Yes,' she replied, no longer surprised that her great-aunt seemed to know all her plans. 'He has finally decided he must face the future he's avoided all these years. Although, I'm sorry to say, not because he reconciled with his father. A delegation from the townspeople in one of the villages on the estate begged him to start becoming involved with their community.'

Aunt Lilly nodded approvingly. 'About time he started acting like Viscount Lyndlington. Since his attics-to-let father refuses to see to teaching him how to run an estate, someone must. Julian will set him an excellent example.' The dowager raised an eyebrow. 'You had some hand in this decision, I'm sure. Well done of you! I hope he appreciates it.'

Maggie chuckled. 'He certainly didn't at first! I did rather lecture him about it, though, which he was kind enough to forgive. Of course, I can't wait to show off Huntsford.'

'I'll leave you to your preparations,' the dowager said,

setting down her teacup. 'Just remember, I'm here to help, should you need it.'

Maggie walked her to the door and gave her a hug. 'Dearest Aunt Lilly! What would I do without you?'

'Heaven knows, child,' her great-aunt said with a chuckle. 'I won't tell you not to do anything I wouldn't, for that would give you far too much leeway.' With a little wave, she allowed Rains to escort her down the hallway.

Smiling, Maggie climbed the stairs back to her chamber to instruct Polly in some packing. And put a word in her ear!

She had to marvel again at her great-aunt putting in place someone to watch over and guard her, a fact which still touched, gratified and outraged her. She felt the world somehow tilted: her great-aunt knew of and approved her having a lover, would help her should there be any consequences—heaven forbid!—and had been a secret presence, watching over her most of her life.

While she'd thought she had been fending for herself.

Shaking her head, she entered her bedchamber, where Polly was spreading layers of tissue paper over her gowns. Halting, she stared at the woman until the maid looked up, a question in her eyes.

'You might have told me.'

Predictably, Polly showed neither surprise nor remorse, her expression more the patience of a mother trying to quiet a troublesome child, than guilt for having reported on her mistress for years.

'Tell you what—that her ladyship obtained me this position? That she begged me to let her know if a child who was virtually motherless and fatherless needed help? I'll not apologise for that, missy!'

'How often did you call upon her?'

'Only once—when your Robbie died. I knew to survive that, you'd need all the loving arms you could get
surrounding you. I considered telling her about that last…
incident, but that resolved itself before any intervention
was necessary. This time, with no wedding ring in the
offing, I wanted her prepared to help, in a way I cannot.'

Polly rose and came over and touched Maggie's cheek.
'My dear Lady Maggie,' she said softly, 'don't you know
I would do anything in my power to keep you safe and
happy?'

It might have been a conspiracy, but it had been one
of love and concern. Blinking back tears, Maggie gave
the maid a hug. 'Very well,' she conceded, letting go the
last of her anger. 'But no contacting her in future, without letting me know first!'

'As long as you're doing what's best for you,' Polly
replied.

'In whose opinion?' Maggie muttered, knowing that
half-concession was the best she'd get from her independent, irrepressible, but loving caretaker. 'Very well, let's
get the packing finished. I can't wait to get to Huntsford!'

'Or get Mr Handsome to Huntsford,' Polly said. 'Remember, those are country folk. Promise me you won't
scandalise them by carrying on while you're in the neigh-
bourhood.'

'Under the eyes of my mother and brother?' Maggie
replied. 'I haven't a discreetly hidden away house of my
own to use there, you know.'

'You have Raven's Cliff.'

Maggie froze, the sudden pain so intense, it robbed her
of breath. 'I couldn't go there,' she said when she could
speak again. 'And I could never take…anyone else there.'

Polly looked at her, an echoing sorrow in her eyes.
'Then I am sorry to have mentioned it.' She pressed Mag-

gie's hand, then returned to the gowns. 'You'll need to see to your papa's dinner soon. How many are to dine tonight?'

Whether she'd meant to or not, the maid's mention of her home with Robbie and the immediate anguish of remembering his loss had a cautionary effect, underscoring Aunt Lilly's warning.

She must be careful not to let herself get too close to the far-too-charming Giles Hadley. Even if she had begun to suspect he might be a man who could keep her intrigued—and tantalised—for a very long time, she couldn't bear to open herself again to the prospect of such pain.

As Aunt Lilly had said, one broken heart was enough for a lifetime.

## Chapter Fourteen

A week later, anticipation buoying her up like a boat on a wave crest, Maggie sat beside Giles in the post chaise for the final leg of their journey to Huntsford. Protesting that he didn't like being cooped up in a vehicle, he had ridden most of the way beside the carriage, keeping pace by her window. But with the prospect of seeing her beloved home soon, she'd asked him to stay in the carriage, so she might point out aspects of the view as they neared the house.

He was an excellent rider, with an easy command of his various mounts, she'd noted—so not just a park-strutter, who could maintain his seat well enough to walk a job horse around Hyde Park during the fashionable hour. Although they had met in the park several times, they had never actually ridden together, so until this journey, she hadn't known what his level of horsemanship might be.

Maggie wondered whether he'd been put on his first pony before he and his mother were exiled from Abbotsweal, or whether the uncle who had sponsored him had taught him equitation, as one of the skills required of a gentleman. It had to be one or the other; an exiled woman living in a simple cottage wouldn't have possessed the means to keep a riding horse.

Not until they began the journey had she wondered whether returning to a great landed estate would be painful for him, even though Huntsford was probably quite different from Abbotsweal, nor would visiting it require meeting the estranged father who had rejected him. Amiable but rather reticent during the transit, Giles had given her no clue to his feelings.

Perhaps he was normally a quiet man, when he wasn't debating political issues. Their few long conversations had focused on that topic, and at Upper Brook Street, their time was mostly spent in conversation of a different sort. Just as she'd not known until the drive here how good a rider Giles was, she had to smile again at how ignorant she was about the man with whom she'd become so quickly intimate.

But she would not have postponed intimacy for an instant in order to get to know him better.

A dearly familiar stretch of road outside the carriage window brought her back to the present. A few moments later, the carriage passed through Huntsford's elaborate iron gates and entered the Long Drive through the parkland.

Maggie clutched Giles's sleeve. 'Watch, now,' she said, pointing out the window on his side of the carriage. 'As soon as we round the next curve, you'll have a view of Huntsford in the distance.'

Almost as she spoke, peering around his shoulder as he turned to the window, she made out the brick-gabled outline of her beloved family home. As they did every time she returned, no matter how short her time away, her spirits soared with a thrill of gladness.

'Tudor brick work, isn't it?' Giles asked, watching the

vista pass before them, before the road took them back into the shelter of the Home Woods.

'Yes, an ancestor who was one of Queen Elizabeth's courtiers gave it that Tudor façade, but inside, it's a hodge-podge—medieval Great Hall, Tudor antechambers, and a new wing behind the façade added by my grandfather in the Georgian style, rooms with larger windows and French doors that open to the garden.'

'It sounds quite impressive. You'll have to lend me a footman for a guide, so I don't get lost on my way from my bedchamber to breakfast.' He turned back to gaze at her. 'Unless, by happy chance, our bedchambers are adjacent?'

Oh, that they might be! But to be safe, she'd instructed the staff to assign him a chamber that was a temptation-resistant distance from the family wing. 'Regretfully, no. I'm afraid we'll both have to be on our best behaviour for the duration.'

'A pity. Then I must seize what might be my last opportunity.'

With that, he tilted her chin up and claimed her mouth.

Ah, how well she knew him now, the contours of his chin and face under her exploring fingers, the wine-sweet taste of his mouth, the raspy softness of his tongue stroking hers. With the sudden realisation that it might be their last moment of privacy, by wordless consent they deepened the kiss, Maggie moving his hand to caress her breast while she dropped hers to trace the length of him, rigid under her fingertips.

And then, before she could reconsider what she was doing, Maggie slid to her knees in the cramped carriage, popped open the buttons on his trouser flap, and took him into her mouth.

Giles uttered a garbled sound and batted at her shoulder. But any motion towards stopping her quickly ceased, and a moment later, he arched his back against the cushions, giving her full access.

With the plethora of detail needing to be accomplished before he could leave London, Giles had cried off their last two mornings, and was obviously as starved as Maggie to savour the explosive attraction between them. For though she prided herself on having learned the range of touch and pressure that brought him the greatest pleasure, she needed none of that expertise for him to swiftly reach his peak.

As he subsided against the cushions, gasping, she crawled back up beside him, shaky herself with unsatisfied desire. 'No,' she whispered when his vision cleared and his eyes refocused on her. 'Don't even think of returning the favour. We're much too close to the house now.'

'What, leave you unfulfilled when you have just pleased me so thoroughly?'

'There's no time to undo my bodice, and I can't—'

Stopping her words with a kiss, Giles coaxed her lips open and began an assault on her tongue, sending her quickly back to full arousal. While she whimpered against his mouth, he laid her back on to the seat.

Kissing her still, he threaded a hand under her skirts and began caressing her leg slowly, from ankle, to knee, to thigh.

He spent a maddeningly long time running his fingers along the tender junction between leg and torso, flicking a fingertip just to the edge of her nether lips, until she was on fire and desperate for him to finally caress her there.

Squirming under him, she moved her hips, trying to bring his stroking fingers closer to the centre of her desires, aware in the dim recesses of her mind that within moments they'd be arriving at the house, a footman running up to open the carriage door…

Finally, finally, Giles eased his fingers to her slick centre. He must have been studying her, too, for he stroked right to the most sensitive place along the little nub, then into her passage, then back, until she convulsed against him.

He pulled her up into his arms, cradling her against him while her heart tried to beat its way out of her chest. Chuckling, he placed little butterfly-light kisses over her nose, her eyes, her chin, while she struggled to control her breathing and recover some semblance of wit.

A few moments later, he eased her upright on her seat, gave her a critical inspection and straightened her bonnet. 'Well, my sweet love, it appears we are about to arrive at Huntsford.'

He peered out the coach window, then pulled out his small travelling flask and offered it to her. 'Have a quick sip to settle your nerves. If my assessment of the lady's appearance is correct, I'm about to meet your mother.'

To her surprise, standing beside her brother Julian on the entry steps to welcome them was Lady Witlow. Joy—mingled with a bit of alarm—filled her at the sight of that dear face. Just what message had Papa sent to Julian, that the lady who seldom ventured further from her chamber than the morning room or its adjacent parlour had been prompted to come greet her?

And her charming guest.

Hoping Papa wasn't reading too much into her friendship with Giles, Maggie let the footman hand her out.

Julian bounded up to wrap her in a hug as Giles exited behind her. Pulling away, Maggie said, 'Lord Lyndlington, may I present my brother Julian, Lord Esterbrook.'

The two men bowed, then walked with her to where her mother awaited them on the doorstep. 'How sweet of you to greet me,' Maggie said, giving her mother a kiss, then stepping back to inspect her. 'You're looking very well, Mama. Are you feeling better?'

'How could I not feel splendid, when my dearest daughter has come for a visit? Bringing such a handsome escort, too,' she said, as Giles bowed to her.

*Isn't he?* Maggie thought. *And, oh, so clever with his hands.*

Gesturing to Giles, she said, 'Mama, may I present Giles Hadley, Lord Lyndlington. My mother, the Marchioness of Witlow.'

'A great pleasure, Lady Witlow. Thank you for allowing me to visit your magnificent home.'

Knowing how much the walk must have strained her mother's fragile strength, Maggie said, 'Shall we go to the morning room? Breakfast at Maidstone was hours ago! I could use some refreshment, and I dare say Lord Lyndlington could as well.'

Giles looked at her and grinned. 'It was a very... taxing journey.'

Giving him a frown, she tucked her arm in her mother's and steered her in the direction of the morning room. 'Did you stop at The Soldier's Rest?' her mother was asking Giles. 'We always found it a most excellent coaching inn.'

'Is that where you stayed when you accompanied Lord Witlow to London?' Giles asked.

With a few more questions, Giles engaged her mother in a conversation about inns, travelling, and the delights of returning home. Maggie smiled approvingly; Mama could be reticent with strangers, but Giles was doing an excellent job at drawing her out.

Her suspicion that her mother had pushed herself to

her limit was confirmed by the ever-increasing weight that lady put on her arm as they progressed. A little anxious, Maggie hurried to seat her mother on the sofa, brought a shawl for her shoulders and hunted for her favourite footstool.

'Don't fuss, Maggie,' her mother scolded gently. 'I'll be quite restored, once we have some tea. Lord Lyndlington, I understand that Julian is to show you around Huntsford and give you an idea of the workings of a large estate, such as you will manage once you inherit Abbotsweal?'

'Yes, ma'am. I'm going to Romesly later, my first visit to any part of the estate since I left it as a child.' Maggie noted how smoothly he passed over the circumstances of that departure. 'Lady Margaret was kind enough to suggest that I visit your estate and observe first-hand the most important tasks in its management, so that I can be evaluating those aspects of Abbotsweal during my visit.'

'You haven't reconciled with…'

'Regrettably, no,' Giles answered, his expression bland.

Maggie wondered at the pain, resentment and anguish that must hide behind that carefully emotionless façade. A simmering resentment of her own bubbled up that the earl couldn't have shown himself more a *man*, getting over his pique and stepping forward to heal the breach with the child who deserved no part of the blame for the estrangement of his parents.

'Are you too taxed from the journey to ride this afternoon?' Julian asked.

Avoiding Maggie's gaze, Giles said, 'I believe a bit of tea will be sufficient to revive me. We travelled all the way to Maidstone yesterday, so there would be daylight enough to see some of Huntsford after our arrival. As much as I would enjoy a longer visit, I can't afford to be gone from London more than a few days.'

'Excellent! Maggie, I thought we would ride out first to the Home Farm and show Lyndlington the cattle barns and sheep pens, then back through the oak forest. Tomorrow we can drive by some of the tenant farms, the church at Wexford and Tarney Village.'

'An excellent plan. After tea, I'll change into my habit and join you.'

So, for the next few days, Julian showed their visitor around Huntsford, explaining the purposes of different types of cattle and sheep, looking over the Home Wood's supply of oak and walnut that was harvested for building and furniture making, and explaining the crops grown on the farms. They stopped by several, Maggie greeting by name the tenants who hurried over. While the men talked of ploughs and grain and crop rotation, she enquired about the health of the family, complimented mothers on new babies, and teased children who'd grown several inches since she'd seen them the previous autumn.

After passing through hop gardens and fields of barley, past oast houses where the grains were malted for making ale and beer, they called on the vicar of the Wexford church, a Romanesque building dating from ancient times. Julian ended their tour at the village of Tarney, where they lifted a mug of home brew at the Lamb and Calf.

As her brother walked off to consult with the innkeeper, Giles raised his mug to him.

'Huntsford is a vast enterprise indeed, yet Esterbrook seems to have every detail in hand.'

'He has been working at it all his life. If you can write

and steer a complex bill though Parliament, you can master this,' she assured him.

'I don't doubt I can—eventually. But it will take time to learn it all. In the interim, I don't want to make mistakes that might injure the people I'm supposed to protect. Not to mention, I know nothing about cattle or sheep.'

'The men who tend them will know. Or you might ask your Whig colleague, Mr Coke of Norfolk—it's said he's the foremost expert on sheep breeding in England.'

'I'd heard he's a great agriculturalist. All our previous conversations have centred around politics; he's been a Foxite Whig and supporter of Parliamentary reform for years. Very well, I shall ask him.'

'So you see now why it is so important to have a skilled manager tend the land, someone who loves and is invested in it, who can oversee and co-ordinate the whole? Maybe you will be not quite so radical a Republican, ready to take it all away from the owners and distribute it to the masses.'

'A skilled manager is necessary, yes; but if the man who owns it isn't knowledgeable, or doesn't care about the welfare of his people, they might be better off if it were confiscated and parcelled out to the masses,' he countered.

Maggie shook her head and laughed. 'I don't suppose we will ever agree on that.'

Julian paced back to rejoin them. 'Maggie, would you mind if I turn you over to Lyndlington to escort you home? The village solicitor has obtained deeds for land whose ownership is being disputed by two neighbours. I should look at them.'

'Of course, Julian, I'll be fine.'

'Thank you, Esterbrook,' Giles said, shaking her brother's hand. 'These last two days have been…illuminating.'

Her brother chuckled. 'Not fair to give it all to you in one big swallow. It's much easier to take, I promise, when you can gnaw at it a bite at a time.'

'I'll keep that in mind.'

'I'll see you at dinner. Don't worry, Lyndlington—Maggie still knows the way home.' Giving her arm a pat, Julian nodded to Giles and walked off.

Their ale drunk and the afternoon light beginning to fade, Maggie headed them back to Huntsford Manor on a less-travelled route that wandered in and out of the Home Woods. They emerged a second time into the sunlight near a field of barley.

An elderly farmer hoeing at the edge of the field looked up, then trotted to the fence, hat in hand. 'Mistress Maggie, it's good to see you!'

'And you, Mr Grey! The field looks in excellent form.'

'Yes, if the weather holds fair, we should have a bountiful crop.'

'Won't you welcome Lord Lyndlington, a family friend who's come to consult with my brother? We've been riding him about Huntsford today.'

'Welcome, my lord,' Grey said. 'Will you be taking the gentleman to see your land, too, mistress?'

She closed her eyes at the sudden, sharp pain in her chest. 'Maybe on another visit,' she said after a moment. 'Lord Lyndlington's time here is rather short.

'Can you stop for some home brew?'

'Thank you, but we've just had a pint at the Lamb and Calf. If I have any more, I won't stay in the saddle long enough to make it home.'

'As you wish, mistress! Though I'd stake you in the saddle against anyone, whatever you've drunk. All those times you and the boys raced across these fields! Well,

God's blessing on you both,' the man said, doffing his cap before turning back to his hoe.

As they rode away, Giles said, 'Mr Grey treated you with surprising familiarity. Sure you're not secretly a Republican at heart?'

'Hardly! Farmer Grey has known me since I was a tot, mounted in front of Papa as he rode about visiting the tenants.' Maggie laughed. 'I had to get you away before he recounted any embarrassing episodes from my misspent youth.'

'Riding *ventre à terre* with your boys.'

'Among other things I don't intend to confess.'

'What did he mean, "your land"?'

They'd surmounted the crest of a hill that gave a wide view over the fields and farms, strips of velvet green and burnished gold divided by the deeper hue of hedgerows and the green-shaded mix of woodland. Dismounting, Maggie dropped her reins to let the horse graze and walked to the edge of the summit, Giles following behind her.

She pointed across the valley to a hill in the far distance, where one could make out the outline of a stone manor surrounded by an embrace of woods.

'That is mine. Or rather, Robbie's—my late husband's. His father died when he was quite young, naming my father as guardian and steward over the land. We grew up together. These last few years, Julian has watched over the property for me. I haven't been able to go back since I left after Robbie's death.'

Giles stood quietly, watching her, and she made herself go on. 'They brought him back to the manor after... after the carriage accident.' She closed her eyes, trying to shut out the memory of the bloody, mangled body that had been her last glimpse of him.

'His injuries were…'

'Catastrophic.'

'I'm so sorry. Bad enough to lose him, but like that—'

She nodded. 'I felt as if someone had tried to rip my heart out through my throat. There was such a weight on my chest, I couldn't breathe. Even thinking of going back to that house, where we were so happy—the old sensation returns, and I can't force any air into my lungs.' She laughed shortly and shook her head. 'Silly, I know, but there it is.'

'It never gets much easier, does it? When one loses… someone dear, one goes through life as if walking through London on a foggy morning—the shapes and patterns recognisable, familiar, and yet somehow…distant.'

She nodded. 'One goes through the motions of life, without ever feeling a part of it.' She looked up to catch his gaze. 'Except with you. That's the gift you given me, even greater than the pleasure, which has been treasure enough. When you touch me, for the first time in a long time, I feel fully alive. Thank you for that.'

He reached over to take her hand and kissed it.

'It's a gift you've returned in full measure.'

He looked for a moment as if he would say more. Maggie held her breath, waiting, but when he said nothing further, she chastised herself for a fool.

He didn't need to say anything more. She wouldn't really want to hear it.

'Even when I chide you about matters that are none of my business?' she asked at last.

'Even then. I needed to be chided, whether or not I appreciated it at the time.'

'What will you do now?'

'I'm not sure. This visit has certainly shown I need to learn a great deal more about Abbotsweal, and to do that, I must spend time there. If I nose about Hampshire without calling on the earl, it will look like I'm sneaking behind his back, afraid of him, or trying to tweak his nose by inserting myself into estate business before I have the right. I'm not afraid of Telbridge, but neither have I any desire to meet with him. However, it looks more and more like I must.'

Maggie nodded, pleased that he'd come to the conclusion she'd reached at the outset. 'Can you be civil?'

Giles laughed. 'Davie says I have the hottest temper of all the Hellions, and I'm afraid he's right. But I'll do my best.'

Maggie bit her tongue on an offer to accompany him. How she wanted him to learn and love the land that was to be his! But it wasn't her place to go with him as peacemaker; there was nothing official between them that gave her such a right, much as she might wish to help smooth things over.

She needed to stop thinking herself into his life, and limit herself to the friendship they shared. 'Maybe you should ask Davie to go with you.'

'I'd prefer to take someone else,' he said, giving her a significant look, 'but doing so would occasion too much comment. I might consider asking Davie—if it wouldn't make things worse with the earl from the outset, my bringing with me as advocate to the mighty earl's house the humble son of a farmer.'

'The earl need only know he's a standing member of Parliament,' Maggie replied. 'But the sun's nearly down; we should get back. I shall need to wash and change, and if I'm late for dinner, I'll earn one of Polly's scolds.'

'Your maid again? She sounds like a tyrant!'

'Definitely. She's been with me since I was so young, she's used to ruling with an iron fist.' Maggie paused, thinking ruefully of the discovery she'd made the week before. 'But I can't resent it—she truly does look out for my good. It was Polly who insisted I come back to London and start running Papa's household again after... after Robbie died. She practically dragged me back into life single-handedly.'

'If she had not, I would never have met you. I must leave her a generous vail.'

Leading their mounts, they walked back to the trail. As Giles paused to help her remount, she spied a clump of her favourite wildflowers on the verge. 'The first rose campion of the season! I must bring some home.'

'Did you pick your mama posies as a child?' he asked.

'Of course! Didn't you?'

'Always.'

While Giles held the reins of her mount, Maggie bent down to pluck a handful of stems. An instant later, she heard the blast of a pistol shot, a fiery whoosh of air right above her head, and a soft thud as the ball buried itself in the tree behind her.

## *Chapter Fifteen*

Watching with horror as a shot streaked through the air where Maggie's head had just been, Giles dropped the reins of the startled, rearing horses, grabbed Maggie and dragged her into the woodland, pushing her down behind the trunk of an ancient oak and covering her with his body. His heart racing, he peered around the tree in the direction of the shot.

He saw and heard nothing—no thrashing and snap of branches, no swaying of tree limbs as someone pushed their way back into the undergrowth.

'What could that have been?' he whispered. 'A poacher?'

'I don't think so,' she replied as softly, squirming to a sitting position behind his protective body. 'It was a pistol shot, wasn't it?'

'Yes.'

'A poacher's mainstay is lairs and traps. A pistol would be too expensive for a farmer or cottager to own.'

'You're right,' he realised suddenly. 'None of the families on the downs where I grew up had one. Ben, who served with the army, told me his rifles were all hand-made, the best from a skilled gunsmith who left his mark, and quite expensive. But if it wasn't a poacher… Stay here and stay down!' he commanded.

He darted across the trail and into the woods in the direction from which the shot had come. This time, he heard a faint rustling in the far distance, and stealthily made his way towards the sound. If the weapon had been a pistol, it couldn't have been fired from very far away.

Almost at once, he came upon a place where the branches had been bent back, the ferns on the ground trampled. Looking back towards the trail, he had a clear line of sight to where he and Maggie had been standing.

A shiver running through him at the implications, he looked all around, trying to find the perpetrator's trail. Studying the ground closely, he found a trace of boot prints, and followed them onward…to a series of shallow and then deeply cut hoofprints that showed a horse had set off at a gallop in the direction from which it had come.

He'd never be able to catch up to them on foot. Convinced that whoever had fired on them was now far away, Giles abandoned any attempt at concealment. Picking up his pace, he continuing past where the deeper fresh prints cut out of the woods to follow the shallower hoofprints—which showed that the rider had been shadowing them along the trail, keeping just out of sight under the cover of the trees.

Having learned all he was going to, Giles retraced his steps. To his exasperation, if not surprise, when he emerged from the woods, he saw Maggie waiting on the opposite verge, the reins of their mounts in hand.

At his raised eyebrows, she explained, 'I thought it would be better to track down the horses, in case we needed to get away quickly. They did run in the opposite direction from which the shot came.'

'Unless the shooter had gone in the direction they fled.'

She shook her head, unwilling to concede the point. 'Then the horses would have run another way. Horses are intelligent like that. Besides, a pistol only holds one shot.'

'And can be reloaded.'

'I ran. And I didn't run in a straight line. Robbie always told me it's hard to hit a moving target. But will you stop arguing, and tell me what you discovered?'

Giving up the point, he said, 'It appears someone was following us.'

She paled as the implications registered. 'But who, why? I can't imagine anyone wishing to do me harm.'

Giles chuckled. 'You did just refuse George's suit, didn't you?

Instead of laughing at his joke, her face clouded.

'What?' he asked sharply.

'Well…' she said slowly, 'He did threaten me when I refused him.'

'He *threatened* you?' Giles echoed, incredulous.

'Yes,' she admitted. 'When I gave him his *congé*, he was…quite ugly, as you'd warned me he might be. He went so far as to say that if I allied myself with you, I would put myself in danger.'

Remorse, chagrin, fury and shame churned in him. 'Why did you never tell me?'

She shrugged. 'I thought it the rant of a spoiled child denied his sweetmeat. But you can't really think…?'

'I would hate to think it! But neither can we afford to rule it out.' Sickened by the possibility, he tried to push it out of his mind and concentrate on what must be done. 'A man with pistol would have to be hired; he would likely not be local, and therefore he might be traced. But first, we must get you safely back to the manor and keep you there. No more riding out in the open.'

'You can't mean to keep me trapped in my own house!'

He held out his hands to give her a leg up. 'We can debate that later. Now, let's get back to Huntsford.'

He threw her into the saddle and remounted. 'Take us back the fastest way, at the fastest pace possible.'

'There's a path down this trail that goes straight back to the stables. Can't do more than a trot on that.'

'Lead the way.'

The pound of cantering hoofs and then the necessity of going single file on the path put an end to any further conversation.

Not until they'd turned their horses over to a groom, did Maggie speak again.

'You're going to tell my brother, aren't you?'

'I think we have to, though we will spare your mother, if you wish. I'd like Esterbrook's assistance in deciding how best to protect you while we try to figure out who did this.'

Maggie sighed. 'So I'm to be hidden away like a bottle of laudanum concealed in the pantry, while you two figure it out?'

'You can certainly help with the figuring, but it would be foolish for you to go about, putting yourself at risk. I'm sure your Polly will agree.'

Maggie shuddered. 'If Polly finds out, she'll lock me in my chamber and sit at my door with a kitchen knife. But promise me, no conferring about all this without me in attendance. I'm not some package for you men to dispose of.'

Giles stopped and looked at her. Could she even imagine how precious she was to him? 'Hardly a package,' he replied gruffly. 'But consider how I feel! Just the possibility that George might be behind the attack sickens me. I castigate myself for arrogance and selfishness in casually dismissing his malice, so I could do what I wanted. Have what I wanted. You, regardless of the consequences.'

'It was what I wanted, too,' she answered softly. 'If it *is* George—still a very large "if", you must concede— we will face those consequences together.'

Hearing her repeat the possibility out loud just hung another leaden weight of guilt on him. His chest tight with the anger and remorse, he said, 'I should have broken with you the night he accosted me at Brooks's.'

'Then I would have had to track you down and seduce you in your rooms. Where Davie would have discovered us, and only think what a scandal that would have been!'

When he could not make himself respond to her attempt at lightness, she tilted his chin down until she could look him in the eye. 'Giles, I'm a part of this, too. It's not all your responsibility.'

'You didn't know how vicious he can be.'

'You don't know for sure he's involved.'

Giles shook his head. 'No. But I've got a bad feeling in my gut.'

'Whatever the cause, we'll find out and put a stop to it. I'm not about to meekly submit to coercion and give up the best thing that's come my way since…for a very long time, because of your idiot of a brother. Not unless or until you tell me you don't want it any more.'

Caution, regret and his sense of responsibility urged him to say just that. 'Would you believe it if I told you so?'

She shook her head. 'Not now. At this moment, I would only think you were being stupidly chivalrous and annoyingly high-handed, making that decision "for my own good". For however long we both want to be together, we will *be* together.' She held out her hand. 'Agreed?'

Suddenly it struck him that after being fired upon and learning the attack was probably deliberate, most females would have swooned or dissolved into hysterics. His fierce Maggie looked angry, annoyed, and ready to ride down the perpetrator all by herself.

'What a marvel you are,' he murmured, and seized her for a kiss.

He let her go after the merest brush of their lips—they were much too close to the house for more—but that fleeting taste left him ravenous.

No, he wasn't ready, either, to bow to coercion and give her up.

As long as he could keep her safe.

For now, there would be no more tasting. Not until he figured out what was going on—and, he hoped with all his soul, confirmed that it was not because of him that she'd come into danger.

He couldn't bear the thought he might be responsible for bringing harm to yet another woman he cared for.

In a sombre mood, they returned to the house. As soon as he reached his bedchamber, Giles penned a note to his host, asking that they meet before dinner to discuss an urgent matter. When the footman he'd dispatched to deliver it returned with a reply, inviting him for a brandy in the Blue Parlour as soon as he was dressed for dinner, he wrote another to Maggie, informing her about the rendezvous.

She was already in the parlour with her brother when a footman guided him there. 'Maggie told me what happened,' Esterbrook said as he handed Giles a brandy, his expression troubled. 'I've agreed it's unlikely the assailant could have been a poacher with bad aim. If he wasn't from the county—and I can't imagine anyone around Huntsford being persuaded to fire at Maggie, regardless of how lucrative the inducement—someone probably will have noticed him. Strangers are pretty rare, here in the country. I'll ride out to the farms and villages tomorrow and send messengers to all those I can't reach, asking if anyone has seen someone lurking about.'

'If I ride south, across the downs, while you ride north through the forested part, we could cover more ground,' Maggie said, holding up a hand to forestall the men's instantaneous protest. 'Giles, you admitted yourself that a pistol would have to be fired at close range, and the fields there are very open. I'd be able to see anyone in the area while still well out of range.'

'Out of the question!' Giles replied. 'Just because the shooter used a pistol today doesn't mean he might not also have a rifle.'

'Then I'll bring along some of the dogs. If there's anyone within a thousand yards, they'll sniff him out and give the alarm. Surely that's far enough away for me to be safe.'

When he and Julian looked at each other and gave their heads a negative shake, Maggie said with exasperation, 'You can't expect me to just sit here cooped up and do nothing! Besides, how are you going to explain to Mama that you two went out riding, and I decided to stay at Huntsford? She'll never believe I suddenly developed a taste for sewing samplers! And I absolutely don't want her worried about this.'

'Couldn't you say you needed to—oh, I don't know, inspect the still room or something?' Julian said.

'Why would I need to look at the still room, or the silver, or the attics, during a visit that is only supposed to last a few days? And you know I'm a terrible liar.'

Julian sighed. 'That's true enough. I'm not much better at it—not with Mama. It probably would be wise to keep you away from her.'

'You could ride with me, Giles,' Maggie said, with a look of appeal. 'The shooter must know that after the failed attempt, we will be looking for him. If he's a stranger, he must also know he will stand out. My guess is that he won't chance making another try. It's just too risky—even the attempt is a hanging offence, after all. If you consider the circumstances dispassionately, the danger to me is small.'

'I would prefer the danger to be "zero",' Giles said flatly.

Maggie shook her head. 'Life itself makes that impossible! I could be thrown by a spooked horse, or hit by a falling tree limb, or trip on the stairs. Be reasonable!'

'And do it your way?' Julian said wryly. 'I have to admit, Lyndlington, what Maggie says is probably true. If I were the miscreant, I'd be halfway to London or Dover by now.'

'So we'll ride out tomorrow, together, with the dogs?' Maggie asked.

Julian looked at him. Giles wanted to insist she stay home—he'd like to lock her in a windowless inner room with three stout footmen outside to guard the door, until they learned who had fired at her today and why. But if her brother, who knew the countryside and its residents much better than he did, agreed the risk of her riding out was acceptable, he supposed he'd have to bow to their wishes.

There was the problem of keeping the incident from her mother, which, he conceded, would be rather difficult if she were locked in a room with footmen guarding the door.

'Very well,' he said at last. 'I still don't like it. You'd better tell all your outriders, if anyone she doesn't recognise even looks like they are riding in her direction, I'm going to blow a hole through them first and ask questions later.'

Maggie shook her head at him. 'Very well, we'll send out a warning. Just don't shoot one of my dogs.'

That settled, they went into dinner, a tense affair for Giles as he tried to respond with appropriate lightness to the banter she and her brother maintained to avoid having Lady Witlow sense that something was wrong. To his relief, the ladies left them to their brandy immediately after the sweet course, and he could finally relax.

He and Julian shared another brandy in solemn silence. 'You're sure she won't be in danger tomorrow?' Giles asked.

'Sure enough not to try to stop Maggie doing what she wants,' Esterbrook said. 'Besides, I know how I'd feel, left to twiddle my thumbs, and there is the matter of concealing things from Mama. Maggie so rarely comes to Huntsford while Parliament is in session, Mama would find it very odd for us not to spend the day together, if she doesn't ride out. Dinner tonight was enough of a strain; I'd not ask Maggie to have to prevaricate for the entire day. If I'm wrong…' He shuddered. 'I don't even want to contemplate being wrong.'

'Nor do I,' Giles said sombrely. Especially since, if anything did happen to her, it would almost certainly be his fault.

## Chapter Sixteen

The skies dawned clear the next morning, with an excellent visibility that made Giles feel a bit better. At least he'd not need to worry about fog or mist veiling a miscreant. They breakfasted early, since there was a great deal of territory to cover, agreeing to meet before supper at the Lamb and Calf in Tarney to share what they'd discovered.

Maggie seemed entirely unconcerned as they rode out, calling to the dogs and laughing at their high-spirited antics. She sat relaxed in the saddle as they rode across the open downs, identifying the first farmer they encountered from far enough away that Giles relaxed the hand he'd been keeping on his pistol.

They waited for the man to approach, and after a warm exchange of greetings—it appeared she *did* know every farmer, tradesman and tenant at Huntsford by name—she related the story they'd invented about a problem with a poacher shooting birds in the marsh.

The farmer frowned. 'Don't see why there'd be poaching, mistress. Lord Esterbrook is always good about giving permission, if anyone wants to go out after birds. Besides, none I know but the squire, and such gentry as his lordship invites, go out with guns.'

Maggie nodded. 'Yes, we're pretty sure whoever it is doesn't live on Huntsford land. You haven't seen any strangers about, have you? Asking directions to the village, or for a drink of water on his journey?'

'We get a few pilgrims from time to time, lost or misdirected on their way to Canterbury, but nobody in the last several months. Sorry I can't help, Lady Margaret. Don't need nobody out there, shooting willy-nilly.'

'We certainly do not! Thank you, and please do keep an eye out.'

The farmer assured them he would, they said their goodbyes, Maggie called the dogs to order and they set off down the road.

They visited half-a-dozen farms that morning, but none of the farmers or their families or labourers had seen anything amiss. After stopping for bread and ale at the inn in the village of Hillendon, they inspected another dozen farms over the afternoon.

Finally, Maggie pulled up her mount, Giles reining in his horse beside her. 'What is it?' he asked, his anxiety instantly ratcheting up.

Obviously reading the tension in his face, she sighed. 'We've found nothing all day, Giles. Couldn't you relax now, and enjoy the ride? We have this very rare chance to spend the whole day together. Don't waste it fretting! I know,' she said, raising a hand to stop him before he could speak. 'You feel somehow responsible for the attack. But you shouldn't. And in any event, by now we can be reasonably sure that whatever danger there might have been, it's now over.'

'You are probably right,' he admitted. 'But as long as there is even a small chance, I can't let down my guard.'

'Would you try, for me?' she coaxed. 'If I did get

shot, I'd hate to think the last day we had together wasn't joyful.'

'Don't even say that!' he snapped, unable to appreciate her attempt at humour.

'Very well. I shouldn't tease you to talk with me. I wondered on the drive down if you were naturally a quiet man, not speaking unless the topic under discussion was a matter about which you are passionate, like your politics. Not that I mind!

'Robbie and I often shared quiet evenings together, reading or playing cards, without the need for constant chatter.'

He laughed. 'I can promise I won't give you that. I spent far too much time alone growing up, with only myself and the dogs for company. Not that *I* minded. There were endless wonders for an inquisitive boy to explore, and I needed nothing more than a pole, some line, and a stream to keep me happy. I do wonder how my mother endured it. She had been raised in a fine house with servants, then married into an even grander one, where family and guests milled about and entertainments went on constantly.'

'Did she like to chat?'

Giles thought back, then shook his head. 'I can hardly remember her having callers, and she certainly never paid calls. She liked to read, and she painted—watercolours. I don't know where she got the books and supplies that sometimes appeared. Perhaps her sister sent them. None of her family ever visited us, though.'

His anger over that slight still smouldered, hotter perhaps because he'd not known he *should* be angry until much later.

'Too intimidated by the earl?' she suggested.

'Or too guilty, after accepting Telbridge's blood money.

My aunt told me the earl settled all the family's extensive debts when they married.' He sighed. 'But I shouldn't castigate them too much. To a small boy too self-absorbed to be inquisitive, Mama seemed happy to me.'

'I'm sure she was. She had her son.'

Something Maggie never had, Giles thought suddenly. It must be a great grief and an added source of regret that the husband she'd loved so deeply had not given her a child.

One of the dogs darted off after a rabbit, and with an apologetic look, Maggie rode off to fetch him.

What would it be like to have a son? he thought curiously at he watched her chase after the hound. Would being with the child of the woman he loved be enough to keep him content, living in a remote cottage on the Hampshire downs?

Maybe—if it were the right woman, he thought, smiling at Maggie, who laughed as she herded the errant pup back to the group.

Though he hardly had the right to consider such a thing, after putting her in danger.

As his very existence had caused his mother's ruin. Maybe George had been right about taunting him after all.

Some hours later, having found out nothing, Giles and Maggie rode into Tarney to meet with Esterbrook at the Lamb and Calf. The excitement in his bearing as they walked in told them immediately that he must have learned something useful.

'What did you discover?' Giles asked as soon as innkeeper moved out of earshot.

'Farmer Adams told us he saw a man he didn't recognise riding back and forth along the section of trail the two of you rode yesterday. Mr Williford, the innkeeper here, says he served a stranger in the taproom day before yesterday. He's given us a description of the man, and the ostler at the stable identified his horse, a black-and-tan gelding. Williford said he returned here in the late afternoon yesterday, in a tearing rush. Declining an offer of supper, he asked for his horse to be rubbed down, then set off.'

'Excellent!' Giles said, both relieved that the man was gone, and anxious to catch up to him. 'Did he mention his destination to anyone?'

'Unfortunately, no. But the ostler said he took the London road. I've already sent one of my grooms after him on my fastest horse, armed with a description of rider and mount, to see if he can pick up the trail.'

'There must be hundreds travelling that road,' Maggie said.

'If someone hired him out of London, he'll most likely return there.'

'Yes,' Maggie said. 'To a metropolis that shelters thousands.'

'True, but finding him might be easier than you'd think,' Giles said. 'He's certainly not gentry, and if he accepted a task like this, he probably resides in one of the shadier parts of the city—Seven Dials, maybe. Even there, he might stand out. He's not just a petty thief or housebreaker—he knows how to ride and can handle a weapon. Might even be a former soldier. I'll contact a friend who has connections with Bow Street; they might suggest someone we could hire to ferret him out. Lady Margaret, it would probably be best if you remain here while we investigate.'

Maggie looked at him in exasperation. 'And just how are we to keep my mother from learning about the incident if I stay at Huntsford? With debate raging over the Reform Bill, and Papa busier than ever with the meetings and dinners, she'd think it extremely odd for me to linger in the country. I won't hear of taxing her limited strength by having her worry about my safety. I shall return to London as planned.'

Neither Giles nor Esterbrook could argue with her desire to protect her mother. 'Maybe you should return to London, to keep from upsetting Mama,' her brother agreed.

'Even so, I don't think it wise for you to resume your hostess duties,' Giles said, conceding reluctantly.

'You think some assassin is going to sneak in with the dinner guests?' Maggie asked with a grin. 'Highly unlikely, I assure you.'

'True, our assassin would never pass as a guest,' Giles replied patiently, 'but he might gain access to the stable or the kitchen by posing as a guest's groom or coachman, or as a lackey from a supplier bringing ices or crab or champagne for a dinner.'

'You're right, Lyndlington,' Esterbrook said, looking troubled. 'Once Papa is acquainted with the circumstances, he'll probably forbid Maggie from acting as hostess anyway.'

'I still can't remain at Huntsford,' Maggie insisted. Then her eyes brightened. 'Why don't I stay with Aunt Lilly? Mama wouldn't have to know I'm not at Papa's. I could still co-ordinate his events from her house, much as it will pain me not to act as hostess. We'd use only our own footmen as messengers back and forth, and all the supplies would be delivered to Cavendish Square.'

'That might work,' Esterbrook said, looking encouraged.

'Aunt Lilly would continue to attend entertainments,' Maggie said. 'She hears all the gossip, so although I still cannot imagine who might wish to do me harm, if someone in the *ton* were behind it, she would be more likely than anyone I know to hear the rumours. Though I warn you, I don't intend to live in isolation for ever, so you'd better figure out what happened quickly! Well?' She looked from her brother to Giles and back.

'It seems as good a plan as any,' Esterbrook said. 'Will it do, Lyndlington?'

Giles still preferred the windowless room with three armed footmen outside…but that was as impractical as letting her remain at Huntsford. 'I wish I could think of something more secure…but I suppose that will have to do until I can. But no going out—not to a *musicale* at a friend's, not to pick up some item for the night's entertainment that Lord Witlow's housekeeper forgot. No morning rides in the park.'

She looked at him, stricken. 'No rides?'

'Certainly not!' her brother said. 'If it's dangerous to ride at Huntsford, it's even more so in the city, where there are buildings and alleyways all along the route to conceal a miscreant!'

'No visits to Upper Brook Street?' she asked, watching Giles.

'Regrettably, that would not be prudent,' he said, only that moment realising the full implications of her confinement.

'That will be a grievous loss indeed,' she said quietly. 'And, I devoutly hope, a temporary one.'

'I hope so, too,' he said fervently.

'I'll ride in the coach with you back to London,' Esterbrook said. 'I can easily find an excuse for the trip that will satisfy Mama. I'll send some of our footmen to Aunt Lilly's, too—I'll tell her Papa needs them. They can provide extra eyes to watch over the stables and the kitchens.'

'I'll ride outside the coach,' Giles said. 'How soon can you leave?'

'Let me check with the estate agent to make sure there is no other pressing business; otherwise, I could be ready day after tomorrow.'

Giles nodded. 'That will give me time to send a note to my friend in London.' He turned to Maggie. 'So we can clear this matter up speedily, and let you return to your normal life.'

'I surely hope so,' she said. 'It will be hard to be away when Papa needs me—and not be able to visit Upper Brook Street.'

It was going to be bitterly difficult for him as well, Giles thought.

Esterbrook finished his ale. 'If we're agreed on the details, I must visit that land agent. Maggie, I'll see you at dinner tonight. Lyndlington, walk with me a moment, won't you?'

Once they were out of the taproom, where his sister could not overhear them, Esterbrook said, 'Whoever had the audacity to target Maggie, I want him found.'

'You can't want that any more than I do,' Giles replied.

'I want him found, and I want to know why—for I find it incomprehensible.'

Unfortunately, Giles knew one possible assailant whose motives were all too understandable.

'It will take a number of men to canvass a city the size of London. I want you to hire as many as Bow Street recommends. I'll transfer funds into an account at my bank for you to draw on—'

'Please, that won't be necessary. I can fund this.'

Esterbrook shook his head. 'I appreciate the offer, but Maggie is my sister—*my* responsibility. Besides, in your present situation, I imagine your funds are more… limited.'

'I still can't allow you—' Giles began.

'But you will,' Esterbrook interrupted, for the first time acting like the landed autocrat he was.

Esterbrook could make funds available. He couldn't make Giles use them. 'Very well.'

'Good.' Esterbrook gazed into Giles's eyes. 'I'm depending on you to keep her safe, Lyndlington.'

'I'd rather die than see her harmed.'

Esterbrook nodded, a glimmer of a smile on his lips. 'I rather thought so. Very well, I'll see you at dinner.'

Soon after, Giles and Maggie collected the dogs from the stables and left the Lamb and Calf. Once they were away from the village, she said, 'Now that we know for certain there's no danger at Huntsford, let's enjoy the ride home—especially,' she added with a grimace, 'since it will apparently be the last ride I have for some time. I don't want to be foolhardy, but being cooped up at Aunt Lilly's will be very difficult.'

'I'll send you some books.'

'You will call, won't you, and keep me informed? Even though we can't…indulge in anything more satisfying than conversation, while I'm stuck under my greataunt's roof.'

'We won't be indulging in anything more satisfying until this matter is cleared up for good and all,' he said flatly.

Maggie sighed. 'Why is it that while I didn't do anything, I feel like *I'm* the one being punished?'

If it turned out George was responsible, *he* was the one who should be punished—for ignoring the possible danger, and proceeding anyway. 'Try to think of it as safe refuge, rather than punishment. And know that I won't rest until we uncover the truth.'

They rode on in silence, Maggie taking a trail through the forest, rather than proceeding back across the open downs. Once under the cover of the leafy canopy, she pulled up her mount.

Immediately concerned, Giles reined in beside her. 'What is it? Do you hear something?'

'No. The dogs would let us know if anyone or anything were lurking in the woods.' She slid off the saddle and dropped the horse's reins. 'If I'm going to be incarcerated *and* deprived for the indefinite future, with Julian at my side all the way back to London, I at least need one final kiss.'

He was on his feet in an instant, drawing him to her, all his frustration and roiling guilt and worry over her safety intensifying the passion of his kiss. She replied in kind, apparently as voracious and driven as he was.

The dogs milling curiously about their feet, Giles kissed her until they were both panting for breath. 'Curse those hounds!' he gasped.

She chuckled unevenly. 'Bringing them was a good idea at the outset. Now, however… If I tried to do what I'd like to do, they'd be all over me.'

'Or me, I if went down on my knees.'

She turned him so his back was against the trunk of an ancient oak. 'Oh, I wish,' she whispered, looking like temptation itself with her lips red from his kiss, her gaze passionate and her face hot under his caressing fingers.

'What?' he whispered.

'It would be so easy… Unbutton your trouser flap. Pull up my skirts. Have you lean back and pick me up, so I could wrap my legs around your waist and rock into you. Rock you into me.'

Listening to her naughty scenario made his member surge. The idea of taking her, finally tasting full possession, was so intoxicating, it required every bit of self-control he could muster not to urge her to act out what she'd just described.

While he wavered, fighting temptation, he felt her fingers stroking him, tugging at his trouser buttons. Control unravelling, of their own volition his hands reached for her skirts, began shimmying them up her legs.

Then one of the hounds jumped up, knocking her away from him. He steadied her before she fell, both of them gazing at each other, their panting breaths the only sound in the wilderness.

'Faithful, indeed,' she murmured, stepping back to shake out her skirts. 'It's his name,' she explained, rubbing the hound behind his ears. 'Thank heavens he was there to keep me from catastrophe! Now that we are both thoroughly frustrated, we'd better return. It's a feeling we—or at least I—will have to get accustomed to.'

Not sure whether he wanted to toss the hound a bone or shoot him, Giles walked Maggie back to the horses and helped her remount.

'Goodbye, my lover,' she said. 'Please, may it not be long before I can say "hello" again.' With that, she kicked her mare to a trot.

'Amen to that,' Giles muttered, and followed after her.

## Chapter Seventeen

In the early evening three days later, after seeing Maggie safely to the door of her great-aunt's town house, Giles returned to his rooms at Albany. Before he bathed and changed, he sent their man-of-all-work to the Quill and Gavel in search of Davie with a note requesting that his friend join him as soon as possible.

By the time he'd washed and dressed, Phillips returned with the welcome news that Mr Smith would follow him directly.

Giles poured himself a brandy and sipped it, pacing impatiently until at last he heard Davie's step in the hallway.

'Welcome back to London,' his friend said, holding out his hand to shake. 'I hope you had an instructive visit to Huntsford. Was this summons designed to avoid, for the present, the ribbing sure to be directed at you by Ben and Christopher for having sojourned at the home of the lovely Lady Margaret?'

Davie's teasing tone faded as he looked up at Giles's face. 'No, I can see it's more serious.'

'Didn't you get my note?' Giles asked.

'No, but frankly, we've been so busy the last few days I've hardly been back to Albany. Shall I look for it?'

'Never mind,' Giles replied, shrugging off his annoyance. Fortunately, he had new information that should make up for the delay in Davie's not having read his earlier missive.

'I'm sorry, Giles. Pour me some of that brandy, and tell me all about it.'

Just the presence of his quiet, meticulous, competent friend lightened Giles's anxiety. If anyone could help him clear the muddy waters of this mystery, it was Davie.

When they were both seated with glasses in hand, Giles said, 'It would have been merely an instructive visit to Huntsford. Except that, while we were out riding, someone took a shot at Lady Margaret—and came within a hair's breadth of hitting her.'

'Hell and the devil!' Davie exclaimed. 'Did you find the man?'

'No,' Giles said grimly. 'I found tracks that indicated he'd been shadowing us for some time, under cover of the woods. When we dismounted, he had a clear line of fire—and took it. By the time I found his trail, he'd galloped off. Lady Margaret, her brother, Lord Esterbrook, and I made an exhaustive canvass of the area the following day, and discovered that a stranger who left by the London road had passed through the local village. Esterbrook sent a groom after him with a description. We learned just as we reached the city tonight that the groom had in fact picked up the trail, and tracked the man back to London.'

'Excellent! Does the groom have any idea where he went after he arrived?'

'The innkeeper where he stopped just outside the city said the man told him he'd send the horse back from the

Green Dragon in Seven Dials. He's been using the name "Teddy Godfrey", by the way. Now we need to find him, and I'm hoping you can direct me to the right people to help me look.'

Davie shook his head. 'Why would anyone want to shoot Lady Margaret? Granted, there have been Swing Riots in the countryside around Manchester, Liverpool and Leeds, even some houses of the aristocracy burned, but nothing in her area. Witlow is known as a fair and concerned landlord who looks after his land and his tenants. Although,' he continued, his voice troubled, 'she has campaigned for Tories in areas that are far more volatile. Still, I can't imagine any radical, no matter how extreme, targeting a *female*.'

'It may be worse than that,' Giles said, guilt and anger scouring him anew. 'After the attack, when I jokingly teased her about having refused George's suit—which, by the way, she did—she told me after she rejected him, he threatened her.'

Davie waved a hand. 'Surely that was just George being George, frustrated at being denied something he wanted. You don't seriously think he would *harm* her for refusing him?'

'I don't know what to think. I certainly hope not. That would make it worse.'

Davie, ever perceptive, understood immediately. 'Yes, I see. Knowing how George can be, you'd feel responsible for not avoiding her after George quarrelled with you over her.'

'It's too late to change that now. All I can do to redeem myself is figure out as quickly as possible who was behind the attack.' He grimaced. 'I would have preferred to incarcerate her in an inner room at Huntsford, but both she and her brother insisted that leaving her there while we deal with the threat would make it impossible to hide the incident from her mother, whom they don't wish to upset—she's in delicate health. As a compromise, Lady Margaret has returned to London, but will remain in seclusion at the home of her great-aunt, Lady Sayleford.'

'At least she'll hear all the latest gossip. How can I help?'

'I remember you told me when you first met your mentor, Sir Edward, in Hazelwick, you helped rescue Lady Greaves—she wasn't Lady Greaves then—from the radical who kidnapped her, working with a prosecutor and a government agent, as well as some men from Bow Street?'

'You want me to look up Mr Albertson, the Home Office man who presented the evidence to the prosecutor,' Davie said, immediately making the connection. 'But that was years ago. He's probably long retired.'

'A mention of his name should get you referred to someone of equal authority, who can recommend some agents to work undercover. We have a name, or at least an alias, an excellent description, and know the general area to which our suspect returned. With that, I'm hopeful we can turn up something.'

Davie nodded. 'There'd be a money trail, too. From what Albertson told me, agitators are usually advanced a sum up front, to fund their activities, but receive the bulk of the payoff after they complete their assignment.'

'If the task was to murder Lady Margaret, he didn't accomplish it. He might not want to meet his employer and admit that.'

'That won't wash,' Davie said, frowning. 'It's extremely unlikely anyone would be foolish enough to agree to murder the daughter of a marquess, no matter how much he was promised! He'd have to know that a person of wealth and position like Lord Witlow would never give up until he found the perpetrator—which would mean the gallows. It would make more sense if the man was only supposed to fire at her.'

'As a warning? But why—and for what? What good is a warning if you don't know what you're being warned about?'

'I didn't say I had the answers,' Davie retorted. 'But you're right; with an alias, a description and a destination, we may well be able to trace the gunman.' He tapped his finger on his glass. 'I believe Albertson's assistant, a Mr Farnworth, still works in the office; I called on him a few years ago to settle a matter for Sir Edward. I'll look for him tonight. Maybe we can get this moving forward immediately.'

Giles clapped him on the shoulder. 'Thank you, Davie. I knew I could count on you.'

His friend smiled. 'I like and admire Lady Margaret. I'm honoured to do all I can to find the man who fired on her. Just one more thing before I go.'

'Yes?'

'Are you having an affair with Lady Margaret?'

Caught off guard, Giles froze, scrambling for an answer.

Before he decided whether to confess or deny it, Davie said, 'You are, aren't you? Everything pointed to your being involved with a lady—the missed meetings, the late mornings—' Davie gave him a smile '—the air of bliss about you. Christopher and Ben are convinced of it, and you may thank me for keeping them from pestering you about it. But…I just couldn't wrap my mind around the idea of your paramour being Lady Margaret. She's always been the very model of propriety, passing up numerous opportunities for dalliance, to say nothing of offers of marriage, since her husband's death. She just…doesn't seem the sort of woman for a casual affair.'

Stung, Giles said, 'Isn't that her business?'

'And yours, not mine,' Davie agreed. 'It does explain why you feel the threat to her safety more keenly. Especially if George is involved. But don't worry, I'm not about to whisper my conclusions into the ear of anyone, even the other Hellions.' He laughed. 'Besides, it's much too amusing to listen to their daily changing theories about who your mystery lady must be.'

'Thank you for your discretion, at least,' Giles said, still irritated.

Davie nodded. 'You're welcome. I'm off to find Farnworth. Are you staying here, or going to the Quill and Gavel?'

'Here, probably. Esterbrook said he'd send word if he heard anything else, and I'm too weary to fend off questions from Ben and Christopher.'

'Probably wise, given that they know you summoned me. At the whiff of mystery, they'd tear into you for answers, like starving hounds with fresh meat.'

'I may involve them, too. Just not tonight.'

'Get some rest. You look exhausted.' Scooping up his greatcoat, Davie headed out the door.

Giles took another deep draught of his brandy. He *was* exhausted—not from the ride, for he'd ridden further, but from the need for constant vigilance that intensified every mile they got closer to London. Scanning each passer-by, rider and coachman, always watching for a hand on a weapon, even though he knew the possibility of encountering danger was slight, had taken its toll physically and mentally.

He resented the hint of disapproval in Davie's tone when he spoke of Giles's relationship with Maggie, even as it smote his conscience. By the stars in Heaven, she wasn't some innocent he'd lured away and debauched! Initially, *she* had propositioned *him*. Though he *had* coaxed her afterward to go through with it, after she'd panicked and withdrawn her offer, he recalled uncomfortably.

Davie was right, though: she wasn't the sort of woman who indulged in casual affairs. Could she be hoping for more? The thought further unsettled him. If so, she'd never even hinted about it.

If he were to marry, he couldn't think of a woman who would make a more interesting, intriguing and passionate partner. But he *wasn't* thinking of it—no matter how special Maggie was. His mother's experience of the institution hadn't inspired in him much enthusiasm or respect for it, or any desire to try it for himself.

Besides, he'd told her from the outset, with his tenuous position and limited income, a union with him could bring her nothing but harm. What a come-down, from daughter of a marquess to wife of a simple Member of Parliament!

Suddenly he recalled the disparaging remarks his half-brother had made about Maggie's age and possibilities when she'd refused his offer. Was their dalliance robbing Maggie of the chance to make an advantageous alliance while she still could, one that would provide her with companionship, passion and protection into a ripe old age?

He certainly didn't want to be the means of destroying her chances, as he had destroyed his mother's.

Even though the idea of her marrying anyone else sparked an immediate sense of outrage.

But no need to think that far ahead. All that was required now was to eliminate the threat to Maggie's safety.

With that conclusion, telling Phillips to wake him if a message came from either Davie or Esterbrook, Giles sought out his bed.

Two days later, Maggie restlessly paced the back parlour Aunt Lilly had given her for an office. She'd dispatched the notes to Papa's housekeeper and Cook about the guest list and menus for tonight's entertainment; supplies had been ordered from their usual providers. The gathering was to be a meeting of her father's closest Tory advisors, which she probably would not have played hostess for anyway.

Still, she chafed at her confinement and struggled to concentrate on the book of travels Giles had sent—reading of someone else's journeys only made her feel more imprisoned. Though she knew it wasn't prudent to risk going out, as the memory of the incident faded, she had a harder and harder time believing someone wished to harm her, and a greater and greater impatience about hiding away as if *she* were the criminal. She wasn't sure how much longer she could stand it, before she rejected all the good advice and returned to Cavendish Square to resume her life.

Would Giles then resume their liaison? She knew even the possibility that his half-brother might have been responsible for the shot fired at her had deeply shaken him. Deeply enough for him to feel he must distance himself from her? Had this unpleasant incident destroyed the sense of magic that had enveloped their relationship, making him ready to move on?

Just thinking about the possibility that he might not visit Upper Brook Street again struck her like a kick to the gut. The blow should be a salutary one, she told herself. It would probably be better if they did end this before she became any more attached—not just to the passion, but to the man.

She'd been woefully naïve in thinking she could become intimate with Giles without also gradually entangling herself deeper into his life and concerns. Wanting to assist and smooth and facilitate, where she had no right and no invitation.

Very well, she conceded, ending it sooner rather than later might be wise.

But she didn't want to end it yet.

On that stubborn resolve, her great-aunt's butler bowed himself in. 'Viscount Lyndlington to see you, Lady Margaret. I've shown him to the Great Parlour.'

Oh, how her heart's leap of gladness ought to alarm her! But too excited about seeing him to spoil the prospect with worry, she said, 'Thank you, Harris. Will you tell him I'll be there directly?'

Rushing to the mirror, she tucked an errant curl back into her *coiffure* and smoothed her gown. Too impatient to bother with any further primping, she hurried to the parlour.

'Giles, what a wonderful surprise! So you've come to check on the inmate?'

At his smile, her stomach did another happy little flip. 'Feeling restricted, are you?'

'"Restricted" hardly describes it! It reminds me of when I was ten, and was caught riding a stallion Papa had forbidden me to go near. He incarcerated me in my room on bread and water for three days.'

'Wanting to make sure you never disobeyed such an order again?'

'I was furious, though secretly I knew he was right. The stallion was a beast, and I was lucky to have made it back to the stables without breaking my neck. However, being cooped up for three days, for someone who rode for miles about the countryside every day, was a torture I've never forgotten.'

She gestured him to the sofa, savouring his closeness as she settled beside him. Oh, how she'd missed him, even more keenly than she missed her freedom!

'You'll be encouraged to learn that we've made enough progress that your liberation may be near. My colleague consulted his Home Office sources, who referred us to several Bow Street operatives. One of them has, we believe, tracked down our man. As we suspected, Godfrey's a former soldier who drifted to London after his family lost their land in the enclosures. He's been hired out on several questionable projects in the past. Hines, our Bow Street man, is going tonight to a tavern in Seven Dials Godfrey is known to frequent.' After a pause, he added, 'I'm going along.'

'You are?' Maggie said with alarm. 'Is that wise? You've no more expertise in dealing with the type of people who frequent Seven Dials than I do. How could you pass unnoticed?'

'Of course, I don't flatter myself that I could handle this on my own—rousting about on the downs as a boy is a far cry from navigating the seamier parts of London unnoticed. But I'll be roughly dressed, and will stay with another of the Bow Street men, who is to provide reinforcements for Hines, if necessary. I want to be near in case we discover…something it would be more proper for me to pursue. Because if we do, I shall pursue it immediately.'

'How I wish I could go, too!' She raised a hand to forestall his protest. 'I know that's not possible—it would be selfish, as well as imprudent, to trail along and end up deflecting Mr Hines from his mission with the need to shield me from danger. But oh, how just *waiting* chafes at me! Promise me you will return and let me know what happened—no matter how late! There's no way I will be able to sleep until I know the outcome. Until I know you are safe.'

He laid his hand over hers, and she closed her eyes, a little sigh of pleasure escaping her lips at even that small measure of contact.

'You mustn't worry, Maggie. If I end up in harm's way, it's no more than I deserve, for placing you in danger.'

'If you feel you deserve retribution for that, only think how I would feel if you were injured, trying to protect me!' she retorted.

He lifted her hand and placed a lingering kiss on it, his gaze as he raised his eyes smouldering enough to dispel her worries that he was ready to end their liaison.

'How I've missed you every morning,' she whispered.

'Not half as much as I've missed you,' he assured her.

'Then may your mission tonight go well, so we may resume our visits to Upper Brook Street.'

'Nothing would give me greater pleasure.'

He stared at her mouth, the intensity of his gaze making her lips tingle and firing her body with need. She closed her eyes and raised her chin, hoping he would follow with his lips the path of his gaze.

She sensed him leaning closer, and her senses exulted. But just as she felt the warmth of his breath and parted her lips to welcome him, he jerked away, cold air replacing that warm promise.

'I'd better go before I do something we'll both regret,' he said, his voice strained.

'Have you taken some sort of holy vow not to kiss me until this quest is completed?' she asked, aware she sounded more than a little sulky. '*You* might regret it. *I* would just enjoy it.'

'Temptress!' he said as he rose from the sofa. 'I will make you pay for teasing me…later.'

'Now that,' she replied, struggling to silence the complaints of her frustrated body, 'sounds a great deal more promising.'

She walked with him to the parlour door. 'You will call later tonight—promise me?'

He nodded. 'I promise.'

With that, she let him go. Tonight, she knew as she walked back to her study, the time would crawl more slowly than ever.

## *Chapter Eighteen*

Maggie tried to stay calm as the night progressed, concentrating on conversing with her great-aunt at dinner, then forcing herself to scan the novel she'd told her great-aunt she intended to read when she'd insisted Aunt Lilly attend her evening entertainments as planned.

By the time her great-aunt returned after midnight, Maggie had become less and less successful at diverting herself. No longer able to concentrate, she abandoned the book to take up some cards. Quickly tiring of playing against herself, she tossed down the pasteboard in frustration and jumped up to pace about the room.

By the time the clock struck one, she was swearing oaths under her breath her great-aunt would have been shocked to discover she knew. If she'd had any idea where Giles could be found, she would have gone out in pursuit.

Finally, as the mantel clock stuck the half past one, a drowsy footman knocked at her door. 'Lady Margaret, there's a gentleman begging to see you. I told him it was—'

'Show him in at once,' she cut the lad off, so relieved she exhaled in a rush that left her dizzy. With her next breath, she vowed she would throttle Giles for making her wait so long.

But the tart words died on her tongue when the door opened to admit, not Giles, but his friend David Tanner Smith.

Fear like an icy hand clutched her heart. 'What happened? Where is Giles?'

'Don't worry!' he assured her. 'He's hurt—but not seriously,' he added at her gasp. 'I'm so sorry you had to wait so long. Apparently after Hines left the inn, Godfrey and some others circled behind them as they made their way out of Seven Dials. Giles sustained a knife wound to his hand, but is otherwise unharmed—he gave as good as he got, he told me. He's already had a doctor clean the wound and bandage it.'

'Thank Heaven for that!' Maggie cried, glad for the doctor's treatment, but not at all reassured that the result would not be serious. A knife puncture could fester, become inflamed...

'Unbeknownst to Giles,' Smith continued, 'the doctor slipped some laudanum in the wine he gave him as a restorative. He'd written you a note—badly, with his left hand—but fell asleep before he could instruct Phillips to deliver it, and only woke up when I came in. Knowing by now you'd probably be frantic, I offered to come in person and reassure you, since a note written in a wobbly hand that admitted he'd been injured might have been alarming. Shall I relate the whole of what happened?'

She tried to tell herself this was Giles, not Robbie. Not the lover who'd been brought back to her broken, battered—and dead.

Trying to stem a rising panic, she said, 'Never mind, I'll ask Giles. I'm coming back with you. I want to see that wound myself.'

Smith stared at her for a moment. 'I don't suppose I need to remind you how…improper it would be for you to visit a gentleman's rooms? Or the result to your reputation, should the visit become known.'

'You do not,' she snapped. Not even to herself could she fully explain the urgent need to fly to him. 'Don't you understand? I must see for myself that he's not in danger! Do you think I care if the ladies of society cut me from their invitation lists or gossip behind my back? I have no desire to remarry, and I doubt my father's political associates care in the least what I do. Papa—well, I can bring him around. And that's only if someone finds out. If I am in and out again before daylight, most likely no one will ever know.'

Her determination must have been written on her face, for after another glance, Mr Smith made no further attempt to dissuade her. 'Then we must see that you are back before dawn.'

She nodded. 'I'll get my cloak.'

A half-hour later, slipping along like proverbial thieves in the night, Mr Smith and a heavily veiled Maggie walked into Albany towards the rooms Giles shared with his friend. Ushering her into the common area, Mr Smith whispered, 'He may be sleeping. I'll be in my chamber. Call if you need anything, and when you're ready to return, let me know.'

Her hands trembling with anxiety, Maggie hurried to the door of the chamber Mr Smith indicated, and quietly let herself in.

A candle burned at his bedside. In the flickering light, Maggie could make out Giles reclining against the pillows, still wearing torn and soiled breeches and a ragged shirt. His hair was dishevelled, cuts and what appeared to be developing bruises shadowed his chin and cheek-bone, and his injured hand, wrapped in a bloodied bandage, lay propped on a pillow.

Despite herself, Maggie uttered an involuntary cry of distress.

Giles opened his eyes to squint up at her. 'Maggie?'

'Yes, Maggie,' she replied, rushing to his side. 'You look a fright! First I shall clean you up, and then I will abuse you for scaring me to death. That was the longest night of my life!'

He seemed to come fully awake then, sucking in a breath with a hiss as he struggled to sit up straight. 'Stars in Heaven, what was Davie thinking? He shouldn't have brought you here!'

'Don't blame him. I would have come on my own, if he hadn't escorted me.'

'But, Maggie—'

'Hush, and don't give me any treckle about propriety. Where can I get clean water?'

'Phillips left some in the basin, there on the dresser. I'd intended to finish washing up, but apparently that damned sawbones drugged my wine.'

'He probably wanted to make sure you rested until the bleeding stopped. And don't get up now, lest you start it again,' she said, putting a hand on his chest to restrain him.

His bare chest, where some of his shirt had been torn away. Despite her anxiety, deep within, a current of response stirred at this touch of flesh on flesh.

For a moment, they both stared at her hand, resting there so intimately.

'Really, sweetheart, I'm not that badly hurt,' he said at last.

'I hope not,' she replied, pulling herself back to her

task. 'But I'll reserve judgement until we get you out of those filthy garments and re-bandage that hand.'

Following his direction, she fetched water, soap, and clean rags. Helping him to sit at the side of the bed, she tugged up the ruined shirt and carefully eased him out of it.

There were cuts and scrapes on his shoulder, but minor enough that he didn't even flinch as she gently washed away the dirt. There was indeed a bruise on his cheek and another on his chin, but the skin was unbroken, nor did he protest when she pressed on them.

'It's been a long time since I've taken a right to the chin,' he said. 'A glancing blow, fortunately.'

'Mr Smith told me your group was attacked. What happened?'

'Hines went to the tavern to find Godfrey, posing as an intermediary for someone who needed a problem "disposed of", and was willing to pay handsomely. Godfrey agreed to consider it, and named a price. But he must have been suspicious to be sought out again so soon after the…incident in Kent. After Hines left, he gathered some mates to follow us. But Hines had warned us about that possibility, so we weren't totally unprepared for the attack. Unluckily for them, all three of us once had aspirations to the fancy, and we weren't the prime pigeons for plucking they must have expected. After a bit of a dust-up, we overcame them and marched them off to the constable. If it hadn't been for Godfrey pulling out a knife at the last, I'd have walked away with nothing more than a few bruises.'

While he talked, Maggie moved her ministrations from his back to his chest and arms, washing off the dirt and patting him dry with the soft cloth. As she stroked over his arms and shoulders, Giles fell silent. 'It's worth a little cut to the hand, to have you do that.'

'We'll see, when I get to the hand! Now, out of those breeches. I'm afraid both they and the shirt are only fit for the rag-and-bone man.'

She tugged at his waistband, urging him to stand long enough for her to peel down the trousers, but he hesitated.

She looked up into his eyes. 'Surely you're not shy! It's not as though I haven't see you—or parts of you—before.'

'True, you've not seen the whole package unwrapped at once,' he said with a chuckle. 'And when you do, you'll know immediately that I find the idea—very arousing.'

Her breath hitched and expectation swirled in the pit of her stomach. But she did need to get him out of his dirty garments and under his blankets, with his bandages changed so he could rest—and she could chastely return to Aunt Lilly's.

'I promise not to stare—more than I have to,' she added.

He stood then, and let her tug the trousers down and pull off the socks. Only then did she raise her eyes—to find him, as he'd hinted, fully erect.

She'd had glancing views of his rigid member as she caressed him within the confines of his breeches, or under and through the linen of his shirt. But to see him completely naked, from toes to collarbone, every handsome well-made line of him, the curve of calf, strong-muscled thighs, flat belly, broad chest, strong arms and shoulders…

Her mouth dried and her heartbeat galloped. Conflicted between desire and duty, Maggie tried to remind herself that, no matter how ready he might appear, he'd sustained an injury and needed to avoid any exertion that might start it bleeding again.

He simply stood there watching her, his blue eyes molten in the candlelight, every muscle taut, temptation incarnate, waiting for her to decide.

Near cursing with frustration and regret, she stuttered, 'W-we'd better get you u-under the bedclothes, before you catch a ch-chill.'

He laughed, something between a chuckle and a groan. 'I'm not likely to be chilled any time soon.'

Instead of making her smile, his attempt at humour reminded her of the danger his wound might pose. 'Let's just hope you don't turn feverish, either.'

He let her help him back into bed. She was proud that, though it took gritted teeth and incredible will-power, she managed to keep herself from running her fingers over any of that glorious naked flesh before she hid it under the blankets.

Taking a deep, shuddering breath to refocus her mind, she pulled a chair close to the bed. Bringing the candle nearer to shed the most light on the injury, she gently unwound the bloody bandage.

She gasped, tears starting to her eyes. A long, jagged cut slashed across his palm, biting deep beneath the thumb, where the doctor had closed the gap with tiny stitches. Blood still seeped from the edges, but the wound appeared stable, the skin scraped and reddened, but not warm with fever. Yet, anyway.

'You should sprinkle yarrow powder on it, to keep it from b-bleeding,' she said, a hitch in her voice as she swiped a wrist across her eyes, having unaccountable difficulty trying to stem the trickle of tears.

'Don't worry, sweetheart,' Giles said, his voice tender. 'It was a clean cut, fortunately done after we finished rolling about the alleyway. It's going to pain me for a while, but it will heal.'

Out of memory, the images attacked her. Broken bones that left the limbs at odd, unnatural angles. And blood— blood everywhere.

'I'm sorry—I'm sorry!' she said, trying to hold back the sobs. 'It's just…midnight, shadows, and candlelight, and blood… It b-brings it all back.'

'When they carried your husband home,' he guessed.

'Yes,' she whispered.

'Poor sweetheart,' he murmured. With his good hand, he pulled her up on the bed and hugged her against him.

The frustration of being confined, the strain and worry of waiting, and the nightmare images of blood and injury must have worn her down, for the tears fell harder and faster until she was clinging to Giles, sobbing uncontrollably. He held her tightly, caressing her back and murmuring soothingly.

At last, the tears were spent. 'I'm sorry,' she said again, embarrassed at her lack of control. 'I promise, I'm not usually such a watering-pot.'

'Nor are you often called to tend dirty and bleeding gentlemen in the middle of the night,' he replied. 'You're tired, sweeting. Rest here a bit, and we'll send you home.'

She snuggled against him. But as the misery ebbed and calm returned, she became more and more aware that the arms that cradled her were bare, and the body beneath the bedclothes completely naked.

Little chills chased up and down her arms, and simmering arousal boiled back up. Could she leave without paying homage to that glorious manhood?

'No, I shouldn't,' she murmured, only half-aware she'd spoken the words aloud. 'You need rest, too.'

She looked at him, to see his eyes blazing again with heat and need. 'Thanks to the good doctor, I've already had a rest.'

Wavering, she said, 'I should kiss you goodbye, and go. Your poor hand!'

'I have one good one,' he said, and pulled her to him. His lips met hers—and she was lost.

Their days of separation and abstinence seemed to have created a boiling cauldron of desire that required only that small nudge to spill out of control. She couldn't get enough of the taste of him, thrusting into his mouth, laving tongue against tongue, deep and hard and fast.

While they kissed, she tugged at the bedclothes, until she could reach within and run her hand over the bare flesh, as she'd yearned to since the moment she unclothed him. He caught her hand and brought it down to his erection, guiding her fingers over and around him.

She wanted more, closer. Lifting herself up, still kissing him, she dragged the covers aside, baring his body to her sight as well as her touch. But she craved the feel of skin against skin.

Too impatient for the slow process of undoing all the pins and fastenings of her bodice, she simply pulled up her skirts and lay against him, sighing with delight as she rubbed her bared legs against his.

But that wasn't enough either—she burned to *feel* him, around and within her, inside that aching needy place that had wanted for him for weeks. Rising up on her knees, she parted her legs and straddled him, stroking her hot centre over the slick velvet of his hardness.

He broke the kiss, his eyes wild, half-focused. 'Are you...sure?'

'Yes,' she murmured. 'Yes.'

Clutching his shoulders, she leaned down to kiss him as she thrust down with her hips, and sheathed him within. He pulled her close and she rubbed against him, savouring the delicious stretch and fullness.

Ah, this was paradise, the exquisite feel of him buried deep, pulsing within her. She heard a moan, not sure whether it was his or hers.

He rocked, just a slight movement within her, and suddenly it was impossible to remain still. She thrust down, pulled back, thrust down, the pleasure of it almost unbearably intense. And then they were moving together, one body, one flesh, one need, one purpose, racing each other to glorious completion.

Afterwards, Maggie lay trembling against him, listening to the frantic beat of his heart that echoed her own. An indescribable peace settled over her, satiation and fulfilment and something more, something profound and tender that penetrated to the depths of her soul with a sense of its beauty and rightness.

'Maggie mine,' Giles whispered in her ear. 'What a wonder you are.'

She kissed his neck. 'You're rather wonderful yourself.'

'You'll not think so, if Davie finds you here tomorrow morning.'

Her eyes flew open. Davie! Albany! A midnight misadventure that could end in disaster if she did not get back to Aunt Lilly's before dawn lit the streets.

As she considered the other possible consequences of her rashness this night, panic fluttered up, like a crow flapping its wings to take flight. She pushed the feeling away; time enough, when she was safely back at Grosvenor Square, to sort this out.

Regardless of what rational reflection revealed in the cold light of day, she would never regret this night.

'You're right, I must go,' she said, scooting off the bed. 'Don't get up!' she said as he made motions to follow her. 'Mr Smith told me he'd see me safely home. You should rest—especially after that unintended exertion.'

'I could do with an unlimited amount of that "exertion",' he said, catching her hand and pulling her back for a quick kiss. 'It was…glorious.'

Maggie felt ridiculous tears threaten. 'It was,' she agreed softly. *And it must never happen again.*

Pulling free, she inspected his hand, noting with relief that the bandage appeared dry. 'Heaven be praised, I don't think you re-started the bleeding.'

'You mustn't come here again,' he warned. 'I'll visit you soon in Grosvenor Square and let you know what they learn after they question Godfrey. Hines seemed to think that when they tell him he assaulted a sitting Member of Parliament, he'll sing like a meadowlark. I'm hopeful we'll know the full story soon.'

'It will be good to know the truth at last.' She finished tidying herself and smoothed down her skirts. 'Goodnight—or rather, good morning. Recover quickly, my dear Giles.'

With one last kiss to his forehead, she walked out of his bedchamber.

## Chapter Nineteen

Later that same morning, Maggie sat in her bedchamber, sipping coffee. Though she'd not returned until nearly dawn, and despite the peace satiation normally brought, she'd not been able to sleep.

She wasn't too concerned that there would be dire consequences from the previous night's folly. Her courses were due any day, and she was usually quite regular, so the chance that she'd conceived was small enough that she wouldn't worry over the prospect now.

Not when there was a devastating task she must steel herself to perform.

Breaking off her liaison with Giles Hadley.

Last night had proven what she'd secretly known in her heart from the beginning: despite her fine words to the contrary, she couldn't trust herself to be sensible with Giles Hadley. She wanted him too much, and that single taste of completion only whetted her appetite to experience it again and again.

She simply couldn't risk that.

When they'd begun this, she'd hoped that when the end came, they could part as friends. She didn't think that would be possible now—not when the mere thought of him brought a rush of desire and a deep craving to be with him. What she felt for him was too powerful and too all-encompassing to confine within the narrow, polite box of friendship.

Attempting to chat with him over a cup of tea in someone's drawing room would be to sustain a thousand tiny cuts of loss and longing that would bleed for ever. Better one sharp, deep slash to sever the bond cleanly.

No matter how debilitating that single blow was likely to be.

Doing something difficult never got easier by putting it off. Setting down the barely tasted cup of coffee, she drew out a piece of paper, and began to write him a note.

Maggie spent the day gathering her belongings and preparing to return to her father's house in Grosvenor Square; with Godfrey in custody, she intended to resume her usual duties, whether Giles believed it safe or not.

Nor, at the moment, did she particularly care. Why bother worrying about her safety when the man she'd wanted to spend time with when her freedom was restored she must no longer see?

It wasn't until late afternoon that Giles replied to her summons. She'd almost hoped he wouldn't come today, so she might put off the final break. She felt his name like a punch to the gut when Rains announced that Mr Hadley awaited her in the Great Parlour.

Rejecting the impulse to delay, she made herself walk from her study, each footfall like a bell tolling of doom.

The smile that lit his face when she walked in just twisted the knife deeper.

'I'm sorry it took me so long to respond,' he said, coming over to kiss her hand. 'I've been at Bow Street and the magistrate's most of the afternoon.'

Motioning him to sit, she took a chair, rather than a place beside him on the sofa. Might as well begin distancing herself.

'Tell me what you discovered.'

'Godfrey did finally give up the name of the man who contacted and paid him. An intermediary; the Bow Street men are tracing him now, and once they locate him, they are confident they can establish who ordered the attack.'

'So it *was* ordered. I still find it hard to believe.'

'Godfrey claims he was paid just to fire at you, not to hit you. Insists his aim is true enough that if he'd intended to strike you, he would have.'

'What will happen to him?'

'If the charge were attempted murder, he would hang, which is why he tried to silence us all after he left the tavern. Hines subdued him in part by telling him he might get clemency instead of the noose, if he co-operated. That will be up to you and your father.'

Maggie sighed. 'Papa was livid when I told him what happened. He'd probably prefer thumbscrews and the rack, but I'll work on him. How is your hand?'

'Hurts like the very devil, but the wound is dry, with no sign of heat or suppuration.'

'Good. I'll have Rains get you some powdered yarrow from the still room; use it each time you change the bandages.'

'You looked tired, sweetheart—as well you might, after so...vigorous a night. And about that—'

'Please, don't apologise! I couldn't bear that. It might have been regrettable, but I don't regret it at all.'

'Nor do I. Although, I suppose when we begin again, we're going to have to think of some measures to prevent a recurrence of so delightful but dangerous an interlude.'

'I've already given that a great deal of thought.' Forcing herself to say the words, she continued, 'I can't meet you at Upper Brook Street any longer, Giles.'

He recoiled, shock on his face, but she made herself continue, 'I hate to end what we've shared, but last night showed I simply can't trust myself to be prudent. And the consequences of that failure could be catastrophic, for both of us.'

He opened his lips as if to speak, closed them, and sprang up. She watched him pace around the room, drinking in the sight of him, imprinting it on her memory. Even as she died a little with each glance, knowing it was the last time she would see him alone.

He halted in front of her, his face grim. 'I'd like to argue with you, but I cannot. My fault, probably, to think we could place limits on passion, which by its very nature defies limits.'

She shook her head. 'It was just as much my fault as yours. Sadly, wanting something very badly doesn't make it possible. I'd thought to take the coward's way out and send you a note, but then I decided I must tell you face to face. And kiss you goodbye, one final time.'

He seized her as she rose to meet him, crushing her against him with his one good arm, kissing her with intensity and conviction. She kissed back just as fiercely, putting into that final kiss all her passion, love, and regret.

After several moments, his kiss gentled, and ended in a series of gentle brushes of his mouth against her forehead, her eyebrows, her cheeks. He wrapped his arms around her and simply held her, while she battled despair and tears.

'Are you sure?' he whispered against her hair. 'I certainly don't want to give you up! If it is the matter of conception, there are ways…'

'I don't trust them,' she said, slowly detaching from his

embrace, each lost bit of contact—his shoulder, his chest, his hand, and the final release of his fingers—another hammer blow at her heart.

Suddenly it seemed important that he understand how hard this was for her—by knowing the reason she couldn't take even the smallest risk. Before prudence could prevent her from revealing what no one on earth but Polly knew, she said, 'You may think me ridiculously cautious, but I know…I know I could not face the consequences again.'

It took a moment before the meaning of her words registered. 'Again?' he repeated.

Wrapping her arms around herself, she walked to the hearth, facing away from him. 'You asked me once about my being engaged, and I told you we broke it off because I was sure we would not suit. But there was much more.'

'More…what?'

'I suppose, even after Robbie died, I looked at the world with the *naïveté* of a child. Several years had passed since I lost him, and I was lonely. I convinced myself that marrying again might help me finally bury the grief. With Papa's position and my wealth, there were always suitors milling about. Sir Francis Mowbrey was the most persistent and devoted.'

She grimaced, the details humiliating, even at this remove. 'I'd grown up with Robbie, and never doubted his devotion or the sincerity of his love. When Sir Francis gave me the same vows of love and constancy, I accepted them without question, even though I knew that worldly considerations of wealth, position and politics certainly figured into his desire to make me his wife. After I'd accepted his suit and we'd set a wedding date, he…pressed me to become intimate, and I agreed.'

She laughed without humour. 'As I said, I was incredibly naïve! It never occurred to me to wonder why Sir Francis happened to have a house in Chelsea we could use for our trysts. It wasn't until several months later, when I decided to surprise him on a day we were not to meet, that I arrived to find the house…already occupied.'

She paused while he took in the meaning. 'Did you confront him?'

'Not then. I ran off, hoping, I suppose, to find some innocent explanation for what I'd discovered. There wasn't, of course. When he called on me later, we had a terrific row. I was hurt and angry, he defensive and rather insulting—something like George, when I refused him. He left after telling me that, as a widow nearly past her prime without any great beauty to recommend her, I ought to think again before breaking our engagement over so "trivial" a matter.'

'What a fine gentleman,' Giles said derisively.

'Hurt, confused, and bitterly disappointed, I had no intention of reconsidering, at first. Until I learned that… I was increasing.'

His eyes widened. 'Merciful heavens!'

'With that realisation began the most wretched month of my life. How could I marry Sir Francis—who, I'd discovered, didn't really love me after all, or at least not with the devotion I desired? But how could I bear a child out of wedlock, condemning him or her to the stain of bastardry, when all that was needed were a few words of contrition, and the child could be born within the confines of marriage? A miserable union for me, perhaps, but one representing safety for the child. Or if I were prepared to birth a bastard, how could I carry a child and give her up, be forced to deny her existence and never see her again?'

At that, he walked over to pull her into his arms. 'I'm so sorry. So, in the end, you did choose…'

'In the end, God had mercy, on me at least. I went back and apologised to Sir Francis—though I did not tell him about the child. Two weeks later and just before the wedding, I lost the babe. As soon as I recovered from my sudden "illness", I broke off the engagement for good. He was furious—I believe he incurred a number of debts, expecting that he would soon have my fortune at his disposal...to fund his gambling and his mistresses,' she finished bitterly. 'He never forgave me, and only his awareness of the damage Papa could do him if he maligned my name tempered the nastiness of the comments he made about me to society.'

'Did none of your family suspect?'

'Aunt Lilly may have, though she never asked me about it. I told Papa only that I'd discovered Sir Francis did not love me as Robbie had, and I wouldn't settle for less. Of course, all the world but me knew of Francis's little house in Chelsea, so Papa wasn't surprised. He even confided that he'd almost told me about it himself, to make sure I was aware what sort of husband Sir Francis was likely to be.'

She pulled away to take a turn about the room. 'After that, I was never tempted to respond to another suitor, since they were all of Sir Francis's stamp—Tories, who could use my wealth and connection to good advantage. How could I trust anything they said?'

'Surely you can't doubt how witty, intelligent, and captivating you are! Completely deserving of any discerning gentleman's love and devotion.'

His praise eased her bruised heart. 'It shook my confidence at first,' she admitted, 'but I recovered—left with only one deep regret.'

When he raised an eyebrow in enquiry, she continued, 'Glad as I was to have my dilemma resolved without having to marry Sir Francis, I still feel…guilty. Would I have carried the child to term, had I been thrilled, instead of filled with dread about it?'

'I don't think anyone knows how much influence one's feelings have over such a thing. I do think it beyond reasonable that you should blame yourself for it.'

'As I believe it beyond reasonable that you should feel in any way responsible for the fate of your mother?'

He smiled. 'You have me there, I suppose.'

'So you understand now why I can't continue? Of course, it goes without saying that I trust you will never reveal to anyone what I've just confessed.'

'Of course not,' he assured her, then halted. After a long pause, as if he were weighing his words, 'I'm only sorry you had to suffer so devastating an experience.'

She waited, perhaps in the very depths of her heart hoping he would say more, that though he understood why she must break it off, that he couldn't imagine not seeing her, that he cared too much to say goodbye.

Of course, he did not. While she mentally flayed herself as a fool, Giles said, 'You will let me know if there are any…untoward consequences from last night.'

'You agreed to an affair, nothing more,' she replied, the words as much to emphasise that truth to herself as to affirm it for him. 'That's all that was or is required of you. Besides, the timing is such that there is very little likelihood of any "untoward consequences".'

'But you would let me know if there were,' he repeated, gazing at her.

She shook her head. 'I was married once, to a man who loved me completely and wanted to spend the rest of his life with me. I won't settle for less than that.'

'You think I don't care for you enough.'

She gave him a sad little smile. 'Love comes to us,

unbidden. Like a wild fawn, it cannot be saddled and bridled and directed the way we want it to go. It simply happens…or it does not. I bear you no ill will because it did not happen for you, but I…I cannot be just your friend.'

'So you are saying…you don't want to see me at all,' he said slowly.

'Yes. I'm sorry, but that's exactly what I'm saying.'

'I see.'

He stared past her, as if he were having difficulty making sense of her words.

The little knives were sawing deeper, and Maggie didn't think she could bear much more. 'Then we've said all that needs to be said. Goodbye, Giles. God keep you safe.'

She curtsied, and looking shocked and disbelieving, he bowed. When he still did not move, she gestured towards the door, both frantic to end this and wanting to savour his presence until the last possible moment.

At length, he nodded and crossed the room, then paused on the threshold. Turning back to her, his expression troubled, he said, 'I still intend to discover who hired Godfrey to shoot at you. Shall I send you a note once I've uncovered the whole?'

'If you wish. And thank you,' she added belatedly. He would probably expect thanks for trying to figure out who had endangered her.

Somehow, that threat didn't frighten her nearly as much as the sight of Giles Hadley, about to walk out of her life for good.

Once the echo of his footsteps in the hallway faded, Maggie staggered back to the sofa, numb and stunned, like a boxer who'd just taken a powerful blow to the chest. She hadn't felt so bereft, so absolutely devastated and hopeless, since she lost Robbie.

The obvious implication finally occurred to her. It seemed so clear and simple now, she wondered why she'd not recognised it much sooner.

Of course she was bleeding inside. Of course the world without him seemed an agonising emptiness. Of course she'd wanted to belong to him completely, everywhere and as often as possible.

It was why she'd felt so strongly driven to intervene in his life and smooth his path. Why she was utterly content, just to listen to him speak about the politics that consumed him, though his opinions were so different from her own. Why, when she'd told him she meant to terminate the liaison, that still naïve child deep within had hoped he would refuse, proclaiming that he couldn't go on without her.

No point trying to deny the fact any longer: despite assuring herself she'd never let herself be vulnerable again, she'd fallen in love with Giles Hadley.

She didn't know when fascination had deepened into love, though if she were honest, she'd been tumbling deeper into enchantment from the moment they met.

Perhaps she'd secretly hoped, if she didn't call what she felt by its name, she might save herself some of the anguish now coursing through her.

She'd been wrong.

She allowed herself to retain only one tiny crumb of hope: if Giles cared as much for her as Robbie had, he would come back. If he did, then and only then would she confess that she loved him.

If he didn't, it was just as well for them to end it now. Continuing on would only entangle her heart and hopes more completely into his life and make the inevitable parting more difficult.

This was hard enough.

Aunt Lilly had been right to warn her, Maggie thought, struggling to get air in and out of her lungs. Hearts *could* break twice. And the second time was looking to be no easier than the first.

# *Chapter Twenty*

Giles found himself back at his rooms at Albany without being able to recall precisely how he'd got there. He ached like the very devil, and he wasn't sure it was his hand that hurt the most.

He still couldn't believe that Maggie had ended their liaison. He'd been so focused on removing the threat to her so she could resume her—and their—normal routine, his chief worry the possibility that he'd have to shoulder the guilt of learning his brother was responsible for the attack, he'd never remotely considered it ending.

Not that he could be angry with her—not when her reasons were so undeniable and compelling. If he were honest, he had to admit that he had coaxed her into suppressing those very misgivings to win her agreement to begin the affair. She'd honoured him by trusting him enough to reveal the deeper reason behind those misgivings—a personal tragedy of which even her closest family wasn't aware.

His lip curled with derision when he thought of Sir Francis Mowbrey. How stupid and selfish the man must be to have remained ignorant of what a treasure he'd been offered! Concerned only with availing himself of her wealth, her connections and her body while giving her nothing but honeyed lies. Giles grieved for the innocent girl whose trust and self-confidence had been so callously shaken.

Small wonder she'd held herself at a distance from all subsequent suitors, too disillusioned to trust the love promises of prospective husbands who stood to gain so much by beguiling her into marriage.

Perhaps that was why she'd chosen him, Giles thought wryly. Her Tory connections were no help to him politically, and he wasn't on the catch for an heiress. As she'd said, he'd signed on only for a mutually pleasurable interlude with an interesting and attractive partner.

So why did he feel like he'd just been gutted?

He'd get over it, he told himself—just like the throbbing in this curst hand would end, eventually. Deciding some medicinal brandy might be good for all that ailed him, he hunted for the decanter and poured himself a glass.

His mind wandering, unable to focus on what he should do next, he automatically began to pick up the glass with his right—injured—hand. He dropped it at once, cursing at the excruciating pain.

Fury far beyond anything merited by that small miscalculation engulfed him. Seizing the glass with his good hand, he threw it into the fireplace, watching as the crystal shattered into pieces.

Like his world.

A week later, Giles was reading through some papers in the committee room when Ben entered with a stack of law books. His vision obscured, he bumped the table, knocking over an empty tankard that fell against Giles's injured hand.

After a stream of curses, he snapped. 'Watch where you're going, lunkhead!'

Ben set down the books with a thump. 'Here's all of Blackstone, as requested,' he told Davie, who sat at the table beside Giles. 'As for you, Giles, in future would you make sure you don't injure yourself while Parliament is in session? You've been like a bear with a thorn in its paw for the last week.'

Irritated and out of sorts, but knowing his friend was right, Giles was working up the will to apologise when a knock sounded, followed by the entrance of a runner, who handed Giles a message.

He read through it swiftly, then rose, going over to claim his hat and greatcoat. 'It's from Hines,' he told them. 'He has the information we've been seeking.'

'Shall I go with you?' Davie asked.

'No. One way or the other, I'll be fine. I'm just happy to end this at last.'

Ending it would mean he'd be able to write to Maggie, he thought as he hailed a hackney, giving the driver Hine's Bow Street address. He might even chance going to Cavendish Square to deliver the news in person.

His spirits rose at the idea of seeing her. Much as he hated to acknowledge it, missing her had been an ache as painful as his wound. Except, he expected, *that* pain would prove much more enduring.

A short time later, he climbed out of the carriage and hurried into Hines's office, eager to have the mystery cleared up at last. The investigator came straight to the point.

'Godfrey was hired by a Tom Brown—not his name, almost certainly. Brown hovers about the edges of society, along with the cent-per-centers and dealers in pawned merchandise, specialising in making discreet arrangements for gentlemen down on their luck who need to sell a family bauble that might not be theirs to sell, settle a bastard child obscurely in the country, or otherwise make inconvenient problems disappear. His reputation for doing so came to the attention of a gentleman who had such a problem, who contacted him to take care of it.'

'And that gentleman was?'

'As you suspected, your half-brother, George Hadley.'

Even though Giles had never been able to imagine anyone else being responsible, having the news confirmed still shocked him like a slap to the face.

'Shall I write and inform Lord Esterbrook?' Hines asked.

'Yes, he will want a full report. Thank you for your good work, Mr Hines. And for letting me come along for that dust-up we enjoyed the other night. Reminded me of my misspent youth on the Hampshire downs.'

Hines smiled. 'I imagine speechifying and law-making must sometimes seem a bit dull for an active man.'

He was about to participate in another dust-up—as soon as he ran down his half-brother. 'Total your bill and present it to my bank, and they will draft you the reimbursement.'

'Thank you, Mr Hadley. Right sorry about your half-brother.'

After exchanging bows, Giles quit Hines's office and raced down to the waiting hackney. Now to track down George at Abbotsweal House, and settle this for good and all.

But to his frustration, Giles arrived at the family town house to find the knocker off the door. Proceeding to the kitchen entrance, he roused a member of the skeleton

staff, who informed him that Mr Hadley had been summoned home by his sire two weeks previous.

Thanking the man, Giles walked slowly out. Unfortunately, he'd not have today the reckoning he burned for.
Even more unfortunately, he was going to have to make
that long-delayed journey to Abbotsweal.

Three dusty June days of travelling later, Giles arrived
at the village of Romesly and engaged a room at the local
inn. Later, he would call on Mr Angleton and meet with
the committee that had requested his presence. But first,
he would visit Abbotsweal Hall and settle the business
with his half-brother. And his father.

Following the directions of the innkeeper, Giles chose
to ride to Abbotsweal, rather than take a carriage. Before anyone at the manor noticed a visitor approaching
and gave the alert, he wanted to get a good look at the
land that would eventually be his and the house he'd not
seen since he was a small boy, and barely remembered.

To his surprise as he drew nearer to the house, bits
and pieces of memories surfaced in his mind—a curve
of road that seemed familiar, a sunny, open copse in the
woodland where he must have played. Then the Georgian manor itself, vast as he remembered it.

The scent of roses brought back hazy images of a
walled garden—which he spotted to the west of the main
building. Then he was approaching the entrance, handing his horse over to a footman, being admitted by an elderly butler. 'Please inform Lord Telbridge that Viscount
Lyndlington is here to see him.'

The old man drew in a breath. 'Master Giles? Is that
really you?'

Giles looked over to find, to his surprise, an expression
of gladness on the old man's face. 'I'm sorry, I don't—'

'I'm Wilson, sir, and of course you don't remember me! You were only a babe when you and...when you left us. I'm so glad you've come home, at last! Your father prefers to receive callers in the library—won't you follow me, sir? I'll let his lordship know you are here at once!'

'Is Master George here as well?'

'I believe he is out riding at present, but due back before dinner.'

Very well, Giles thought, following the old man into a large, long room whose walls were lined with cases filled with leather volumes. He'd deal first with Telbridge, then with his half-brother.

What a handsome room it was, he thought, idly picking up a book at random. It was disorienting to consider that, at some future date, this handsome library would be his, as well as this vast Georgian edifice and all the land he'd ridden through, including the village.

He was still trying to wrap his mind around that notion when the butler returned to announce Lord Telbridge.

Walking in behind him was the father Giles had not seen in over twenty years. For a long moment, they simply stared at each other.

Giles could see the resemblance to George: the same square jaw and hazel eyes, the silver hair that must once have been his half-brother's sandy-brown hue. Whereas he, with his blue-black hair and blue eyes, was entirely a reflection of his mother.

No wonder Telbridge had banished him with her.

'Telbridge,' he said, bowing. *They could at least begin with courtesy.*

The earl paused, apparently unsure what to call him.

'I'm Lyndlington,' he said pointedly, though he knew the butler would have passed on the visitor's name.

'Lyndlington,' his father repeated. 'I suppose we ought

to sit down.' Gesturing Giles to a wing chair, he took the chair behind the large desk.

A sudden memory surfaced—a young boy playing fortress in the wing chair, while a man looked on indulgently from behind that massive desk.

Pushing it away, Giles turned his attention back to the most important matter: the attack on Lady Margaret.

'I suppose you wonder why I've come here uninvited,' he began. 'It's not the obvious reason, although I will get to that in a moment. My primary purpose is to talk with George about an attack on Lady Margaret Dennison Roberts—a lady he courted, but who rejected him.'

'An attack on Lady Margaret?' Telbridge echoed. 'What do you mean? And what has that to do with George?'

'In brief, George had aspirations to the hand of the Marquess of Witlow's daughter, and when she refused his advances, he threatened her with retribution. I count myself fortunate to be a friend of that lady and her father. George previously warned me to stay away from her, and the knowledge that she persisted in befriending me after rejecting him certainly would have increased his anger and disappointment. However, no amount of outrage justified his hiring a man to take a shot at her while she was riding at Huntsford.'

'He hired someone to shoot at her? But that's madness! I know there is ill feeling between you. Surely that enmity has coloured your interpretation of the facts, for I cannot imagine—'

'Lord Telbridge, the *facts* are not in dispute. Lady Margaret's brother, Lord Esterbrook, had the incident thoroughly investigated by Bow Street. The perpetrator was tracked back to London, where he was apprehended and confessed. He had been hired and paid by an intermediary, who had in turn been hired by George. I am not speculating; if you doubt my word, you may apply to Lord Esterbrook for a copy of the report Mr Hines of Bow Street prepared for him.'

'But that is...fantastic!'

'Fantastic, indeed. Ill-judged, certainly, and prosecutable in a criminal court, definitely. Though I myself would favour a trial and punishment, to spare the lady and her family embarrassment, I imagine Lord Witlow will prefer to proceed privately. But George must be dealt with; the marquess will stand for nothing less.'

'I had some...prior knowledge of a problem between them,' the earl admitted. 'I summoned George home after receiving a note from Witlow informing me that George had been harassing Lady Margaret; the marquess wrote that he would consider preferring charges if I didn't bring George home and exercise more control over his behaviour. But to endanger Lady Margaret...'

At that moment, the butler bowed himself back in. 'Master George just returned, my lord. Shall I have him join you?'

'At once,' Telbridge said curtly.

There being nothing further he needed to say, Giles remained silent as they waited for the earl's second son to arrive. Davie would caution him to remain calm and curb his temper—so he did not succumb to his strong inclination to stalk over and floor George with a roundhouse punch to the jaw the moment he entered the library.

'You wanted to see me?' George said as he walked in. He stopped short, the smile on his face fading when he saw Giles. 'You!' he spat out incredulously. 'What are *you* doing here?'

'Surely you didn't think you could get away with this,'

Giles said, fixing his half-brother with a hard look. 'Don't pretend you don't know exactly what I'm talking about.'

Breaking eye contact with Giles, George looked over at his father. 'I don't know what sort of rubbishing story he's told you, but I assure you, it is false and exaggerated! What's he doing in our library anyway, as if he were a welcome guest? I would have expected you to show him the door!'

'That's quite enough, George,' Telbridge said. 'Take a seat. I'd meant to discuss this matter ever since you returned home, and now it can be put off no longer.' He nodded to Giles. 'Lyndlington, if you would explain?'

'George needs no explanation, being fully aware of the facts,' Giles replied. 'Which are, that at O'Malley's Gaming Emporium in one of the more…questionable areas of London, he sought out a Mr Tom Brown, who has a reputation for arranging matters of dubious legality for gentlemen who don't wish to dirty their hands doing them personally. George hired Mr Brown to find someone who would fire on Lady Margaret—or that's what the shooter, Mr Godfrey, insists. Unless you really intended to have her killed for refusing your suit?'

His expression stony, George remained silent, staring straight ahead.

'Well, George?' Telbridge demanded. 'Please tell me that Lyndlington is mistaken, and that you had nothing to do with this tawdry episode.'

When he still made no answer—trying to come up with an explanation for the unexplainable—Giles felt almost sorry for the man. But not quite.

'I require an answer,' Telbridge said, as if George's silence wasn't confession enough. Perhaps to accept that his beloved son could be responsible for such shocking events, he needed to have them confirmed by the man himself.

'Of course, I didn't intend for Lady Margaret to be harmed,' George said sulkily. 'Only to frighten her—maybe enough to realise that keeping company with *him* was dangerous—for such it proved, didn't it?' he added with a laugh. 'I thought she might come to her senses, and think again about my proposal. Although if the shooter's aim had been bad, and he struck *him* instead, I wouldn't have shed any tears.'

'If the shooter's aim had been bad, he might have struck *her*!' Giles retorted. 'He came shockingly close as it was! And if he did kill me, you'd have led a man into committing a hanging offence, just to soothe your injured dignity!'

George turned to Giles, frustration and fury in his gaze. 'If *you* had kept out of the matter, the proposal would have been accepted! Why shouldn't Lady Margaret marry me? I'm of impeccable lineage, belong to the correct party, and could maintain her in a position she prizes, as a leading political hostess! Whereas *you* only wanted to trifle with her. I tried to warn her!'

Giles sucked in a breath, needing all his willpower not to grab his half-brother and throttle him. Perhaps George's insidious words, added to the cautious scepticism she'd developed as a shield after her betrayal by Sir Francis Mowbrey, explained why Maggie had not seemed to believe how much he cared for her.

'So it's true, what Lyndlington told me,' Telbridge said, pinning George with his gaze.

'Well, yes, but there wasn't any harm—'

'No *harm*?' Giles cried, unable to restrain himself. 'You put Lady Margaret's life at risk, alarmed her family, and forced her into hiding! Not to mention, your hirelings could be brought up on offenses that could get them transported, if not hung. All so Lady Margaret might— *reconsider your suit?*'

'That's enough from you, too, Lyndlington,' the earl said. 'George, you will go to your chamber and wait for me to decide how I wish to proceed. It will require careful arranging to avoid having our family name tarnished by seeing you brought up on charges!'

'Very well, Father,' George said, bowing. 'I know you will figure a way out of this.'

While Giles shook his head in disbelief, with a great deal more nonchalance than a man in his position should be feeling, his half-brother walked out.

'You don't really think you can get him out of this,' he asked the earl once the door had closed.

'No,' Telbridge said quietly. 'I've…overlooked some questionable activities before, things I see now I should have put a stop to, but this appalling lack of judgement and consideration passes all limits. I fear I must implement the plan I'd been considering since I got the marquess's earlier missive. The family has mercantile interests in the Americas; I shall send George to our head office in the Bahamas to learn the business.'

'Lord help the office in the Bahamas,' Giles muttered.

'This time, he must act like a man and learn to make his own fortune. He's not an unintelligent lad. If he works hard and masters the details of the export business, he could earn a tidy income from it some day. As you will… eventually inherit here, he will need another source of income.'

*Since you won't be here to siphon off funds from the estate for his benefit any longer,* Giles thought. 'I had to come to Abbotsweal to find George anyway, but I did intend to also discuss the matter of the succession. After the election last month, a delegation from Romesly invited me to the village to meet the electors and the tenants hereabouts, wishing me to start becoming acquainted with them and their needs.'

'Doing for yourself what I had not done?'

Giles couldn't tell from his tone whether that was meant as comment or accusation. Refraining from answering, he continued, 'I never meant to tread on Abbotsweal land behind your back; I planned to call here first, and inform you of my intentions.'

'I'm glad you did call. I should have summoned—requested—you to return to Abbotsweal long since.' The earl smiled sadly. 'Inertia, I suppose. Plus, it is hard to admit one is wrong.'

Before Giles could recover from his surprise at that remark, the earl said, 'I admit, I've indulged George too much. And that, without any help from me, you've made an impressive name for yourself.'

'I'm glad you approve,' he replied, unable to keep an edge of sarcasm from his tone.

The earl laughed. 'I imagine you don't give a tinker's damn what I think—nor have I given you any reason to.' He paused, his gaze going to the far distance, as if his thoughts had wondered miles away. 'Did your mother ever give you an explanation for why I sent you away?'

Startled at the change of subject, Giles said, 'No. Until my aunt came to take me away to school, I had no idea we *had* been sent away. Aunt Charlotte explained it to me afterward, but…Mama died that same winter, before I could see her again and ask her anything.'

'Then it's time you heard the truth. All of it. Which will require some courage.'

The earl went to the sideboard and poured them each a brandy. Sitting back down, he took a long swallow and began. 'The cottage where you grew up was rented by an old friend, who used to go there for the shooting. My best friend, Richard Kensworthy, and I used it, too. A few years after your mother and I were married, I chanced upon the friend, and he asked me how I'd enjoyed the little taste of honeymoon before my wedding. I must have looked puzzled, for he reminded me that my wife had asked to borrow the cottage just before the wedding. I played along as if I recalled the incident, but I knew she hadn't gone to the cottage to meet *me*. It was Richard, of course.'

'I was in a rage when I returned and accused her. She made no attempt to deny it—it wasn't adultery, she said, because we were not yet married. And when I asked her if she could assure me that you were my son, she replied that she could not.'

'I *had* heard that part. And that because of it, you banished us both.'

The earl sighed. 'Actually, I didn't. It was Lydia who no longer wanted to continue our marriage. She said that she still loved Richard, she'd always loved Richard, that she'd only married me because of pressure from her family. I'd pledged to pay off her father's debts, you see. She said she'd tried to be a good wife, but if I was going to despise her for loving Richard and treat her son with contempt because he might not be *my* son, she would rather leave.'

'*She* wanted to leave?' Giles echoed, incredulous.

'Yes. Since you *might* be Richard's son, she said she wanted you all to herself. I see now that I should have waited, let us both have time to calm down and think rationally. But I was young, and stupid, and ferociously jealous. Because I did love her, you see. I always had, even though I knew she preferred Richard. I felt almost…

guilty, taking advantage of her situation to win her hand, knowing her family would never allow her to marry a penniless younger son. I thought I could make her love me, and when she confirmed I had not, I was furious. She told me she was going to take you and leave, and advised me to divorce her.' He smiled bitterly. 'So I might marry again and have a son I was sure was mine.'

'So you did,' Giles murmured.

'So I did.'

'Why did you allow society to believe you'd cast her out?'

'Pride. How could I admit to the world that my wife would rather live in a cottage on the downs than with me—' he gestured around them '—in this great old manse? The only concession I won from her was her agreement to live with you in that cottage. Where I could make sure you were both all right, with enough food and such few presents, like books and art supplies, that she would allow me to give her.'

As memories returned in a rush, Giles felt like George had punched *him*. Mama, receiving a wrapped package with a new book, or some watercolours. A merchant from the nearest village, arriving with a basket of vegetables, a side of beef, flour and supplies to make bread.

The truth dawned in a horrifying rush. '*You* own the cottage on the downs?'

The earl nodded. 'It's part of the estate. You will own it one day, which is why I was not willing to sell it to you when you made enquiries, some time ago.'

'Did your second wife know?'

'I think she suspected. She knew I never loved her, but there was no pretence of that union being anything more than a marriage of convenience. I wanted a son I knew was mine, and she wanted to marry an earl.'

'Why did you not come forward when my aunt sent me to school? I know my uncle paid my fees and expenses.'

'My second wife was still alive then. I knew I could always reimburse Lord Newville later, which I intend to do.'

'Does no one else know about your connection to the cottage?'

'The friend who used to rent it—but he was killed at Waterloo. And Richard, of course, but he died in India. I recognised almost immediately that remarriage had been a mistake, but by then it was too late. And by the time my second wife passed away, Lydia was already dead, too. I tried to transfer all my love and devotion to George.'

He shook his head, his expression full of grief. 'In the process, I ruined him and created a breach with you I didn't know how to heal. For so long after Lydia died, I didn't have the heart to try. So you see, the son I loved too well turned into selfish, shallow, reckless man concerned only with his own wishes; the son I spurned has become a man any father would be proud of. After this business with George, you have no reason to like or even respect me, but the estate will one day be yours. It's past time I began showing you how to run it. I'd like to begin again, if you'll let me.'

With everything he'd ever believed about the relationship between his mother and the earl turned on its head, Giles hardly knew what to think. Regardless of the maelstrom of conflicting emotions raging inside, the earl's offer was a reasonable one—the best resolution he could have wished for, for the good of the estate and himself.

'I'm not sure how to begin over either,' he admitted. He might never be able to conquer his anger and resentment for the man who'd allowed him to grow up fatherless all those years. 'I will try. And I will certainly accept your offer to acquaint me with the estate.'

The earl held out his hand. Giles shook it.

'Can you stay?' Telbridge asked. 'I'll have the house-keeper prepare rooms for you.'

'No, I must get back to London as soon as I've spoken with the delegates in Romesley. I've hardly held my weight the last few weeks on finishing the final preparations for reading the Reform Bill out of committee. If it's agreeable to you, once it's passed—it will pass—and Parliament adjourns, I'll return.

'Besides,' he added ruefully, 'you had better not trust me under the same roof with George. Perhaps by the time Parliament dissolves, you'll have dispatched him to those poor unwary souls in Bermuda.'

The earl held up a cautionary hand. 'As you've not given up on me, after all my poor decisions these many years, I'm not yet ready to give up on George. He may yet find the tiller that can right his ship.'

'I will pray he does,' Giles said. *Although that transformation would be a daunting task even for the Almighty.* 'Now, I need to return to Romesly. I sent Lord Witlow a note before I left London, promising to return as soon as possible and let him know what would be done about George.'

The earl nodded. 'I will write him as well, offering my sincere apologies and assuring him George will cause no more trouble. Also, to give him my thanks for choosing not to resolve this in a public manner that would cause embarrassment to us both. Will it be possible to obtain mercy for the two men George hired?'

'If the marquess chooses not to press charges, probably.'

'I will request it in my note. Perhaps they, too, can be…relocated.'

Giles stood, and the earl stood, too, offering his hand again. Giles shook it firmly.

'Goodbye, Lord Telbridge. I'll send you a note when I know when I can return.'

'Do that. Goodbye…my son.'

## *Chapter Twenty-One*

Giles rode back to Romesly, almost dizzy from the velocity of the thoughts and questions whizzing around in his head about what the earl—his father—had just revealed.

His *mother* had wanted to end the marriage.

The earl had always loved her, had watched over and protected them all the years he was growing up.

The earl would have forgiven her and continued the marriage—but she had wanted to live apart. To treasure her son by herself.

*He was not the cause of her ruin and banishment.*

He'd always told himself he didn't believe George's taunt, but as he began to fully assimilate the truth of the relationship between the earl and his mother, his entire soul felt suddenly light, as if a terrible burden had been lifted. Perhaps, he thought wryly, he'd believed it more than he'd realised.

Mr Angleton and the voters of Romesly would be thrilled to learn he'd reconciled with the earl—removing any worry about possible retribution against them for ousting George from his Parliamentary seat.

He knew one other person who'd be thrilled to know

he would be taking up his proper role for the estate. His chest expanded with anticipation and delight at the thought of telling her.

But…Maggie had asked him not to call on her again. Because she believed, deep down, he was only 'trifling' with her, as George had warned? How *could* she believe that, after all they had been to each other?

He'd been so shocked and dismayed when she'd broken with him, he'd hardly made sense of her words. Suddenly, some of them recurred to him: *Love simply happens… or it does not. I bear you no ill will because it did not happen for you…*

For *you*. Was that to say love *had* happened, for her?

He had missed her as he'd never missed any other woman, longed for her as he'd not longed for any other woman. And he could not imagine wanting any other woman by his side when he took up the tasks that would be his destiny.

'I love you, Maggie mine,' he whispered with incredulous delight, and then laughed out loud for the joy of it. Perhaps it had taken learning the full truth about his mother's love and the earl's heartache, to free himself from the past and leave him open to recognising a love of his own.

Whatever the reason, he suddenly knew, with as much certainty as he knew his own name, that he loved Maggie Dennison Roberts.

*Love comes to us, unbidden.*

So it had, but given the earl's salutary example, he wasn't going to let his slip away from him.

And he was prepared to use every weapon at his command, including that explosive passion they both had so much difficulty resisting, to woo his shy fawn back to him.

* * *

A week later, Maggie sat in the little study at Cavendish Square, planning out the seating arrangement for Papa's dinner. It had been two weeks since she'd given Giles his *congé*, but she'd made little progress in banishing the aching sadness that afflicted her during every waking moment and haunted her sleep.

With the danger of further attack removed, she'd thrown herself back into her duties as hostess for her father and mistress of his household. She'd tried to fill up any odd spare moments shopping for new gowns, perusing the shelves at Hatchards, and making calls on acquaintances in town she normally never bothered with. All to keep herself from brooding about how much she missed him, and how dreary her life was, now that she'd banished him.

But new gowns only reminded her of how he'd unlaced her out of her bodice, and Hatchards of the books they'd discussed, and making calls of their secret rendezvous, she waiting with breathless anticipation for him to ride from the park and slip up the stairs at Upper Brook Street and join her.

Only by recalling the memory of Francis and the dire consequences of succumbing to passion, could she keep herself from summoning him back.

She'd fobbed off Papa, when he'd asked in concern what was ailing her, by saying she was still recovering from the shock of being shot at. The shock of loving and losing Giles was far greater, of course, but she *would* get through it, she kept telling herself. It *would* get better.

She pushed away the depressing thought that she'd never really got over losing Robbie. What made her think recovering from this second blow would be any easier?

Would Giles come, if she summoned him?

Exasperated, she squelched the useless speculation. She would not summon him. If he ever returned, it would be because he could not stay away. Because he'd belatedly realised he loved her, as she'd finally come to realise she loved him.

As she reached that conclusion, Rains walked in. 'Viscount Lyndlington to see you, Lady Margaret.'

So completely wrapped up in thinking about him had she been, at first she wasn't sure she hadn't just imagined hearing his name.

'W-who did you say?'

'Lord Lyndlington,' Rains repeated.

'Oh,' she said faintly, her heart commencing to beat so hard in her chest she had difficulty thinking. 'Show him into the Blue Salon.'

Rains peered at her with concern. 'Are you all right, my lady?'

'Quite all right,' she replied unsteadily, knowing it was a lie. 'Tell him I'll be right in.'

After the butler went out, Maggie rose from her desk, unsure what to do next. *Check your* coiffure, *make sure there are no ink smudges on your nose or fingers,* she told herself, having difficulty recalling what would normally be second nature.

*Go to him.*

She tried to ground the great, ravenous bird of hope that was flapping its wings in her chest, trying to take flight, making it hard for her to breathe.

He'd probably come to tell her the final results of the shooting incident. Though her father had already shown her Mr Hines's report.

*Go in and see, looby.*

She walked to the parlour on legs that seemed stiff and awkward. When she opened the door and saw him waiting for her, joy consumed her, and it took every bit of restraint she possessed not to run across the room and throw herself into his arms.

'Giles, what a pleasant surprise,' she said instead, making herself walk at a decorous pace. 'So, have you finished your quest?'

He came over and took her hand, those marvellous blue eyes scanning her face as he brought her fingers to his lips. She bit her lip against a whimper of delight.

'It's wonderful to see you, too, Maggie. Yes, the quest is complete. I'd thought to write you a note, but there was so much to say, I decided to come in person. I hope you don't mind.'

Oh, she minded! Torn between telling him to leave, before the ache of needing him grew any sharper, and begging him never to leave, she simply nodded and gestured towards the sofa.

Prudently seating herself on a chair, she got her unruly thoughts under control. 'What did you discover?'

'As your father might have told you, the investigation showed that George had indeed paid for Godfrey to fire at you. When I went to confront him, I discovered he'd returned to Abbotsweal, so I was obliged to follow him there.'

'So you met your father at last—and survived, I see. I assume you did not murder George?'

'No, though I certainly considered it. It turned out to be a…surprising meeting, in many ways.'

'Can you tell me about it, without violating any confidences?'

'I intend to.'

They paused then, Rains returning with wine. While

he poured, Maggie thought how wonderful it was to have Giles sitting in her parlour, confiding in her as they had so often when they lay in each other's arms at Upper Brook Street. How she ached for the precious hours she had not appreciated nearly enough when she had them!

After the butler walked out, Giles said, 'I'd feared Telbridge would support George, despite the evidence of his wrongdoing. The threat of possible prosecution by your father might have influenced him, but for whatever reason, of his own volition, he's decided to send George to the Bahamas to learn the management of the earl's export business there, with the possibility of running it himself one day, if he does well.'

'Perhaps he will, with a change of place and occupation. And a knowledge that he cannot count on the earl to support him for ever.'

'Yes. However, what I learned about my mother was even more surprising.'

He proceeded to tell her what the earl had revealed about his relationship with Giles's mother. 'It seems your belief was accurate,' he concluded. 'I was not responsible for my mother's divorce and banishment. The earl would have forgiven her lapse, and taken us back.'

'I knew you could not be responsible. I hope now, you believe it, too. So you reconciled with the earl?'

'Yes. I'll return to Abbotsweal after the session is over—at the earl's invitation. You'll be pleased to learn he has decided to do his duty, as you always insisted he should, and begin showing me around Abbotsweal himself.'

'That's excellent news!' she said, truly happy that the man who should bring Giles back into involvement with his birthright had finally accepted the responsibility. She smiled. 'How does it feel, knowing you're about to join the opposition?'

'Strange,' he conceded, smiling back. Oh, how charming his smile was, setting those compelling blue eyes aglow! 'But not all peers oppose the Reform Bill. I may have some company, when I finally enter the Lords. But that, please God, won't be for many years.'

'You may manage to get the institution disbanded before then,' she said with a twinkle.

'Perhaps I will,' he replied. 'More importantly, though, the startling news about the earl and my mother made me think more deeply about my own…relationships. About how much I missed you—and I missed you dreadfully. About what an amazing, intelligent, passionate woman you are. I realised it had been a mistake to let you send me away, and I wasn't going to follow the earl's example and let you go.'

The bird inside was flapping harder. 'You aren't?' she whispered.

'Several things you said in that final interview, that I only half-heard in the shock of the moment, gave me hope. That you'd been married to a man who loved you completely, and wouldn't settle for less. That you bore me no ill will because love hadn't happened *for me*. Which, can I believe, implies that love *did* happen for you? And that you would consider marrying me—if you believed I loved you enough in return?'

She hardly dared trust what she thought she was hearing. 'Are you trying to tell me that you *do* love me?'

'Absolutely, totally. Even if I was such a nodcock, it took me far too long to recognise it. Could you love me back, Maggie mine? Teach me to run an estate, stay by my side, in my parlour, in my bed, now and always?'

A happiness she'd never thought to experience again suffused her.

'Yes. I can teach you to be a good Tory, too.'

He laughed, the joyous sound an echo of her own joy. 'I won't go that far! Perhaps I'll teach you to be a good Radical.'

She chuckled, so delirious with gladness she wanted to run to the window and shout her happiness to everyone in the street. 'Sounds like we shall have to debate that.'

'That, perhaps, but never this: I love you, Lady Margaret Elizabeth Charlotte Dennison Roberts. I want you to be my wife and live with me all my days.'

With that, he dropped to one knee. 'Will you marry me, Maggie mine, and make me the happiest man in Christendom?'

She clasped his dear face between her hands, gazing down into the blue, blue eyes that had captivated her from their first glance. 'Yes, my darling Giles, I will.'

With a whoop, he jumped up, seized her hands, and danced her around the room. Stopping at last to kiss her soundly, he said, 'Shall we summon Rains? This calls for champagne!'

'I had a better celebration in mind. Why don't we repair to Upper Brook Street?'

His eyes blazed with excitement of another sort. 'In the middle of the afternoon? What about your elderly cousin?'

'Remember, I told you she's very deaf.'

Chuckling, he bent to kiss her nose. 'She's going to need to be. Shall I ask your father for your hand first?'

'He'll say "yes"; ask him later. I've already waited long enough to return to Upper Brook Street.'

He lifted her in another hug and whirled her around,

then set her back on her feet. 'Come with me now, then, Maggie mine. Come with me, and never leave me again.'

With that, he clasped her hand and led her from the room.

* * * * *

# STOLEN
# ENCOUNTERS
# WITH THE DUCHESS

To Sue Ballard

You light up a room with your smile and brighten my day with your cheerful optimism. Thank you for being the inspiration for my Faith and for me.

# *Chapter One*

Setting off at a pace brisk enough to clear the wine fumes from his head, David Tanner Smith, Member of Parliament for Hazelwick, headed from the Mayfair town house where he'd dined with some Whig colleagues towards his rooms at Albany.

The friends had urged him to stay for a few more rounds, but after a day of enduring the mostly irrelevant objections the opponents of the Reform Bill kept raising to delay bringing it to a vote, he was weary of political talk. He was also, he had to admit, somewhat out of spirits.

His footsteps would echo loudly once he reached the solitary rooms of his chambers. Though he rejoiced that his best friend, Giles Hadley, had found happiness with Lady Margaret, he'd discovered that losing the companion with whom he'd shared rooms since their student days at Oxford had left him lonelier than he'd anticipated.

Since the only woman he'd ever loved was far beyond the touch of a lowly farmer's orphan, he didn't expect he'd ever find wedded bliss himself. Being common-born, but sponsored by a baronet and a marquess, put him in an odd social limbo, not of the gentry, never acceptable to the *haut ton*, but as a rising politician in the Whigs, not a nonentity either.

Rather a conundrum, which spared him attentions from marriage-minded mamas who couldn't quite decide whether he would be a good match for their daughters or not, he thought with a wry grin.

The smile faded as he recalled the stillness of Giles's empty room back in Piccadilly. Who might he marry, if he were ever lonely enough? The daughter of a cit who valued his political aspirations? A politically minded aristocrat who would overlook the lack of birth in exchange for elbow room at the tables of power?

He was rounding the dark corner from North Audley Street towards Oxford Street when the sounds of an altercation reached him. Slowing, he peered through the dimness ahead, where he could just make out the figures of two men and what appeared to be a young woman draped in an evening cloak.

'You will release me at once, or I will call the watch,' she declared.

'Will ye, now?' one of them mocked with a coarse laugh.

The other, grasping the woman's shoulder, said, 'The only thing you'll be doing is handing your necklace over to us—and the bracelet and earbobs, too, if you don't want that pretty face marred. '

'Aye, so pretty that maybe we'll take you to a fancy house after,' the other man added. 'They'd pay a lot for a tender morsel like you, I reckon.'

'Take your hands off me!' the girl shrieked, kicking out and twisting in the first man's grip, as the second pulled on the ties to her cape.

Davie tightened his grip on his walking stick and ran

towards them. 'Let the woman go!' he shouted, raising the stick menacingly. 'Now—before *I* call the watch.'

For an instant, seeing his imposing size, the men froze. Then, city blokes obviously having no idea of the damage a strong yeoman could do with a stout stave, they ignored him and resumed trying to subdue the struggling female.

He'd warned them, Davie thought. After having to restrain himself around buffoons all day, the prospect of being able to deliver a few good whacks raised his spirits immensely.

With a roar, he rushed them, catching the first man under his ear with the end of the stick and knocking him away. Rapidly reversing it, he delivered an uppercut to the chin of the second. The sharp crack of fracturing bone sounded before the second man, howling, released his hold. Wrenching free, the lass lifted her skirts and took to her heels.

Davie halted a moment, panting. Much as he'd like to round the two up and deliver them to the nearest constable, he probably ought to follow the girl. Any female alone on the street at this time of night was likely to attract more trouble—at the very least, some other footpad looking for an easy mark, if not far worse.

Decision made, he turned away from the attackers and ran after her. 'Don't worry, I won't hurt you!' he called out. 'It's not safe, walking alone in London at night. Let me escort you home.'

The girl gave a quick glance over her shoulder, but apparently unconvinced, fled on. Hampered by her skirts, she wouldn't have been able to outrun him for long, but before he could catch up to her, she tripped on something and stumbled. With a cry, she fell to her knees.

Reaching her in a few strides, Davie halted at her

side and offered a hand to help her to her feet. The girl took it, but then suddenly jerked away with such violence that, when Davie hung on instead of releasing her, the force of the ricochet slammed her back into Davie, chest to chest.

Swearing under his breath, Davie held fast to the lass, who immediately began struggling again. 'Stop it!' he said sharply. 'I told you, I don't mean to hurt you.' Lowering his voice, he continued, 'We'll sort this out, miss, but not on a public street. Let me take you somewhere safer, and you can tell me how to get you home to your family.'

With a deep sigh, the girl ceased trying to pull away from him. 'Please, Davie,' she said softly, 'won't you just let me go?'

The dearly familiar voice shocked him like the sharp edge of a razor slicing skin. 'Faith?' he said incredulously.

To his astonishment, as he turned the woman's face up into the lamplight, Davie recognised that it was, in fact, Faith Wellingford Evers, Duchess of Ashedon, he had trapped against him.

Before he could get his stunned tongue to utter another word, the lady pulled away. 'Yes, it's Faith,' she admitted. 'I was on my way to find a hackney to take me home. Couldn't you pretend you hadn't seen me, and let me go?'

As the reality of her identity sank in, a second wave of shock, sharpened by horror over what might have happened to her, held him speechless for another moment. Then, swallowing a curse, Davie clamped a hand around her wrist and began walking her forward. 'No, Duchess, I can't let you—'

'Faith, Davie. Please, let it be Faith. Can't I escape, at least for a while, being the Duchess?'

It shouldn't have, but it warmed his heart that she would allow such familiarity to someone who'd not been a close friend for years. 'Regardless, I can't let you wander on your own, chasing down a carriage to get you back to Berkeley Square. The streets in Mayfair are better, but nowhere in London is truly safe after dark, for anyone alone. To say nothing of a woman!'

'You were alone,' she pointed out.

'Yes, but I was also armed and able to defend myself,' he retorted. 'I *was* going to take the young lass I'd rescued to a tavern and discover how to help her, but I can't do that with you. Not around here, where we are both known. You'd better let me summon the hackney and escort you safely home.'

She slowed, resisting his forward motion. 'You're sure you can't just let me go?' After his sharp look of a reply, she said softly, 'I didn't set out to be foolish or irresponsible. I *am* sorry to have inadvertently got you involved.'

She swallowed hard, and the tears he saw sparkling at the edge of her lashes hit him like a fist to the chest. *How it still distressed him to see her upset!*

'Well, I'm not. Can you imagine the uproar, if you *had* summoned the watch, and they discovered your identity? Far better for it to be me, whose discretion you can depend upon. If you *don't* want to find out what society would say about a duchess wandering around alone on a Mayfair street, we better return you to Ashedon Place as soon as possible, before someone in a passing carriage recognises you.'

When she still resisted, a most unpalatable thought occurred. 'You...you do trust me not to harm you, don't you, Faith?'

She uttered a long, slow sigh that further tore at his heart. 'Of course, I trust you, Davie. Very well, find us a hackney. And you don't have to hang on to me. I won't bolt again.'

Without another word, she resumed walking beside him. The energy that had fuelled her flight seemed to have drained out of her; head lowered, shoulders slumping, she looked…beaten, and weary.

Good thing he had to be mindful that some *ton* notable might at any minute drive by, else he might not have been able to resist the strong impulse to pick her up and carry her. After a few more minutes of brisk walking, they arrived at a hackney stand where, fortunately, a vehicle waited. Still not entirely believing he was accompanying his Faith—no, the widowed Duchess of Ashedon, he corrected himself, never *his*—he helped her in, guiding her back on to the seat.

After rapping on the panel to signal the driver to start, Davie looked back at the Duchess. 'Are you all right? They didn't hurt you? What about your knees? You took quite a fall.' *If they had harmed her, he'd track them down and take them apart limb from limb.*

'No,' she said in a small voice. 'I was frightened, and furious; my arm got twisted, but I've nothing more than bruises. I think I landed a few good kicks, too.'

'Thank heaven for that! Before we get back to Berkeley Square, can you tell me how you ended up alone on the street at this time of night?'

'Can't you just let me return, and spare the exposition?'

He studied the outline of her profile in the light of the carriage lamps. 'I don't mean to pry. But finding you alone, practically in the middle of the night—well, it's disturbing. Something isn't right. I'd like to help fix it, if I can.'

To his further distress, the remark brought tears back to her eyes. 'Ah, Davie. You've always wanted to make things better, haven't you? Compelled to fix everything—government, Parliament, society. But this can't be fixed.'

She looked so worn and miserable, Davie ached to pull her into his arms. Nothing new about that; he'd ached to hold her since he'd first seen her, more than ten years ago. Sister-in-law of a marquess, she'd been almost as unattainable then as she was now, as the widow of a duke.

Unfortunately, that hadn't kept him from falling in love with her, or loving her all the years since.

'What happened?' he asked quietly. 'What upset you so much, you had to escape into the night?'

She remained silent, her expression not just weary, but almost…despairing. While he hesitated, torn between respecting her privacy and the compulsion to right whatever was wrong in her universe, at last, she shrugged. 'I might as well tell you, I suppose. It wasn't some stupid wager, though, if that's what you're thinking.'

'I'm sure it wasn't. You may have been high-spirited and carefree as a girl, but you were never a brainless ninny, or a daredevil.'

'Was I high-spirited and carefree? Maybe I was, once. It's been so long.'

Her dull voice and lifeless eyes ratcheted his concern up even further. Granted, these two unlikely friends had grown apart in the years since the idyllic summer they'd met, he twenty and serving his first stint as secretary to Sir Edward Greaves, she a golden-haired, sixteen-year-old sprite paying a long visit to her cousin, Sir Edward's wife. But even on the occasions he'd seen her since her marriage, her eyes had still held that warmth and joy for life that had so captured his heart the first time he set eyes on her.

'You *were* carefree,' he affirmed. 'Which makes the fact that I found you alone on the street, seeking transport home, even more troubling. What drove you to it?'

'Ever since Ashedon's death—by the way, thank you for your kind note of condolence—his mother, the Dowager Duchess, has been making noises about how she must support "the poor young Duchess and her darling boys" and see that the "tragic young Duke" receives the guidance necessary for his elevated status in life. A month ago, she made good on her threat and moved herself back into Ashedon Place. She's been wanting to do so for years, but though his mother doted on him, Ashedon knew how interfering she is and wouldn't allow it. It's enough that I must tolerate the sweetly contemptuous comments of other society matrons at all those boring, insipid evenings I've come to hate! Now, I have to live with the Dowager's carping and criticism as well, every day. Then, tonight, when I accompanied her to the party she insisted we attend, I discovered her younger son, my brother-in-law Lord Randall, was there. When he caught me alone in the hallway on my way to the ladies' retiring room and tried to force a kiss on me, I'd had enough. I knew the Dowager wasn't ready to leave, and would never believe anything derogatory about her precious son, so there was no hope of persuading her to summon the carriage. But remaining was intolerable, so I decided to walk towards Oxford Street and look for a hackney.'

She gave a little sigh, the sadness of it piercing his

heart. 'Ashedon and his doxies were bad enough, and now this. Sometimes I don't think I can bear it any longer.'

His heart ached for the gentle spirit whose girlish dreams of being loved and cherished had been slowly crushed under the heel of her husband's indifference, leaving her trapped, a lonely and neglected wife. As Davie was trapped in his place, unable to help her.

Except, always, to be a friend.

To his dismay, the tears he'd seen on her lashes earlier began to silently slip down her cheeks. Putting up a hand to try to mask them, she turned away.

And then, somehow, she was in his arms, cradled against his chest. She clung to him and he clutched her tightly, almost ready to bless the ruffians he'd rescued her from, for without that incident, the marvel of holding her would never have been his. It was a dream come true; oh, far better than any dream, to feel the softness of her pressed against him, her lavender scent filling his nostrils, her silky blonde curls under his chin. He could die right now, and be content, for he would never get any closer to heaven.

And if his body burned to possess her fully, he rebuked it. He'd never expected to have even this much bliss; he'd not ask for more.

Inevitably and all too soon, she got herself back under control, and pulled away.

Letting her go, when all he wanted was to hold her for ever, was the hardest thing he'd ever done.

'Sorry,' she said gruffly. 'Usually I'm not so poor-spirited.'

'Don't be sorry. I'm only glad I was here, to stand your friend.'

'My friend. I have few enough of those. I did try to be careful tonight, I assure you! I suppose…I suppose

I was just too tired and preoccupied, because I never noticed the two men who must have followed me. They seemed to appear out of nowhere.'

Davie shook his head with a shudder. 'I'm only glad I happened along. What they might have done to you, I don't even want to contemplate.'

She nodded. 'They threatened to take me to a brothel. Could they drag a woman there against her will, or were they just trying to frighten me?'

'I'm afraid it's quite possible. A little laudanum, and you might have awakened to find yourself locked in a room in some den of vice somewhere,' he answered grimly.

'Except for not seeing my sons again, I'm not sure I'd have cared. I thought of leaving Ashedon, oh, so many times! But I couldn't have taken my boys with me—legally, they belonged to him, of course, and Edward is the heir. Though I saw little enough of them; the Duke didn't think children should be spoiled by having their mother dote on them. Now that he's gone, I've tried to alter that, though I must continually fight against the Dowager and their tutor to do it. As long as I get to be with my boys, one way or another, I will endure it—for now, anyway.'

'Have you talked with your family, your sisters? Do they know how unhappy you are?'

She smiled wryly. 'I...I'm not that close to them any more. The Duke actively discouraged me from seeing my family at the beginning of our marriage. Silly me, I thought it was because he wanted me all to himself. Which he did, in a way. He didn't want anyone around who might interfere with his authority. So over the years, we...drifted further and further apart. As you and I did.'

He nodded. 'I'm sure they regret that as much as I do. Could you not try to re-establish ties?'

'I suppose. But there isn't anything they can do to help me, either. Most of the time I manage better.' She tried to summon a smile for him. 'It's only rarely that I feel as if I'll…burst out of my skin if I don't get away from all of it.'

'As you did tonight.'

'As I did tonight.'

He looked at her, frowning. 'At the moment, I don't have any clever ideas on how to make things better. But will you promise me something?'

'What?' she asked, tilting her head at him with an enquiring look, and instantly, he was catapulted back into the memories.

How many times that summer had she gazed up at him just like that, her eager mind probing further into whatever they were discussing—poetry, politics, agriculture? As if the whole world excited and enthralled her, and she could not learn enough about it.

Fury fired in him again to realise how much of that joy had been squeezed out of her.

Suppressing the anger, he replied, 'The next time you feel you cannot stand it a minute longer, please, don't go wandering around the streets by yourself! Send me a note; I'll meet you somewhere, anywhere, and we can talk. You're not alone, Faith. You'll never be alone, while I still draw breath. Promise me?'

She studied him for a moment. 'You mean that?'

'Of course. I never say anything I don't mean.'

She nodded, the faintest of smiles on her lips. 'Yes, I remember that about you. And how you were always a loyal friend. Very well, I promise.'

'Good,' he said, troubled still, but feeling a bit better

about her situation. 'We should be at Berkeley Square shortly, which is fortunate—especially if your mother-in-law noticed you were gone, and rushed home to find you.'

She shrugged. 'She'd probably rejoice to have me gone. Except, she'd no longer have so ready a target for her complaints.'

'You're just weary. Everything will look better in the morning, when you're rested.'

'Will it?' She smiled. 'Maybe for a man who's set out to change the world. I do hear some of what you're accomplishing, by the way, even in the wilderness of the *ton*. Not that anyone talks about it to me directly, of course—politics being too intellectually challenging for a woman. No, we are left to discuss trimming bonnets, managing servants, and perhaps, if we've very bold, speculating about who might make the best lover, or which dancer in the Green Room has become the latest mistress of which nobleman.'

He grimaced. 'There could be so much more than that! As you doubtless know, my friend Giles Hadley, Viscount Lyndlington, recently married Lady Margaret Roberts. She has played political hostess to her father, Lord Witlow, for years; not only does she understand politics, she and her father frequently bring together the best minds in government, science and art to debate all manner of topics at their "discussion evenings".'

'That sounds wonderful—and so much more stimulating that anything I get to experience. Unless...' Her dull eyes brightened. 'Did you really mean what you said, about meeting me? '

'Didn't I already answer that?'

'Then...would you meet me tomorrow afternoon? I usually drive with the Dowager during the Promenade

Hour in Hyde Park, but after tonight, I would rather not endure the hour-long lecture she will surely subject me to about my improper behaviour in leaving that wretched party. Would you meet me instead—at Gunter's, perhaps? No one we know should be there at that hour, so we won't be disturbed. I would love to hear more about what you are doing in Parliament. Perhaps I will even understand it.'

He ought to be in committee meetings, but when she looked at him with that appeal in her eyes, he'd have agreed to miss the final vote on the bill. 'Yes, I'll meet you there.'

The carriage slowed, indicating they were about to reach their destination. Davie felt a stab of disappointment; he could have ridden about London, talking with Faith, all night.

Bowing to the inevitable, he hopped out as the vehicle stopped and reached up to hand her down. 'I'll wait until you're safely inside,' he said as she descended.

'Very well.' She took a step towards the front door, then stopped, as if she couldn't quite bring herself to re-enter the Duchess's realm. Turning back to him, she went up on tiptoe and gave him a quick kiss on his jaw.

While his heart stuttered, then raced in his chest, she said, 'Thank you, Davie. For your rescue, and much more. For the first time in a long time, I have a "tomorrow" I can look forward to.'

*As did he*, he thought as she ran up the steps. The privilege of escorting her about probably wouldn't last long. He intended to relish every second.

# *Chapter Two*

The following afternoon, after dispatching a note to her mother-in-law, a late riser who had not yet left her rooms, informing her a previous engagement would prevent her driving to the Park, Faith let her maid put the finishing touches to her coiffure. 'There, *madame*,' Yvette said, her eyes shining with pride. 'Who could find fault with such an angel?'

'A great many,' Faith muttered. But knowing the soft-hearted girl was only trying to encourage her, she gave her a smile. 'The new arrangement is lovely. Have you a name for it?'

'Trône de la Reine,' the maid replied. 'And *comme ça accord, madame*!'

'Thank you. I shall be the loveliest lady present.' Thankfully, not at the Park, Faith added silently as she descended to the hackney the butler had summoned, her spirits buoyed by knowing she'd not have to grit her teeth while the Dowager recited the long litany of offences she'd committed last night. Instead, anticipation rising at the thought, she would have Davie to talk to.

She'd missed the company of the young man to whom she'd grown even closer than she was to her sisters during the time she'd spent as a guest of her cousin, stretching a visit planned for a month into a summer-long idyll. His calm counsel, his stimulating ideas and his zeal to create a better future had inspired and excited her. Truth to tell, she'd fancied herself a bit in love with him by the time she'd been summoned home to prepare for her upcoming Season.

Only too aware that he was no fitting match for a daughter of one of the oldest families in England, she'd nonetheless hoped she might share with him some of her thoughts and observations of London, but he'd remained at Oxford during her Season. Instead, mesmerised by the Duke's assiduous and flattering attentions, envied by every other unmarried female on the Marriage Mart and their resentful mamas, she'd allowed herself to believe she'd fallen as much in love with her noble suitor as he had with her.

Why had she never noticed how cold and calculating his eyes were, compared to the warmth and compassion in Davie's?

Far too late to regret that now.

With a sigh, Faith let the footman hand her into the carriage. Glancing back towards the shuttered windows of the town house, she felt a pang of foreboding. She was likely to draw enough fire for not attending her mother-in-law's daily ride through the Park; were the woman to learn Faith missed that important event to associate with a man so far beneath her station, she'd be harangued for a month.

Still, it was time to wrench herself out of the influence of her mother-in-law and the misery that evoked. The Dowager had no real control over her; without the dictates of a husband to prevent it, she could involve herself more in the wider world.

Just talking with Davie, she knew, would help her do that. With each street that brought their rendezvous closer, her excitement and anticipation grew.

At last the carriage arrived, Faith so impatient she could hardly wait for the vehicle to stop before climbing down and hurrying into the establishment. She spotted Davie immediately, seated in an alcove on the far side of the room. The appreciation on his face as she approached his table made her glad she'd decided to wear the new grey gown that flattered her figure and showed her complexion to advantage.

'Duchess, what a pleasant surprise,' he said, rising and giving her a bow. 'How lovely you look!'

'How kind you are, Mr Smith,' she replied. 'Though as a mother of three, I'm afraid I've lost the bloom of youth you probably remember.'

'Nonsense, it would take more than a brace of boys to erase that,' he replied, helping her to a seat. 'Tea? Or would you prefer ices?'

'Tea, please.'

After sending the waiter off for refreshments, he looked back to study her.

'You do look rested. Truly fresh as a young girl, and not at all like the venerable mother of three.'

She laughed. 'I'd hoped for more children, but with three boys making the succession secure, Ashedon… lost interest.' *Or had he kept mistresses all along, and she'd just been too stupid to notice?* 'Somehow, growing up with a brother and all those sisters, I expected when I had a family of my own, I'd be surrounded by children. But as their mother, I spend much of the day in my world, and they in the nursery, in theirs.'

Davie chuckled. 'Unlike growing up in a farm family, where the children are underfoot all day, learning from their mamas or doing chores for their papas. Close even at night, stuffed as they are in the loft just above the main room, like sausage in a casing! Maybe you should have been a simple farmer's wife.'

'Maybe I should have.'

She looked up into his eyes, those kind eyes she remembered so well—and suddenly, saw a flash of heat there, so intense and sudden it shook her.

It shook her even more to feel an answering heat from deep within. Suddenly she was brought back to last night, where despite her fatigue and misery, she'd been intensely aware of being held against his chest.

His broad, solid chest. The tall, rangy youth she'd known had grown into a tall, well-muscled, physically impressive man. Not fitting the wasp-waisted, whip-thin dandy profile now so popular among society's gentlemen, he was instead big, sturdy, and solid, built more like a…a medieval knight, or a boxer. Strong, powerful, and imposing.

For a time, while he held her, she'd felt—safe, and at peace. If she were still the naïve and trusting girl she'd once been, she might even have said 'cherished'.

But that was merely an illusion born of need and wishful thinking.

Still, she hadn't mistaken the desire she'd just seen in his eyes before he masked it, nor the physical response he evoked in her. That unexpected attraction would… complicate a renewal of their friendship, yet at the same time, she was fiercely glad of it. The realisation that he wanted her was a balm to her battered self-esteem, reviving a sense she'd nearly lost of herself as a desirable woman.

She cleared her throat nervously. Welcome as it was,

the unexpected sensual tension humming between them was so unexpected, and she had so little experience dealing with it, she felt suddenly awkward. 'Thank you for meeting me,' she said at last. 'I was so relieved not to have to ride in the Park today and feel all those eyes on me, while the Dowager harangued.'

'I suppose that's the price of being a Duchess. You will always be the focus of attention, wherever you go and whatever you do.'

She wrinkled her nose. 'Yes, and it's so distasteful. I don't know why that fact didn't occur to me before I wed a duke, but it didn't. I've never enjoyed the attention.' She sighed. 'Especially as Ashedon and his women provided so much scandal for society to watch my reaction to.'

His jaw tightened and a fierce look came over his face before he burst out, 'Your husband was a fool! Even if I shouldn't say it.'

Gratified, she smiled sadly. 'I didn't mind him being a fool. I just minded that he never loved me. But I didn't come today to whine about poor, neglected little me. I want to hear about something of real importance. Tell me of your work! I always hoped we would maintain our friendship, but after the wedding, and with you at Oxford...I do know that, with Sir Edward and my cousin Nicky's support, you were elected MP from Hazelwick shortly after leaving university. And I seem to remember something about "Hadley's Hellions"? What was that?'

He chuckled. 'Fortunately for a commoner like me, I met Giles Hadley soon after arriving at Oxford. As I imagine you know, although he's Viscount Lyndlington, until very recently he'd been estranged from his father, the earl. After growing up in an isolated cottage, he didn't form friendships with anyone from the *ton*, bonding instead when he was sent to Eton with other outsiders—Ben Tawny, the natural son of Viscount Chilford, and Christopher Lattimar, son of Lord Vraux.

'That name I do know,' she said. 'One of the "Vraux Miscellany", siblings supposedly all fathered by different men?'

Davie nodded. 'With those backgrounds, you can understand why all of them felt that society and government needed reforming, with the power to change not left in the tight-fisted hands of a few whose only qualification for the job was that their families had always held it.'

'A view of reform you always supported,' she inserted, recalling their spirited discussions of government and politics that long-ago summer.

'I did. When Giles stumbled upon me, reading alone in one of the pubs, he immediately drew me into his circle. First, out of kindness for a commoner whom he knew would never be invited into any of the aristocratic groups. But once we began discussing what we hoped to accomplish once we left university, we soon discovered we aspired to the same goals.'

'And those aspirations, in the eyes of the powerful, were enough for you to be labelled hellions?' she guessed.

'They were bad enough, but we didn't win that label until some of the dons, churchmen all, discovered we aimed to eliminate the clergy's seats in the Lords. An intention, they felt, that could only have been inspired by the devil.'

She tilted her head at him. 'Was it only that? Or was the name partly earned for exploits more scandalous than you care to mention to my innocent ears?'

Had he been a hellion? A little thrill went through her as she studied him from under the cover of her lashes.

He was certainly virile enough to excite a woman's desire. Had he cut a swathe through the ladies of Oxford?

She found herself feeling jealous of any female he'd favoured with his amorous attentions.

'Having served with the army in India,' his words recalled her, 'Ben was something of a rabble-rouser, and Christopher was always a favourite with the ladies. Giles and I generally didn't have enough blunt to kick up too many larks, one of the reasons we pooled our resources and began rooming together early on. We helped each other, too, once it came time to campaign. As you may know, your brother-in-law, the Marquess, gave me his generous support when I stood for the seat under Sir Edward's control in Hazelwick, for which I'm grateful.'

'How could Nicky, or anyone else, listen to you explain your views, and not be persuaded? You certainly convinced me that summer! How close are you to accomplishing your aims?'

'A new Parliament convened in June, filled overwhelmingly with supporters of reform. We're very hopeful that by later this autumn, we'll finally get a bill passed.' He gave her a wry grimace. 'There are still recalcitrants who seek to delay us by bringing up an endless series of irrelevant discussions. Sometimes I'd like to knock a few heads together in the committee room, like I did last night on the street!'

'You were certainly effective there!' she declared, shuddering a little as she recalled how close to disaster she'd come. 'So there will be a change in the way the country is governed, for the first time since the medieval era? How exciting!'

'It is exciting, to know you can influence the governance of the nation.'

She gave a wry smile. 'I have enough difficulty exerting influence in the mundane matters of everyday life.'

'As duchess? Surely not!'

She hesitated, tempted to continue, though she really shouldn't confide in him. She'd had to struggle these last miserable years to transform the open, plain-spoken girl she'd once been into a woman who kept her own counsel. But the warmth of his regard, and that inexplicable sense of connection that seemed to have survived the years they'd been apart, pulled at her.

How long had it been since she'd had anyone to talk to, anyone who truly cared about her feelings or her needs?

Compelled by some force she didn't seem able to resist, she explained, 'Ashedon's housekeeper has been there since his mother's day, and is ferociously competent. Since my husband supported her authority, I barely had more to do than arrange flowers and approve menus. Now that my mother-in-law has returned to Ashedon Place, challenging Mrs West's years of unopposed domination, the two are in a constant battle for control, a struggle that frequently traps me in the middle.' She sighed. 'And then, there's the boys.'

'Your sons? Is your mother-in-law trying to take them over, too?' he guessed. 'How difficult that must be for you.' Almost absently, he put his hand over hers, giving her fingers a reassuring squeeze. 'But as their mother, you must make sure your will prevails.'

She ought to remove her hand. But that simple touch evoked such a powerful surge of emotion—gratitude for his compassion, relief at his understanding, and a heady wave of sensual awareness that intensified that sense of connection. She could no more make herself pull away than she could march back home and evict the Dowager.

'I am *trying*,' she said, savouring the titillating, forbidden feel of her hand enclosed in his. 'As I told you before, the Duke didn't consider it proper for his Duchess to hang about the nursery, an impediment to Nurse and the maids going about their duties.' She gave him a wry smile. 'I was reduced to visiting at night, tiptoeing past the sleeping maid to sit at the foot of their beds and study their little faces in the darkness. Since Ashedon's death, I've worked to find ways to spend more time with them, but I've had to fight Carlisle, the tutor Ashedon installed, at every turn. My increased involvement with the boys was the first thing the Dowager criticised when she invaded us. I've held my ground—the first and only time I've defied her—but she reinforces Carlisle as much as she can, making it as difficult as possible.'

'Bravo for resisting her! That can't have been pleasant. Now you just need to figure out better ways to get round the tutor.'

'Yes. And to keep the boys away from their uncle—an even worse example of manhood than my late husband, which is the truth, even if it's not kind of me to say so.' She grimaced, remembering the feel of Lord Randall's hands biting into her shoulders as he tried to force her into that kiss. 'Since his mother has taken up residence, he seems to think he can drop in whenever he wishes, usually to dine, or to borrow money from his mother. One of the few things Ashedon and I agreed on was that his brother is a wastrel who will spend as much of the family fortune as he can get his hands on.'

'Then you definitely need to get the boys away more. There are so many places they might enjoy—the British Museum, riding in the parks, Astley's Amphitheatre— even Parliament.' He lifted a brow at her. 'The young Duke will take his place in the Lords there, some day.'

'Ready to persuade him to join your coalition?' she teased, immeasurably cheered by his sympathetic support.

'It's never too early to start.' Smiling, he raised her hand, as if to kiss it. And only then seemed to realise he'd been holding it.

He sucked in a breath as he looked down at their joined hands, then up to meet her gaze, and his grip tightened. In an instant, a touch meant to offer comfort transformed into something more primal, as heat and light blazed between them, palpable as the flash of lightning, the rumble of thunder before a storm.

In his eyes blazed the same passion she'd glimpsed earlier. The same passion she felt, building in a slow conflagration from her core outward. Struck as motionless as he, she could only cling to his fingers, relishing every atom of that tiny bit of contact between them.

Slowly, as if he found it as difficult to break the connection as she had earlier, his grip eased and he let her go. His ardent expression turned troubled, and for a moment, she was terribly afraid he would apologise.

Which would be beyond enduring, since she wasn't sorry at all.

He opened his lips and hesitated, as if searching for words. Watching his mouth, her mind obsessed by imagining the feel of it against hers, she was incapable of finding any herself.

At last, he cleared his throat. 'Perhaps you could take your sons to call on your sister, Lady Englemere? She's in town with the Marquess for Parliament, I expect. Let the boys become better acquainted with their cousins?'

He looked back down at their now separate hands as he spoke, as if he regretted as much as she did the need to break that link between them.

Forcing her attention back to his words, she replied, 'At the moment, they aren't acquainted at all. I don't even know if Sarah is in London; she may still be in the country.' Faith grimaced. 'Lucky her. The thing I've hated most about life as a duchess is being trapped in London, far from the "unfashionable" countryside Ashedon despised and I love so much.'

Davie nodded. 'I seem to remember a penchant for riding in breeches and climbing trees.'

That observation brought her a smile. 'Yes. We used to climb that big elm in Cousin Joanna's garden, and I'd read you poetry. There were a few early-morning races on horseback, too, I recall, before Joanna found out and made me ride at a more decorous pace, on side-saddle.' Nostalgia for that carefree past welled up. 'How I miss those days,' she said softly.

'Avoid looking back by building something better to look forward to,' Davie advised quietly.

She glanced back at him, seeing sympathy overlay the passion in his eyes. 'Like you are doing for the nation.'

'Like you can do for yourself. You are free now, Faith. Free to remake the future as *you* choose.'

And what would she choose, if she *were* completely free? Desire resurged, strong and urgent. *What if I said I wanted you, now?*

But of course, she did not say that. 'I may be *freer*,' she replied. 'But with the Dowager, and my sons' futures to protect, I'll never truly be free of the shadow of being Duchess. Never truly free to choose *only* what I want.'

She gazed at him, willing him to understand what she could not say. Perhaps he did, for his face shuttered, masking whatever response her answer aroused in him.

'Then, as in Parliament, you must strike the best deal

you can get with the opposition, so all can move forward. Speaking of which, I'm afraid I must get back.'

A sharp pang of regret made her want to protest. Suppressing it, she said, 'Of course. You have important work waiting. Which just reinforces how trivial my little problems are. How I wish I could observe you making those real, significant changes!'

'There's nothing more important to the future of the nation than you raising your boys properly! But if you *would* be interested in hearing some conversation about the Reform Bill, Lady Lyndlington still plays hostess for her father. I'm sure she would be delighted to include you in one of their discussion evenings. With it being hosted by a marquess, I don't think the Dowager could object to your attending. Shall I ask Lady Lyndlington to send you an invitation?'

Oh, to spend an evening where people talked about important ideas, where, among statesmen and diplomats, a mere society female whose opinions were of little value would be ignored. Where she'd be able to sit quietly and just observe. And escape, for an evening, all the petty problems that pricked at her daily.

'It sounds fascinating, but...would you be there, too? It would be rather intimidating to attend such a gathering of intellectuals, having only a slight acquaintance with all those present.'

'I'm sure you'll have met most of them at various society gatherings. But, yes, if it would make you feel easier, I could make sure I'm invited as well.'

'Then, I should love it! If you're certain Lady Lyndlington wouldn't find it impertinent of me to request an invitation? I've met her, of course, but could hardly claim to call her a friend.'

'I imagine she would be delighted of your company,

but I will ask. Now, we should probably be getting you back as well. Shall I send you a note after I've spoken to Lady Lyndlington?'

Glancing over at the clock, Faith noticed to her surprise that they had been chatting for some time. 'Yes, I should go, too. I'd prefer to already be at home before my mother-in-law returns from the Park, and the inquisition begins.'

Hating to bring their time together to an end, Faith made herself rise. 'How can I ever thank you enough? Rescuing me not once, but twice, and then offering the promise of a stimulating evening.'

'It would give me the greatest delight to stimulate you.'

Her eyes flew to his face, and though it coloured a little at the blatant *double entendre*, he didn't apologise, nor did he retract the remark. Instead, he simply looked at her, giving her another glimpse of heat before masking his gaze.

Arousal returned in a rush. How easily she could imagine the delight his 'stimulation' would bring her!

She wanted to reply in kind, to make clear she understood and shared his desire. But so inexperienced was she in flirtation, before she could come up with some cleverly suggestive remark, he said, 'I hope you'll enjoy a political evening at Lord Witlow's even half as much as I have enjoyed this conversation. I'll send you a note as soon as I've spoken with Lady Lyndlington.'

She suppressed a sigh, irritated that she'd let the opportunity slip. Accepting his redirection of the conversation back into proper channels, she said, 'Thank you again. I've enjoyed our conversation, too. We mustn't let our friendship lapse again, must we?'

Friendship...and perhaps more? He offered his arm,

and she took it, a little surge of energy flashing between them the instant her fingers touched him. As he escorted her out, she was once again intensely aware of his virile presence beside her, the strength, confidence and sense of purpose that seemed to radiate from him.

Ah, yes, her Davie had grown up, and the man he'd become fascinated—and attracted—her. Regardless of the potential danger of that attraction and the possible objections from her mother-in-law about being in his company, she couldn't wait to spend more time with him.

# *Chapter Three*

After seeing the Duchess safely off in a hackney, Davie started walking. He *should* go back to the committee room, but after spending time with Faith, he was too energised, excited—and aroused—to be able to recapture yet the calm and imperturbable mask he wore when doing political work.

And partly, he admitted to himself, he wanted to savour the rare experience of spending time with her. Let himself linger and recall each moment, like a collector taking a precious object out of a treasure box, to admire and examine again and again.

As a girl, she'd glowed with an infectious joy in life that drew people to her, like an inn's beacon attracts travellers on a cold, dark night. He recalled her fixing that warm, intense gaze on him while he spoke, as if he were the most fascinating individual in the universe. To feel like the sole focus of attention of so beautiful and intelligent a girl—small wonder he'd tumbled head over heels.

It hurt his heart to see how sadness had dimmed that glow. But though the fire might have burned low, embers remained. He felt compelled to give her the encour-

agement and opportunities that would fan those sparks
to a blaze again.

Just this one short meeting proved to him it was possible. Offered his understanding and support, and the
prospect of an evening away from her usual society
duties, she had unconsciously straightened, her expression brighter, her smile warmer, while in her eyes, a
guarded enthusiasm grew.

He couldn't wait to see that progress continue, when
she actually attended such a gathering.

He shouldn't have made that remark about 'stimulating' her, though the desire coursing through him had
been too strong for him to rescind it, inappropriate as it
was. She'd been lovely enough, swaddled in her cape in
the dimness of lamplight last night; upon seeing her in
full daylight, in that grey gown that accented her curves
and brought out the brilliance of her blue eyes, he would
have to have been made of stone not to have wanted her
more than ever. The slender beauty he'd loved for so long
had grown into a powerfully alluring woman.

Though she'd not known how to reply to his suggestive remark, she hadn't rebuffed him. Quite the contrary;
leaning closer, her lips parting slightly, her gaze heating, he had read in her response that the passion he felt
was reciprocated.

Probably not with the same intensity, he conceded.
Still, he couldn't help feeling a primal masculine satisfaction upon discovering that the lady he prized above
all others found him attractive, both as a friend and as
a man. But knowing that she would welcome his touch
would also make it harder to hold under control a body
already ravenous to taste her.

Because that absolutely could not happen. An affair
between two individuals from such radically different

levels of society was too delicious a piece of gossip not to eventually become known, no matter how careful they were about meeting. Much as he wanted her, he loved her more. He would not tarnish her honour—or his—with an affair that would make her the target of the malicious, or give her mother-in-law further reason to disparage her or question her fitness to bring up her sons.

Besides, an affair would never be enough for him. Having all of her for a time and then being forced to give her up would be unendurable.

Better to live with the ache he knew, re-establish their friendship, and use that position to enrich her life as best he could. Even if she would never be his, he wanted her to be happy.

Still not ready to return to the committee room, where he would have to banish Faith's image and the memories of today's meeting, he considered going back to Albany to write Lady Lyndlington a note. But then he'd have to wait upon her reply before he could communicate with Faith, and he didn't want to wait.

Why not call upon his friend's wife now? She would most likely be either at her town house in Upper Brook Street, or her father's home in Cavendish Square.

Energised by the prospect of being able to move forward his scheme, Davie hurried to the hackney stand and engaged a jarvey to take him to Upper Brook Street.

To his relief, Lady Lyndlington was at home, although the butler informed him this wasn't a day when she would normally receive guests. Insisting that he was close enough a friend of the master for that restriction not to apply to him, he persuaded the butler to convey him to the Blue Salon and to enquire whether her lady-ship could spare him a few minutes.

Davie paced the parlour, too agitated to sit. He was certain his friend's wife would take the Duchess under her wing, and impatient to learn when they could begin.

'Davie, what a pleasant surprise,' Lady Lyndlington said as she walked in, giving him her hands to kiss. 'That is, everything is all right? Giles hasn't suffered any injury—'

'No, no, Giles is fine! I'm sorry if my sudden appearance worried you, Maggie. It's just, I had a favour to ask, and since I was out, rather than send you a note, I thought I'd try to catch you at home and deliver the request in person.'

Her worried countenance relaxed as she waved him to a seat. 'If it's within my power, I would be happy to grant it. What do you need?'

'I recently ran into—almost literally—an old friend. Faith Wellingford—you would know her as the Duchess of Ashedon.'

'The Duchess? I didn't know you were acquainted!'

'She's a cousin of my sponsor's wife. We developed a friendship many years ago, when I first began working as secretary to Sir Edward, and she was visiting her cousin. We grew to be close, though of course, there was never any question of a warmer relationship between us. I've only seen her a few times since her marriage, and we've grown apart. But upon meeting her again, I was struck by how…unhappy she is.'

'Having been married to Ashedon, I'm not surprised,' Maggie said bluntly.

'She wanted to know what I'd been doing, so I told her a bit about the Reform Bill. We used to have quite spirited discussions of politics. She seemed so intrigued, I asked if she would like to attend one of your political dinners. She was quite enthused by the idea, so I said I would approach you to ask for an invitation.'

'Of course I will include her, if you think she would enjoy it.'

'She has a lively mind, which apparently doesn't get much use during her usual society functions. I do believe she would enjoy the debate.'

'I will send her a card, then. And you, of course.'

'Thank you, Maggie. I'll be very grateful.'

Davie's mind immediately moved to evaluating options for conveying the news to Faith. Should he send a note, asking her to meet him? Or just write, letting her know that an invitation from Maggie would be forthcoming?

Meeting her, of course, would be his preference, but...

'How long have you loved her?' Maggie's quiet voice interrupted his racing thoughts.

Shocked, he jerked his gaze back, to find her regarding him, sympathy in her eyes. He considered for an instant returning a denial, but as she had just granted his rather odd request for help, there seemed little point in dissembling. 'Since the moment I set eyes on her, I suppose,' he admitted. 'Is it so obvious?'

'Probably not, unless one already suspected it.' She smiled. 'Leaving aside the fact that you seemed to be unusually concerned about the well-being of a lady who was merely a friend from long ago, your whole face lights up when you talk about her. There's this intensity in your eyes, and an urgency in your words.'

He sighed. 'I've been avoiding going back to the committee room for that very reason, suspecting I might not be able to hide that I'd seen her again. I'll tell Giles privately, but the last thing I want is for Ben or Christopher to find out. They've harassed me enough over the years about my obsession with the "Unattainable One".'

'They all know about her?'

'At some point, I had to explain why I was always turning Ben and Christopher down when they wanted to go carousing, or when Christopher offered to have his current lady find a friend for me.'

She nodded. 'Better to remain alone, than be disappointed in yourself and your partner, when she can't compare to your lady.'

'Exactly!' he cried, surprised and gratified to discover someone who understood. 'No one else *can* compare. Coming upon her again unexpectedly, the difference was…shocking. As if I'd been living in a grey world under cloudy skies, and suddenly, the sun came out, painting everything with vivid colour. Not that I've found my life dull or purposeless up till now, I assure you. But she just makes things…different. More beautiful.'

'I know. I lived in just such a dull world—before I found Giles to illumine it.'

He gave a rueful sigh. 'Ben and Christopher keep insisting that if I really wanted to, I could forget her and turn my attention to someone more suitable. But just because one knows one can't have something, that doesn't mean one can make oneself stop wanting it.'

'I know. I am sorry.'

'Don't be. Loving her is an old ache, and I've known from the beginning that nothing could ever come from it. A penniless farmer's orphan does not marry the well-dowered daughter of a family whose ancestors came over with the Conquest.'

'And why should the daughter of an ancient family

be valued any higher than a commoner who, by his own efforts, has risen to a position of power?'

He smiled at her. 'That sounds like Lord Grey and the Friends of the People. Has Giles been converting you?'

'I should hope I always appreciate individuals for what they themselves accomplish, not for their pedigree. However, you…you do not intend to attempt more than rekindling a friendship, do you?'

He didn't pretend not to understand her. 'No. I wouldn't tarnish her honour—or mine—by attempting an affair. Goodness knows, nothing more is possible.'

She sighed. 'It makes me sound a terrible snob, after just stating how much I value you—and I do, you are worth ten of her wretched Duke!—I have to agree. Hadley's Hellions are doing their best to make the world a more equitable place, but we are nowhere close to being a society that would react to a duchess's remarriage to a commoner with anything but shock and derision. Not so much for you, of course. But for her… I never had any desire to move in the late Duke's circle, but like most of society, I heard enough of his exploits—and the falsely sweet "sympathy" expressed for his "poor little Duchess". She's suffered enough. I'd not be a party to anything that would bring more scorn upon her, or result in her permanent banishment from society.'

'I assure you, all I wish is to offer her is the chance to meet other individuals from her own rank, whose company she may find more interesting and fulfilling than the endless rounds of idle society parties she told me she's come to hate.'

'With all the snide remarks her husband's infidelities must have forced her to endure, I can understand why she detests them. Just promise me you won't complicate her situation. She has already had enough to bear, married to Ashedon all those years.'

'That's an easy promise to give. I want to lighten her burden, not make it heavier.'

'In that case, I shall be delighted to include her in the dinner I'm planning for next Friday. Giles and Papa are assembling some men of less radical views, with the hope of building a moderate coalition that will see the Reform Bill passed more swiftly. I'll send her a card. And one to you as well.'

'Thank you, Maggie. I very much appreciate it. I think you'll like the Duchess, and I know she will enjoy your gathering.'

'I hope you will as well.' She looked at him, her face troubled. 'You did me a very good turn once, bringing me back to the man I loved. I only wish I could conjure a magic spell, so I might create as favourable a result for you.'

'Helping Faith is the best thing you can do for me.'

'I'll do all I can.' She walked him to the door, halting on the threshold to give him a kiss on the cheek. 'Have a care for yourself, too, Davie. As I know only too well, hearts can break more than once.'

'But only once for the same person,' he replied, and walked out.

He certainly hoped so, anyway.

In the afternoon two days later, having received a note from Davie informing her that Lady Lyndlington would be sending her a card of invitation for a dinner the following Friday, Faith ordered a hackney and went to pay a call on her erstwhile hostess. She'd suffered the expected dressing-down from the Dowager over her dinner-party flight—and her absence from the obligatory drive in the Park the next day—in a silence meek enough not to call down more criticism on her head. She felt safe enough attempting this errand; as Davie had said, even the high-in-the-instep Dowager couldn't fault her calling on the daughter of a marquess.

Knowing how persuasive Davie the politician could be, she wanted to assure herself that Lady Lyndlington truly wished to include her in the gathering...and to discover whether she would feel comfortable enough with her hostess to want to attend.

In the early years of their marriage, Ashedon had done a very effective job in isolating her, distancing her from her family while at the same time actively discouraging her developing friendships with anyone else. At the time, still radiantly in love and certain of his love in return, she'd been too preoccupied trying to learn the duties required of the mistress of numerous properties and a multitude of servants, then waylaid by a succession of pregnancies and the delight of newborns, to fully realise just how alone she'd become.

But as the boys grew and her husband's attentions dwindled, she'd become only too aware that she had virtually no friends of her age and class. The society women in whose company she often found herself all seemed to have already established circles of friendship, which were not interested in admitting any newcomers. And even if they had, most of the members were either indifferent to or contemptuous of the country life and activities that she prized so much more highly than the idle amusements of London.

She could tell that Davie admired Lady Lyndlington, and she valued his opinion. But a man's view of a woman could be very different from one woman's view of another. Would this marquess's daughter, with her superior intellect and expertise in politics, hide beneath polite words the same contemptuous pity for simple little Faith Wellingford that made her association with other sophisticated ladies of the *ton* so unpleasant?

The carriage slowed to a halt, the footman coming over to open the door and hand her down. Heading to the front steps of the Upper Brook Street town house, Faith took a deep breath, suppressing out of long habit a too-often disappointed hope. One way or another, she was about to find out.

The butler showed her into an elegant room done in the Adam style in shades of white and blue. Several bookcases stood against one wall, filled with a variety of volumes. Perusing the shelves to discover several plays and novels she had enjoyed, Faith felt a renewal of the hope she'd tried to squelch.

Perhaps Lady Lyndlington might be someone of similar interests after all.

A moment later, the lady herself entered. 'Duchess, how kind of you to call! I do hope you didn't do so to convey your regrets for the Friday night gathering! I'm very much looking forward to becoming better acquainted. Davie—Mr Smith—is my husband's closest friend, and we both have a very high regard for him— and for anyone of whom he speaks with as much warmth and respect as he did of you.'

'He is very kind.'

'Indeed. Would you take tea?'

'If I wouldn't be imposing, or taking you away from other duties.'

'Not at all. I should like it very much.'

*As would I*, Faith thought, her cautious optimism increasing as her hostess rang the bell pull and informed the butler to bring refreshments. She'd spoken briefly with Lady Lyndlington at several society balls, among a crush of other attendees, but meeting her here in her own parlour, she was immediately drawn by her warm, open friendliness.

She'd already seen enough to decide she could safely accept the dinner invitation. She'd try not to hope for more.

'I understand you've known Mr Smith since you were very young,' her hostess said as she took a seat on the sofa.

'Yes, before I even made my come-out. I was spending the summer with my cousin, and Mr Smith had come to serve as secretary to her husband.' Faith gestured to the bookshelves. 'After dinner one night, we found ourselves both in the library, searching for a book. Which led to a discussion about favourite authors that lasted the rest of the evening. After that, we met in the afternoons when he'd finished his work, and talked or rode. I'd read him poetry; he'd tell me about history and politics and his plans for the future—to become a parliamentarian, and help to change the government of the nation. He was so…intelligent, and caring, and full of conviction! I'd never met anyone like him.'

Lady Lyndlington smiled. 'It sounds as if he hasn't changed very much. He's still intelligent, caring and full of conviction.'

*He's changed in one way*, Faith thought, conversation lapsing as the butler brought in the tea tray. *The romantic young hero has become a compellingly attractive man.*

'Yes, he seems much the same as I remember,' she continued after Lady Lyndlington handed her a cup. 'Foolishly, I suppose, I expected we would maintain our friendship over the years. But of course, once I married and he began his career we…didn't see each other very often.'

'I expect not. Running such a large household, a duchess must have many duties.'

Declining to correct that erroneous assumption, she said, 'Mr Smith tells me that you've managed your father's household for years, and arrange his political dinners. How fascinating it must be, to literally have a seat at the table of power as matters of national interest are discussed!'

Lady Lyndlington laughed. 'Along with a smattering of gossip and personal anecdotes. But you are right; it *is* stimulating. Not that I did anything special to deserve being so blessed, other than having the good fortune to be born my father's daughter. I do hope you will find the evening enjoyable.'

'I'm sure I shall! I expect to do no more than listen, which I hope will be acceptable. What's the old saying— 'Better to be silent and be thought foolish, than to speak and remove all doubt'? I shall refrain from displaying my ignorance!'

'Listening to the discussions, you will soon have a fairly accurate picture of what's transpiring. Please, feel free to ask questions! Coming into the debates with no preconceived ideas, you will have a fresh perspective that could be most helpful.'

'Well, I don't know about that, but I shall certainly listen most carefully.'

'The discussions often become quite lively—and I hope they will be, for there's no cards, or singing, or other entertainment. I would hate to bore you on your very first evening with us.'

'I don't care at all for gaming, and I shall be quite content to listen to intelligent discussion of issues that matter, rather than the snide, biting comments that so often form much of the conversation.' She shrugged. 'Perhaps because I have been so often the subject of them.'

Lady Lyndlington frowned. 'Surely people are not disrespectful to a duchess!'

'Oh, no, they are obsequious—to my face.' Perhaps it was the ready sympathy she read in the other woman's expression, but once she'd started, Faith couldn't seem to keep herself from adding bitterly, 'But I often "overhear" comments made, I'm sure, deliberately just within my hearing. About what a poor little dab of a thing I am, how it's no wonder, after getting his heirs on me, my husband looked elsewhere. And now that my mother-in-law has moved back in, I am treated daily to a recital of all the ways in which I fall short of being worthy of the high position I occupy.'

'I feel so fortunate in my family, who have supported me through the worst of times!' Lady Lyndlington shook her head. 'I'm so sorry you haven't experienced that, and I wish I could protest that most in society are kind. But as I know only too well, many are not.'

Faith grimaced. 'They seem to assume I don't have the wit, or the courage, to toss back some biting response. I *could* answer in kind. I just don't want to. Isn't there enough heartache and cruelty in the world, without deliberately adding to it?'

Impulsively, her hostess seized her hand. 'I so agree! And I understand more than you know. Before I met Giles, after being a widow for several years, I began to think about remarrying. I'd been acting as Papa's hostess for some time, and had a number of interested suitors. Sadly, having married my childhood best friend, I was completely naïve, never questioning that the admiration a man expressed might be due more to my wealth and family connections than to the charms of my person.'

'Now that, I cannot believe!' Faith protested.

'Believe it,' Lady Lyndlington said with surprising bitterness. 'One particularly ardent suitor, who had political aspirations my father's support could assist, convinced me of his love, and I persuaded myself I returned his regard. Just before we were to wed, I discovered that he maintained a little love-nest where he continued to entertain *chère-amies*. Apparently I was the only one in London who didn't know about it. I broke the engagement, but you can imagine the titters behind fans and malicious comments I "overheard". But you may know this already; it was quite the *on dit*.'

Hardly believing so lovely, confident, and intelligent a lady could have been subject to such treatment, Faith said, 'I didn't know. So you truly do understand.'

'Yes. By the way, I did, quite inadvertently, discover a way to respond to the malicious that did not require descending to the same level as the speaker. Soon after the…incident, I overhead a comment that so infuriated me, I couldn't utter a word. I simply turned and stared at the perpetrator, as if she were a worm I'd discovered on one of my prize roses and intended to crush. She ended up looking away first, and never bothered me again. The technique worked so well, I used it on several other occasions during that awful time, to good effect.' She patted Faith's hand. 'I recommend the tactic.'

Faith had to smile. 'As a marquess's daughter, you were probably born to it, but I doubt I could manage the "look". Papa lost all our money when I was still so young, I grew up with no expectations of making a grand match, more comfortable climbing trees and riding in my brother's old breeches than mastering curtsies and clever drawing-room conversation. But thank you. I'm sure I'll have occasions I could try out the technique, whether or not I can carry it off.'

Lady Lyndlington nodded. 'Practise it in front of your glass. I did.'

At the idea of this elegant lady practising set-down looks in a mirror, Faith had to laugh out loud. 'No! I don't believe it!'

'Oh, it's true. I'd remember the remark that so incensed me, and look into the mirror until I perfected an expression that should have made the glass shatter and vaporise into dust. You must try it.'

Subsiding with a giggle, Faith set aside her cup. 'Perhaps I will. But now, I've taken up enough of your time.'

She rose, and her hostess rose with her. 'You will come to dinner on Friday?'

'Yes. I shall be looking forward to it.'

'Excellent. I think we should be friends. After all, we principled ladies must stick together.'

Drinking in the warmth and encouragement like a wilted plant responds to water, Faith could almost feel her withered optimism and trampled hope begin to stir. 'That would please me very much.'

'Until Friday, then.'

After an exchange of curtsies, the ladies parted, Faith returning to her carriage with more anticipation for the future than she'd felt in years

Bless Davie! Not only had he given her a stimulating evening to look forward to, he might have steered her towards something she hadn't had since she'd been distanced from her sisters.

A close female friend.

If only she could keep them both.

## *Chapter Four*

On Friday night, Davie arrived early at Lord Witlow's town house, already so energised at the idea of seeing Faith again, he'd been more or less worthless in committee that afternoon. Once or twice he'd seen Giles send an appraising look in his direction, from which he'd turned away without acknowledgement. But, arriving as far in advance of the appointed hour, he knew that sooner or later his hostess's husband was going to take him to task.

Lord Witlow's butler showed him to the Blue Drawing Room, remarking with a touch of reproach as he directed him to the wine decanter on the sideboard, that, it being so far in advance of the hour for dinner, the host and hostess had not yet come down. Chuckling at that veiled set-down about his poor manners, Davie began pacing the handsome chamber, trying to dispel some of his nervous excitement and anticipation.

As luck would have it, the first to join him in the drawing room was Giles. The look of enquiry on his friend's face told him that he was about to be taken to task for his renewed interest in 'the Unattainable'.

Considering that he'd volunteered a few judicious words of caution to his mostly unappreciative friend when Giles was first pursuing Maggie, he figured it was only fair that he suffer Giles's comments with good grace. Particularly as he knew whatever Giles might say would stem from a genuine concern for his welfare.

'So, Maggie tells me that you asked her to invite the Duchess of Ashedon to our little gathering?' Giles asked, confirming Davie's expectations.

'Yes. I ran into her unexpectedly a week or so ago. She still…hasn't found her feet since the death of her husband, and seemed very low. Years ago, when we first met, she had a lively interest in politics. I thought attending this evening would help draw her out of grief, and let her focus on something other than her own cares for an evening.'

'From what Maggie tells me about the character of the late Duke, I doubt the Duchess is experiencing very much grief.'

'More like regret for what might have been, probably,' Davie admitted, advancing to the wine decanter on the sideboard. 'I understand the Duke…frequently availed himself of the company of other women, particularly after the Duchess had borne him several sons to secure the succession.' Choosing two glasses, he poured them each some wine.

'Now that I've reconciled with my father and been more or less forced to attend *ton* gatherings, I've had to listen to a lot of gossipy rubbish,' Giles said, accepting the glass from Davie. 'One bit, from that fribble Darrow, said the late Duke met his demise while attempting to… copulate with his current doxy while racing his high-perch phaeton. A drunken wager, apparently.'

Shocked, Davie froze, the wine glass halfway to his lips. 'The devil he did!' he exclaimed a moment later. Faith told him she'd never enjoyed the attention paid to a duchess. *Especially as Ashedon and his women provided so much scandal for society to watch my reaction to.* How embarrassing and degrading it must have been to face down that bit of salacious gossip! 'I hadn't heard. Poor F—poor Duchess.'

'Not much to lament about the passing of such a man,' Giles said acerbically.

'I don't believe he ever truly cared for her,' Davie said, trying to mask the anger that fact always aroused in him. To have been able to claim the beauty and innocence and joy that was Faith, and not appreciate it, was stupidity of such colossal proportions he could never forgive it.

Why couldn't that gift have been tendered to a man who would have treasured it? Not him, of course—it could never have been him—but surely there was *some* man of suitable birth and station who could have loved her and made her happy.

At least now she was free of the husband who hadn't. He squelched the little flare of excitement that resonated through him. *Free, maybe, but not for you.*

Ah, but a man could dream, couldn't he?

He surfaced from that thought to find Giles frowning at him. 'Maggie told me two days ago that you'd asked her to invite the Duchess tonight, so I made sure Ben and Christopher were occupied elsewhere. You ought to tell them, before they find out from some other source, that you're…involving yourself in her life again. I'll make sure they don't harass you about it. But…be careful, Davie. Don't let yourself hope too much from this.'

'I'm not!' he assured Giles—and maybe himself? 'If I can help her break free from the unhappiness of her life with Ashedon that will be enough.'

'Will it?' Giles asked, giving him a penetrating

glance. 'I'm not sure how much she can "free" herself from that life. Don't forget, Davie, she's a rich widow, her oldest son now the Duke, her minor children protected by a trust. Her family may well have further plans for her.'

A fierce protectiveness rose in him as the austere, disapproving face of the Dowager surfaced in his mind. 'As long as she has a say in making those plans, rather than have them imposed on her.'

'As long as you remember it's not your place to determine that.'

'I just want to stand her friend. She has few enough of them.'

'Well, here comes one who should be.'

Davie looked over as a tall, well-dressed gentleman entered the parlour. 'Englemere,' Giles said, walking over to shake the Marquess's hand. 'Good to see you. Perhaps tonight we can make some progress on hammering out that coalition.'

'I hope so,' the Marquess replied. 'If your lovely wife has anything to do with it, there will certainly be a lively discussion. Good evening, Mr Smith. You'll add your voice of reason to that debate, I'm sure.'

'Always,' Davie answered, reaching out to shake the hand the Marquess offered. He owed a great deal to Englemere, the best friend of his sponsor, Sir Edward Greaves, and one of his backers for his Parliamentary seat, and respected him even more. Did the Marquess know his sister-in-law was going to be present this evening? he wondered.

Almost before he'd completed the thought, the lady in question appeared at the doorway as the butler intoned, 'The Duchess of Ashedon.'

For a moment, everything in Davie's world halted

while he took in the loveliness that was Faith. Her gown, a lavender confection of lace and silk, hugged her tiny waist and moulded itself over her rounded bosom in a way his hands itched to trace. Her golden hair, pinned up in an elaborate arrangement of curls, made him yearn to rake his fingers through it, freeing the heavy mass to cascade around her shoulders, as it had when she was a girl. She wore only simple diamond drops in her ears, the soft expanse of bared skin and shoulders rising above the bodice of her gown her only other adornment.

She married the look of the angel she'd always been with the allure of a siren. Davie wasn't sure which was more powerful—the ache of his love for her, or the burn of desire.

While he simply watched her, spellbound, Englemere answered his question as he paced forward to take her hand. 'Faith! What a delightful surprise! I didn't know you would be here tonight. How are you? It's been far too long.'

He took her hands, and Faith leaned up to give him a kiss on the cheek. 'Lady Lyndlington was kind enough to invite me. I didn't know you'd be here either, Nicky. How lovely to see you! How is Sarah?'

'Still carefully nursing Elizabeth, our youngest, who was very ill with a congestion of the lungs last winter. Gave me quite a scare, I have to admit. With Lizzie so slow to regain her strength, I wanted her out of the noise and smoke of the city, so I've taken a house near Highgate Village, with a large garden for her to walk in and fresh country air to breathe. If you have time, I know Sarah would love to have you call.'

'Fresh country air? How Sarah must love that, and… and I would, too. I will try to visit her, Nicky.' She raised her chin, almost defiantly, Davie thought. 'We've grown apart, and I'd like to rectify that.'

'As would we,' Englemere said, giving her hands a squeeze before releasing them. 'But I mustn't monopolise you. You know Lyndlington? And Mr Smith, of course.'

'My lord,' she said, making a curtsy first to Giles, then to him.

'Duchess,' he said, taking the hand she offered. Savouring the contact, he retained her fingers for as long as he could without exciting comment before forcing himself to release them. To his delight, she gave his hand a brief squeeze as he let hers go.

'Who else can I expect to see tonight, my lord?' she asked Giles.

'Elder statesman and your host's political sponsor, Lord Coopley, whom I'm sure you know. Lord Howlett, another member of Witlow's Tory coalition in the Lords. Two of my Reform MP colleagues, Richard Rowleton and John Percy.'

'I'm acquainted with all of them,' she said, her apprehensive smile steadying. 'Particularly Lord Coopley. He used to take Ashedon to task about his behaviour, which annoyed my husband exceedingly.'

Bravo for the baron, Davie thought. Counting on his age, lineage and position to protect him from retribution for criticising a gentleman of higher rank? Or too principled and courageous to care?

Laughing, Englemere said, 'I'm sure it did, though I wager Ashedon didn't choose to respond. Coopley has never shrunk from calling a spade a spade, and he's too intelligent—and belligerent—for most men to willingly argue with him.'

'As I've experienced on several occasions, when promoting ideas he does not favour,' Giles inserted wryly. 'But you mustn't worry, Duchess. Lady Lyndlington has you seated beside her father, and near Mr Smith, so you'll have a dinner partner you know well to chat with.'

'And to assist me, I hope!' Faith replied, darting a look at Davie, to which he returned an encouraging nod.

'I doubt you'll need any assistance, but Mr Smith will certainly provide it, if necessary,' Giles said. Then his eyes lighting, he said, 'Here's my wife and her father! Excuse me, please.'

Davie watched Faith, who was watching the alacrity with which Giles hurried to meet his wife, giving her a kiss on the cheek and murmuring a few words that made her blush. Sadness washed over her face, and he saw the shimmer of tears in her eyes.

'They look very close,' she said. 'How wonderful for them.'

'They're all April and May, like two young lovers. Ben, Christopher and I heckle Giles all the time about it.'

Just then, the butler announced the arrival of the other guests Giles had mentioned. Spotting her, Lord Coopley walked over to Faith.

'How kind of you, Maggie, to invite another beauty for an old man to talk with!' he exclaimed, making Faith a courtly bow.

'You are very kind, my lord,' Faith replied. 'But I intend to do more listening than talking.'

'Nonsense, say whatever you like—I know it will be clever!' As Giles and Davie exchanged startled looks— both well aware how merciless the baron often was to inexperienced souls who dared venture opinions about the political topics that obsessed him—the old gentleman added, 'Always enjoyed chatting with you, my girl. Talked about books and horses and hunting. Right fancied you for my eldest, before Ashedon swept you away. Would have made you happier.'

As a blush of embarrassment tinted Faith's cheeks at that too-frank assessment, Lady Lyndlington inserted smoothly, 'Since we all know each other so well, we can dispense with formal introductions. Shall we proceed to table? Lord Coopley, will you escort me in, before I succumb to jealousy over your attentions to the Duchess?'

Chuckling, the older man clasped the arm she extended. 'Of course, Maggie! You know you'll always be first in my heart. The daughter I never had, much as both your papa and I might have wished you'd been a son who could have carried on our work in the Lords.'

'Oh, but I provided you a magnificent husband to take that place,' she teased.

Since as the leader of Reform, Giles was the man to whom the baron was most often opposed, her remark earned a laugh from the entire assembly.

'Minx,' Coopley reproved, wagging a finger at her. 'If I thought he could be seduced into it, I'd send *him* off in a horse cart with a doxy.'

'No chance of that,' Lady Lyndlington flashed back. 'If I thought he could be seduced into it, I'd murder him first.'

Davie watched Faith anxiously, but rather than causing her additional distress, the light-hearted remarks touching on her late husband's ignominious demise drew the group's attention away from her, giving her a chance to recover her composure. Before he could add a quick word of encouragement, Lord Witlow walked over to claim her arm.

'I'm so pleased you joined us this evening, Duchess,' he said with a warm smile. 'My daughter tells me you are quite interested in the work we're now doing in Parliament, so I trust we won't bore you this evening.'

'Oh, no, my lord! I'm sure I will be informed and—' she shot Davie a mischievous glance '—stimulated.'

At her words, the arousal he'd been trying to ignore hardened further. Devil's teeth, but he needed to master the always simmering, ever-increasing desire her nearness evoked! *Concentrate on making sure she feels comfortable and included,* he instructed himself.

'I hope so,' the Marquess said as he led Faith into the dining room. 'My Maggie lives and breathes politics, but she's never had a female friend who shared that passion. She's thrilled to find that you have an interest. You must come visit us more often—even if, as I expect, your association with Mr Smith would have you favouring the Reform agenda. With my daughter now married to a reformer, I shall be beset on all sides!'

'Mr Smith and I used to debate politics, but that was many years ago. As you know, the late Duke was not politically inclined, so I know much too little about the bill under consideration to "beset" anyone with my opinions,' Faith said as her host seated her.

'You've come to the right dinner party, then,' Lord Coopley remarked from his end of the table. 'With these rum customers present—' he gestured to Giles and the Reform MPs '—you'll hear every point of view, worthless as some may be.'

'I trust, my lord,' Giles said, taking a seat adjacent to Coopley, 'we shall eventually hammer out a compromise even you can agree with.'

'Are they always at loggerheads?' Faith murmured over her shoulder to Davie, who had followed her in protectively and halted beside her chair.

'Always, though now that Giles has married his friend

Witlow's daughter, Coopley isn't quite so brutal,' Davie replied softly. 'Giles used to feel lucky to return to our rooms with his skin intact.'

'I know so little about the discussion tonight,' she said, once again sounding apprehensive. Impulsively, she reached out to touch his hand. 'You will help me, so I don't make a complete fool of myself?'

Davie's toes curled in his shoes as he resisted the to desire to link his fingers with hers. 'You could never do that. But if you get confused, send me a look. I'll insert some explanation. Don't worry—you'll be fine.'

She gave him a tremulous smile. 'Thank you, Davie. You're always so kind.'

Though, as the highest-ranking woman present, Faith was seated as was proper beside their host, Davie was surprised to find their hostess had indeed fudged protocol by placing a commoner adjacent to her, rather than further down the table. As he looked at Maggie with a lift of his brows, she smiled and said, 'As a Member of Parliament, you should rank with the others. And besides, isn't the ranking of men based on their talents, not their birth, a tenet of your beliefs?'

'Humph.' Coopley sniffed. 'An excuse to give any upstart with a glib tongue the power to agitate the rabble! Though in fairness, I must grudgingly agree that Mr Smith possesses considerable talent.'

'Far more than some men of exalted rank,' Giles observed.

Coopley gave a bark of laughter. 'Far more than the one we mentioned earlier tonight, that's for certain! No matter, we'll tend you now, girl,' he said, turning to Faith. 'Only sorry I don't have any unmarried sons to send courting.'

Much as he'd wanted her to have a husband who appreciated her, Davie felt an immediate stab of protest at the idea of Faith marrying again. *Please Heaven, not yet. Not until...*what future could he possibly envision?

'I don't need that sort of "tending",' Faith was replying, the blush returning to her cheek. 'I'm not even out of mourning yet.'

'Not much to mourn for,' the irrepressible baron declared. 'Ah, here's the first course. Always know there will be fine food on your table, my dear!' he said to his hostess. 'Need to fortify myself before the hard bargaining starts.'

For a time, as the various courses came and went, conversation was general. Davie ate little and talked less, his attention focused on Faith. Urged on by their skilful host, she was induced to talk about her sons, a topic about which she soon became animated, describing them and asking the Marquess's advice about their upbringing.

'I would certainly recommend getting them into the country more,' Lord Witlow replied to her question. 'Never too young for the little Duke to start learning about his land and tenants. Though I regret he never developed an interest in politics, I'm proud of the work my son Esterbrook has done on our estate, which he began running when he was still a boy. Besides his duty to Parliament, there's nothing more important than a landlord's care of his land.'

'I would like to get Edward to Ashedon Court more often, but now that the Dowager has moved back with us, it's no easier than when her son was living. Both much prefer staying in town.'

'Take them on your own, then,' the Marquess advised. 'They no longer have a father whose permission you must secure, and I imagine the trustees will approve any decisions you make about their care that seem reasonable.'

'I really may?' Faith asked, her eyes lighting. 'I would love that! Although we visited so seldom, I know almost as little about Ashedon Court as my sons.'

'Time to learn more,' Witlow said.

'Might have a care, though,' Coopley added from his end of the table. 'It's a hotbed of radicals, from Liverpool and Manchester, out into Derbyshire and Nottinghamshire.'

'Is that a problem?' Faith asked.

'Those are the cities and the areas that currently have no, or limited, representation in Parliament,' Davie explained. 'Over the years, there have been demonstrations and protests.'

'Riots and destruction of property, more like,' Coopley countered. 'Depending on how close Ashedon Court is to the disturbances, I could see why your late husband might not have wanted to install his family there. Though proximity to his London doxies rather than his family's safety is more likely the reason for his remaining in town,' he added, mirroring thoughts Davie wouldn't have been tactless enough to voice.

Apparently armoured now against the baron's bluntness, Faith barely blushed. 'Mr Smith told me the new industrial cities of the north, having not existed when Parliamentary districts were drawn up in medieval times, were among those most vocal in calling for revamping the way Members are chosen. There were also towns and districts from that old assessment who now have very little population, yet retain their representatives, aren't there?'

'Exactly,' Rowleton, one of the Reform MPs, said. 'For instance, Dunwich has thirty-two voters, Camelford twenty-five, Gatton seven, yet each of these send two representatives to Parliament. While Liverpool and Manchester, with thousands of souls, send none! It's a travesty we must address, and the Reform Bill does.'

'Perhaps, but you would take away votes from some districts that have always had them,' the Tory, Lord Howlett, said. 'That's not just, either.'

Normally, Davie would have launched into the discussion himself, but tonight, he was much more interested in watching Faith, her eyes sparkling, her lips curving into a smile as she followed the banter and debating points being scored up and down the table.

All too soon for his liking, the meal ended, brandy was brought in, and Lady Lyndlington rose. 'Before anyone comes to fisticuffs, we ladies shall leave you gentlemen to sort out the details. Duchess?'

'A fascinating discussion, which I am so pleased you allowed me to witness,' Faith said. 'I can now claim to be much more knowledgeable about the great work going forward.'

'Yes, and you can warn those drawing-room idlers like your late husband that they need to get their lazy arses to the Lords,' Coopley added. 'Find out what is going on, with the most important decisions to be made in four hundred years about to voted on! A crusty old curmudgeon like me couldn't persuade them half so easily as a lovely and eloquent lass.'

'I appreciate your confidence, my lord,' Faith said. 'I shall certainly do my possible to encourage every peer to attend.'

At Lord Coopley's endorsement, Davie could almost

see Faith's self-confidence grow. More appreciative of the crotchety old gentleman than he'd ever been previously, Davie felt as proud as an anxious tutor whose student has just passed a difficult exam. How right he'd been to encourage Faith to attend this gathering!

How sad he was that the ladies were about to withdraw, ending this special evening with her. But there was no way he could leave now and escort her home without arousing a great deal of unwanted speculation.

'Will you stay for tea, Duchess?' their hostess was asking as Faith walked over to meet her.

'No, I should return to my boys.'

'Then I shall retire as well. Shall I have Rains summon your carriage?'

'He could have a footman find me a hackney. The Dowager was using the carriage tonight.'

'Ah, I see. I'll have him get your wrap. Mr Smith, would you be kind enough to keep the Duchess company until her hackney arrives? I'm sure these gentlemen could spare you for a few minutes.'

Davie's gaze shot to his hostess, who gave him a quick wink. 'I'd be honoured. Duchess?' He offered Faith his arm, stifling the sigh of delight that nearly hissed through his teeth when she laid her hand on it.

As he led Faith out behind their hostess, Giles gave him a concerned look, Coopley a questioning one. After the courtesy of farewells, however, the other gentlemen ignored them, becoming consumed once again by their debate.

'Thank you, Maggie,' he whispered to his hostess a short time later, while the butler was assisting Faith into her evening cloak. 'For dinner, and this.'

She nodded, but her look was speculating and her

eyes were sad. 'Just remember your promise. Friendship only.'

'Friendship,' he repeated, even as his traitorous body stirred and hardened. Memories of holding her flashed through his head—the softness of her body against his, her golden hair under his cheek—and sent desire spiralling.

The butler exited to order the hackney, Faith walked back to them, and their hostess turned to her. 'I'm so pleased you enjoyed the evening, Duchess. I hope you will join us for many more—and call here often. There is work we can do together!'

'I would like that very much. But you must call me Faith, then.'

'I would be honoured! And you must call me Maggie, as Mr Smith, does.'

'I, too, would be honoured by your friendship.'

Maggie nodded. 'That's settled. I'll bid you both goodnight—and count on seeing you both again soon!'

With that, bows and curtsies were exchanged, and Maggie ascended the staircase, leaving him alone with her.

How to best use these precious few minutes?

A radiant smile on her face, Faith stepped nearer. It took every bit of self-control he could muster not to close the distance between them and take her in his arms. Or at least, take her hands in his.

Somehow, he made himself stop. The mere inches of air separating them vibrated with sensual tension, making his heart pound so hard in his chest, he thought surely she could hear it.

Slowly, while he gritted his teeth with the effort to remain motionless, she reached out a hand and gently stroked his cheek. 'Thank you for tonight, my sweet

Davie,' she murmured. 'I haven't felt so…energised, and appreciated, and alive, since…'

*Since I held you in my arms a week ago*, he thought, consumed with the need to take her again. But he'd promised…something.

'Well—for a long time,' she finished. She went up on tiptoe, and for an instant, he had the wild hope that she would kiss him again, as she had when he'd escorted her home that night. Then, as if realising how inadvisable that was, she returned to her feet.

For long, endless moments, they stood frozen, staring at each other from a hand's breadth apart. He devoured with his gaze every curve and angle of her sweet face, every plump contour of the lips he hungered so much to taste, the desire pulsing through him stronger than he'd ever experienced.

And then, with a little sigh, she angled her head up, offering her lips, her eyes drifting closed, as if she were as helpless to resist the force between them as he was.

Heaven knew what idiocy he might have committed, had the butler not chosen that moment to stomp back in, announcing the arrival of her hackney.

The man's voice sent a shock through him, and they both stepped back. 'Your hackney, Duchess,' he repeated inanely, seized by a looming sense of loss.

'When will I see you again?' she whispered, voicing the thought that consumed him.

'Perhaps…perhaps,' he replied, thinking rapidly, 'I could escort you to visit your sister, in Highgate. Englemere doesn't come to town every day, I imagine. I could…bring him some committee reports.'

'Yes!' she said, her eyes lighting with enthusiasm. 'I would like that.'

'Bring your boys, too. They could become acquainted with their cousins.'

'Witlow said I should be able to take them where I like, now that I don't need their father's permission. When shall we go?'

'Arrange what is convenient for you, and send me a note.'

She nodded eagerly. 'I will. Tonight was wonderful! Thank you again.' With a glance towards the waiting butler at the open front door, she said, 'Goodbye, Davie. I'm so glad I'll be seeing you again.'

'Make it soon.'

'I will.' She turned to leave, hesitated, then gave his hand a squeeze before hurrying over to the door.

As she disappeared into the night, Davie raised his hand, inhaling her faint scent of lavender. The skin she'd touched still sparked and tingled, the aftermath of a desire so powerful he'd almost done something foolish and irreparable.

It shook him to realise how swiftly being with her, alone, had unravelled his control.

Maybe it wasn't wise to see her again, lest his hold over himself crumble altogether, leading him to commit some irreversible act that would tarnish his honour and hers and sever for good this tenuous revival of their friendship.

And yet… With her sons along to play chaperone, they wouldn't be alone on the road to Highgate. After they arrived, she'd most likely be closeted with her sister, while he could discuss the latest compromise position with Englemere, focusing his mind on business and away from her enchanting face. With her within the protective embrace of her family, there would be no opportunity for passion to get out of hand; he'd be able to enjoy the delight of her company without fearing for his sanity or his honour.

Besides, he knew in the depths of his soul that he could never stop himself from seeing her unless she herself forbade it.

## Chapter Five

Faith's euphoria buoyed her through the short hackney ride back home. She hadn't felt so energised, challenged, and *alive* since the early days of her marriage—before she discovered what a tragic farce her dreams of being loved and cherished had become. To attend a society function and meet encouragement and appreciation, rather than smug or pitying glances, made it seem as if she'd suddenly emerged from the dark room of isolation and sadness in which she'd been trapped for so long into a glorious dawn of new possibilities.

And then there was that thrilling, titillating connection with Davie. How could so strong a bond re-establish itself so quickly with a man she'd seen only half a dozen times over the last ten years?

She couldn't thank him enough for this evening, where he'd stood beside her, encouraging with a glance, assisting with a helpful comment, supporting her with his silent presence. And always, simmering underneath—until it had nearly erupted into action in Witlow's front hall—was the powerful physical link that seemed to strengthen each time they were together.

How could she find words to thank him for the sense

he gave her of being attractive, desirable, and wanted, nurturing her crushed and battered spirit to a renewed confidence? His obvious desire unleashed an unprecedented, heady sense of feminine power—and an urge to use that power to satisfy the increasing demands of desire.

Ah, yes, *desire*. Having endured so many years of unhappiness made her a little reckless. She'd never be permitted to marry a man like Davie—if marriage were in fact on his mind, which it probably wasn't. Lust certainly was, as it was on hers.

Dare she yield to it? Would he let her?

She didn't know. Continuing to associate with him would lead her into a maze full of risks and dangerous choices—but also to the possibility of fulfilment, even joy. She wasn't prepared yet to decide whether to proceed down that path. For the present, she'd seize every opportunity to be with him, and just enjoy.

*Make it soon.*

She'd write a note to Sarah this very night, seeking a convenient time for a visit.

Still aglow with energy and optimism, she sprang down from the hackney and waltzed up the front steps. Not until the butler admitted her, informing her that the Dowager had returned from her entertainment and would enjoy a glass of wine with her in the Blue Salon, did her soaring spirits make an abrupt descent.

She was home again, and back to being the much-maligned Duchess.

But not any longer, she told herself. Not that she would be rude to her mother-in-law, but she did not intend to meekly endure her criticism. Though she wasn't sure Lady Lyndlington's 'stare' would work to silence so overbearing and self-important a woman, she would certainly excuse herself, if her husband's mother decided that a 'chat over wine' meant a litany of reproof for her behaviour today.

Bracing herself, she entered the Blue Salon. 'Did you enjoy the opera?' she asked, seating herself and accepting a glass from the footman the Dowager waved to serve her.

'It was tolerable. Although it had to be more entertaining than a dull political evening at Lord Witlow's. I can't imagine why you accepted that invitation.'

'I didn't find it dull at all. Conversation about the new Reform Bill was fascinating, and Lady Lyndlington is a very gracious hostess.'

'Lyndlington? Ah, yes—Witlow's daughter, Lady Margaret, married that jumped-up by-blow of the Earl of Telbridge—who is to inherit, despite the fact that the earl divorced his harlot of a mother! Quite the scandal!'

Just like the Dowager, to have some bit of disparaging gossip to divulge about every person one could mention. Avoiding any response that would allow her to elaborate, Faith said instead, 'My brother-in-law, Lord Englemere, was also present, and asked me to call; his youngest child has been ill. I shall send my sister a note directly to see when is convenient. You mustn't be alarmed,' she added quickly, when the Dowager held up a hand in protest. 'I know what a dread you have of illness, so there is no need for you to accompany me.'

'Very well, if you feel you must, although I think it is very *inconsiderate* of your relations to ask you to visit a sick house, especially as you are a mother with three children of your own to protect!'

'I believe the child is recovering, and most of my visit will be spent with my sister.'

'I still think it encroaching. But I didn't ask you

to stop by to discuss some dull political gathering—I have exciting news that will certainly raise your spirits! Which have, quite properly, been downcast since the demise of our dear Edward—' The Dowager paused, her voice wobbling as she wiped her eyes with a bit of muslin. 'Well, no longer must we suffer being a household of women. My dear Randall has consented to live here with us! Now we shall have a gentleman's escort to any entertainments we find proper to attend!'

The memory of her brother-in-law's leering face, drunken smile and hard, grasping hands swept over her, followed by a wave of revulsion. Faith set down a glass that suddenly wobbled in her hand.

'How…useful,' she said at last.

'I would have expected you to exhibit a bit more enthusiasm,' the Dowager said tartly.

'I'm tired, and the news is…shocking.'

'Shocking? What is so unusual about a son coming to care for his mother?'

Faith bit down hard on her lip to stifle the replies that immediately sprang to mind. That the arrangement was probably more about the estate taking care of Lord Randall's needs, than him caring for his mother. That he was highly unlikely to escort them to a gathering unless he wished to attend, and since he preferred spending most of his evenings at gambling hells, bordellos, and other establishments of dubious repute, they would be as often without masculine escort as they were currently.

The appalling news settled in, setting other thoughts careening back and forth in her head like a shuttlecock in a lively game. She'd never be able to convince the Dowager that her younger son was an unreliable, dissolute wastrel—or that he'd made advances towards Faith. Was there any way to prevent Lord Randall from installing himself, a leech upon the estate? Did she have the power to eject him, or would, upon her appeal, the trustees do so?

Gulping down the last swallow of wine, she said, 'I know you will be much comforted by his presence.'

'But you're not?' the Dowager said with a frown. 'Heavens, you're always the most ungrateful child! All excited about running off to visit your sister's sick brat, and no enthusiasm at all about having your dear departed husband's precious brother coming to bear us up in our hour of grief!'

*She would not stay here and be harangued.* 'Grief does exhaust me, and it's late,' she said sharply. 'I'll bid you goodnight.' Nodding to the Dowager, she rose and paced out of the room, blocking out whatever response the Dowager might have made.

A sick hollow in the pit of her stomach, she took the stairs up to her chamber. Having to tolerate her mother-in-law was bad enough—but Lord Randall's presence was much worse.

Had his amorous attentions been inspired by the drunken boredom of an idle evening—or would she now have to watch her back, every minute, in her own home?

A shiver went through her as she reached the dark hallway outside her chamber. Sighing, she stood surveying the stout oak door. Could she obtain a key to double-lock it? One that he could not duplicate?

She was about to unlatch the door when the all-too-familiar smell of strong spirits alerted her to his presence an instant before she recognised Lord Randall's voice, approaching out of the dimness.

'Well, well, if it isn't my sweet little sister-in-law.' Reaching her, he leaned a hand against the doorframe and peered down into her face. 'Looking surprisingly energised after an evening of political discussion. Or is it some politician you're lusting after, now that Edward isn't here to keep your depths well plumbed?'

Outraged by his crudeness, she remained silent, staring at his hand on her doorframe. After a moment, he removed it.

'What are *you* doing outside my room?' she said at last.

'Didn't our esteemed mother tell you? I live here now. When I confessed my current…pecuniary difficulties, dear Mama insisted I should become your houseguest, for as long as needful.' He laughed. 'And with Mama footing the bills that should be a long time indeed.'

'The estate footing the bills, you mean. Edward would never have permitted it!'

'True, but he's not here, is he? Might be a little dab of a thing, but you were never a hypocrite, so you'll not convince me you're sorry about that. Still, I shouldn't object to our giving each other a little comfort in our bereavement.'

He leaned towards her, the liquor fumes threatening to make her gag. 'Life with two widows should be far too dull for your taste,' she said, stepping back. 'Why not move in with one of your doxies?'

He rubbed thumb and fingers together. 'Takes the ready to support those doxies, m'dear sis. Which I'm alarming short of at the moment.'

'More gaming losses?' she said derisively.

'Lady Luck's as unfriendly as you are at the moment. Maybe you should give me a kiss, to console me for my losses.'

'Have you no sense of decency at all? Speaking like this to your own brother's widow?'

He shrugged. 'Never any love lost between us. Had

the same inclinations, so why must he be the heir, and the one with the deep pockets to fund them? Besides, I know he wasn't giving you as much of it as a lusty young woman needs. While I wait for something better to happen along, I'm happy to fill the empty well.'

'You disgust me!'

He merely laughed. 'Maybe. But I could also pleasure you. Suckle those sweet little breasts, taste that—'

Revolted, she slapped his face as hard as she could. 'Get out of my sight!'

He stumbled from the force of the blow before righting himself, rubbing the cheek she'd struck. 'My, what a little wildcat you are. Didn't know you had it in you! But that will make taming you all the sweeter. Maybe not tonight. But soon. And afterwards, you might find yourself begging me for more.'

'You might remember that I have a pistol, and know how to use it,' she retorted. Pushing past him, she went into her room and closed the door. To her infinite relief, he did not try to follow her.

This time.

With trembling hands, she turned the latch. At the sound of the lock clicking into place, Lord Randall laughed. 'Sleep well, sweet sister,' he called through the thick wooden panel.

Faith leaned against it, her heart pounding, furious—but worried. Would he try something, or was he just playing with her, the tomcat toying with the defenceless mouse? What if he were able to get into her chamber in the middle of the night, while she was sleeping and unaware?

She would shoot him in a minute with no regrets. But if he chose to, could he force himself on her before she could defend herself?

Why this, just when life finally seemed to be offering her alluring new possibilities? Tears threatened, and angrily she brushed them away.

She'd have to think of something. She was done being the pawn of some idle aristocrat who thought his position entitled him to take whatever he wanted.

And she'd rather shoot *herself* than let that slimy ferret have his way with her.

## Chapter Six

In the morning three days later, having overruled the protests of the boys' tutor about his charges missing their lessons, Faith went up to the schoolroom to fetch her sons for the journey to visit her sister. The carriage was ready; Davie was walking his horse in the mews, waiting on them, and the boys were almost as excited as she was to be meeting their cousins for the first time since the birth of five-year-old Colin, her youngest.

For today, at least, she could put out of mind the unpleasant fact that her brother-in-law was now in residence, a worry that seldom was far from her mind. Though, as yet, Lord Randall had provided no reinforcement for her fears. As far as she could tell, he'd been absent from the house since she'd encountered him that first night.

She suspected that his mama had provided him with funds, which he was happily occupied in spending on women, spirits, and games of chance. Since in that case, he'd probably not return to Berkeley Square until he ran out of blunt, she sincerely hoped his luck would hold.

'Will there be a pond, and horses?' seven-year-old Matthew asked when she entered the schoolroom.

'Dogs? Trees?' Colin piped up, pulling away from the nursery maid who'd helped him into his jacket, and running over to her.

'I don't know about a pond,' she said, ruffling his blond curls, 'but there will certainly be trees, horses and dogs. Probably ponies, too, which the grooms might help you ride while I visit with your aunt Sarah. The older boys will probably be with their tutor, but your younger cousins will be able to show you about.'

'I should not like to be helped by a common groom,' eight-year-old Edward said, standing with his arms crossed.

'One should never refuse the help of an expert, even if he is a commoner,' Faith replied. 'If we'd spent more time in the country, Edward, you would already be a proficient rider, with your own pony. I hope soon, we will go to Ashedon Court, and you may begin lessons.'

'I want to climb a tree!' Colin announced. 'Mama's climbed lots of trees. I want to be up in the branches, taller than everyone!'

'Looby, Mama is a duchess,' Edward said with an exasperated look. 'She doesn't climb trees.'

'I don't know—I might still be able to manage it,' she replied, a bit disconcerted by her eldest's pronouncements. 'I certainly climbed any number while I was growing up. We shall see about that later today, Colin. Now, into the carriage, boys. Mary, bring their extra things.'

Excitement rising higher, Faith helped the nursery maid usher the boys from the room. Though she was disappointed to learn from his note that Davie planned to ride escort, she could understand why he'd not want to be confined for several hours in a carriage with three active boys. He'd keep pace at her window, his missive said; they would be able to chat.

But not touch, her frustrated senses knew. Although she was thrilled to be taking her sons to meet the family they hadn't seen in so long, having them with her meant that she would have no time alone with Davie.

Which might be a good thing, she acknowledged as she descended the stairs behind her sons, the younger two whooping as they chased each other. She was still undecided on what to do about this…passionate connection between them. It would be a good deal safer to content herself merely with a revival of the camaraderie they'd shared long ago.

In truth, Davie's unfailing good humour, intelligent conversation, and supportive concern were so many miles beyond what she'd experienced in these last meagre years of isolation, despite the frustration of her senses, she felt blessed enough to have that.

'Mary, take Colin's hand and help him avoid the puddles,' Faith instructed as they caught up with the boys and exited the back stairs into the garden. Reaching over to snag Matthew's, she added, 'I'd at least like to begin the journey with the boys not all-over mud.'

But puddles and mud and boisterous boys fled from her mind as they walked out the gate to the mews where the carriage waited—and she saw Davie, dismounted beside his horse.

He was dressed for riding in breeches, jacket and boots, a simple neckcloth knotted at his throat and a modest-sized beaver hat on his head. The coat sat easily across his broad shoulders, the breeches loose-fitting enough that they suggested, rather than outlined, his powerful thighs. Neither garment was fashionably tight enough to have required the efforts of a valet to force him into them, and for a naughty instant, she regretted his body was not encased in garments that would have more closely outlined his form.

Then he was bowing before her, smiling. Her hands itched to brush the dark hair off his forehead as he straightened, and for a moment she allowed herself to focus on nothing but the steady warmth of those blue, blue eyes.

'Even the weather smiled on you today, Duchess,' he said. 'I was afraid we might have to journey in the pouring rain, which would have made conversation impossible.'

'Then I am glad, too, for the fair weather. But let me make you known to my boys. Mr Smith, may I present Colin Evers, Matthew Evers, and my eldest, Edward, now Duke of Ashedon. Boys, this is Mr Smith, a Member of Parliament for Hazelwick. He graciously agreed to escort us today since he has matters of government business to discuss with your Uncle Nicholas.'

After the men large and small made their bows and exchanged greetings, Edward said, 'You have no title, Mr Smith?'

'No, Your Grace,' Davie replied.

Edward looked over to his mother. 'Carlisle says that a duke and duchess should travel with outriders. Not a simple "mister".'

Faith frowned, not pleased with the pattern of her eldest's comments this morning. She suspected that his tutor, almost as toplofty in his opinions as the Dowager, must have stepped up his efforts to instil in the boy a sense of the consequence due his position, now that he was the Duke. Quite prematurely, in her opinion.

'Perhaps, during Tudor times, when the whole court went on progress, there were outriders and equerries,' she replied. 'But not for a simple visit to your uncle's house, a short drive out of London.'

'Can we go now, Mama?' Matthew said. 'I want to see the horses and dogs and ponies.

'Up with you, lads,' Davie said, helping Matt and Colin to clamber into the carriage, his good humour seeming not at all affected by Edward's slighting remark. Her annoyance with her son, his tutor, and her intentions to challenge the man faded as Davie stepped over to assist her.

Pushing all problems aside, she let herself savour the pleasure of his one hand on her arm, the other pressed against her back to steady her as she mounted the steps. She had a sudden notion to lose her balance, so he might catch her in his arms.

She was seated, regretting the loss of his touch, before her mind wrenched control back from her senses. *Behave yourself*, it reproved. *You're a mother of three, not a silly, swooning girl—or a doxy on the stage.*

Her cheeks burning as she acknowledged the truth of that assessment, she nonetheless couldn't keep her gaze from veering back to Davie, as, with an easy grace, he threw himself up into the saddle. Then the coachman snapped his whip, and they set off.

The narrow streets and congestion of the city prevented Davie's riding beside her window until they'd reached more open country. While her boys crowded the windows, pelting him with questions, Davie pointed out pastures, woods, grazing cows, inn signs and, once, the excitement of a mail coach passing with a blare from its horn. Even Edward relaxed his demeanour, becoming once again an eight-year-old excited by an excursion into the country, rather than a peer preparing to don his ducal coronet.

Fortunately, before Davie tired of their barrage, the carriage turned off the main road and headed down a drive that led to a red-brick manor house set at a distance in a pretty park. The drive threaded around old trees and crossed a rushing brook before passing a stable block and approaching a handsome porticoed entrance.

'Would you ask the coachman to stop here?' Faith called to Davie. 'I'd like the boys to stretch their legs before trooping into the house, and I could do with a short walk myself.'

Davie passing on her request, the coach halted. 'Can we visit the stables, Mama?'

'Will the dogs be out?'

'Can our cousins take us to fish?' the three boys' questions overlapped as they jumped down.

'To the house, first, boys,' she replied. 'You must greet your aunt properly before you go haring off across the property.'

With a collective sigh, the boys fell in line, Colin skipping as he followed his older brothers. Faith slowed to relish the feel of her hand in Davie's as he helped her down, then began walking beside him. 'I'm sorry about Edward's impertinence,' she murmured.

Davie waved a disparaging hand. 'He's just a boy, and mimicking what he hears, I suspect.'

'Yes, I believe it's his tutor's influence. Carlisle has a starched-up sense of consequence which my late husband appreciated, and I don't. I would wish my poor son the freedom to be a boy before he has to shoulder all the responsibilities of a duke. Which I would like him to shoulder responsibly, without the toplofty sense of superiority his father and uncle possess.'

'If you don't like the tutor, dismiss him.'

Faith halted, surprised. 'Can I do that? Would the trustees allow it?'

'Find a respectable replacement and notify them. If they do object, you can always apologise and promise not to exceed your authority in future.' He grinned. 'Ask forgiveness, rather than permission; that's always been my motto. In the meantime, you'll be rid of an employee who doesn't please you.'

'Perhaps I shall,' she said, cheered by the idea of dispensing with the impediment Carlisle had become. 'But I don't have any idea how to find a replacement.'

'Ask Englemere, or your sister. Surely they've engaged several tutors for their sons over the years.'

By then, they'd reached the entry steps, the butler holding open the front door to admit them. Before Faith finished handing over her wrap to the butler, her sister Sarah came hurrying out.

'Faith! My darling Faith! I'm so delighted to see you! And your sons—my, how they've grown. Come give your Aunt Sarah a hug, boys!'

As she knelt down, her smile warm and her arms open, the boys scampered over like eager puppies, even Edward unbending to accept her embrace.

She rose, leaving her arms loosely around the shoulders of the two youngest. 'Mr Smith, how kind of you to escort my family here safely. And to bring out those committee reports, sparing my husband one day's ride in and out of London. We both very much appreciate it.'

'It was my privilege. Your princess is doing better, I hope?' Davie said.

'Yes, Lizzie seems much improved this last week. With it being so sunny today, I may even let her go outside with her cousins—I've given them all a holiday from their lessons, in honour of your visit. Cook made some special jam tarts, too. Once you boys have had some tea in the nursery, you can go outside.'

'To see the horses?' Matthew asked.

'Horses, ponies, dogs. I think we have some hoops and sticks in the stables, too. A pond with frogs, or you might drop a line in it.'

'Fishing?' Edward said, his eyes brightening.

'Whatever you wish,' Sarah replied. 'It's not often that my nephews visit. Now that you know the way, I hope you'll come back.'

'Me, too,' Colin said. 'I love tarts!'

'We will come back, won't we, Mama?' Matthew asked.

'Yes. Yes, we will,' Faith replied, meeting her sister's questioning regard, a wave of warmth and affection sweeping over her. This was *her* family, the older sister who'd been more mother than sister to her, whose children she barely knew. Freed from the shadow of her disapproving husband, she intended to rectify that error.

'I'll leave you to your family party,' Davie said. 'Though I will regret missing those jam tarts! Is Englemere in the library?'

'Yes, I'll have Wendover show you the way. And don't worry, I'll have some of those tarts sent in for your tea, too.'

'Thank heavens! You're an angel, Lady Englemere. Duchess.' Giving Faith a nod and a little wink, Davie walked down the hallway after the butler.

Faith stared after him as he disappeared. The pang at the loss of his company was eased by a growing sense of warmth and well-being—the feeling of coming home again, she realised with a little shock.

She looked back to see her sister watching her watching Davie. Colouring a little, she turned to her sons. 'Shall we go up to the nursery and meet your cousins?'

'Yes, yes,' the boys chorused as, laughing, Sarah took each of the younger ones by the hand. 'Follow me, then.'

'You must tell me how they are doing,' Faith said as they climbed the stairs. 'Aubrey, Charles and Nicholas will be studying with their tutor, since you chose not to send any of the boys to Eton. And Elizabeth is still with Nurse, recovering?'

'Yes, I've kept Elizabeth away from her brothers, so she's not tempted to exert herself too much yet, though as I told Mr Smith, she is much better. Charles and Nicholas are very much anticipating taking a holiday from study today with your boys, but Aubrey isn't with us; he left for Oxford earlier this year.'

'Oxford?' Faith exclaimed in shock. 'Impossible! He can't be old enough yet!'

'He's turned seventeen,' Sarah said, a mingling of pride and sadness on her face. 'A young man now, off preparing himself to enter a man's world. I miss him dreadfully. Charles is fifteen, and even little Nicholas is now seven. My babies are growing up!'

Faith shuddered. 'I'm happy my eldest is only eight!'

The party reached the schoolroom, where Sarah's sons bounded out to meet them. As the sisters reintroduced the cousins to each other, Edward gravitated towards the oldest of his counterparts. 'Do you have a tutor?' he asked Charles.

'I do, although Mama and Papa read with us, too,' the boy replied, then halted, dismay on his face. 'I'm so sorry—Mama told me you lost your papa this year. You must miss him awfully.'

Edward shrugged. 'I never saw him much.'

Charles's eyes widened. 'Did you not? How unlucky! I get to see mine every day, unless he must stay overnight in London for a meeting. I suppose your papa travelled a lot.'

'I guess,' Edward answered vaguely.

Regret, anger and anguish stirred in Faith's gut. How long would she be able to shield Edward before he discovered just what sort of 'travelling' had led to his father's premature demise?

After a concerned glance at Faith's face, Sarah said quickly, 'Boys, I've sent for your tea to be brought up—'

'With jam tarts, Mama?' Nicholas interrupted.

'Yes, with jam tarts.' While he and his brother Charles cheered, she continued, 'After tea, you must take your cousins to the fishing pond and the stable. I think all the boys would like to take a turn on your ponies.'

'That would be beyond everything wonderful, Aunt Sarah!' Matthew cried.

'I would like to see that fishing pond,' Edward admitted.

'You boys enjoy yourselves, while your mama and I have a comfortable coze.' Sarah leaned over to give her two sons a kiss. 'Don't let them break anything important, like an arm or a leg.'

'Nothing bigger than a finger, Mama,' Charles promised with a grin.

Leaving the boys in the schoolroom with the nursery maids, Sarah led Faith to her private sitting room. 'We'll have our tea here, and catch up.'

'Oh, Sarah, it is so good to see you and the children again! I am sorry I stayed away so long.'

'So am I. I did call on you several times in those early years, when Nicholas was in London for Parliament. I was always told you were "unavailable". Which I know was on Ashedon's instructions, not yours.'

'"Unavailable"?' Faith cried. 'You truly came to the

house, and were turned away? That's—that's incredible!' She seized her sister's hand. 'I'm so sorry! And, no, it was certainly not on my instructions. I would never have been too busy to see you!'

Sarah squeezed her hand before releasing it. 'I thought as much. I wasn't angry, just sad, and worried about Ashedon exerting so much control over your life—just as I'd feared he would.'

'He'd certainly discouraged me from contacting any of my family. How like him to make sure that dictate was enforced, by forbidding the staff to let me know you'd called,' Faith said bitterly. 'And how gracious you are, not reminding me that you'd strongly advised me not to marry him.'

Sarah gave her a sympathetic look. 'It's hard to dissuade a girl as much in love as you were.'

'A girl too stupid to recognise the truth when her sister told it to her.'

Sarah waved a disparaging hand. 'Not stupid at all! Even I, who was suspicious of his intentions, had to admit his display of affection was convincing. For your sake, I'd hoped it was genuine. But from what I knew of his character, I suspected it was not.'

'He got exactly what he wanted—a girl so bedazzled she tried to anticipate his every desire, a girl too meek and obliging to resist him even long after she realised he'd only married her to get a well-bred brood mare to produce his children, one spineless enough not to create scenes or tax him about his affairs.'

Sarah gave her a hug. 'You are too hard on yourself. You offered him the love and warmth and sense of joy you radiate to everyone around you. It was his loss that he did not appreciate such a gift.'

'Well, enough about the sorry past. We're seeing each

other again, and I intend that we shall continue to. Bad enough I didn't begin until it was too late for my boys to know Aubrey; I want to make sure the rest of the cousins can become as close as we siblings were, growing up.'

'I should love that, too! So, what do you intend to do with yourself, now that you no longer have to please a husband? You…haven't given a thought to remarriage yet, have you?'

Recognising that as a subtle enquiry about her relationship with Davie, Faith felt her face flush. 'Having just got out of one highly unsatisfactory marriage, I'm not sure I ever want to risk the institution again. I doubt that my powers of discernment are much better now than they were at seventeen. How could I trust that a man valued me for myself, and not for my wealth and position? And even if I could trust his affection—' in her mind's eye, she saw Davie's face '—how could I trust that it would endure, once he spent as much time with me as a husband would?' She shook her head. 'I think I would do better to content myself with mothering my boys.'

*And what of passion?* her senses demanded. She pushed the question away, not ready to make a decision about that yet.

'Nicholas told me that you'd attended a dinner at Lord Witlow's,' Sarah's voice recalled her. 'And seemed to enjoy discussing politics. Don't I remember you used to discuss that, and all manner of things, with Mr Smith?' She laughed. 'For six months after the summer you spent with Cousin Joanna, I heard nothing but "Mr Smith thinks this" and "Mr Smith said that".' She pinned Faith with her frankly assessing gaze. 'You seem to have resumed your friendship.'

'Yes,' Faith replied. 'But don't give me that *look*. I've already said I have no interest in remarriage; even if I did, I know that Mr Smith, despite his rise in politics, wouldn't be considered suitable. But surely now I am free to choose whatever *friends* I like! And friendship is all I'm interested in.'

*And maybe something warmer than friendship?* the sharp voice of honesty added.

'You can't fault me for wishing, after all the unhappy years you spent, that you might find the same happiness I have with Nicholas,' Sarah protested. 'But as long as you are getting out, mingling with friends and engaging in activities you enjoy, I shall be content.'

'As long as I can do that, and spend time with the dear family I have been estranged from for too long, I shall be content, too,' Faith replied.

'Speaking of family, shall we go see what the boys are up to?'

Comforted and encouraged by their talk, Faith rose. 'Yes, let's join the children.' Arm in arm, they descended from Sarah's salon to the terrace and down the gravel path to the tree-bordered garden.

They encountered the boys, a pack of dogs running and barking around them, as soon as they turned the corner at the edge of the walled kitchen garden—all except Colin. A spurt of alarm zipping through her, before she could ask Charles what had become of her youngest, she spotted him, proudly perched on the first branch of a nearby oak tree. 'Mama, look!' he called. 'I can do it! Charles only had to help me a little. I'm taller than everyone!'

'So you are. Bravo!' she replied, smiling with fond affection at her fearless, adventuresome son.

'Can you climb up, too, Mama? There's room.' He patted a place on the limb beside him.

'Since this is a day for finding my roots again,' she said, grinning at Sarah, 'maybe I should.'

'Oh, Mama, don't be silly,' Edward said.

Irritated at his dismissive tone, she turned to him. The look of distaste on his face, the disparagement of his tone, made him seem the image of his late father—who'd been so unappreciative of who she was, who'd tried in every way to squelch the freeness of spirit she was finally rediscovering, or smother it by forcing her always into company with those just as disapproving.

Sudden fury filled her. Before she knew what she intended, she'd marched to the base of the tree, kicked off her slippers, and reached up to grasp the lowest branch. After examining the trunk to find the best toe-holds, she steadied her grip, swung herself up and dug her feet into the furrowed trunk.

While the boys whooped and clapped, Colin laughed in glee and Edward looked on, astonished, as she managed to pull, push and shimmy herself several feet up the trunk, where she eased to a resting position on the branch beside her son. A beaming Colin scooted over to give her a fierce hug. 'You're the bestest mama ever!'

'It appears I still have the knack!' she announced, hugging him back.

'So it does.'

Shocked at the sound of Davie's voice, Faith twisted, nearly losing her balance. She felt her cheeks flush as she watched him and Englemere stroll into the garden, suddenly aware of the dirt on her hands, what would doubtless prove to be stains on her skirts—and the fact that her climb had ruched up those skirts so she was now displaying a very indecorous amount of ankle and leg.

'Well and truly caught, my dear sister-in-law,' Nicky said, coming over to wrap an arm around his wife.

'You do climb as well as you did as a girl,' Sarah said, laughing.

'Not quite,' she replied, still embarrassed. But as she saw Davie's gaze trace her leg from the stockinged toes to the curve of her calf, heat of a different sort washed through her. Suddenly breathless, she said, 'It—it was much easier to climb in breeches. I'm not sure how I shall get down without creating a spectacle.'

'Let me help.' Davie walked over to the tree and stationed himself below her. Raising his arms, he said, 'Lean down a little, and give me your hands. I'll have you safely on the ground in a trice.'

Looking down, she was surprised to realise he was indeed tall enough that she needed to stretch down only a small distance to reach his extended hands.

'Slide forward off the branch,' he coached. 'I won't let you come to any harm.'

'I know you won't.' She leaned forward and placed her hands in his.

'I have you now. You can push off.'

And he did have her. She couldn't take her eyes from the face, confident, slightly smiling, that gazed up at her encouragingly. He tightened his grip, pulled, and then she was falling, falling into the void—and into his arms.

He cushioned her descent, letting her slide down his strong, solid body until her feet touched the ground, and then steadied her, his eyes never leaving her face.

She stared up at him, suddenly unable to draw a breath, the memories racing back. He'd rescued her once before, when in the gathering darkness of a summer evening long ago, she'd misjudged her descent from the tree in cousin Joanna's back garden where she'd been reading to him, and slipped. Waiting below, he'd caught her and eased her to the ground, bracing her until she found her footing.

And then, as a spangle of stars sparkled over them, he'd leaned down and kissed her.

From the sudden tightness of his grip, the blaze of heat in his eyes, she knew he was remembering it, too. The babble of the children's voices, the gambolling dogs, the presence of her sister and brother-in-law watching them—all of it faded, until she could feel only the energy pulsing between them, see only his rapt gaze focused on her face, her lips.

With every fibre of her being she yearned for him to kiss her again. Even though she knew it was impossible.

He must have concluded that, too, for he stepped back and pushed her away, breaking the spell. 'Safe on the ground again,' he said gruffly.

On the ground again, perhaps, she thought. But not at all safe.

'How about you, young lad?' Davie called up to Colin. 'Are you ready to hop down?'

'Will you catch me, like you did Mama?'

'Of course.'

'Here I come!' With that, Colin launched himself from the branch.

Davie caught him easily, then swung the boy round and round while he shrieked with glee, before setting him on his feet again.

'I love climbing trees! Will you bring us again tomorrow?'

*Oh, how I would love that!* Faith thought. 'I'm afraid Mr Smith has to work, Colin.'

'Climbing trees would be heaps more fun,' the boy coaxed.

Davie laughed. 'You must know the committee members I have to deal with.'

'All right, boys, back to the house,' Sarah ordered. At the sighs and protests of dismay, she added, 'Did I mention that Cook might have an additional treat waiting in the nursery?'

'More jam tarts?' Matthew exclaimed. 'Bet I beat you there, Nicholas!' With that, he took off running, the other boys pelting behind him.

'Did your discussions go well?' Sarah asked, turning to the gentlemen.

'I think we're getting ever closer to a compromise Englemere will be able to persuade his colleagues to accept,' Davie said.

'That's excellent news!' Sarah exclaimed.

'We'll take up the work again when I ride in tomorrow,' Englemere said. 'Thank you again for bringing out the latest documents, so I might be prepared, Mr Smith.'

'It was my pleasure.'

'And mine,' Faith said. 'Let me add my thanks, for allowing us to accompany you. It was so wonderful to spend time with my family again!'

'You must visit them often,' Davie advised.

*Every day, if I could claim your escort*, Faith thought.

'Shall we join the children back at the house?' Englemere said. 'Much as I hate to break up the party, it's probably time to call for your carriage, if you are to return to London for the boys' supper.'

'I should do some additional work on those documents before tomorrow, too,' Davie said.

Realising with regret that their interlude together was nearly at an end, Faith recalled Davie's earlier advice. 'Nicky, Sarah, could I ask your help?' she said, taking her sister's arm. 'I've never got on well with the tutor

Ashedon engaged for the boys. Then, since Ashedon's death, he seems to be trying to instil in Edward an excessive concern for his own consequence. Though I am sure the Dowager encourages him, I cannot like it.'

'You must have someone who agrees with your ideas for the boys' education,' Englemere said. 'Edward has plenty of time to develop a sense of what is owed to him as a duke. Shall I make enquiries and send you some recommendations?'

'That would be wonderful! I'd like to give the current tutor his notice immediately.'

'Then do so,' Englemere said. 'Edward's only eight; he'll not suffer any permanent damage from missing a few lessons while you look for someone who will suit you better.'

'Thank you!' *And you, too, Davie, for encouraging me*, she thought, giving him a grateful nod.

All too soon, they had collected the boys, who begged to be allowed to walk down to the stables to meet the coach before being confined again for the journey back to London. Bidding her sister's family goodbye with vows to visit again soon, Faith and Davie set off behind the boys for the short stroll to the stables.

'You have a fine horse, Mr Smith,' Matthew said as they walked. 'Did a groom teach you to ride?'

Davie laughed. 'No, I grew up on a farm, my first mount a gentle old plough-horse.'

'A farm?' Colin said. 'With trees and horses and dogs?'

'And fields and chickens and goats and ducks and pigs, too.'

'You could ride and fish every day?' Matthew said, awe in his voice. 'That must have been wonderful!'

'There was a lot of ploughing and weeding and milking and feeding stock, too, along with the riding and fishing,' Davie told him. 'But it *was* wonderful—for a time. When I was still young, there were bad harvests, and my family lost the farm. My parents went into the city to work in a factory, and were killed in an accident.'

'How awful for you!' exclaimed Faith. Though she knew Davie had been orphaned, he'd never before mentioned the circumstances.

'The tragedy did allow me to get back to the country. An older widow took me in to help her with her cottage and the farm work.'

'Where Mr Smith later encountered Sir Edward, who was so impressed by his abilities that he sponsored him at Oxford and, with your Uncle Nicholas, supported him to become a Member of Parliament. He now has a very important role in the governing of England,' Faith told the boys.

'Do you not have any land?' Edward asked, frowning. 'My tutor said every gentleman must own land.'

Before Faith, once again annoyed at Carlisle's officious teaching, could rebuke her son for his implied criticism, Davie said, 'I didn't for many years, Ashedon. But I was recently able to buy back from Sir Edward the farm my parents used to own.'

'So you have a farm, too?' Matthew said. 'Can we visit it?'

'Some day, if you like,' Davie replied, giving Faith a wink to forestall her objections. 'It's rather far away, though.'

'Do you have horses and trees and dogs?' Colin asked.

'Yes. In fact, the horse I'm riding today was bred there. A tenant manages the land for me, since I spend most of the year in London, working on government business.'

'I'm sorry you don't have a title,' Edward said. 'But I s'pose it's all right, if you own some land.'

They'd reached the stables by then, the boys running off to have one last look at the horses before being corralled into the carriage for the journey home. Turning to Faith, Davie said with a smile, 'I think I've just been accorded the ducal approval.'

'Please, don't encourage him!' Faith said with a groan. 'I'm going to give Carlisle his notice tonight! I shall do everything I can to make sure Edward doesn't grow up to be a replica of his father.' Looking up into Davie's strong, kind, handsome face, she added softly, 'I shall try to help him grow up to be like you. Compassionate towards his fellow man—those of his own rank, and those who are not. Diligent in his duties to his land and its tenants. Responsibly involved in the governing of his country.'

Davie reddened under her scrutiny. 'I appreciate the compliment, but I certainly don't deserve it. I'm no paragon, Faith. I have just as many flaws and faults as any man.'

'Don't disillusion me by pointing them out,' she said with a smile.

'Carlisle might turn…unpleasant when you dismiss him. Are you sure you want to tackle that now? You could wait until Englemere finds you a replacement.'

'It won't be any easier then. I'm not always a meek little mushroom! I can be hard, even toplofty, if the reason to be so is compelling enough. No matter how unpleasant the interview, knowing Carlisle will be gone at the end of it will make the experience worth it!'

'How fierce you are,' he teased.

'Fiercer than you might expect,' she tossed back. 'Now, before the boys return and the groom brings out your horse, let me thank you one last time for escorting us today.'

'You seem to thrive, back with your family, here in the countryside you've always loved. You certainly haven't lost your talent for climbing trees!'

'I do sometimes have difficulty climbing down, though.'

'Ah, that's the part I like best. The climbing down.' He stepped closer, close enough for her to feel the heat radiating from his body.

The coachman and grooms were still in the stable with her boys. For this moment, blocked from view by the coach, they were almost…alone.

'I liked the "getting down", too,' Faith said, her throat suddenly so constricted that the words came out in a whisper. The passion that had been simmering beneath the surface all day flared up to envelop her in heat and need. Helpless against his appeal, she closed the distance between them and angled her head up.

For a moment, he hesitated. 'This is madness,' he muttered. But even as she whimpered with frustration and urgency, he cupped her face with his hands and leaned down to kiss her.

His touch was gentle, tender, his lips tracing hers almost with reverence, the contact so sweet, she felt the burn of tears. But then, as she clutched at his coat, he coaxed her lips to part and delved inside.

She gasped as his tongue found hers, laved and stroked at first lightly, then with increasing force. Desire flaming hotter, she brought her hands up to clasp his neck, urging the kiss harder, deeper.

He tasted like tea, with a sweet echo of jam. She

couldn't get enough of the strength of his body against hers, the tender hold of his fingers on her face such a contrast to the fierceness with which he was devouring her mouth. She wanted more, closer—

And then he was stepping back, thrusting her away, keeping her at arm's length when she would have closed the distance between them again. Only then, her senses swirling in a vortex of desire, did she hear it—the gruff tones of the grooms in counterpoint to the soprano of her sons' voices, the whinny of the team being led to the traces.

Davie cleared his throat. 'Shall I assist you into the coach, Duchess?' he said loudly, his voice a little ragged. Not meeting her glance, he thrust out his arm for her to take and led her to the door, which one of the grooms trotted over to open.

Still beyond speech, she could only look back mutely at him as the groom took her hand from Davie and helped her up the steps. Then, before she could recover, he turned to accept his horse's reins from another groom, and swung himself into the saddle.

'I'll ride ahead for a while,' he told her over the giggles and chatter of her sons as they climbed up, agile as monkeys. 'I feel the need of a good gallop.' Giving her a nod, he put spurs to his mount and set off.

Her heartbeat only now beginning to slow, Faith watched him ride away. How she, too, would have appreciated the freedom of breeches and the possibility of a hard gallop, with a sharp wind to cool passion's fire and clear the fog of lust from her brain!

She hoped he wouldn't regret the kiss, for she certainly did not.

No, it had not been prudent; had they been caught, explaining it away would have been difficult, and she would place no reliance at all on the willingness of Ashedon's servants, whose master had for years provided them with so much delicious fodder for gossip, to refrain from whispering about it.

But all she could think about was how wonderful it had been. And how, in a more discreet place and time, she could induce him to repeat it.

## Chapter Seven

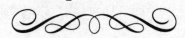

*Idiot, idiot, idiot.* The words echoed in Davie's head with the cadence of hoofbeats as he pressed his mount hard.

Fiercely as he repeated to himself all the reasons why his rash act in kissing Faith was regrettable, he couldn't make himself feel sorry.

Not being sorry didn't mean he didn't recognise that he absolutely could not repeat such recklessness. He'd been given a trust in escorting her, offering his guarantee in turn to care for her and keep her safe. And then, he'd risked that very safety and reputation because, with opportunity and, admittedly, her encouragement, he hadn't been able to control himself.

He'd told her he had the same failings as any man. He was only human, and a man could stand only so much temptation. But was he a man of honour, or a cad, to indulge himself in brief carnal satisfaction at the cost of her good name?

It was more than lust, his heart rebuked. How could he have resisted, when the girl he'd loved for so many years turned her angelic face up, inviting his kiss? He could no more have refused that invitation than he could stop himself from breathing.

So he'd better learn to hold his breath. Or not see her again.

Everything within him revolted in furious denial at that alternative. He would be better, his senses coaxed his implacable sense of honour.

For Giles was right. The family of so rich and high-ranking a widow, still so young and beautiful—and perhaps the lady herself—would be formulating plans for her future, once a decent period of mourning was over. Plans that sooner rather than later would sweep her out of his orbit again.

He had one brief, precious chance to enjoy her company. He wanted to soak up every minute before it was no longer possible.

Could he trust himself?

He would have to do better. Because he had to see her. He wouldn't squander this only-once-more-in-this-lifetime opportunity to be with her.

Freshly resolved, he rode back to the coach.

With no real possibility of private chat, any awkwardness between them soon dissipated. Daylight was fast fading, allowing him to point out to the boys scenes they'd observed on the drive out, but in a different aspect. Torches burned outside inn entrances, casting their flickering light on the roads; the carts of merchants unloading the day's remains of goods impeded travel, while other business owners were closing and latching the shutters on their shops. Boisterous voices rang out from the taverns they passed, townspeople and farmers stopping at the end of the day for a convivial round of ale before travelling home.

* * *

All too soon, their little caravan reached the mews behind Berkeley Square.

While he dismounted, one of the grooms ran in to summon the nursery maid, who hurried out to lift the sleeping Colin off his mother's lap.

Matthew bounded over to shake his hand. 'Thank you ever so much, Mr Smith, for taking us to Aunt Sarah's! You will take us again soon, won't you? And maybe to visit your farm?'

'That will depend on your mama, but I will if I can,' he said, smiling at the eager boy.

Edward also lingered, waiting his turn to shake Davie's hand. 'Thank you, Mr Smith. And I'm sorry for what I said earlier. You were a very good escort, and so I shall tell Carlisle.'

'A handsome admission, Ashedon,' Davie said, his lips twitching as he masked his amusement at the boy's serious manner. The child certainly did need a tutor who could encourage a bit more liveliness in him.

And then Faith stood before him, looking up at him gravely. Staring into her beautiful blue eyes, words failed, and everything within him turned to yearning.

He gritted his teeth to stifle it, sternly reminding himself of his pledge.

'A marvellous day at Sarah's,' she said. 'And an even more marvellous ending to it.'

'The ending was marvellous,' he replied, glad she was addressing the matter so openly. 'But it can't happen again. You know that, Faith! It's much too dangerous. How can I pledge to protect you, and then put you at risk of falling victim to the worst sort of gossip and conjecture? Haven't you suffered enough of that at Ashedon's hands?'

She shuddered, and he knew his words had struck home. 'Yes, but it wasn't like that, Davie! Not like his… amusements.'

'Maybe not. But society wouldn't see it any differently.'

'That's so unfair,' she said softly.

'That he might "amuse" himself as he chose, but you must be circumspect? Unfair, certainly, but the way of the world. And remember, even Ashedon, for all his high rank, ended up forfeiting his reputation for his actions.'

'I suppose you're right,' she agreed with obvious regret before her eyes widened, her expression turning alarmed. 'You aren't going to tell me that you won't see me again, are you?'

'I probably ought to…but I can't,' he admitted. 'I will tell you that I intend to do much better. I couldn't live with myself if, through my own weakness, I endangered your reputation, or generated the slightest bit of gossip about you. Perhaps it would be best if we met only at Lady Lyndlington's.'

'Or in the company of my sons? They all like you so much, even Edward! I know they would enjoy it immensely if you could accompany us to the park, or on an outing—I intend there to be many, once I get rid of Carlisle! Of course, I know you are busy, so it's presumptuous of me to assume—'

'No, I enjoyed spending time with them, too, and would like to spend more.'

'Family time. That will be…safe, won't it, Davie? Now that we have met again, it would be very hard for me to give up a friendship that, despite our…indiscretion, our outing today showed how much I've missed.'

'Family time,' he repeated. 'Friendship. Yes, I can agree to that.'

She gave him that beautiful Faith smile, the one that seemed lit from within and warmed him to his toes, as if he stood before a blazing hearth. 'Good. So...I'll see you at Lady Lyndlington's? I got a note today, inviting me to another dinner later this week. You will be there?'

'Thursday? Then, yes,' he said when she nodded.

With a moue of distaste, she said, 'Unfortunately, I must go in. Thank you again, Davie. For taking me back where I belong, to what I should never have left. After today, I can just begin to see my way back to my family. To who I truly am.'

*How he wished there might be a place for him in that life!* 'In the country, climbing trees,' he teased to ease the ache in his heart.

'Especially climbing trees. Maybe we can even get my far-too-pompous Edward up in one.'

'He's still so young. Take away the pompous tutor, and you'll likely see a change.'

'I hope so. Well—again, thank you, and goodbye.'

'Goodbye, Duchess.'

Holding the reins of his horse, Davie lingered, watching her until she was lost from sight beyond the wall into the garden. Then, sighing, he remounted his gelding and nudged him to a trot.

Could they remain friends this time, as they had failed to do when she married Ashedon?

Probably not. When she wed again, which she surely would—much as it stabbed his heart like a dagger to think of it—he imagined her husband would frown on her friendship with another man.

Unless she married a political figure.

Which was possible. She was certainly lovely and

intelligent enough to make an excellent wife for a man with a government or diplomatic post.

Could he stand remaining just a friend, knowing that some other man could taste the lips he'd tasted tonight, bind against him the softness of her bosom, that delectable warm round of bottom…possess her completely? His arousal, which the gallop had barely dissipated, hardened again.

Unthinkable to turn away from her, and torture to imagine her with another.

*But if she were to wed a politician, why not you?* an insidious little voice whispered.

*Impossible*, he answered it. A duchess does not wed a commoner. A man, as her son succinctly put it, without a title or a grand estate.

Maybe not now… He'd already been awarded some profitable government sinecures, whose income had allowed him to purchase back his family's farm and provided a steady source of funds greater than he'd ever expected to earn. If the Reform party swept the next few Parliaments, he might well rise to a Cabinet post, even the Prime Ministership.

Where commoners were often knighted.

A widowed duchess might be able to marry such a man.

Except a young, beautiful widowed duchess wouldn't remain unmarried long enough for him to become a man worthy of her hand.

Uttering an expletive that made his horse shy, Davie set his jaw and headed for the livery. Enough anguishing over impossible alternatives. He'd put it all from his mind, concentrate on going through the dossiers he must discuss tomorrow, and think no more of Faith.

At least, not until next Thursday.

\* \* \*

Buoyed by her time with her family and heartened by
Englemere's and Davie's support, Faith marched back
into the Berkeley Square town house ready to do battle.

She had her first opportunity at dinner. When the
Dowager began to complain again about her visit to
the country, Faith interrupted with a reminder that, as
her brother-in-law was a marquess, the Dowager surely
would not wish her to insult such a high-ranking peer
by failing to respond to his invitation. As the Dowager
sat, mouth gaping in surprise at being cut off in mid-
sentence, with a great deal of satisfaction, Faith added,
'Besides, now that the boys are older, it's time they became better acquainted with their cousins. I intend to
visit my sister at Brookhollow Lodge quite frequently.'
Then, after calmly sipping her soup, she enquired in a
pleasant tone what her mother-in-law had done with herself over the course of the day.

The heady sense of accomplishment she felt after
sparring with her husband's mother made her positively
relish the interview with Carlisle. Summoning the tutor
after dinner, she told him in the same pleasant but firm
voice that, much as she appreciated his efforts on behalf
of her sons' education, she now wished it to go in a different direction. She would see he was paid the rest of
his quarter's salary and be happy to write him a character, but she would very much appreciate it if he could
vacate Ashedon House by the end of the following day,
as her cousin, the Marquess of Englemere, was sending
her a replacement and she wished to have his quarters
made ready. Before the stunned and hapless man could
stutter out a reply, she nodded graciously, said, 'That
will be all,' and waved the footman to usher him out.

The alacrity with which the servant complied told her the tutor hadn't been a favourite with the rest of the staff, either. Probably always puffing off his superior position as an intimate of the new Duke.

*Not any longer*, she thought. As soon as the sound of their footsteps faded down the hallway, she bounded out of her chair, hugged herself and did a little dance around the room. If she hadn't been afraid she might be overheard, she would have given a whoop of triumph that would have done her sons proud.

After that interview, she capped off the pleasure of the evening by waltzing into the Dowager's sitting room to inform her that, as the country air had made her sleepy, she would not be joining her for tea and cards, but would repair to the library to do some reading. While her husband's mother stared at her as if she had grown two heads, probably wondering if some actress off the stage was impersonating her normally meek and obedient daughter-in-law, she danced to the library to choose a book, startling the butler by ordering a most out-of-the-ordinary celebratory glass of wine.

Now, if she could just master as well the conundrum of what to do about her fascination with Davie…

That being as yet beyond her ability, she settled in with a sigh to enjoy the wine and the novel. Not until she'd read long enough to truly become sleepy did it occur to her that, with Carlisle on his way out, there was no one to countermand her reading a story to her boys.

Energised by the thought, she sprang up, her step only slowing when, at the bong of the mantel clock, she realised it was rather late. Her sons were probably long abed.

At the least, she could look in on them. Picking up a volume of stories, she took the stairs up to the nursery.

Once there, she discovered, as she'd suspected, that the boys were already asleep. As she tiptoed through the room, her spirits soared at the realisation that her days of having to sneak into the nursery were over. She would now direct her sons' education. She would now be fully involved in their lives.

Where would she take them for their first excursion? she wondered as she halted by each bed, smoothing a curl off Matthew's forehead, straightening the covers Colin had tossed aside. To see the antiquities at the British Museum...the menagerie at the Tower?

So many possibilities, and they were still young enough that she would have years to spend with them before she was confronted by the necessity, as Sarah had just been, to send Edward off to Oxford. She intended to savour every moment, reviving those old dreams that, despite her husband's discouragement, she'd never relinquished of having them grow up a close and loving family like her own.

Thinking the day could hardly have been more perfect, she closed the nursery door softly behind her and descended the stairs to her chamber. Humming to herself, she was walking down the hallway towards her own door when the voice emerged from the dimness behind her.

'If you're ready for a cicisbeo, you needn't resort to some low-bred politician. I'm quite ready to accommodate you.'

A shiver of shock, anger, and unease rippled through her as she turned to face Lord Randall. 'Vastly obliging of you, but that so-called "low-bred politician" is a friend of long standing. Which you are not. Goodnight, sir.'

She resumed her walk, but moving with cat-like speed, he slipped in front of her and crowded her up against the wall, one arm raised to prevent her passing him. 'Not now, maybe. But I could be. I could be a very…intimate friend. Show you some things that farmer's whelp could never imagine.'

'Learned in the most expensive brothels in London?' She looked down at his arm blocking her progress. *Never show weakness, never show fear.* 'I believe this conversation is over. You'll remove your arm, please.'

'Of course. After I've had a little taste of this.' Trapping her against the wall, he forced her chin up and kissed her.

Furious, she resisted the tongue pushing at her lips, trying to part them. Though she twisted and turned, she wasn't able to wriggle out of his hold.

Struggling only increased the tightness of the grip that was bruising her arm, so she changed tactics, letting herself go limp instead. He gave a mutter of satisfaction as she raised a hand, as if to stroke him through his trousers, and eased his hold, moving back a fraction to give her access.

It was just enough. With all the strength she could muster, she brought her knee up and slammed it into his groin.

With a howl, he released her and backed away, clutching himself. 'You little bitch! You're hardly better bred than he is! Daughter of a bankrupt gamester, the only reason you caught a duke was the extravagant dowry Englemere furnished you.'

'I may not be better bred than he is,' she retorted, 'but I'm better bred than you—who would try to seduce your own sister-in-law! I expect you'll remember for some time how I am good with a knee. Don't give me reason to show you how much better I am with a pistol.'

Turning her back on him, she walked into her chamber and slammed the door behind her.

She turned the latch and leaned against it, shaking, but this time Lord Randall stomped off without whispering any further provocations through her door. She hoped his private parts pained him for a week.

How had he known that Davie had escorted them to Sarah's? she wondered—before she recalled the room his mama had assigned him looked out over the back garden, towards the mews. He must have seen them return this afternoon.

She shivered a little, remembering the strength of his grip. After all the experience she had arm-wrestling with her brother Colton growing up, he an adventuresome boy just a year older, she a pest of a tomboy always tagging at his heels, she'd thought she'd be able to break free of dandified Lord Randall.

As her anger faded, the concern engendered by their previous confrontation intensified. It appeared he did not intend to leave her alone. She was still confident of her ability to wing him with a pistol in whatever part of his anatomy she aimed at—assuming she had enough notice of his intent, and her weapon at hand.

She rubbed her fingers over the lock of the latch. Would it be sturdy enough to keep him out—or loud enough, if he forced it, to give her time to react?

He was a bully, and like most bullies, only picked on those he thought weaker than himself. Tonight she'd showed him she wasn't easy prey. Would he slink away and leave her alone now? Or would he, with his overweening sense of masculine superiority, still believe she was easy *enough*? Had her getting back some of her own only angered him and strengthened his resolve to have his way with her?

There wasn't any point complaining about him to his mother. She'd immediately assume Faith had tried to entice her son; if she even bothered to ask him about it, Lord Randall would certainly claim the same.

Maybe she should take the boys and go stay with Sarah until she could figure out a way to evict Lord Randall. But she'd hardly begun to re-establish her ties with her family. Sarah would think it extremely odd if she were to suddenly appear on her doorstep with her children in tow. Faith wasn't a very good liar, and the idea of confessing what had happened to her was so shameful and mortifying, she knew she couldn't do it. Just thinking about Lord Randall having his hands on her, trying to force his tongue into her mouth, made her feel *soiled*.

There wasn't anywhere else she could go.

She'd not leave Berkeley Square—not yet. Not unless things progressed to the point where she no longer had any confidence that she could protect herself.

Suddenly she was conscious of her stinging lips. Licking them, she tasted the metallic edge of blood, and a noxious mix of tobacco and strong spirits that could only be Lord Randall. Revolted, she rushed to the washbowl on her dressing table, poured in water, dipped a rag in it and gently scrubbed her mouth and lips.

How much different Davie's kiss had been! Tender, gentle, his passion controlled, taking the kiss deeper and harder, but at the pace she invited. His caress made her feel cherished, rather than defiled.

Tears stung her eyes, and angrily she brushed them away. She would not let Lord Randall make her feel like a victim. This was her house, not his. And he would be the one who must leave it.

Even if, as yet, she had no idea how she was going to make that happen.

## Chapter Eight

$\mathcal{O}\!\!\!\!\!\!\!\!\!\!\!\!\!\!\!\!\!\!\!\!\!\!\!\!\!\!\!\!\!\!\!\!\!\!\!\!\!\!\!\!\!\!\!\!\!\!\!\!\!\!$

The following Thursday night, Davie stood in front of his glass, knotting his cravat in preparation for walking to dinner at the Lyndlingtons'. He smiled at his image, recalling the scornful predictions of his fellow Hellions that, now that he had income and a position, he would get himself a proper valet and turn into a veritable Macaroni.

'No, my friends,' he'd answered. 'At heart, I will always be a simple farm boy.'

As Faith would always be a duchess.

And there they were.

Sighing, he completed the knot and shrugged into his coat. Those unalterable facts might not have changed, but neither had his resolve to seek out—in a more restricted environment—and enjoy her company for as long as he could.

Which would make the inevitable parting even more wrenching, the voice of prudence warned.

*So be it*, he answered. *You don't refuse to hang a borrowed Rembrandt in your study just because you can't keep it for ever.*

Catching up his hat and walking stick, he set off. A stroll through the cool night air would calm him, let him distance himself from the complex and tedious business of managing the reform legislation and concentrate instead on the anticipation of spending time with Faith.

Giles was in the drawing room to greet him when he arrived, once again unfashionably early. Handing him a glass of wine, he said, 'Did I mention this was to be mostly a family party? Maggie's father, Lord Witlow, and her great-aunt, the Dowager Countess of Sayleford, are coming—and also Ben and Christopher.'

Davie stifled a groan. 'The very friends who have most strenuously urged me to forget "the Unattainable". Do they know I've been seeing her again?'

'Not unless you've told them. That's your business, and I try not to meddle. Though I did recommend you let them know before they found out some other way.'

Davie shrugged. 'Then they'll find out tonight. I only hope they will behave themselves.'

'I don't think you need to fear any embarrassing disclosures at table. But when we meet for our usual conference tomorrow morning at the Quill and Gavel—I can't predict their response, but if I were you, I'd be prepared with answers to some hard questions.'

Davie smiled wryly. 'I only wish I had some.'

Giles hesitated, then took a sip of his wine before saying, 'Are you sure seeing the Duchess is wise?'

'I'm sure it is not,' Davie replied. 'But, having unexpectedly been handed the opportunity to do so, I'm also sure there is no way I could have refused it. And I do think I can help her.'

'As long as you emerge from it with a whole skin.'

'I gave her my heart long ago. There's nothing more I can lose.'

'I only hope you're right,' Giles said cryptically before the butler announced the arrival of the next guests, Benedict Tawny and Christopher Lattimer.

Having been forewarned, Davie wasn't unsettled by the appearance of their fellow Hellions. In fact, in the few minutes between learning of their impending appearance and their actual arrival, he'd decided to take Giles's advice and tell them about Faith straight away, before the rest of the party made its entrance.

'Just a convivial dinner tonight—we'll save the politics for another time,' Giles said as he handed each a glass of wine.

'No politics?' Ben rejoined. 'What, you would have us miss an opportunity to continue pressing—very politely, of course—Lord Witlow on moving forward with the Reform compromise?'

'I would. I want my father-in-law to relax and enjoy the company. There will be other females present besides Maggie, so the two of you start thinking of something that could be considered acceptable conversation for a lady's dinner table.'

'One lady attending is someone you won't be expecting,' Davie said. 'The Duchess of Ashedon.'

Both Ben and Christopher turned to stare at him. '"The Unattainable"?' Ben asked. 'But how—why?'

Quickly Davie summarised the events that had brought them together, and his intentions for the immediate future. 'She should be arriving any moment. I didn't want her presence to take you by surprise—'

'Leading us to make some…inappropriate remark,' Ben inserted.

'Like calling her "the Unattainable" to her face,' Christopher added.

'Yes, that,' Davie said, having a hard time not snapping back, though he knew his friends were trying to goad him. 'Or tasking her about her intentions, now that Ashedon is dead, or referring in any way to the...unfortunate circumstances of his passing.'

'Were they unfortunate?' Ben asked, raising his eyebrows. 'How so?'

'Later,' Davie ground out.

'Actually, she's not so "Unattainable" now,' Ben remarked.

'A widowed duchess?' Christopher said. 'Of course she is, halfwit.'

'Only if Davie has *marriage* on his mind,' Ben said, giving Davie a sly look. 'Whereas, after worshipping her from afar for so many years, the Saint might just be ready for something a little more car—'

'Pray do not transfer your lustful ambitions to me,' Davie said, holding on to his temper with an effort made more difficult by knowing there was more truth than he'd like in Ben's assessment. 'Unlike you, I don't feel compelled to seduce every woman I meet.'

'Be a sight more affable if you did,' Ben shot back, unrepentant.

At that moment, the butler announced the arrival of the rest of the party. Giles's wife walked in on her father's arm, following by her great-aunt, Lady Sayleford, who was chatting with the Duchess.

'Can't wait to meet your paragon,' Ben murmured as Giles walked over to take his wife's arm, then turned to make the introductions.

'Just make sure you behave yourself,' Davie muttered.

'Oh, around ladies, I always do.' Ben flashed him a smile.

Knowing what his friend always did around ladies, Davie stifled a curse. Ben loved females, and they returned the favour, responding to his practised charm and tall, lithe, handsome form with universal gratification and approval.

Whereas Davie, who confined most of his conversation to politics, had never developed the art of strictly social conversation. On the few such occasions he had joined his friends, Ben's flattering attentiveness and clever wit with the female guests made him feel like a large, backward, doltish farm boy.

The idea that Ben might try to captivate Faith made Davie want to wrap his hands around his friend's throat and throttle him. Surprised at the intensity of that reaction, he made himself take a deep breath. Ridiculous that he should be jealous of his friend.

Fortunately, Ben was only barely more suitable a match for a widowed duchess than he was.

Then Faith stepped out from behind the Dowager Countess, and smiled at him, and every other concern slipped out of mind while his whole being responded to her. She looked glorious, as always, gowned tonight in dark grey overlaid with a silver net that seemed to twinkle and glow as she moved in the candlelight. Small diamond drops winked at her ears, and something equally sparkly was threaded through the curls pinned atop her head. She looked like a chef's iced confection, good enough to eat.

He wasn't aware of walking towards her, but suddenly he was at her side. To his annoyance, so too was Ben. 'Duchess,' his friend drawled, 'I'm so delighted to make your acquaintance at last. Davie has sung your praises on innumerable occasions over the years.'

Faith smiled at his friend. 'Mr Smith has told me about you, too, Mr Tawny. You served in India, did you not?'

To Davie's relief, before Ben could launch into one of

the amusing army stories that always delighted female listeners, the Dowager Countess said, 'Shall we go in at once, Witlow? I'm famished, and it's not good to keep an old lady waiting. Might faint dead away.'

Lord Witlow laughed. 'If you like. Although I'd wager you possess as much vigour as all of us put together. Duchess, if you're ready?'

'Certainly, Lord Witlow. I'm sure we will talk more later, Mr Tawny,' Faith said, before going over to take her host's arm. Giles led in the Dowager Countess, Maggie took Davie's arm with a smile, and they all followed, arranging themselves as directed. To his delight, Davie was once again seated adjacent to Faith, while Ben and Christopher flanked Maggie at her end of the table.

'Duchess, I'm pleased to see you looking so well,' Lady Sayleford said to Faith. 'My niece tells me you have an active interest in politics, which the late Duke did not share. How fortunate that you can now attend events that may provide more stimulation than the usual society party. I must warn you, though, politics is somewhat of an obsession with Maggie and my nephew. Given the least encouragement, she will have you riding to the hustings with them.'

'I can't think of anything more vital to the well-being of our country,' Faith replied. 'Lord Coopley urged that more society ladies encourage their relations and acquaintances to take an active part, and I shall certainly do that. If I could be of any use on the hustings, I'd be happy to assist.'

'I'm making a note of that offer,' Maggie warned from her end of the table. 'I shall certainly call on you when the time comes!'

'You're in for it now,' the Dowager Countess said with a chuckle. 'Maggie is a force as powerful as one of those new steam locomotives when some political business needs to be done. But don't I recall that you began debating politics with Mr Smith some years ago, when he was secretary to your cousin, Sir Edward Greaves?'

'Why, yes—but that was quite long ago, before I made my come-out,' Faith said.

Maggie laughed. 'Aunt Lilly knows everything about everyone—or soon finds out. So, gentlemen...' she looked over to Ben and Christopher '...if you have any secrets, beware.'

Faith blushed a little, and Davie wondered if she were remembering that forbidden kiss. A timely reminder that nothing in society ever remained secret, providing helpful reinforcement of his intention to be more prudent in future.

Conversation became more general, a smattering of politics interspersed with some of the stories Ben was induced to tell about his army days in India, which led to a lively discussion of the relative merits and peculiarities of society in England and the subcontinent. Davie was content mostly to watch Faith, but as the evening went on, that enjoyment became tempered with concern.

To Davie, it seemed that she was somewhat...withdrawn, for though she smiled, and answered any questions put to her, she made no attempt to initiate conversation. When the conversation was centred elsewhere, her smile faded and a quiet, almost troubled look took over her countenance.

What could be causing her unease? Surely not some gossip about their lapse at her sister's earlier this week—something that scandalous would be so volatile, Giles would have heard of it and warned him.

Some confrontation at her home?

'You seem preoccupied tonight,' he said quietly, under

cover of the larger conversation. 'Is Carlisle giving you trouble?'

To his relief, she brightened. 'Oh, no! As I was planning to tell you, that interview went off very well. I was firm, and purposeful, and didn't let him get in a word of response. Very duchess-like! Even better, he vacated the house yesterday. Until I finish reviewing the dossiers Englemere sent and choose someone to replace him, I'll have the boys all to myself.'

'That's wonderful! Where do you mean to take them?'

'We went to Green Park today, watched the milkmaids with their cows and bought some fresh milk. Tomorrow, if the weather is fair, I may take them to the Tower of London.'

'They should enjoy that! Especially if you embellish the visit with stories of the famous inmates, mentioning scaffolds and beheadings.'

She laughed. 'Yes, the more bloodthirsty the story, the better.'

Dinner concluding, Maggie stood. 'This being a family party, we'll not leave you gentlemen to port and cigars, but all go in to tea directly.' Waving them to the salon, she took her husband's arm. Lord Witlow walked with his aunt, allowing Davie to claim Faith.

After cups had been filled and emptied, Lord Witlow said, 'We don't have any formal entertainment planned, but Maggie did promise to play for me. Normally after dinners in company, I'm stuck with a bunch of loquacious old politicians fighting some old election or arguing for a new.' He gave Giles and the other Hellions an amused glance. 'Listening to music is a treat I get too rarely.'

'Yes, I did promise,' Maggie said. 'But though my fond papa enjoys my piano, I'm competent merely. If you gentlemen would rather seek more skilled entertainment, there's still time to make the theatre or the opera—or your favourite gaming house.'

'Or house of another sort,' Lady Sayleford said with a pointed look at Ben.

'Aunt Lilly!' Maggie said with reproof. 'In any event, we very much enjoyed having all of you to dinner, but you mustn't feel obligated to remain.'

'Not that I don't appreciate your playing, my dear, but these old bones are longing for their sofa,' Lady Sayleford said.

'Ben and I arranged to meet some associates later. *Political* associates,' Christopher emphasised, with a smile for the Dowager Countess.

'Is that what they're calling them now?' she responded with a twinkle.

'Off with all of you, before you put me to the blush,' Maggie said.

'If it won't seem to be intruding, I should like to stay and listen,' Faith said. 'I'm no good at all, but my sisters used to play for us in the evening. It's one of the things I missed so much after leaving my family,' she concluded, her voice wistful.

'We should be delighted to have you stay,' Maggie said. 'And Davie, if you like.'

'You know how much I enjoy hearing you play.' Although he'd stay for a caterwauling soprano, if Faith remained.

With expressions of thanks for the fine dinner and congenial company, Ben, Christopher, and the Dowager Countess took their leave. Lord Witlow, Maggie, Giles, Davie and Faith moved into Maggie's private parlour, where a piano stood near the window. Lord Witlow chose a wing chair near the hearth, while, declining to sit beside Faith on the sofa, Davie angled a straight chair next to it. That put him close enough to feel her nearness, but saved him the torture of sitting next to her, knowing with one subtle movement in the candlelit dimness, he could slide his leg over to touch hers.

'I'll start with your favourite, Papa,' Maggie said, and launched into Beethoven's *First Piano Concerto*. With a little gasp, Faith leaned forward.

Before Davie could enquire what the matter was, she turned to him to whisper, 'Lady Lyndlington was far too modest. How wonderfully she plays!'

'She is very good, isn't she?' Davie agreed, delighted that the company he'd introduced her to was providing another unexpected treat.

For the next hour, while Lord Witlow tapped his toe in time to the music before eventually nodding off, Maggie played and Giles sat beside her on the bench, turning the pages for her. From time to time, Maggie looked over at her husband and they shared a smile; once, as she paused between one passage and the next, he whispered a 'bravo' and kissed her cheek.

As Faith became more immersed in the music, the tension Davie had noticed in her at dinner seemed to ease. Though he was relieved that the music's magic had driven from her mind whatever was disturbing her, he still fretted over the cause. He would have to try again to get her to tell him.

With the tutor gone, was she having more problems with the Dowager, who didn't approve her sending Carlisle away or spending so much time with her sons? As he speculated about what the problem might be, he heard the echo of Giles's voice warning that Davie couldn't solve Faith's problems, that she and her family would direct her future.

Despite Giles's well-meant advice, he didn't seem able to keep himself from wanting to make everything smooth in her world. It might not be his responsibility or his privilege, but during the short time they had together, he would do what he could.

At that moment, Maggie paused again, the piano falling silent before she began the next movement. She looked over at Giles, who returned a glance so tender, Davie felt a stab of envy and longing. He gripped the arms of his chair to keep his hand from reaching out for Faith's.

Just before the music began again, Faith sighed. To his infinite delight, in the dimness of the candlelight, while their host and hostess remained absorbed in the music and each other, and Maggie's father dozed, she moved her hand from the arm of the couch and reached for his. Both of them still watching at the musicians, conscious of sharing a guilty pleasure, he let his hand slip from the chair's arm and reached over to link his fingers with hers.

'They look so happy,' she whispered.

'They are,' he murmured. 'Well suited, and perfectly attuned to one another.'

'It must be wonderful, to be in a marriage like that.'

'They are certainly a good advertisement for the wedded state.'

She nodded. 'My sister and Englemere as well.'

'Maybe you will find that one day. No one deserves it more.'

She looked back at him then, her melancholy gaze sharpening, her eyes sparking with some more powerful, physical reaction.

'Maybe I want something else just as much. Something more…immediate.'

He felt it, too, the pulse of desire that seemed to vibrate around them, in the music, with the music, urging them together. They were like Beethoven's sonorous chords, he thought, distinct and separate notes that could blend into a harmonious whole, something new, more powerful and more beautiful than the single note alone.

'I want that, too,' he whispered, tightening his grip. 'But we dare not have it.'

'I know.' She sighed again and detached her fingers from his as the movement ended with a final triumphant chord.

They both clapped, the sound waking Lord Witlow, who added his applause. Much as Davie enjoyed the music, he felt more like protesting its conclusion than applauding its performance.

The end of the piece meant the end of his time with Faith. Though, unlike at the political dinner, he might leave when she did, even offer to see her safely home without anyone present thinking his behaviour suspicious, he knew he didn't dare subject himself to the temptation of riding alone in the coach with her.

After the music ended, Giles would take his wife up to their bedchamber and make sweet, slow love to her. The spell of the music having only intensified the connection of mind and attraction of body he already felt to Faith, Davie couldn't keep himself from envisioning doing the same.

Seeing her sitting there, the candlelight sparkling off the spangled silk of her gown, he could imagine leaning over to worship the bare skin of her neck and shoulders with his lips. Wrapping her in his arms, angling her head up for another mesmerising kiss…

Sweat breaking out on his brow, he wrenched his mind from the images. Maggie belonged to Giles in a way Faith would never belong to him, he told himself angrily. Could he not keep that one simple thought in his head?

Faith rose, and he followed her lead, bludgeoning his disobedient mind into performing the normal rituals of politeness, complimenting Maggie on her playing, thanking her for a fine dinner and a lovely evening. After giving her hostess an impulsive hug, she turned to Davie. 'I suppose I must have my carriage summoned and go home.'

'I don't want the evening to end either,' he admitted. A sudden thought occurred, and he frowned. 'Are you worried that you'll have to endure another of the Dowager's harangues?'

'No. That's actually better, too, now that I've stopped meekly following all her commands. Every time she begins to criticise, I either interrupt her or leave the room. I don't think she's yet figured out exactly what to do about it. It's lovely, to finally feel I have some power within my own house.' Her bright smile faded. 'Though not enough, I fear.'

Before he could question her about that, Lord Witlow finished his conversation with his daughter, and looping her arm in Giles's, Maggie walked over to them. 'We've sent for your carriage, Faith. Papa is so fatigued, he's decided to spend the night with us. Davie will wait with you until it arrives. Would you like him to escort you home, too?'

'No, that won't be necessary. John Coachman and the grooms will see me safely to Berkeley Square.'

'I'll bid you goodnight, then, and see my father to his room. You will call again soon, won't you? I already have some ideas about some political work we could do together.'

'I should be delighted to help in whatever way I can.'

'Good.' Maggie reached out to give Faith a hug. 'I knew we would make great allies!'

Each footfall as they descended the stairs seemed like the bong of a clock sounding the hour marking the end of their time together. Unwilling to part without knowing when he might see her again, Davie said, 'With the special election and Parliament reconvening last June, many members with agricultural interests haven't been home to see to their tenants and crops. We'll soon be taking a brief recess so they can check on the upcoming harvest before the vote is called later this month. If you'd like, I could take you and your sons for a walk around Hyde Park. In the morning, of course, when we're less likely to get trampled by horsemen and carriages.'

She turned to smile at him. 'That would be lovely! I know the boys would enjoy it.'

'Shall I meet you at Hyde Park, or call for you in Berkeley Square? Maybe I could help you review the dossiers of tutors Englemere sent you before we go out.'

To his surprise, that offer brought the anxious look back to her face again. 'I don't really need to review them. Englemere has already ensured all those he recommended possess the proper credentials. I only need to interview the candidates to see which one seems the best fit. Perhaps it would be best if we meet you in the Park.'

Taken aback, Davie couldn't help feeling a little hurt. Obviously, Faith didn't want him appearing at her front door. Was she embarrassed that some other society caller might discover she had received him?

Immediately, he rejected the thought. He knew Faith cared little for the opinions of society. But the Dowager would certainly not approve of her associating with someone so far beneath her station. Most likely, she was reluctant to invite him into her mother-in-law's domain, thereby almost goading the Dowager to give her a lecture on the proper behaviour of a duchess.

'Very well, the Park it shall be. Hyde Park Corner, day after tomorrow at ten o'clock, shall we say?'

'At ten, yes.' She smiled, her look of anxiety fading, confirming to him that he had correctly interpreted the reason for her disquiet. 'How can I thank you enough? Taking me to see Sarah, bringing me into a circle of congenial friends, and then, tonight, reminding me of a joy I'd almost forgotten. I only wish I could provide something so special for you.'

*You do—just by letting me be near you.* But that sounded too hopelessly besotted, so he said instead, 'Being a friend is special enough.'

Her smile grew tender. 'It is indeed.'

Then the butler walked over, announcing the arrival of her carriage, and helped her into her evening cloak. 'Goodnight, Davie. I shall be looking forward to the Park!'

'I'm determined to get a laugh out of Ashedon, if I have to play hopscotch through the mud with him. He needs to learn to act like a boy again.'

'A dignified Member of Parliament, hopping through the mud?' she laughed. 'Now that, I truly must see.'

The butler was holding open the door for her. Giving him one last smile, she walked out, leaving him staring after her. Leaving him bereft, with only his lonely room and lonely bed to return to.

But he had the park to look forward to, the day after tomorrow. Which would give him time to make the outing something truly memorable.

## Chapter Nine

In the middle of the morning two days later, Faith sat at the desk in the small salon adjoining her bedchamber, making notes on the dossiers of prospective tutors Englemere had forwarded her. It was rather difficult to imagine, from sterile lists of academic backgrounds and previous references, which candidate might be most amenable to the freer, more egalitarian system of education she wanted for her sons, particularly Edward. She would have appreciated Davie's help in narrowing the field of those to summon for interviews.

Before he'd quickly masked the expression, he'd seemed—offended, that she'd turn down his offer. Another iniquity to lay at the feet of her worthless brother-in-law, she thought, scowling. Since she never knew when or whether Lord Randall would appear, she didn't dare invite Davie to call. The very idea that he might meet Randall, and what Randall might say to him if they did, made her feel queasy.

She made a final note and assembled the dossiers into a neat stack, then wearily dusted off her hands. She'd barely slept lately, worried that she'd hear his footstep in the hallway, the rattle of the door she kept securely locked, with a chair pushed up against it for extra measure.

As far as she could tell, however, her unpredictable brother-in-law had once again taken an extended leave from the house. Though the Dowager had complained last night that he'd not shown up to escort them to the rout given by one of her closest friends, an event she'd most particularly informed Randall she'd wanted him to attend with them, Faith was relieved by his absence and could only hope it would continue.

As the mantel clock bonged the hour, her spirits rose. Finally it was time to collect her sons for their trip to the Park...where she would see Davie again. Impressed by her old friend during their trip to visit her sister, her boys were almost as excited to have his company again as she was.

After a quick stop to gather up her pelisse and gloves, Faith went to the nursery, to find the boys eager and ready. They trooped to the waiting carriage in an excited cascade of voices, and as soon as the vehicle started on its way, began assaulting her with a volley of questions.

'One at a time!' she protested, laughing.

'Mr Smith said he would take us riding again. Is he bringing ponies, Mama?' Edward asked.

'No, we're to walk today.' As his eager expression faded, she added quickly, 'There will be a pond, with ducks. Cook made me a packet of breadcrumbs to feed them.'

'Will there be cows, too, Mama?' Matthew asked.

'No cows—and no fresh milk. Although I imagine we might find some meat pasties somewhere, before we venture home again,' she added, chuckling at his whoop of enthusiasm anticipating that treat.

'There are trees in the park, aren't there?' Colin asked. 'Can we climb some?'

Anger and sadness coursed through her, that though her children had been in London for years, apparently their tutor had not been moved to take them beyond their own back garden.

'Yes, there are trees, but no climbing today. There are also long gravel paths, and you may have a foot-race. We're passing Green Park now; we'll be entering the park gates soon.'

At that, the boys crowded the window, eager to inspect this new playground. As the carriage passed under the arches at Hyde Park Corner to enter the grounds themselves, Faith scanned the paths for Davie.

The vehicle slowed, beginning a circuit down the carriage row, then stopped altogether. Leaning out over her sons' heads, Faith spied Davie, who'd waved down the carriage, and her heart leapt.

Fatigue, the burden of responsibility she felt to make the right choices about her sons' tutor and education, her worries over the Dowager's interference, and the looming danger posed by Lord Randall—all faded away, washed from her mind by a rush of joy and anticipation at being able to spend the morning with the men who brought light and happiness into her life—her sons, and Davie.

What a blessing it would be, to have Davie's kind, clever and alluring company every day, the wistful thought occurred. Sighing, she banished it; she would treasure today and not repine that she would not be able to experience such treats more often. All too soon, Davie's responsibilities—and probably boredom with the company of a matron of no particular talents and her three rambunctious sons—would put an end to such adventures.

She intended to suck every iota of joy out of the ones she managed to grab.

As he approached, the footman handed her down and the boys tumbled out of the coach and ran to meet him. With affection and pride, she watched Edward hold up a hand to halt his brothers before they reached Davie, make him a proper bow, and wave his brothers to copy that behaviour.

Not to be restrained any longer, Matthew tugged at Davie's sleeve. 'Mama said we would only walk today, but might there be ponies later?'

'We are going to the Serpentine to feed the ducks,' Faith inserted, not wanting her children, who had no idea of the cost involved in renting ponies or hiring grooms, to wheedle Davie for expensive treats.

'An excellent idea, Duchess,' Davie said, making her a bow. 'How nice to see all of you again.'

'And you, Mr Smith.' As he straightened, their eyes met, and for a moment, Faith let her tremulous smile and the intensity of her gaze convey all the longing and delight she dare not put into words.

He seemed to understand, for he stared back just as intensely, and for a moment, Faith thought he might take her hand.

Instead, he gave her a tiny nod and turned to Matthew, who was once again tugging at his coat sleeve. 'Shall we go see those ducks, young man? As for ponies, I thought afterward, we might go to Astley's Amphitheatre.'

Edward's eyes widened and he gave a gasp. 'Where the riders do tricks on horseback? That would be splendid!'

'How kind of you to offer such a treat, Mr Smith,

that's not necessary; the tickets must be rather dear, I should think.'

Being led forward, as Matthew tugged at one hand and Colin the other, he looked back over his shoulder. 'I'm not a penniless orphan any longer, Duchess.'

Her cheeks coloured. 'I didn't mean to imply—'

Then he chuckled, relieving her of the fear that she might have offended him. 'No worries on that score. I can stand the ready, and I'd very much like to offer them that treat.'

'Then, we accept with pleasure.'

'Have you seen the horses there, Mama?' Edward asked.

'Your Aunt Sarah took me once, while the late Mr Astley still performed. They presented "The Battle of Waterloo"; it was quite a spectacle.'

'A battle?' Matthew cried. 'With guns and horses and fighting and everything? That would be splendid!'

'I'm afraid they don't do the battle scene in the afternoons,' Davie said. 'But there are acrobats, and lots of horsemen doing tricks while they ride.'

'Let's feed the ducks fast!' Colin said, picking up the pace.

A few minutes later they reached the verge of the Serpentine, Faith pulled the cloth-wrapped crumbs from her reticule, and the boys began vying to see who could attract the most ducks with their treasures.

Edward, who emptied his handful first, grew bored waiting while his youngest brother painstakingly tossed his bits down, crumb by crumb, giggling at the ducks who rushed around his small feet, gobbling down the morsels.

When one of the ducks, stymied of winning some of Colin's last crumbs, waddled over to nudge at Edward's feet, he picked up a branch and pushed it away. Apparently encouraged by the squawk and flapping of wings that ensued, he began hitting the duck on the back.

Before Faith could say anything, Davie reached out to stay his hand. 'Don't, Ashedon,' he said. 'You mustn't hurt him; smaller creatures are here for us to enjoy and protect.'

'It's only a duck,' Edward said with a shrug.

'Every creature, no matter how lowly, has value,' Davie said quietly. 'Only men with small minds and hard hearts treat cruelly or slightingly those of lesser estate than themselves. A man of high position, as you will one day be, has a responsibility to protect those who are poorer and less fortunate.'

'Like you do in Parliament?' Edward said. 'Uncle Nicholas said your Reform Bill wants to give all men a voice in running their government.'

'That's right. Wouldn't you rather Nurse asked if you wanted bread—or jam tarts—with your tea, rather than just bringing you what she thinks is best for you?' As he nodded, Davie continued, 'Most men don't mind following reasonable rules, but they do like to have a say in making them. Now, are we out of breadcrumbs, Master Colin?'

When her youngest nodded, Matthew gave a shout. 'Now we get to see the ponies! C'mon, Colin, I'll race you back to the coach!'

Rather than run ahead with the others, Edward chose to walk beside them. Her son was even more impressed with Davie than he'd been on that first excursion, Faith realised. But how could he not be? His own father had spent little time with him, never bothering to talk to him about anything that mattered, like a great man's duty to those around him.

Probably because he didn't feel any.

How she wished her sons could grow up with a man like Davie to model themselves after!

'Won't you ride to Astley's with us, Mr Smith?' Edward asked.

'Thank you, Ashedon. If it's all right with your mama, I will. But after we arrive,' he continued, turning to address Faith, 'why don't you send your coach home? No need for the staff to hang about, walking the horses, while we watch the show.'

'Very well, I'll instruct John Coachman,' Faith said, wishing she could take Davie's arm, but too mindful of Edward keeping pace beside them.

The boys were, of course, their excuse to spend time together, but oh, if only she could find some way for them to steal a few minutes alone! How she longed for an obliging screen of trees, a gardener's hut, a conveniently placed empty coach—anything that would allow her to glide close to him, lift her face, and beg another kiss.

Of course, there was nothing in Hyde Park but well-tended pathways...and once they reached Astley's, there would be several hundred additional witnesses surrounding them, she thought, sighing.

Replying, 'No!', rather more sharply than she'd intended when Davie enquired whether something was wrong, she had to settle for the much-less-satisfying pleasure of laying her hand on his arm as he helped her into the coach.

The carriage ride to Astley's was a mixed blessing. Moving her boys on to the forward seat, she was able to sit beside Davie. But trying to maintain a proper distance between them, when all she wanted was to snuggle up against him, strained both patience and decorum, while the bumps that jostled them enough for their knees or hands to touch set off sparks that made keeping away even more difficult.

A sidelong glance at his set jaw and a sensual tension so strong she wondered that even the boys didn't notice something, told her he found this almost-but-not-quite togetherness as difficult as she did.

Still, she would rather burn in his presence than pine for his absence.

Not sure whether to be relieved or sorry when the carriage stopped at their destination—freeing them from frustration, but removing the tantalising possibility that any moment, another rut might throw them together— she let the groom hand her down, while Davie went to obtain their tickets.

*Enough amorous thoughts*, she scolded herself. *You're a mother, on this excursion primarily for your sons' benefit. Concentrate on making sure they enjoy it.*

Which didn't require much effort, once the boys took their seats in the grandstand and the show began. Totally enthralled, they gasped at riders standing upright on the backs of their galloping horses; a female dressed like a ballerina poised on one foot as her horse circled the ring; others who jumped their horses over fences while standing upright. They marvelled as the manager, Andrew Duclow, performed his famous 'Courier of St Petersburg' stunt, standing astride two white horses while mounted riders carrying the flags of countries travelled through on the journey from England to Russia rode beneath him. With the rest of the crowd, they laughed at the shenanigans of the clowns, applauded the skill of the acrobats, and shouted approval at the finale when a group of riders entered the arena and raced their ponies round and round.

'They will talk about this for weeks,' Faith said over

their heads. 'You rose high enough in their estimation for the trip to Brookhollow Lodge; after this, it's fortunate you will be occupied with business, for they would plead with you to take them out again and again.'

'It would be hard to equal the excitement of Astley's.'

'For them, perhaps. I found the end of our day at Brookhollow even more satisfying. I only wish I could repeat *that*—again and again.'

Her words sparked his gaze to an intensity that promised he could deliver exactly what she burned for. Oh, she wanted…she *wanted*. But could she persuade him to it?

The light of his gaze burning hotter, he said, so softly that with all the noise around them, she could barely hear him, 'Repeat that, and dare more.' Taking her hand, he brought it to his lips for a brief caress.

Faith felt the delicious vibrations move up her arm and radiate throughout her body. How she wished they could leave this spot and go somewhere private! She longed with a fervour she'd never before experienced to kiss him, unknot his cravat and place her lips on his bared throat where the pulse throbbed. To peel him out of coat and waistcoat and shirt and rub her lips, her cheek, against his bare chest. Kiss him from his chest downward, unfastening his trousers to unveil him—

Shocked by the explicit carnality of her thoughts, Faith's cheeks flamed. But she was spared the embarrassment of Davie noticing; he had already looked away, breaking that contact between them. Exhaling a heavy sigh, he said, 'But we must be content with less.'

He wanted her, she was certain, but tempting him to act on that desire wouldn't be easy. Was she even certain yet, despite the force of her desire, that she dared lead him there?

Exhaling a huff of frustration of her own, she turned her attention back to the arena.

What was she thinking, anyway? She was a matron with three sons, not a temptress from the *demi-monde*.

Sometimes, she thought wistfully, she wished she had their skills.

Soon after, the performance concluded. Davie went off to procure their hackney, finding some meat pasties for the boys along the way, which they consumed with gusto. For the length of the drive back to Berkeley Square, they chattered about what a famous time they'd had, what terrific performers the horsemen had been, how beautiful their mounts. Matthew announced his determination to become a skilled rider and open his own amphitheatre, graciously conceding that Colin could join with him, but Edward couldn't, because he would have to be a duke.

Bracketed by exuberant boys, there was no chance for any private conversation. So, when Davie handed her down, after sending her sons up to the nursery, she lingered by the hackney.

'Thank you for another perfect outing.'

He smiled. 'I'm so glad you—and they—enjoyed it. Paragon that you are, no one deserves perfection more.'

'I'm hardly that!' she protested.

'You are to me. The perfect embodiment of joy, purity, and delight.'

She knew she wasn't worthy of such praise, but she couldn't help drinking in an admiration that refilled the reservoirs of self-confidence and self-worth drained so low by years of marriage to a man who'd belittled her.

But the butler still stood at the top of the entry stairs, holding open the door. Hating to end the excursion, she nevertheless forced herself to say, 'I must go now. Thank you again.'

Before she turned away, he caught up her hand and kissed it, the gaze they shared saying they both regretted not being able to end this interlude with the one thing that truly would have made the morning perfect. Faith's lips tingled, imagining that forbidden, longed-for kiss.

Then, with a little nudge, Davie pushed her towards the stairs. 'You must go in, Duchess. Thank you for a wonderful outing.'

'You'll let me know if you have another free morning?' she asked, wanting to hold on to the magic by guaranteeing she would see him again.

'Yes. Or you may be sure that Lady Lyndlington will rope you into one of her political projects, and I'll see you there, or at another of her dinners.'

'It can't be too soon.'

'I hope it is very soon.' With that, Davie tipped his hat, and she reluctantly turned to walk up the stairs.

As she did, someone stirred the curtains at the front parlour window. Focusing on the movement, she realised with a shock that Lord Randall stood there, watching her as Davie's hackney drove away.

# *Chapter Ten*

Her heart pounding, Faith hurried through the hallway, up the stairs past the salon and up another flight to the nursery, one place she knew her brother-in-law wouldn't follow her. She halted outside the door to the schoolroom, panting from her exertions, but relieved at having avoided a confrontation she dreaded.

Perhaps the Dowager was in the salon with him, or perhaps he simply didn't want to accost her yet, for he'd had enough time, while she skipped up the stairs from the street level, to cut off her retreat, had he wanted to. She could only be glad that he hadn't, and that she was now forewarned that he was back in the house.

For how long, she didn't know; hopefully, he'd borrow more money from his mother and be gone for days again. But she'd have to tread carefully, in case he made a longer stay this time.

Anger fired up, overlaying the dread. She hated having to remain constantly on guard in her own home! She simply had to resolve this intolerable situation.

Only she hadn't yet figured out a way to do that. An enquiry of the Dowager, about which solicitor maintained the documents setting out the rules of the trust established for the boys and the details of how income from the estate was provided to them, was met first with a blank stare, and then a querulous enquiry about why she would need such information.

She only wished she'd paid more attention at the reading of the will, but she'd been so shocked and mortified by the circumstances of her husband's death, all she could think about was how those present must be staring at and pitying her.

Englemere would know; standing in for her deceased father, he'd been involved in arranging the details of her marriage settlement. But with momentous changes about to be voted on in Parliament, he was busy with important work in the Lords. Besides which, he would naturally be curious why she was suddenly enquiring about financial details which had never interested her over the many years of her marriage and widowhood.

Confiding in him would be even more impossible than admitting the tawdry circumstances to Sarah.

Maybe tomorrow, she'd try going through Ashedon's desk—though, as she couldn't remember her husband ever troubling himself over financial matters, the search was unlikely to yield her much.

Better still, why not simply ask Cooper, the butler, she thought, brightening. He would probably think the enquiry strange, but since butlers knew everything, he most likely would be able to give her the name of Ashedon's solicitor.

Heartened, as she leaned against the door, recovering her breath, she imagined the interview with the solicitor. That gentleman, who didn't know her at all, was less likely to think it odd of her to make enquiries, especially when she could tell him, quite truthfully, that she was concerned about how the arrangements had been left for the boys' schooling. She could also explain that her husband had feared his younger brother might try to make inroads upon the estate; wanting to honour his wishes and protect her sons' inheritance, she needed to know just what funds and properties Lord Randall could make use of, and which uses she should report to the trustees, should he overstep his bounds.

She'd spend the remainder of the afternoon here, with her boys, she decided. She'd need to venture out of the schoolroom to dress for dinner, and then dine with the Dowager, but with any luck, Lord Randall would have cudgelled some funds out of his mother and be gone by then. If the Dowager did coax her darling son to remain for dinner, she would only be interested in talking with *him*, allowing Faith to remain mostly silent, masking the fact that she had no desire to converse with her despicable brother-in-law.

Fortunately, she'd left in the schoolroom the story-book she'd brought up some nights ago, so wouldn't need to retreat to the library to fetch it. By now recovered, Faith opened the door and walked in.

To her delight, her sons jumped up to greet her with a surprise and excitement that grew more exuberant when she told them she meant to stay until suppertime, reading them stories—and would have Cook send up some more bread and tea for their party.

Even Edward smiled at that. Fetching the book, she gathered them around her at the schoolroom table, and began to read.

The degree of relief she felt upon entering the salon before dinner to find her brother-in-law absent told her she'd been dreading the prospect of dining with him more than she'd imagined. Her relief was so great, she bore with unimpaired good humour the Dowager's criticism of her spending the morning out gallivanting with her sons instead of being home to greet Lord Randall upon his arrival, and her selfishness in remaining closeted with them all afternoon, without giving a thought to whether her mother-in-law might need her.

Most unusually, the Dowager continued her complaining after they went into dinner, decrying her son's lack of feeling in deserting her, too, even after she'd most particularly requested that he remain to dine and escort them to the rout this evening. Then, seeming to realise this description of Randall's behaviour did not fit the rosy picture she'd painted of how he would attend and support them, she made an abrupt conversational about-face. Doubtless, she said, he was very busy; after all, a gentleman of his looks, charm and pedigree was highly sought after by hostesses offering the most select entertainments; they could not fault him for not wishing to disappoint such noble ladies to keep company with two old widows.

Her lips twitching with the effort not to laugh at the sudden change in tune, Faith felt an unexpected sympathy towards the overbearing woman. How painful it must be to realise—even if she could not admit the awful truth to herself—that her son visited her only to obtain something, and was unwilling to even occasionally oblige her by spending an evening in her company.

Never would she end up in that sad position, if there were anything she could do to prevent it! Choosing a tutor who included her in his plans for her sons' studies would be the first step. Spending more mornings 'gallivanting about' with them and more afternoons 'selfishly closeted away with them' would follow, too.

For the first time, she saw the Dowager, who along

with her son had belittled and criticised her for her whole married life, not as the imposing, elegant leader of society who had always intimidated her, but as a lonely old woman with few true friends, whose one remaining child was indifferent to her.

Perhaps it was a re-awakening of confidence, a spirit healing after years of repression, which provided this fresh point of view. Whatever the reason, Faith felt the sense of a burden lifted. No longer would she dread or resent the Dowager's remarks. Her newly minted sympathy wouldn't prompt her to spend much more time than necessary with her mother-in-law, and she certainly didn't intend to brook any interference in the bringing up of her boys, but she would try to make the time they did have together as enjoyable as she could for the woman.

That resolution stayed with her as the Dowager bore her off to a rout given by one of her society friends, the Dowager Marchioness of Hargrave. To Faith's chagrin, one of the attendees was the woman's daughter, Lady Mary—who never let slip an opportunity to diminish Faith in her sweet, falsely sympathetic voice.

'Dear Duchess!' Lady Mary sang out, coming over to clasp Faith's arm and draw her into her circle. 'Are you in good health? You seem—uncommonly ruddy of complexion tonight. I hope you're not sickening with something. Although I can imagine how difficult it has been to get over Ashedon's sudden demise—and especially the *manner* of it.'

Normally, Faith would have shrunk into herself, returning some monosyllabic reply. But at this moment, it struck her that Lady Mary's remarks *always* focused on Ashedon and his women; might her malice stem from having once been one of them, and then discarded? How it must grate to have been displaced by others of lesser birth and consequence—and to know that Faith, whom she thought so meek and useless, had been able to hold on to him as her husband.

'No, I am in the best of good health, after taking my boys to the Park today for some fresh air. And as we both know, Ashedon hadn't been mine to lose for quite some time.'

Mrs Pierce-Compton, one of Lady Mary's cronies, exclaimed, 'Took your sons to the Park *yourself*? Whatever for? Was their tutor riding in the curricle with Ashedon that day?' she added with a titter.

Fury boiled up in Faith—at the woman's crass comment, at the very idea that she would allow someone so deficient in moral character to instruct her precious sons.

Raising her eyes to meet the other woman's, she stared at her, unsmiling and silent. After a moment, Mrs Pierce-Compton looked away, saying with a weak laugh, 'It was only a joke, Duchess.'

Without a word, Faith turned her back on the woman and walked away, head high, leaving the onlookers gaping. Not until she'd marched into the next room and grabbed a glass of wine from the tray offered by one of the servants did she realise she'd just inadvertently applied Lady Lyndlington's 'technique'.

She had to smile to herself. *You were right, my friend. It is effective, and my, how good it feels!* Probably the best moment she'd had at a society party since the early days of her marriage, before her husband lost interest in her.

Quite a banner day. First, a new perspective on the woman who'd been one of the banes of her life since her wedding day, and now stumbling into a way to dismiss those who tried to hurt her without resorting to meanness, a way that left her feeling powerful and in control.

*Thank you, Davie and Maggie, for helping me regain that confidence.*

To her amusement, as it turned out, it wasn't only *her* behaviour that altered. After her cut of Mrs Pierce-Compton, for the rest of the evening, the other matrons who often congregated with her tormentor, piling on disparaging remarks, kept their distance. She was even able to have a halfway intelligent conversation with her host, Lord Hargrave, about the upcoming reform legislation.

All in all, a much more pleasant evening than she'd been anticipating. And if the new degree of respect being awarded her tonight carried over to the other *ton* entertainments she was forced to attend, it would be a banner day indeed.

If it didn't carry over, she told herself, riding high on that new-found assertiveness, she'd just have to deliver a cut-direct to a few more detractors. When it came right down to it, she really didn't care to speak with any of them. If that behaviour reduced the society invitations she received by half, she wouldn't miss them in the least.

Her resolve to be pleasant to her mother-in-law was stretched almost to the breaking point on the carriage ride back to Berkeley Square, during which the Dowager reprimanded her for being impolite to Lady Mary and then went on at length about how poorly she was treated, by the daughter-in-law who embarrassed her with her uncivil behaviour and by her son, who cruelly disappointed her by not appearing at the rout she'd promised everyone he'd attend. It took a great deal of will to refrain from pointing out that, if the Dowager wished to see more of Lord Randall, she should be a little slower in handing him money to fund his gaming habits.

Her high-flying confidence soared abruptly back to

earth once the carriage arrived in Berkeley Square. As they walked up the entry stairs, Faith stiffened, instinctively girding herself for the possibility of encountering Lord Randall in the shadows of the stairway or the hall outside her chamber. But to her relief, he did not appear.

Safely ensconced in some gaming hell or some doxy's bed, she sincerely hoped as she latched her chamber door and dragged the chair in front of it.

She fell asleep to dreams of her sons, shrieking with delight at the horses and clowns and acrobats of Astley's. And the handsome, kind, powerfully attractive gentleman who'd given them that treat, whom she only wished she knew how to seduce.

Some time later, she came groggily awake, aware of light spilling over her bed. The dawn sun, she was thinking, when suddenly the sense of someone in the room pulled her into full wakefulness. Sitting up with a gasp, she saw Lord Randall at the foot of her bed, holding a candle.

'How did you get in?' she demanded.

He chuckled, setting the candle on a side table and walking closer. 'If you want to keep someone out, dear sister, you need to bar the door to the service stairs, too.'

She'd told the staff she left the chair by the chamber door to keep it firmly shut against draughts from the hallway, which was at least plausible. Blocking the service entry would not be so easy to explain, alerting the maids and tweenies, coming to lay fires or bring up coffee in the morning, that something was amiss. 'I didn't think you'd stoop to using the servants' stairs.'

'Needs must, sweet sister.'

'I don't care how you got in, just go.'

'I thought by now, you'd be ready to invite me to stay.'

'Do you still not understand?' she asked, exasperated. 'My continuing mention of pistols ought to convey the clear impression that I will never invite you. I'm tired of your little game; it's time that it ceases.'

Fumbling in her bedside table, she brought forth the small pistol. 'I don't want to wake the house and scare everyone to death, but I really have no qualms about using it. And then telling everyone just why I had to.'

'Oh, I don't think you will, sweet sis.' He stepped closer. 'You won't use that pistol, and you won't breathe a word. If you do, I'll just say I was here at your invitation—and who do you think will believe your denial? My mother?' He laughed. 'That low-bred politician who's been sniffing at your skirts? If you're giving him any, or teasing him that you will, he'll be only too ready to believe you're handing it out to whoever asks.'

She hesitated, stricken. She *had* invited Davie's kiss. He told her he thought her the essence of purity. If Randall were to claim she'd lured him to her bedchamber— after she'd tried to tempt *him*—would Davie believe her a wanton?

The thought of losing his good opinion made her stomach lurch.

Randall took advantage of her distraction to move forward and seize the wrist of the hand holding the pistol. 'I think you can dispense with this, my dear. Then you can show me all the little tricks you've been using with your Parliamentary lover.'

She didn't dare struggle, lest the pistol go off inadvertently. 'The only thing I'm going to show you is the door.'

'I think you'll soon be ready to show me a great deal more,' he said, his teasing tone turning harsh as his face set in angry lines, his eyes glittering with lust. 'Put me out of commission for several days with that trick with your knee. You're going to be using those knees to make amends, kneeling before me to kiss and stroke that poor injured part. I can't wait to see how good you are with that sweet little mouth.'

He ran the fingers of his free hand over her lips. Too distressed and infuriated to remain still any longer, despite the risk, she batted that hand away and gave her imprisoned wrist a savage twist, extracting it from his grasp. Thankful that the pistol hadn't discharged, possibly wounding *her*, she placed it down carefully on the coverlet, out of his reach.

'Say what you will, I'll never give you that.'

'I think you'll be giving me that, and whatever else I want. Because I can talk to more than Mama and society. What if I go to those trustees, the oh-so-concerned uncle distressed to reveal the painful fact that my brother's widow is a wanton who brings her innocent boys with her when she meets her lover? A lover so far beneath her, those good gentlemen would be shocked and dismayed. How long do you think they would leave your precious sons in your charge after they learned how you were dragging your title in the mud, consorting with commoners and taking one to your bed?'

Thrown into dismay and confusion by Randall's threat, Faith had no reply. She knew the Dowager, and most of society, would disapprove of her friendship with Davie. Would Lord Randall be persuasive enough to convince the trustees she was a wanton, so abandoned she took her children to trysts? Would even the fact that she 'consorted with commoners' be enough for the trustees to consider taking her sons away?

There would be any number of witnesses who could testify that they had all been together at Astley's.

'Yes, consider it, sweet sister. If it came to my word

against yours, who do you think society—and the trustees—would believe? The son and brother of a duke, living all his life in the most select ranks of society? Or a woman everyone knows as inept and ineffective, never rising to successfully fill the high position to which she'd been elevated?'

He snatched again the wrist he'd seized and yanked her hand over, forcing it to the front of his dressing gown. Shock and fury pulsed through her as her fingers connected with the hard outline of his erection.

'Ah, yes, this is going to be very good. But I can wait. Let you ponder the situation. You may be a failure as a duchess, but you *are* intelligent. You'll soon realise the truth of it. When I come back next, you'll be ready.'

He leaned over and gave her a quick, hard kiss on the mouth. Then, strolling nonchalantly across the chamber, as if they'd just had a pleasant little chat, he moved the useless chair blocking the door and let himself out.

Scrubbing at her lips, Faith leaned back against her pillows, shaking with revulsion and dismay.

A turmoil of thoughts tumbled around in her head. Though she couldn't remember, from the chaotic episode of the reading of the will, who Ashedon had named as his sons' trustees, she found it hard to believe any would be so high in the instep as to consider her an unfit mother simply for having a well-known, well-respected Member of Parliament as her friend, particularly one with close connections to her family. But a claim that she had made such a man her lover, and brought her children along on her rendezvous with him, could well be damaging enough to make them question her fitness.

Sickness churning in her gut, she remembered the housekeeper turning out two maids who were found to be increasing. Though she was almost certain the poor girls had made no attempt to attract her husband's amorous attentions, it was the females who paid the price for that immorality.

With Lord Randall making the accusation, it was highly likely the trustees, drawn from the same rank of society as her brother-in-law and knowing her not at all, would believe him—and not her counter-accusations. Especially since society commonly believed that a man wouldn't make advances unless a woman encouraged him.

Sarah wouldn't believe it—but she was a woman, without any power. Would Englemere believe in her innocence?

And Davie? She *had* been trying to entice him; indeed, she'd halfway convinced herself to make an all-out attempt to seduce him. Would Randall's assertion that she'd been trying to entice him, too, so shock and disgust Davie that he wouldn't believe her denial, either?

Even worse, she realised that Lord Randall had just checkmated her plan to go to the trustees about him. If she were to accuse him now of making inappropriate financial inroads upon the estate, he would simply claim that she was trying to discredit him because he had refused her advances.

If Sarah couldn't help her, and she couldn't count on Englemere or Davie to believe her, how was she to thwart Lord Randall and keep her boys?

She took a deep, slow breath, forcing her frantic pulse to calm. Just because, at this moment, she had no idea how to do it, she didn't intend to panic.

She'd endured nine years of marriage to a man who'd used and then ignored her. She'd vowed, after his death freed her, that she'd never allow herself to be used or manipulated again. She was not about to let Ashedon's despicable reprobate of a brother coerce himself into her bed and make her break that promise.

There'd be no more sleep for her tonight, at any rate. She might as well spend the rest of the hours before dawn trying to come up with a plan to prevent him.

## *Chapter Eleven*

In the afternoon two days later, Davie hopped down from the hackney at Giles and Maggie's town house, where they were hosting a meeting between officials from the Lords and Commons and some influential representatives of society. At Lord Coopley's behest, they intended to invite those society leaders to encourage their representatives and peers to attend the meetings and the crucial vote soon to come over the Reform Bill.

Excited as he was to see their efforts finally come to fruition, Davie admitted he was looking forward most to seeing Faith again.

It was foolish, and most likely, sooner or later to be the source of anguish, but in every moment not focused on his committee work, his mind was preoccupied by her. And his dreams—ah, in his dreams, she'd completely replaced any strategising about government reform.

In those hazy moments between sleep and wakefulness, his mind and senses were flooded with images of her—the gold of her hair, the precise blue colour of her eyes, the shape of her shoulders, the contours of her cheeks under his hands. The softness of her breasts pressed against his chest, the silk of her hair under his cheek, the velvety fullness of her mouth, the taste of her.

He would come awake hard, throbbing with anticipation, desire and tenderness—only to realise the images, the touch, the taste, were all an illusion. Surprise and disbelief would bring him fully awake, leaving a twist of anger in his gut as passion faded and bitter disappointment settled in its wake.

Conscious, reasonable, he could talk himself out of the disappointment and anger, but in his half-dreaming state, the idea that he could not claim the woman he loved increasingly made him burn with a fierce determination to turn those illusions into reality.

It had become more of a struggle, even when awake, to yield to the hard realities of their world and repress the conviction to claim her that haunted his dreams.

Which was why this afternoon was so precious. In a salon full of other guests, he could see her, talk with her, but with so many witnesses present, have an easier time keeping a tight rein on the growing compulsion to throw caution and principles out the window and make a full-out attempt to win her.

Not as just his lover. As his wife.

Only the harsh truth that marrying her would be a selfish act that would hurt and diminish her allowed him to keep that reckless desire in check. He might have made a place for himself at the tables of political power, but a farmer's orphan could only rise so high.

Handing over hat and cane, he mounted the stairs to the salon, from which emerged a babble of voices. He halted on the threshold as the butler announced him, scanning the crowd for the one face he desired to see above all others.

He spied her at once, standing by Maggie at the

hearth, her glance lifting to his as the butler intoned his name. Along with the zing of attraction and the wash of admiration he always felt as their gazes met, he noticed that her eyes looked tired and there were faint lines of strain on her forehead, so fine that anyone who hadn't memorised her features as minutely as he had probably wouldn't notice them.

Whatever had been troubling her that day they went to Astley's had not been resolved.

Which resolved *him* to somehow carve out a few private minutes this afternoon and find out what it was.

He made himself complete the rituals of politeness, going over to greet his host and hostess and the senior members of Parliament before returning, like a lodestone to the north, to the person whose presence drew him most. 'So glad you were able to attend, Duchess.'

'Very good to see you, too, Mr Smith. I was hoping you'd be present.'

He smiled. 'I was counting on seeing you, else I'd not have attended.'

Her cheeks pinked at the compliment. 'I hope to learn enough to be able to speak knowledgeably about the bill, so I may convince any gentleman I encounter at dinners and routs next week to involve himself in the discussion. Lyndlington and Coopley were telling me they believe the bill will be read in within the fortnight, and will surely pass the Commons.'

He nodded. 'I agree. Which means it will come to the Lords soon after. Anything you can do to encourage attendance at so vital a vote will be appreciated.'

'I will do what I can. I did manage to get a few words in about it to my host, Lord Hargrave, at the dinner we attended two nights ago.' She chuckled. 'I've spent so much time at society events with my head down, trying to remain silent and impassive in the face of snide comments, I believe he was astonished to realise I was capable of intelligent conversation.'

'He can't ever have spoken with you before, and thought that.'

'I didn't generally converse with gentlemen. Or anyone, if I could avoid it, for if I did, I was sure to be treated afterwards by a lecture from the Dowager about what I should or shouldn't have said, or belittling comments from my husband, if he chanced to be present. It was easier to say nothing.'

'Another reason to be glad he's gone—even if I shouldn't say so,' he added, holding up a hand to forestall the objection politeness obliged her to make.

After a reproving glance, she said, 'I meant to thank you.' At his enquiring look, she continued, 'Emboldened by your and Lady Lyndlington's encouragement, I even dared confront some of those who made snide comments.'

She must have been recalling the event, for what began as a twitch of her lips turned into a laugh.

*Her sudden mirth was like the sun brightening a grey winter day*, he thought, warmed to his toes by her delight.

'When I did confront them, the ladies were even more shocked than Hargrave—and wary of me afterwards. Though the Dowager took me to task on the carriage ride home for incivility, warning that if I couldn't curb my waspish tongue, no one of breeding would invite me anywhere, I think quite the opposite might prove true. Society will be curious to see the novelty of meek little Faith Wellingford Evers behaving as imperiously as a true duchess.'

'You are a true duchess—much as I wish you weren't,' he added softly.

A grave look replaced the mirth. 'I wish I weren't, either,' she said with a sigh, her brow creasing again with worry. 'It's such a heavy responsibility, making sure my sons are brought up correctly. I want Edward to have all the training he needs to discharge his duties to the estate and the tenants, while remaining free of the arrogant sense of superiority that afflicted Ashedon. And his brother,' she added in an odd tone, her eyes flashing with something like anger.

More concerned than ever, he wanted to press her, but Giles was calling the group to order, Maggie begging all the guests to find a seat, so that the distinguished members could present their overview of the pending legislation. Though Davie perched himself on a chair near Faith, he had to wait through the exposition and the question session which followed before Maggie invited them all into the dining room, where light refreshments had been set out.

Seizing the opportunity, Davie gave Faith his arm and escorted her in. 'That was a great deal of information packed into a very short time. How about a stroll in the garden, after your tea and cake? By then, you'll have had time to think through what was presented, and can ask me any questions you might have.'

Though the invitation might have been framed to sound to anyone who overheard it as a helpful follow-on to the discussion, by the brightness in her eyes and her quick smile, Davie knew Faith understood it represented their one opportunity for some private time together. To his relief, she immediately replied, 'That sounds sensible. Over tea, I shall carefully consider everything that was said.'

Impatient for that brief sliver of time alone and determined to coax Faith to reveal whatever it was that brought the troubled look back to her face, Davie scalded his mouth, gulping down tea, munched a cake without tasting it, and had to work hard to curb his edginess while Faith daintily disposed of hers. He was nearly pacing with restlessness when, finally, she announced she was ready for a walk.

As he led her from the dining room to retrieve her wrap, he felt Maggie's speculative look on him. *I trust you to keep your promise*, it said.

Recalling his vow not to think of seducing—or marrying—Faith provoked a ferocious rush of conflicted feelings. Honour demanded he never do anything that might harm her, and reminded him that a promise is a promise. The imperatives of love and desire argued they belonged together, no matter what the world might say.

Should he have given such a promise? Would he be able to keep it?

Shaking off those thoughts, as soon as they'd begun to stroll, he said quietly, 'I don't mean to pry, but I couldn't help but notice you've seemed troubled the last two times I've seen you. Is something wrong?'

The surprise in her eyes before she schooled her expression told him he was right, regardless of whether she confided in him at once or not. Which increased both his worry and his determination to induce her to tell him what was disturbing her.

'Nothing, really. That is, there is something—not of great import, so you mustn't feel concerned!—but I think I shall be able to handle it. I shall handle it,' she added, the determined note in her voice at odds with the anxious look in her eyes.

While she spoke, she absently rubbed at the wrist of

her right hand, where the long sleeves of her spencer met the edge of her short kidskin gloves. As she moved her hand away, Davie noticed a darkened area of skin that looked almost like—a *bruise*?

Without a thought for whether or not it was proper, Davie snatched her arm and peeled down the glove—revealing what was indeed a large, deep purple bruise that appeared to entirely circle her wrist.

Shock and fury blasted out of his mind any intention to try subtle persuasion. 'What is going on?' he demanded.

She blanched before managing a tremulous smile. 'I suppose I can't convince you now that n-nothing is going on?' A sheen of tears, hastily blinked away, momentarily glazed her eyes.

'No, you'll not convince me. In fact...' he gently brushed away one errant tear with the finger of his glove '...I'm becoming more concerned by the moment. I imagine you'll say there's nothing I can do. But I can listen, at least. Sometimes just sharing a problem lightens the burden.'

She shook her head. 'There you are, being "Davie" again, wanting to solve the problems of the world.'

'Not all the world's. Just yours.'

'I appreciate that. And I can't tell you enough how much your encouragement has...strengthened me. Made me remember the confident, competent person I once was, long ago. The person I want to be again.'

'I'm not happy with encouraging you, if it makes you soldier on alone with a problem others could help you solve.' He touched his hand lightly over the bruise. 'Don't try to tell me you fell against a cabinet. I've been in enough fights to know someone had to have grabbed you hard and held on, to create such a mark. Is the Dowager violent towards you?'

'The Dowager?' she repeated, and laughed. 'Oh, no!'

'Surely not one of the servants!'

'No, nothing like that.' She pressed her lips together, staring into the distance, obviously debating with herself.

'Please, Faith, tell me. How can I go back into that salon as if nothing is wrong, worried that someone might harm you? Do you need to leave London? Should I take you and the boys to your sister's?'

'No!' she cried. 'No, it's absolutely essential that *you* do nothing at all. I...I probably shouldn't even have agreed to walk in the garden with you.'

Struck to the quick, he must have recoiled, for she took his arm, adding urgently, 'I don't mean to hurt your feelings. If I could, there is no one else I'd rather rely on. But...but in this instance, I just can't.'

Stiffly he withdrew his arm, stung far more deeply than he wanted to let her see. He ought to nod, and bow, and return her to the salon—but he just couldn't let it go. 'Before I remove you from my polluting presence, could I at least be informed why my assistance would be inadequate?'

'You know I don't feel that way about you,' she said softly, her eyes filling with tears, which immediately defused his anger. 'Very well, I'll tell you. But before I do, you must *promise* not to intervene.'

*Another promise he might not be able to keep?*

'If I think my intervention would make the situation worse, then I promise to do nothing,' he said, modifying her request to something he could live with.

She took his arm and led him further away from the house. 'I told you that first night I'd had an...unpleasant encounter with my brother-in-law, Lord Randall. Shortly thereafter, the Dowager invited him to take up residence with us in Berkeley Square. She believed she would see more of him, but he is generally around only when he needs more money. But on those occasions, he has taxed me to…become intimate with him.'

'The devil he has!' Davie burst out. 'The unprincipled reprobate! Making improper advances to his own brother's recent widow?'

'Well, that's Lord Randall,' she said drily. 'Ever on the lookout for his own advantage.'

'I'll take advantage of his impudence to beat him within an inch of his life!' Davie said furiously. 'Then tell him, if he ever darkens the door of Berkeley Square again, it will be the last doorway he ever walks through without the help of a cane.'

'But that's exactly what you cannot do!' Faith cried. 'You can't confront him, or beat him, or have any contact with him whatsoever. He started by just toying with me, or perhaps he really thought I was desperate enough for male company to take him for a lover. But when I consistently refused, he found a more promising approach. He…he has seen us together, me and you and my boys—coming back from the visit to Sarah's, from the trip to Astley's. He threatens that if I don't give in to his desires, he'll go to the boys' trustees and claim I am having an affair with you, and am so devoid of proper motherly feeling that I've dragged my sons along while I conduct it.'

'That's preposterous! Surely no one of sense, who knows you, would believe such a faradiddle.'

'But the trustees *don't* know me. Not personally. Probably all they know is what society thinks, that I never cut an adequate figure as duchess, that Ashedon disdained me, and then humiliated me in the manner of his death. After that, they might be convinced I decided to get back at him, dishonouring my rank and his sons, by behaving in the most flagrantly immoral way possible, consorting with a commoner and bringing my sons along to witness it. If you champion me, it just gives more credence to his claims.'

For several moments, Davie paced the pathways with her, his mind feverishly working over all she'd revealed. 'Surely you don't intend to give in to his blackmail, sacrificing yourself to ensure you keep your sons!'

'Of course not. I'd shoot him, as I threatened to, or myself, before I let that happen. But I have some time to figure out a solution. He's delivered his ultimatum, and believes after I think it over, I will conclude I have no choice but to acquiesce to his desires. He said he would wait a while before confronting me again, and I believe he will. First, because he doesn't come to Berkeley Square until he's run out of money, and his mother funded him again just two nights ago. Second, he enjoys this cat-and-mouse game, and will prolong it as long as he can, confident of my eventual surrender.'

'He can't be confident if he's dead.'

'You shooting him is an even worse solution than me shooting him,' she retorted.

'Not really. Either of us could hang for it.'

'I have no intention of dying—either for his murder, or at my own hands, for giving myself to a man I loathe. I will come up with some other plan. But I will not let him force me from my own house, or force himself on me.'

'I applaud that resolution,' he retorted, not in any way convinced. 'But how, exactly, do you mean to ensure that doesn't happen?' He glanced down at her bruised wrist, almost unhinged with fury at the idea of Lord

Randall hurting her, threatening her. 'Surely you don't think you're strong enough to resist him, if he did try to compel you.'

She sighed. 'I thought at first I could, but you're right. If it comes to brute force, I wouldn't prevail. So I'll have to see it doesn't.'

She must have been able to tell from his expression how inadequate a response he found that statement—and how much he felt like ripping a branch off the unoffending shrubbery bordering the pathway and breaking it over Lord Randall's head. Halting in the pathway, she took both his hands.

'Please, promise me, Davie,' she said earnestly. '*Promise* me you won't do anything to Lord Randall. Don't trail him, harass him, come to fisticuffs with him—in short, don't assault him personally in any way that would confirm a strong connection between us, giving further credence to an accusation that we are lovers. Any number of people—here today, at Astley's—can testify that we've spent time together, and you are even more an outsider to society than I am. Nothing you assert would be believed over Lord Randall's sworn word.'

'Doesn't anyone in society realise he's a liar, a wastrel, and a reprobate?' Davie spat out.

'Yes. But he was born a duke's son, and that's all that will matter,' she replied bitterly. 'We should go back in. Before we do, you will promise me, won't you? Else I'll worry even more than I am now. And…and I probably can't risk any more outings alone with you and the boys, even to Sarah's. Much as I hate to concede even that much to Randall, I should probably see you only at gatherings like these.'

She looked at once both so fierce, and so forlorn, it was all Davie could do not to pick her up and carry her back to his rooms in Albany, where he could keep her safe. But she was right, at least initially. He couldn't intervene now, lest he risk giving the despicable Lord Randall more ammunition with which to threaten Faith.

With the loss of her sons. The phrase settled in his chest like a blow.

It would destroy her.

He couldn't do anything that would lead to that.

He couldn't stand by and do nothing, either.

But for now, he would ease her anxiety with a promise, he thought, his mind already racing through possible scenarios. A very carefully worded promise.

'Very well. I promise I will not personally assault Lord Randall.'

Fortunately, she didn't analyse how much leeway that pledge left him. 'Thank you, Davie,' she said, visibly relieved.

'But I want a promise from you in return.'

'What?' she asked, looking wary again.

'If you're wrong, and Lord Randall confronts you in your bedchamber, scream to raise the roof, shoot first and worry about the consequences later. Or take the boys, today, and go to Sarah. I may be nobody in the eyes of society, but Englemere is a marquess. He can protect you.'

'Your good opinion is everything to me,' she whispered, pressing his hand. 'Knowing that you believe in my innocence gives me the courage to keep on. I won't go to Sarah—yet—but I promise I will shout the house down, if Randall should try to force himself on me. Now, we must go in.'

Knowing he'd pushed her as far as he could, he gave her his arm. Together, they walked back to the house, Davie wondering how he would manage to sit calmly through the rest of this meeting, when all he wanted was time alone to figure out how he would counter Lord Randall's threat without compromising his promise to Faith.

Because he fully intended, before he set eyes on Faith again, to have eliminated the problem of Lord Randall.

## Chapter Twelve

Having had difficulty refraining from tapping his heels for the rest of the meeting at Lord Lyndlington's, for the first time, Davie was content to leave Faith with Maggie as the gentlemen made their departures.

'Keep her here as long as you can,' he murmured in Maggie's ear as she kissed his cheek, adding, 'I can't explain now, and don't ask her,' when she moved to arm's length, her eyebrows raised. 'Can you do that?'

'Of course,' she said, giving his hand a squeeze.

'Duchess,' he said, turning to Faith, 'I trust you will try to bend as many ears as possible this coming week, encouraging attendance at Parliament.'

'Yes, Mr Smith. Thank you again for taking the time to walk with me and fully explain some of the particulars.'

'It was my privilege.'

'Mine as well, to talk with so learned and principled a gentleman. Your electors in Hazelwick must have great confidence in you, knowing you are a man who always keeps his promises.'

While Maggie cast a puzzled look from Faith to

Davie, he bowed. 'I trust that I keep my promises to everyone,' he said pointedly to them both.

Then, telling Giles he had an errand to discharge before meeting him back at the committee room, he walked out.

Already fairly sure of his destination, Davie chose to walk for a street or two, wanting some quiet time to review his preliminary impressions and confirm a plan of action.

He felt only disgust for a man—he wouldn't dignify Lord Randall Evers with the title 'gentleman,' no matter how high his birth—who would try to coerce a woman into his bed. That the woman the man was trying to coerce was his recently widowed sister-in-law made the attempt even more despicable.

That the woman was Faith made him want to take the man apart limb from limb.

There was nothing that would give him more pleasure than *personally* showing Evers what it was like to be confronted by a more physically powerful opponent. Though he was confident that such a man was a self-indulgent bully, who, once he was opposed by someone who could inflict more punishment than Evers could deliver, would back off and not menace her again, he'd promised Faith not to undertake the punishing himself.

That was disappointing, and he'd need a good, long session boxing with a worthy opponent to work off the frustration of having to honour that pledge.

On the other hand, the man was sly enough, and vindictive enough, that if Davie did assault him, he might make his accusations anyway, counting on his elevated status and the evidence of Davie's abuse to give credence to his preposterous claims. To protect Faith into the future, it was probably wiser that the retaliation for Evers's threat not be traced to him personally.

His authority and opinions might not carry any weight in circles more elevated than Parliament. But there were certain places in which he was well known, his proven competence respected, where he would be able to recruit exactly the assistance he needed.

In this instance, he thought grimly as he hailed a hackney and set off for Bow Street, it was useful to have friends in *low* places.

Fortunately, for he didn't want to explain to Giles what had taken him so long to 'discharge his errand', Mr Hines was in his office when Davie arrived.

'Mr Smith, good to see you again!' Hines said, waving Davie to a chair. 'All going well in Parliament, I hear? About to strike a blow for the common man?'

'We certainly hope so.'

'As I imagine you are aware, we got a conviction in the case of the man hired to shoot at Lady Roberts—that is, Lady Lyndlington now. With both families involved strongly urging to the judge that clemency be shown, he was transported, rather than hanged.'

'Let me commend you again for how expeditiously your men handled that case.'

Hines nodded, accepting the compliment as his due—which he should; the man was efficient and fanatically persistent in solving the cases brought to him. 'Always glad to help out a man who has given us so much assistance from time to time. So, what brings you to me today?'

'A rather delicate matter, one whose resolution requires discretion and actions that might not precisely follow the letter of the law. Actions, I must warn you, taken against a man of high standing, who could make a lot of trouble for both of us if the business isn't handled properly.'

'So it involves a female,' Hines said, interpreting Davie's euphemisms. 'A woman some high-ranking gent is trying to abuse, like that earl's son in the case of Lady Lyndlington?'

'Something similar. Though I would far prefer to handle the situation personally, if the…actions could be traced back to me, the man in question might be able to make further trouble for the lady. So I'm looking for two or three skilled individuals, who can perform the actual…intervention.'

Hines nodded thoughtfully. 'Them higher-ups been bending the law to suit them for centuries. I reckon it's only fair it be bent a time or two against them—especially if it's to protect a female. I know you got too much respect for the law to ask me for help on this, if the cause wasn't right and just. What type of "intervention" do you have in mind?'

Davie described what he envisioned, Hines making suggestions at various points to improve the plan. Within a half hour, they'd worked out a scenario that satisfied them both with its safety and efficiency, and its ability to be implemented soon, perhaps that very night.

Leaving Hines to put the finishing touches on the scheme, with directions about contacting him later to launch it, Davie thanked the man again and took his leave. Knowing that he most likely would be able to snap off the problem of Lord Randall like the branch he'd wanted to break in the garden this afternoon, he was able to return to the committee room calm, resolved and full of purpose.

* * *

It was mid-evening by the time the committee completed its deliberations, and the Hellions were free for the night. Just as they were finishing up, a boy delivered a note to Davie that greatly relieved his mind.

The very efficient Hines had come through again. They'd be able to put the plan into action this very evening.

'Shall we head off to the Quill and Gavel?' Ben Tawny's question interrupted Davie's thoughts. Rolling his tired shoulders, he added 'After all those hours bent over documents, I could do with a good roast and a large tankard of ale.'

'Before you head off to find refreshment of a more intimate and satisfying sort?' Christopher Lattimer asked with a grin.

'Naturally,' Ben replied. 'You're welcome to come along. Sally has several friends, all of them as voluptuous and playful as she is.'

'I just might,' Christopher said. 'Giles, you're off to your lady wife, I expect. Davie, will you join us for dinner? For as we know only too well, you'll not join us for the festivities after.'

'Certainly not!' Ben said. 'The Saint will return to his empty rooms, to worship at the shrine of "the Unattainable", and find whatever pleasure he can reading musty old legal documents.'

'He's been worse than ever since—for no good reason any of us can tell—he started seeing her again,' Christopher observed.

'Well, having beheld her up close, I can better understand why he's worshipped all these years. Although, Davie, you still know nothing can come of it. Isn't it time you bowed to reality and set your sights on someone more suitable?'

'Isn't it time you both stopped harassing him and let him make that choice?' Giles interposed.

Refusing to be drawn by their banter, Davie simply shrugged. 'I can't join you gentlemen for dinner, either—and not just because you can't seem to stop pestering me.'

'I did refrain from pursuing the Vision myself,' Ben pointed out. 'You owe me something for that, because she truly is delectable. And after all those years tied to a fool like Ashedon, she deserves a little…frolic, with a man who can make sure she enjoys it.'

Finally goaded beyond endurance, Davie sent Ben a thunderous look that had his friend laughing as he raised his hands protectively in front of his face. 'Pax! Don't try that punishing roundhouse punch out on me.'

Reminded of where he wished he could use it, Davie said, 'You push me very close to the edge, but, alas, that's not to be. I do have some urgent business to complete, though.'

'More urgent business?' Giles asked quietly. 'Anything the Hellions can help you with?'

'Not now. Not yet. But if…circumstances develop in that direction, I will certainly let you know.'

'Then all we can do, is hope the enterprise prospers,' Giles said.

'If Davie doesn't need us, I'm ready for dinner. Come, Christopher, let's find a good roast.'

'And then on to more delectable entertainment,' Christopher added as the two friends sauntered out.

Giles lingered, regarding Davie silently until the other Hellions were out of earshot. 'You've been tense as an overwound watch all day. Are you sure I can't help?'

'Not tonight, which I hope will resolve the matter.'

'Then I will hope so, too.' Giving him a clap on the arm, Giles said, 'You've done me a good turn more times than I care to mention. Just know I stand ready to return the favour.'

Davie smiled. 'Considering that, if you hadn't befriended me in that tavern in Oxford all those years ago, I might be toiling away as a lonely law clerk in some barrister's office today, rather than working towards the most significant piece of legislation in the last four hundred years, I think we can call ourselves even.'

'Friends don't keep score. Don't forget the offer, though. I'm off to Maggie.'

'Give her my love.'

'I'll do that.' With a final nod, Giles walked out, leaving Davie in sole possession of the committee room. For a few minutes, he paced the length of it, going over in his mind each step in his plan for the night. Then, satisfied he'd calculated every angle and considered every detail, he squared his shoulders, took a deep breath, and set out.

The initial move had him strolling into an area of London he seldom visited, a slip of a lad trailing him. Until recently, when the government sinecures he'd been awarded had begun providing him with a steady income, he'd not possessed enough blunt beyond what was essential to pay for his food and lodging, to think of wasting any on gaming. Not that, he thought, looking askance at the knots of young men swaggering down the street from gaming hell to gaming hell, their fine garments proclaiming them as gentlemen of privilege, he could ever have been persuaded to throw away good coin on games of chance.

Solid farm boy that he was, he thought with a wry grin, whenever he got a penny to spare, he'd saved it to invest in good English land—and now possessed a fine small estate, a fact that gave him far more satisfaction than the lucky outcome of a frivolous game.

A moment later, he reached his destination. With his imposing size and prosperous look, he was easily granted access to Aphrodite's Dice, a hell known both for its deep play and its lovely—and available—women. When the proprietor, spying a gent who might be a new pigeon for plucking, tried to induce him to join in some game of chance, he politely declined, informing them he was there as a friend of Mr Hine's.

The man's eyes widened before he nodded. 'Very good, sir. Would you like a glass of wine while you wait?'

Accepting that, he followed the proprietor, who led him into the next room and nodded towards a table. There sat Lord Randall, rolling a pair of the dice featured in the establishment's name, the glass of brandy in his other hand continually replenished by the scantily attired lovely at his side.

'The preparations are all made. Did you want to have a word with the gentleman—before?' the proprietor murmured.

'Not as yet.'

'As you wish.'

Giving him a short bow, the proprietor exited, and Davie turned to watch Lord Randall. It appeared, as arranged, he was currently winning, for the stack of counters in front of him had been steadily growing. Intent on the play, his eyes glazed with the feverish look of the hardened gamester, he was oblivious to all else, even the blandishments of the lady wielding the brandy decanter, whom he pushed away when, from time to time, she leaned over to whisper in his ear.

After one particularly successful run, he gave a crow of triumph, leaning back to seize the hand the harlot had rested on his shoulder and pulling it down to rub at his groin. 'Feel that power, Letty?' he crowed. 'Stronger and sweeter than brandy. You'll be getting a mouthful, soon as I finish off this round.'

Davie only hoped the man hadn't used such crude terms with Faith. The very thought made him clench his fists, and he had to force himself to remember all the good reasons he couldn't just walk over and punch Lord Randall in the gut.

Since he'd turned down the offers of the other young ladies who strolled up to accompany him to the card tables, the faro bank—or upstairs—they soon left him alone. He found himself pitying not only the unfortunate women who had to service such clients, but the gaming-crazed young men who seemed unable to walk away from the tables until they'd spent their last coin.

Imagine, he thought—watching as one well-dressed gentleman dropped almost five hundred guineas—having that much blunt, and just tossing it away.

Finally, the moment for which he'd been patiently waiting arrived. Lord Randall, happily finished at his table, pawed up his winnings and staggered upright, leaning on the shoulder of his doxy. As he crossed the room towards the stairway to the chambers above, he finally spotted Davie, and halted.

A slow smile on his face, he patted the doxy on the bottom and said, 'Go on up, honey. I'll meet you in a trice.' Giving her a push towards the stairs, he sauntered over to Davie.

'Well, well,' he said, subjecting Davie to a slow, insolent inspection from his boots to the crown of his head. 'You're that guttersnipe politician who's been sniffing around my brother's wife, aren't you? Wonder they let so low-born a cur in the place. Might have to take my custom elsewhere.'

'I'm sure they'll be delighted if you do. The women, at least.'

'Ah, yes, women.' He smirked. 'Ashedon's doxy wife, in particular, eh? Can't blame you being interested—she's a choice little morsel. So hot-blooded, I'm having trouble holding her off! But she's not available—at least, not until I'm done with her.'

Gritting his teeth against the compulsion to knock the varmint to his knees with one well-placed blow, Davie made himself reply calmly, 'I think you will be "done with her" very soon. Tonight, as a matter of fact.'

'I will, will I? When I haven't truly started yet? No, indeed!' Randall struck an exaggerated pose, hands on hips. 'You're thinking you can make me?'

'I won't need to. Your conscience is going to persuade you it's only right to stop harassing your brother's widow.'

Randall burst out laughing. 'What, she tell you tales? Say I "threatened" her, or some such? Thing is, she's so unsophisticated and simple, she exaggerates or misrepresents what she hears.'

Davie nodded. 'I'm rather unsophisticated and simple myself. But I understand what a bruised wrist represents. So you're not going to see her again. In fact, you're not going back to Berkeley Square—ever.'

Randall's smile faded. 'You know, you're not so amusing any more. Why don't you leave, before I have the proprietor eject you? And if you have the audacity to come around me again, trying to tell a duke's brother how to treat his women, I've got a little warning for you. Persist in this, and I'll tell the trustees overlooking her brats about the little trysts between you two. Yes, I've seen you, bringing her and the sons back in the carriage. Don't think the trustees would hold with a duchess rutting in the gutter with a commoner—while her dear children watch. I'm guessing they'd whisk those boys away faster than she could find herself a handkerchief to boo-hoo in. Face it, guttersnipe. You can't help her. You can only destroy her.'

'Whereas you don't *care* if you destroy her,' Davie said, calling on all the willpower he possessed to keep from pummelling Evers then and there.

Randall smiled again. 'True. But unlike you, I get what I want.'

As Evers waved a hand dismissively, Davie added, 'Perhaps. You'd have to be alive to get it, though. Bullies who try to abuse innocent women often suffer unforeseen…accidents. Goodnight, Evers.'

After the insult of neglecting to accord him his title, Davie turned on his heel and walked away. Having confirmed all that Faith had confessed and more, it was time to initiate the second part of the plan.

Unfortunately for the fury and contempt raging through him, he would have to play a much less active part in that.

Forewarned by the proprietor, the men Davie had hired were stationed by the door as a drunken Lord Randall was helped down the back stairs of the gaming hell some time later. From the place in the shadows where he stood beside his horse, Davie gave the nod, and the driver of the waiting carriage pulled his vehicle up to the bottom of the stairs.

''Ere's your hackney, governor,' one of the men said.

'Get you back to your lodgings all right and tight,'

the other said, grabbing Lord Randall's shoulders and heaving him up the step.

'D-don' need lozzings,' Randall slurred. 'Hav'a house. Berkeley Square.'

'In good time, governor. In good time.' After pushing Evers into the cab and closing the door behind him, the two men hopped up on the box beside the driver and gave Davie a wave.

The carriage set off, Davie mounted quickly, and quietly followed.

After a winding journey from the dubious streets behind Covent Garden to a nicer part of town, the carriage entered through the gates of Hyde Park, continuing through the deserted gardens until it reached a place near the verge of the Serpentine. There, the vehicle halted.

While Davie dismounted and took up his position a short distance from the vehicle, the two men climbed down from the box and opened the carriage door.

'Wakee, wakee, my lord,' one said. 'Time for your walk.'

'Wa—walk?' Evers's drowsy voice repeated.

'Yes, walk. Preacher says, contemplation's good for the soul.' With that, the man reached inside and yanked Lord Randall from the coach.

The full moon illumined them as Randall stumbled out, the second man caught him neatly and held him upright while the first pulled a sack over his head and down his body, securing it with a quick knot of rope about his upper thighs.

'Wha—what are you doing?' Evers cried. Shock and the cool air apparently dissipating some of the drunken haze, he flailed his imprisoned arms inside the sacking restraining his upper body.

As Davie watched, the two men half-pushed, half-dragged the protesting Randall over to the Serpentine, threw him in, and waded in after him.

After a moment, Evers found his feet and surfaced, gasping. 'Whatever do you—?'

Each man taking an arm, they knocked his feet out from under him and tossed Randall into the water again.

Breathing even more raggedly, he emerged a second time. A note of panic in his voice, he cried, 'What do you want? I can pay—'

The two seized him and submerged him a third time—and a fourth, and a fifth.

When they finally allowed him to remain on his feet, Randall sobbed, 'P-pay you! Wh—whatever you want! J-just let me go!'

At Davie's signal, the two grabbed Randall again, dragged him back up the bank, and tossed him to the ground.

'Wh—why are you doing this?' he cried. 'I haven't done anything! You must have the wrong man!'

'Don't reckon we do,' the leader said. 'Heard a lot about you. Lordling's son and brother. Living off his mama in a smart house in Berkeley Square. Got the right of it, don't I?'

'But what—?'

'Threatening his sister-in-law. His poor, widowed sister-in-law. Just ain't right. A man don't do such.'

'*He* sent you!' Randall cried. 'That pox-ridden politic—'

The second man struck Randall on the jaw before he could finish, knocking him to his knees.

While he scrabbled to regain his balance, the leader said, 'Don't need no names. And nobody sent me. Heard a mate repining over a mug of ale, ya see? 'Bout a fine lady being threatened by a greasy muckworm—that would be you—and how angry he was, not being able to grind the muckworm under his boot like he wanted, on account of the muckworm maybe making more trouble for the lady. Now this mate, he's done me some powerful good turns over the years. So when I heard him so agitated 'n' all, I thought to meself, why not do him a favour back, and take care of this for him?'

At his nod, the second man hauled Evers upright. The leader reached out to grip Randall's shoulder with one large paw, his hold punishing enough that Randall cried out. Leaning closer, he said, 'Had to sympathise, ya see. Got a daughter of me own—prettiest thing a man ever laid eyes on. So pretty, a fancy man tried to snatch her for a bawdy house. I 'bout lost my mind when I found her missing, but with the Lord's blessing, I found her right quick. And that fancy man? Well, he won't be snatching no more girls, ever again.'

'No names!' Evers agreed, his voice pleading. 'Just let me go. I'll pay you! And I'll leave the bitch alone, I promise!'

'Here, now, show the lady some respect!' the first man said, nodding to the second man, who punched Evers again.

This time, Lord Randall didn't try to stand back up, but remained cowering on the ground. Between Evers's sobs, the first man continued, 'Don't want your mama's money. Don't believe a muckworm's promises, neither. No, we'll have a little agreement, jes' between me 'n' you. You'll take those winnings Aphrodite's Dice allowed you tonight, and leave London. Go far away as you can get. I hear Calais is a good town for cheap living and high play. And you'll stay there a good long while. Till my agitation with you simmers down. Understand?'

He nodded to the second man, who hauled Randall

back to his feet. 'I understand,' Randall sobbed. 'Leave London, tonight. Won't come back.'

'That's right. Good to know even a muckworm like you has some sense. But just in case you get to thinking, after we drop you at that lodging house to get your spare duds, that maybe instead of leaving, you'll go complain to your mama, or the constable, or some such, remember this. We knew where to find you tonight. When a man don't pay his valet, or his servants, or any what provide him with coats and hats and boots and such, there's a lot of folk eager to tell whatever you want, to get a few coins back on what's owed them. If you don't leave London, I'll know, and the next time I toss you in the water, there'll be a rock in that sack with you. Doubt anyone will miss you, 'ceptin them what you owe money to. Now, think you can remember that?'

'Yes,' Randall gasped. 'Please, just let me go!'

'Dunno,' the man said, his tone considering. 'Not sure your memory's that good. Mebbe need another dunking to strengthen it some.' At his wave, the second man knocked Randall to the ground and started dragging him back towards the Serpentine.

'No, please!' Randall screamed, struggling futilely in the confining sack. 'I'll remember. I'll leave tonight!'

At his leader's nod, the second man halted. The leader walked over to where Evers struggled on the ground and knelt next to him.

'Sure you'll remember? No more trouble for the lady? No recriminations for my mate?'

'No! Nothing! I hope I never lay eyes on either of them again.'

'Ah, yes—yer *eyes*. Now, if after a time you should come to think, from the safety of whatever rat's nest you run to, that you might send yer *money* back to London and try to get someone to find me, save the coins. Oh, someone'd take them, all right. But you'd get nothing else for them. I'm a rather well-connected gent in certain parts; you have no power and no influence there. If you was to want to come back and settle up yerself—now, that's a meeting I'd relish. Got lots of sacks, and there's plenty of lonely riverbank. But I don't think you're up to that. Better you just take your winnings and get your miserable muckworm self out of London tonight, and stay gone.'

'I'll go. I'll stay gone. Just take me away now!'

'Sure you don't need a little more water cure to help your memory?'

'No, no, I'm sure! Please! Just let me go!'

When Randall stopped to take a breath, the leader said, 'Very well. Being a fair man, I'll give you a chance to hold up your end of the bargain.' He clapped his hands, summoning the coachman, who dismounted and came running.

'Take him to his lodgings,' he told the second man. 'And keep watch. Don't report back until you know he's left London.'

While Randall moaned and whimpered, the second man and the coachman half-led, half-carried him to the carriage, dragged him up the step, and tossed him in. After securing the door, the two men scrambled back up on the box, and a moment later, the coach drove off.

Once it was well away, the leader walked over to where Davie waited in the shadows. 'Where do the toffs come up with such scum?' he asked. 'Right tempted to toss him in the water again and leave him.'

'Glad you didn't,' Davie said. 'I wanted him cowed, not murdered. Though I doubt anyone but his mama would miss him, doing away even with a reprobate like

Evers would cause too many problems. My conscience would have required me to fish him out, and I'd have been hard-pressed to make myself do it.'

'Never can tell for sure, but I think he's gone for good. I'll have Jack watch him for a week or so, and keep Hines posted.'

'He'll write his mama and beg for more money, once what they let him win tonight runs out,' Davie said. 'But I don't think he'll be back to make accusations. Sadly, there are too many other women in the world for a man with money to bother, to keep pursuing just one, especially after you made him such a convincing case for moving on. Thank you.'

Davie held out his hand, and the leader shook it.

'Figure what I owe you for the gaming hell, the carriage, your men, and the surveillance, and let Hines know.'

'Some for the lads and the gambling house, but nothing for me,' the man said. 'Putting the fear of God into him was my pleasure. Wasn't bamming when I told him about me daughter. Wish I could bag up all the varmints that prey on females and toss 'em in the river! Good luck to you and your lady. You'll be getting us common men our day in Parliament soon, right?'

'I will keep pressing for it,' Davie promised. Tipping his hat to Hine's operative, he walked back to his horse, while the man disappeared into the night like the phantom he was.

Reasonably sure that Randall had been dealt with for good, Davie rode back towards Albany, as satisfied with the results of the night's manoeuvrings as he could be, without having been permitted the satisfaction of personally planting a few blows in the middle of Lord Randall's smirking face.

Now he had a more delicate task to accomplish: figuring out how to tell Faith what he'd done, and convincing her to visit Sarah until he was sure his ploy had permanently removed the threat of Lord Randall.

## Chapter Thirteen

Encouraged by a note from Hines confirming that Lord Randall had indeed left London that night, followed by a second indicating their man had watched Evers boarding a packet bound for Calais, Davie was able to curb his impatience to see Faith again until a favourable opportunity arose. Which it did in the afternoon three days later, when he learned from Giles that the ladies were going to call on an elderly peer, an old friend of Lady Maggie's father, who'd turned over his estate to his son and lived in a grace and favour apartment at Hampton Court.

'Are you going to escort Maggie there?' Davie asked.

'Yes. Maggie and the Duchess will go to charm Lord Harvey, and I'll come along to provide any details he may demand about the legislation. His lordship's not as healthy or vigorous as he once was, but still takes an interest in Parliamentary doings, Maggie said. With the vote to come next week, we need to involve as many peers as possible.'

'Sure he'll vote with us?'

'Maggie says he's a realist. If we can convince him the vote must pass, he'll want to have a part in doing what will prevent further unrest and distress in the country.'

'Do you mind if I accompany you?'

Giles studied him for a moment. 'Wouldn't it be better if you did not?'

'Not this time. I have some information of a…confidential nature for the Duchess that shouldn't be trusted to a note. The visit to Lord Harvey will allow me to convey it to her personally, upon an occasion in which our meeting will not excite any comment.'

'This "confidential information" is related to the "business" you were so keen to take care of several days ago? Which, I assume, prospered, since you've seemed much more your normal self since then.'

'Yes, and, yes.' Davie gave him a wry smile. 'Thank you for trusting me on this, and making no attempt to pry. And especially for not making any mention of it in front of Christopher and Ben, who would have no compunction about pressing the matter.'

Giles nodded. 'I figured if the Hellions could be of any help, you'd ask, and if we couldn't, it was none of our business. Especially as it seemed to relate to the Duchess.' He hesitated. 'Do you…have some notion of what you envision for that association?'

'There's where I'd wish it to go, and where it will likely end,' Davie admitted.

Giles clapped a hand on his shoulder. 'If there's anything I can do…'

'Noted. When do we meet the ladies?'

Giles consulted the mantel clock. 'We'd best leave now. The Duchess was to take tea with Maggie at Upper Brook Street, with our carriage ordered to come around after.'

Anticipation and trepidation rising in equal measure

at the idea of seeing Faith soon, Davie rose with Giles and went to get his hat and coat. Some time after the meeting, he'd ask Faith to walk with him in the gardens.

It had better be a long walk, he thought wryly. Because after he confessed what he'd done, she might hand him his *congé* this very afternoon.

When they joined the ladies at Upper Brook Street, the light that sparked in Faith's eyes and the warmth of her smile at his unexpected appearance soothed the ever-present ache in his heart with an uplift of joy. Driving deep the hunger to touch and taste her that also leapt to the forefront the moment he saw her, he tried to convince himself he could be satisfied by a life where he met her only as a friend.

'Mr Smith! What a surprise!' she said, coming over to him as Giles and Maggie shared a hug.

Wistfully wishing he had the freedom to share the same with Faith, he said, 'Not an unwelcome one, I hope.'

'Indeed not! I'm so pleased you'll be joining our little expedition this afternoon.'

'You've been well, I trust?' he asked, knowing that Lord Randall had not been around to bother her, and hoping that she'd been able to suppress her anxiety over the threat he posed. 'You look more rested than when I saw you last.'

After this afternoon, she would have no more reason to lose sleep. The certain knowledge that he had eliminated for good the threat posed by her brother-in-law made it worthwhile to have acted without her knowledge or approval, even if it created a breach between them.

Her safety was more important than anything else.

'Yes, thankfully, there have been no…disturbances these last few days.'

'Shall we go?' Maggie turned to ask. 'I told Lord Harvey in my note that we'd be there in time for a late tea. So many of his generation have already passed, he doesn't get many visitors, so I know he'll be waiting for us.'

'Then let us leave at once,' Faith said. 'We'll find an opportunity to talk later, Mr Smith?'

'Certainly. Perhaps we might stroll in the garden after the business is complete, to give Maggie some time for a private chat with Lord Harvey?'

Faith's eyes brightened. 'We could walk in the maze! I haven't wandered through it since I was a child, but I remember being enchanted by it. Although, you are so tall, you may be able to see over the hedges.'

'I've never been; you must show it to me. I promise not to peek and spoil the suspense.'

With that, the ladies collected gloves and wraps and descended to the carriage. Thinking it wiser to avoid the temptation of sitting beside Faith—and any potential awkwardness on the drive back, if she should be furious with him—Davie chose to make the transit on horseback. Not wishing to mar even this limited contact being impatient or anxious, he forced his sense of urgency beneath the surface. Once they were out of the congestion of the city, he rode beside the carriage, keeping up a running conversation with the denizens of the coach, as he had when he'd escorted Faith and her sons to Lady Englemere's.

The day being warm and pleasant, the trip was enjoyable, with autumn wildflowers nodding beside the lanes and just a touch of chill in the air to warn of the approaching change of season. Their vehicle and Davie's horse dispatched to grooms at the palace, they proceeded to the apartment occupied by Lord Harvey, where they found the genial gentleman and tea awaiting them.

After introductions were made all around, the ladies launched into their mission of charming the elderly peer, accomplishing it so successfully that Giles's announcement of the radical changes about to happen in Parliament drew nothing stronger than an exclamation of surprise from Lord Harvey. As Giles presented the major points, he asked a series of sharp, penetrating questions that made Maggie remark with a laugh that she was glad the more knowledgeable gentlemen had accompanied them.

Content to let Giles explain their position, Davie curbed his impatience to get Faith alone and simply appreciated the joy of being around her, watching her with even more than his usual intensity.

The enquiring angle of her head as she listened to Lord Harvey pose a question, or Giles answer it, reminded him again of that summer of debate they'd shared. So full of dreams and purpose they'd been, he thrilled that Sir Edward's patronage would allow him to take part in turning his ideas for a new England into reality, she giddy with anticipation to enter the adult world.

She was just as lovely as she'd been that summer, a girl poised on the brink of becoming a woman. She still lit up the room, and his heart, with her smile. But the struggles of her marriage and the responsibility of motherhood had created layers of reserve and complexity that made the woman even more fascinating than the girl. After enduring heartache, disappointment, and disparagement, she'd raised that little chin, and with a militant sparkle in her eyes, ultimately refused to be defeated by the neglect of her husband, the disapproval of society, the criticism of her mother-in-law—or the crude threats of a reprobate.

Which just emphasised the need for him to be eloquent this afternoon. His newly confident Faith wouldn't be dictated to, or metaphorically patted on the head and told what he'd done without her approval was for the best. He would need to persuade her that his actions had been well thought out, fitting—and effective—in order to preserve her trust.

Would he be persuasive enough?

With tea consumed, Lord Harvey having reached the end of his questions and the personal chat between their host and Lady Maggie beginning, he was about to find out.

'Shall we have that walk now, Mr Smith?' Faith asked, turning to him, obviously eager to begin the stroll he both anticipated—and dreaded. He absolutely hated to spoil their precious time together bringing up something that was sure to make her angry. But he'd rather have her distressed with him, than to have stood by and done nothing as she'd begged him to, and have her still at the mercy of the infamous Lord Randall.

Wraps and coats collected, they exited Lord Harvey's apartment and strolled across the palace grounds to the entrance to the maze.

'Isn't it lovely?' Faith exclaimed, examining the handsome stand of boxwood at the entrance. 'I don't think even you will be able to see over it, Davie.' Taking his arm, she said, 'Though it would be amusing to discover who could solve the key and reach the centre first, I simply can't bear for us to part, and waste this opportunity to be alone, far from prying eyes and listening ears!'

'I doubt we'll be overheard, though we might still be observed from the upper storeys of the palace,' Davie noted. With her perfume infiltrating his nose and the touch of her hand on his sleeve setting his body into a full clamour for more, he was struggling to keep her enchanting presence from distracting him from the serious matter he had to discuss.

'The trees will block the view—or well enough. Oh, Davie, it's so good to be with you again!' Taking his arm with both hands, she marched him at a quick step down the first avenue and around the corner, into the sheltering walls of the maze.

And then before he was aware what she intended, she reached up and pulled his head down for a kiss.

Desire incinerated surprise the instant her lips touched his. Prudence, discretion, the confession he was about to make—all cindered as well, as his whole universe narrowed to the woman pressing her lips to his.

He wrapped his arms around her, drawing her close, sighing as the softness of her bosom contacted his chest. Though he was so starved for the taste of her, he wanted to possess and plunder, he kept himself still, letting her set the pace.

And discovered there was something intensely erotic about letting her initiate and probe and explore, opening his mouth only when she demanded entry, meeting her tongue with his only after she sought it out. Her little gasps and sighs filling him with a tenderness almost as vast as the passion they inspired, he opened to her as she pressed deeper, the vibrations created by the sensuous plush of her tongue rubbing his so intense, he thought he might reach his peak from her kisses alone.

Devil take it, how he wanted her! So much, he blessed this narrow walk, bordered on either side by nothing more comfortable than evergreen shrubbery, else he might lose all control and take her right here, right now.

But her artless passion deserved wine, and wooing, and fine linen sheets, and hours in which to show her how much he desired and cherished her.

She must have been near the brink, too, for heedless of time and place, she wrapped her arms around him and pulled him closer still, bringing his throbbing erection tight against her belly. Knowing if she gave any indication of moving that sweet mouth to the part of him most desperate for her caress, he'd be well and truly lost, he somehow found enough will to break the kiss.

Not enough will to release her, though. They stood with their arms wrapped around each other, the only sound their ragged, panting breaths and the distant call of a bird. Finally, with a sigh, she pushed away.

'Though ending that before it went any further was prudent, it doesn't make me feel any less like slapping you,' she said, taking his arm and starting to walk again.

'Slap away. I didn't like ending it any more than you did.'

She took a shuddering breath. 'Maybe we ought to talk about…going to a place where we wouldn't have to end it.'

Not allowing his mind to explore the meaning behind that comment, Davie said, 'Before we talk of anything else, I have a confession to make, as well as a prediction that I hope will leave you much relieved.'

'A confession? Oh, dear—I'm not sure I like the sound of that.'

'Although, to be prudent, I'd like to have you take your boys and go visit Lady Englemere for a few days, I'm nearly certain your problems with Lord Randall are over.'

It took her only an instant to comprehend the implications. Halting, she dropped his arm and turned to face him. 'What have you done? Oh, Davie, I begged you not to intervene! You haven't shot him, have you? Or beaten him to a pulp?'

'No, though it required a great deal of restraint to resist beating him to a pulp.'

'But you did confront him—thereby providing him all the ammunition he needs to accuse us to the trustees! Which, unless you truly did murder him, he's sure to do. And after you promised me! I wish I *had* slapped you! Now I'll never be free of his menace! And if he ends up getting them to take my boys away, I'll hate you f-for ever!'

Her furious voice breaking as tears started in her eyes, she turned on her heel and stalked away from him. In two strides, he caught up and grabbed her arm.

'Wait, Faith, let me explain! I didn't break my promise.'

She looked up at him, confused and miserable. 'But—didn't you just tell me you'd confronted Randall, hurt him, after I most particularly begged you not to?'

'I promised not to physically assault him myself—and despite the utmost provocation, I did not.'

'But you did confront him.'

'I—talked with him. Predicted that he would cease his unwelcome attentions of his own free will, since it was the right thing to do. Which, in a way, he has. True, there are people at the gaming hell who could testify to seeing us together. But we parted without any altercation, so even if he were to return at some point and try to make an issue of it, no one could claim to have witnessed anything more than a conversation.'

"If he should return at some point?" she echoed. 'What, you had him kidnapped and transported?' A reluctant smile tugging at her lips, she sighed and laid her hand back on his arm. 'You'd better tell me the whole.'

Briefly he summarised the events at the gaming hell and beside the Serpentine, concluding with the reports that Hine's operative had seen Randall safely embarked to Calais.

'I only wish I could have witnessed his dunking in the Serpentine!' she said, laughing as if she were envisioning it. 'I might have been too tempted to let him drown, though.'

'I was tempted as well, I assure you. But a dead duke's son would cause too much trouble.'

'Oh, Davie, what a marvel you are! And so very clever about wording your promises! I shall have to remember that.'

'You didn't truly believe I would just sit on my hands and let him threaten you?'

'Yes—no. Other men might have. But not you, Davie. I should have known you would find some way to thwart him.'

*I would die to protect you*, he thought. Suppressing the words, he said instead, 'Randall's just a bully, Faith. Purposeless, idle, and too much indulged. That sorry breed only preys on the weak. I learned enough about them when I got to Oxford. I wasn't quite so strapping then, but I was still strong enough. They soon learned not to bait the "farm boy", and took their mischief elsewhere.' He smiled. 'My education in fisticuffs progressed rapidly.'

'But you said—ah,' she said, making the connection. 'You stood up for the other boys.'

He shrugged. 'It was only right. Outsiders should stick together. Although, after Giles took me up, I never felt like an outsider again, even though I was. And am.'

'That knack served you—and me—excellently well in this circumstance.'

He chuckled. 'Yes. I doubt Lord Randall will forget the events of that evening for a very long time.'

'Do you think he wrote his mother? She's not complained about him abandoning her, yet. Although, it's not at all unusual for him to disappear for days at a time, without sending her any word, although ostensibly he's living in her house. My *son's* house, I should say.'

'He was warned not to complain to anyone. Being mostly concerned with his own hide, I doubt he'll contact her until he runs out of money. I'm reasonably sure he will remain in Calais for some time, and when he does return to England, he'll avoid you.' Unable to help himself, he added, 'By then, you'll probably have a new champion.'

Suddenly, with a gasp, Faith halted. Taking both his hands, she looked up into his face, her expression eager. 'I just realised the full extent of what you've accomplished! Not only are my boys safe, but now there is truly an opportunity for…for *us*. To come together as one. Oh, Davie, I know it's shocking of me to propose it, but I…I want you so badly! I admire and honour and esteem you as the dearest friend I've ever had, but I want more. More of *this*…'

She flung her arms around him and pulled his head down for another kiss, one that started already hot and needy and quickly intensified. One hand twined in his hair, she pursued his tongue, laving, sucking, urging him deeper. With the other, she slid her hand between them to stroke the iron rod of his erection.

The pleasure was so intense, he thought he would shatter on the spot. But he couldn't, wouldn't, have her making love to him in a garden within view of the palace, where anyone who looked out an upper-storey window might see them.

It still took him several minutes to find the strength to break the kiss. 'Darling Faith, not here,' he gasped.

She leaned against him, trembling. 'Yes, you're right. Not here. I'll come to you at Albany. Or I have money, I can hire a house. We'll have a place to be together, where we can do away with the sham of "Mr Smith" and "Duchess", and be the lovers we were meant to be. I've known it must happen, somehow, since that first summer—haven't you? Oh, Davie, please say "yes". All I've ever known of passion is to be taken by a man who just wanted to breed sons on me. Won't you give me the joy of being loved by a man who truly cares for and desires me?'

His friend. His lover. He'd known it all along, but hearing what she said—or rather, what she didn't say, cut deeper than he'd imagined possible. *She'd take him as a lover, but he wasn't good enough to be a husband.*

Ruthlessly he squelched the anguish and made himself focus on reality. 'There's nothing I desire more, but you must realise, my darling, that eliminating Lord Randall doesn't make our situation that much safer. He's not the only peer who might find a relationship between a commoner and a duchess with minor children objectionable enough to bring it to the attention of their trustees. And this time, it could be someone more reputable, more credible than Lord Randall.'

She waved a hand dismissively. 'With all the affairs going on amongst members of the *ton*? I doubt any would care enough to make a point of it. Would you deny us a chance for happiness over so unlikely an event?'

'Happy, yes—but for how long? A week? A month? Before someone found out, and society started to point fingers? Because it *would* get out, you know that. We'd have to end it, and it would end badly. With you disgraced. Possibly even threatened again with losing control over your sons. And what if you were to conceive? Forcing you to hide away somewhere to give birth in secret, and then give up the child. *My* child. How could I bear for you to give me a son neither of us could ever acknowledge?'

He waited, still unable to relinquish the slender hope that she might suggest the one way they could prevent that from happening. When instead, she drooped against him, crestfallen, he reined in the urge to ask for her hand.

Eliminating Lord Randall hadn't changed any of the hard facts about their relative positions. Marrying him would still be a huge step down in the world for her, turning her into an object of derision. Exiling her from association with her class. And quite possibly, resulting in the loss of her sons.

He couldn't take advantage of her longing and his desperation to urge her into a union she would almost certainly come to regret. A regret that would cripple him with remorse for persuading her into it. A regret that would force him to carry for the rest of his life the burden of knowing he was not considered "good enough".

He'd worked too hard for too many years to remove that taint.

The heat of passion drained away, replaced by an anguish that cut inside like two opposing hussars with blades clashing. 'I won't be the means of diminishing you.'

Two tears slid silently down her cheeks as she stared up at him. 'Then, you'll offer me…nothing? Nothing to live for, to look forward to? Not even a chance for happiness, however fleeting?'

Anger, hurt, desire and the sense of impending loss churned inside him. Much as his body urged him to accept, to salvage something rather than nothing, he knew that having her and giving her up again would destroy him. 'I won't be your "temporary diversion", Faith,' he said, unable to keep the bitterness from his voice. 'Such an affair would be an affront to *my* honour, as well as yours.'

Uttering a curse so vile it startled him, Faith stamped her foot. '*Honour!* How often men dredge up that word to provide noble camouflage for refusing to do—or not do—what they want? With the immorality so rampant in the world, you'd object to our having an affair? Using "honour" as your excuse for denying two people who care for one another any chance to be happy? Oh, Davie, of all times for you to revert to your...your *bourgeois* principles!'

Frustration and rage won out over the hurt and despair. 'Yes, I am *bourgeois*,' he shot back. 'I still care about things like decency and loyalty and honour. I'm sorry that failing displeases you.'

Knowing he couldn't bear any more, he turned and stalked away.

But instead of giving him the space he needed to mourn and lick his wounds, she ran after him. 'Please, Davie, don't go! I'm sorry, I'm so sorry!'

She caught up and grabbed his sleeve, forcing him to halt. 'You'd think by now, I'd be used to humiliation, but having you refuse me, deny what I wanted so desperately—I just...lashed out. I won't importune you, or throw myself at you again. Please, promise me you'll remain my friend. I...I don't think I can go on, else.'

Furious, agonised, he stood, refusing to look at her, battling against the raging desire to throw honour and conscience to the winds and accept her offer. Even now, he could envision the rendezvous, a snug little house where Faith waited for him, clad only in a wrapper. Opening her arms to him when he walked in and picked her up, laid her on the bed where he would cherish every inch of her with kisses and caresses, finally claiming the body of the woman he'd loved for so long.

Better to shrug off her hand and keep walking, then accept "friendship" with its twin burdens of temptation and heartache.

She reached up to angle his face towards hers. 'Please, Davie,' she whispered.

But when he looked down at her, those tear-filled eyes, the misery on that dearly beloved face, he was as lost as the first time he'd set eyes on her.

With a deep sigh, he cupped her face in his hands. 'Never doubt that you are the most lovely, desirable creature on the face of the earth. That it tests my willpower to its utmost limit every time I am alone with you— yearning for what must not be. If there were any justice in the world, you would have been married to a man who appreciated how beautiful you are, inside and out. Yes, I'll remain your friend. But I cannot be more than that, so please, don't tempt me any further. If I broke the vow I made to protect you, I would end up hating us both.'

She kept nodding her head up and down as he spoke. 'Yes, yes, anything. Whatever you want. Just…promise you'll never a-abandon me?' she asked, her voice breaking again at the end.

His heart turning over, he held out his arms and she rushed into them, clinging to him, burying her head in his coat. Her slender body trembled, and he knew she was silently weeping.

Damned if he did, and damned if he didn't, he thought

despairingly, loving the feel of her in his arms, hating that he was the source of her sorrow. Heartbreak was written all over this agreement, but he didn't know what else he could do.

Spurning her when she needed him was unthinkable.

At length, she pushed back, giving him a watery smile. 'I know I should have more resources on my own, and I shall do better, I promise. Just now I was at a… rather low ebb.'

He offered his arm and she took it. 'We shall just have to go about rising the tide.'

'As long as our boats travel together—even if we can't travel in the same one.'

'You must start by doing me that favour I mentioned. As you know, the vote on the Reform Bill should take place any day now, and it's certain to pass the Commons. We'll all of us be occupied then, rallying support for a swift passage in the Lords, so I'm likely to be tied up for the next several weeks. We know Randall has left England, but just to be safe, would you pay an extended visit to Lady Englemere? Rebuild your intimacy with your sister and her family, so you will feel comfortable calling on them in future, should the need arise. Tell the Dowager you want to give your sister a break from the sickroom and spend time with your recovering niece, while you let the cousins become further acquainted. I imagine you want to do all that anyway.'

She nodded. 'It would certainly be nice to be out of the house, once the Dowager starts to worry over Randall's absence. Like you, I don't believe he'll bother to contact her until he is out of funds.'

'With Aphrodite's help, he has a healthy stake with which to begin life in Calais.'

She shook her head, her expression wry. 'I ought to repay you that, at least.'

'Absolutely not. The blunt means nothing; all I truly regret losing was the opportunity to go a few bare-knuckle rounds with him before he was sent on his way.'

'A few rounds?' She stopped walking and took one of his large hands in her small one. 'Randall wouldn't have lasted more than a minute against this.' She raised his hand to her face, rubbing her cheek against it before kissing his knuckles. 'Dearest Davie, can you even imagine how safe you make me feel? How much I treasure you?'

With everything in him, he wanted to pull her back into his arms and hold her for ever. Resisting the urge to embrace her one last time, he took her arm instead and resumed walking.

At least, she felt safe—and treasured him. It wasn't nearly what he wanted, but it was something. It would have to be enough.

As they reached the entrance of the maze, Faith halted again, turning to gaze back over her shoulder. 'I will dream of this, and imagine you gave me a different answer,' she said softly.

'I can't control your dreams.' *Or his own*, he thought.

Would he curse himself later, for letting high principle squander a priceless opportunity? Faith would keep her word, he knew. She'd not invite him into her arms and her bed again.

Honour wasn't honour if you invoked it only when it was easy or convenient, he told himself.

*Repeat that homily in the chill of your lonely bed*, his outraged body replied.

## *Chapter Fourteen*

After attending the entertainment the Dowager wished them to grace with their presence that evening, as their carriage carried them back to the Berkeley Square town house, Faith realised for the first time in several weeks, she was returning home without a sense of dread.

She descended from the coach in a state almost of euphoria, feeling as if an enormous burden had been lifted from her shoulders. She could go to the nursery and read to her boys, or retreat to her chamber and read to herself, even tiptoe into the library later in her robe and night rail to pour herself a glass of wine, without fear of encountering Lord Randall's insinuating voice or groping hands.

Or his threats against her and her children.

*Bless you, Davie*, she mouthed silently as she ascended the stairs.

Though they were probably asleep by now, she'd celebrate by running up to the nursery to see if the boys were awake, sharing her joy with them—and inform them that, faithful to the promise she'd made Davie, they would soon have a prolonged visit with their cousins—the possessors of those oh-so-desirable dogs, horses and trees. Smiling, she was about to continue up the stairs to the nursery when the Dowager's voice recalled her.

'My dear Faith, you'll sit with me in the salon, won't you? I've been so worried about Randall. He's not been home in days, nor have we seen him anywhere when we've gone out in society. I was almost certain he'd be at the Blanchards' tonight, as they are our most particular friends.'

With true nobility, she refrained from pointing out that it was not at all unusual for Lord Randall to disappear until his funds were exhausted, nor, while he was flush in the pocket, did they ever see him at respectable *ton* gatherings.

'Of course, if it will make you feel better.' But, she promised herself, if the Dowager started criticising her while she fretted about her son, Faith was going to instantly develop a headache that required she take to her bed.

'Pour me a sherry, won't you, dear? I'll just send a note with the footman round to his lodgings. Sweet boy that he is, he might be feeling he's imposed too much on us, visiting so often—as ridiculous as that sounds! I'll reassure him that we miss him, and can't have him with us often enough.'

*You'd be welcome to join him in Calais*, Faith thought.

It shouldn't take the footman long to make the transit to and from Berkeley Square and the rooms near Bond Street where Lord Randall resided, when he wasn't sponging off the estate. The interlude would give her the opportunity to warn her mother-in-law of her upcoming trip.

Bringing the Dowager the requested glass, she poured herself one and waited until the woman finished writing her note. With that dispatched, Faith said, 'I shall be off myself, as soon as I've confirmed a convenient date with my sister. My niece has been ill, you may recall. I promised Sarah when I made my first visit that I would return for a much longer one. It will give me an opportunity to become better acquainted with my niece and nephews, let my sister have a break from her sickroom duties, and allow the boys to enjoy their cousins' company.'

'Must you go now?' the Dowager said with a frown. 'Lady Blanchard told me tonight that her husband said this Parliamentary session will be ending soon. With all the best families heading to the countryside for the autumn shooting, there will be such a dearth of good company in town! We must enjoy the parties while they last. Surely you can visit your sister later. You have a duty to your family here, you know.'

'Duty to family is very important,' Faith replied patiently. 'But while you have many friends in town to visit with at various entertainments, my sister has only me close enough to assist with her convalescing daughter. My other sisters are all busy with their families at their estates, far from London.'

'Your responsibility to the ducal line should take precedence,' the Dowager said repressively.

While her husband was alive, much as her soul resisted such coercion, she would probably have acquiesced, as he certainly would have seconded his mother's comments—probably with an added slur on how inadequately she performed her duties as duchess.

Wonderful, she thought, how *freeing* his absence was.

But for one thing, she could almost be happy with her life now.

While the Dowager chattered on about the missteps she'd noted among the attendees tonight, and recounted all the latest gossip she'd obtained, Faith's attention wandered back again to the interlude in the maze this afternoon, an episode to which her thoughts returned every time she wasn't physically occupied doing something else.

Her cheeks burning at the memory, she could still hardly believe what she'd had the audacity to propose. The burn went deeper as she recalled the humiliation of being refused.

But 'humiliation' wasn't truly an accurate description. Davie's denial hadn't denigrated her in the dismissive, contemptuous way her husband had delighted in. Her overwrought reaction stemmed from disappointment, devastation even, that Davie, who'd shown her more appreciation and concern than anyone since her family growing up, had refused her what she wanted so badly.

Indeed, he'd taken pains to affirm it wasn't the woman, or her desirability, he was repudiating. She knew with absolute certainty that Davie desired her and a liaison between them as much as she did. But Davie, honourable-to-the-core Davie, wouldn't take what he wanted, when he knew that doing so would put her good name, reputation, and relationship with her children at risk.

And he was right, much as she hated to admit it. They were not living isolated in some wilderness; in the London of servants and merchants and gossips avid to discover the latest *on dit*, there was no such thing as a 'secret' hideaway, where they could go back to being simple Faith Wellingford and Davie Smith, two kindred souls sharing friendship, as they had that halcyon summer.

Sharing friendship, and so much more, she thought, recalling the kiss she'd all but forced on him. Not that he'd refused it. Oh, no, he'd let her play with his lips, his tongue, taking, retreating, opening himself to her fully. Even as she explored him, she'd sensed the strength of the passion he was restraining, felt the thrill of trying to provoke him beyond the limits of his control.

He'd been teetering on the brink of succumbing as she stroked him. A shudder of arousal and longing went through her as she recalled the hard, thick length of him under her fingers, sharply outlined where it pressed against his breeches. The tremor intensified as she imagined his member teasing at the entrance to her hot, moist centre, then entering her, filling her. She could almost weep with disappointment that she hadn't managed to break through that barrier of restraint and succeed in uncovering him, tasting him…mounting him.

Right there in the maze? Where, as he'd rightly said, a casual observer looking out one of the palace's upstairs windows might have been able to see them?

No, he'd been right to stop her. Right to turn her down. An affair between them would eventually be discovered, probably sooner than later. Even with Randall gone, the risk of someone finding that relationship objectionable enough to broach the matter to her sons' trustees was serious, and losing them too great a catastrophe to contemplate. No matter how much she wanted Davie.

But her sons wouldn't be young and in her care for ever. Sooner than she could imagine—as had happened for her sister Sarah and her eldest, Aubrey—they would be grown and going on with their lives.

Might there be a time for her and Davie then? she wondered, her flattened hopes rising on an updraught of excitement. Truly, the only consideration preventing her from making a full-out assault on Davie's sense of propriety was the threat of losing the boys. The prospect of being 'disgraced' didn't worry her in the least—she'd been a source of mockery among the *ton* ever since her wandering husband made his disdain for her obvious. She didn't care a fig for society's opinion of her, and being banned from participation in its entertainments would almost be a blessing.

Her growing excitement halted abruptly as she considered the man Davie had become. She knew he'd loved her since that long-ago summer. But he was no longer a gangly boy on the cusp of manhood, a powerful intellect who'd attracted a prominent patron, but was otherwise an obscure unknown of no wealth or family. With his sponsor's support, and through his own wits, efforts, and skill, he'd become a force in the Commons and one of the intellectual leaders of the Reform movement.

He'd also grown into a powerfully attractive, virile male. Considering that fact, Faith was astonished some ambitious girl hadn't already manoeuvred him into the parson's mousetrap. As his wealth and fame increased over the years, he'd likely be married long before her boys were old enough for her to be able to truly do whatever she wanted.

As she reached that dismal conclusion, a knock sounded at the door, interrupting the Dowager's monologue, followed by the entry of the footman she'd dispatched with her note.

'Well, Johnson,' the Dowager said sharply as the man simply stood there. 'Did my son give you a reply?'

'Weren't there, Your Grace. I knocked and knocked, thinking his man would answer, but he never did. Finally, the landlord came round and said Lord Randall had scarpered—run off, Your Grace.'

'"Run off!"' the Dowager echoed. 'What do you mean?'

'Lord Randall don't live there no more. The landlord took me up to the rooms to have a look-see, telling me he woulda seized and sold anything Lord Randall left, to cover the unpaid rent, but there weren't nothing. No clothes, no rings or snuff boxes or personal items. Looked like he'd left in a hurry, too—drawers standing open, old newspapers spilled on to the floor. The landlord pressed me, wanting to know my direction—I think he wanted to task whoever sent me with paying the rent—but I didn't tell him nothing.'

'Gone? How could that be? Where could he have gone, with no word to me?' the Dowager cried, wringing her hands. 'Oh go away, man!' she added with exasperation as the servant remained standing. 'You are dismissed.'

'Well done, Johnson,' Faith said quietly before the footman could exit. Her mother-in-law might not appreciate the man's cleverness in preventing Lord Randall's creditors from descending upon them, but she certainly did. 'Stop by my study tomorrow morning, and there'll be a coin or two for your efforts.'

The footman's face creased in a smile. 'Thankee, Duchess. Your Grace.' Bowing, he left the room.

'Honestly, child, I can't imagine why, when you indulge in such reckless generosity, you haven't already run through the household accounts,' the Dowager said sourly. 'Rewarding that impudent fellow, when he didn't even fulfil his duty by actually delivering my note!' Jumping up, she began to pace. 'And where could Randall have gone, and why? Oh, I shall be beside myself until I know his whereabouts, and have word that he is unharmed!'

With an effort, Faith refrained from retorting that Lord Randall was a far greater charge on the household budget than giving a vail to an employee who persisted in discovering her son's circumstances, when he might well have simply knocked once and left. Reminding herself that the mother's anxiety was genuine, despite the worthlessness of the child she worried over, she told herself to hold on to her patience.

And might there be just a wee bit of guilt tempering her indulgence, because she knew Randall's true circumstances but would not reveal them?

She shrugged it off. Randall was perfectly capable of informing his mother of his plans, if he so chose. That it caused his mother distress because he had failed to do so was not her fault.

'I can't imagine what could have caused him to—to flee in the night, taking all his possessions, with no warning to me!'

'He is very fond of gaming,' Faith observed. 'Perhaps he suffered…sudden and distressing reverses.'

'Yes!' the Dowager cried, halting. 'That must be it. Naughty boy, he confessed the last time he visited that he has, on occasion, resorted to moneylenders when he found himself, as he put it, "up Tick Creek without a paddle", and did not find me at home to provide assistance when he called. He must have been anxious to escape the presumptuous importunings of such a person, or his lackeys! There could be no other reason for him to decamp so suddenly.'

That might not be the reason this time, Faith thought, but if Randall had indeed borrowed from a cent-per-center, such an individual would be none too dainty about the tactics he used to recover his loans.

'Even so, where would he have gone, if he did not come here?' the Dowager wailed. Then she stopped short, her worried countenance clearing. 'Ashedon Court, of course! Clever boy! Some unsavoury individual might track him here, but they'd never venture that far out of London. Have your maid begin packing at once, and tell the nursery maids to prepare the boys, too. I shall get Talbot working now, so we can leave for Ashedon Court as soon as possible. I shall not sleep a wink until I am certain about the safety of my dearest Randall!'

With that, she swept from the room, apparently not giving a thought to the fact that Faith might not wish to drop everything and hurry off to Ashedon Court with her.

She was about to follow her mother-in-law out and tell her that she would visit Sarah while the Dowager travelled to Derbyshire when a new notion occurred.

She knew for certain that Randall wouldn't be at the ducal country house. Even if he quickly tired of Calais and made his way back to England, she doubted he'd return to an estate in the middle of the countryside that he'd several times pronounced a dead bore, in which he didn't intend to spend a moment's time until he was buried in the family crypt. So she needn't fear running into him there.

And she'd longed for years to take her boys into the country, acquaint them with the rhythms of a life she so much preferred to the city routine of London. Edward, in particular, needed to learn about the land and tenants whose care would be his duty and heritage.

Instead of rusticating at Sarah's, why not accompany the Dowager to Ashedon, spend some quiet, unhurried time there with her boys, soaking in the peace and beauty she'd missed so much? Meanwhile, she could see to hiring a new tutor, employ a groom to teach the boys to ride, and maybe show them a few tricks about catching fish, catching frogs, and climbing trees she remembered from a long, carefree youth spent running after her brother Colton.

Davie had warned her he'd likely be too busy the next few weeks to find some 'unexceptional' occasion to see her. After their fraught meeting yesterday, she probably needed some time apart to reorder her thinking and convince herself to keep her promise and not try to seduce him again the first chance she got. To persuade herself that she could be content with friendship for the present, while she nurtured the hope they might share something more in future.

As long as he didn't marry. Needy for him as she was, she wouldn't attempt to seduce a married man. Not that her honourable-to-the-core Davie would allow himself to be seduced, once he'd pledged his troth to some other woman.

Dismissing that outcome as too dreadful to contemplate, she forced herself to concentrate on the immediate future. With him so occupied with his duties in Parliament, it was unlikely that some ambitious female would lure him into a liaison now. Surely she could bear being parted from him for a *few* weeks.

He'd already helped her recover much of her former energy and confidence. It was up to her to continue the process, and being in the countryside she loved would further fuel that recovery.

After they were safely arrived at Ashedon Court, she thought with another tweak of conscience, she'd make amends for her bad behaviour by having the Dowager receive an anonymous note informing the woman of her son's whereabouts.

She'd write the note tonight, with instructions that it not be posted until after their departure.

If, after receiving it, her mother-in-law wanted to pursue her son to Calais, she could go with Faith's blessing, but not with Faith's escort.

Oh, to be able to spend several weeks in the country! she thought, the idea filling her with enthusiasm. Having the boys all to herself, to dine with and read to and take walking and fishing and riding. Perhaps she'd even have the gamekeeper start showing Edward how to use a pistol.

She could rise in the morning to fill her lungs with sweet country air. Ride for as long as she liked, without having to worry about returning to dress for callers. And, praise Heaven, delight in evenings spent reading or placing games with her sons instead of being forced to endure boring *ton* parties being polite to sharp-eyed matrons who, though wary of her now, still watched her every move, looking for something to ridicule or criticise.

The only thing that would make a country sojourn more perfect would be having Davie beside her—in her life, in her bed. With a deep sigh, she recalled how safe and cherished she'd felt, wrapped in those powerful arms. The giddy delight of tasting, teasing, stroking him, pushing the limits of his passionate restraint. The heat and burn that simmered deep within whenever she was near him.

Just thinking of him, she burned anew.

But since the ultimate means of satisfying that desire wasn't possible—yet—she might do well with a period away from Davie's frustration-inducing presence. In the meantime, she would do her best to enjoy the unexpected opportunity the Dowager had just given her to introduce her sons to country life.

## Chapter Fifteen

In the evening a few days later, Davie hefted a mug of ale with the other Hellions in the boisterous taproom of the Quill and Gavel, as they and the other patrons, most of them Members of Parliament, celebrated the passage through the Commons of the Reform Bill.

'Almost ten years since we envisaged this, sitting in that dingy taproom in Oxford,' Ben cried. 'Here's to Davie, our intellectual light, to Giles, master manipulator extraordinaire, to Christopher, the voice of doom who helped us find and eradicate the flaws. To the Reform Bill!'

'To the Bill!' they all repeated, raising their mugs.

'We still have a lot of work to do, even if the Bill passes the Lords without alteration,' Christopher pointed out. 'Voting requirements need to be standardised from district to district, and we absolutely must work towards universal suffrage.'

'Yes, towards a day where a farmer's orphan won't need aristocratic patrons to be able to participate in government,' Davie agreed.

'You're a long way from being that penniless farmer's orphan now,' Giles said. 'As a man of property with several sources of wealth, and a growing reputation as a visionary political thinker, *you* have no need for aristocratic patrons any longer.'

Davie waved a deprecating hand. 'If I am even close to being that, it's due to the support and assistance of you all. From the day Giles took pity on the outcast sitting alone, nursing the single glass of ale he could afford at the cheapest of Oxford's taverns.'

'Giles is right,' Ben agreed. 'You're no longer an indigent outsider, but a man of influence within the circles of power.'

'At heart, I'll always be that farm urchin,' Davie said with a laugh. Then, those words instantly transporting him back to his contentious interview with Faith, he fell silent.

She'd accused him of clinging to bourgeois values that prevented them from having a chance for happiness. She'd been right—but in a different way than she'd meant, or he'd realised at the time.

Yes, he prized honour, loyalty and the sanctity of marriage. But, as Christopher and Giles had just reminded him, he was no longer a lowly orphan, alone and powerless. Without false modesty, he could agree with their assessment that he was now a man of substance and a politician of growing influence and authority.

So why, when it came to Faith, was he acting as if he were still that penniless farm urchin? Believing himself unworthy of her hand because he had been born so far beneath her station?

He wasn't and never would be an aristocrat. But the steps they'd achieved with the passage of the bill today would provide the framework on which they would continue to build, towards an England where every man had a vote and every man's vote mattered, where one's birth meant less than what one made of the opportunities one was given. He didn't truly believe himself inferior to the wretched Lord Randall, or even the admirable Marquess of Englemere, simply because he hadn't been born with a title, did he?

If he, who was fighting to change society, didn't think he was equal to the best of those who did have titles—Giles and Lord Witlow and Englemere—how could he hope to sway the opinions of other Englishmen?

The only Englishmen whose opinions mattered on this point *now* were the trustees for Faith's children. If he were to claim her, would they consider her an unfit mother, for marrying too far beneath her?

He didn't know. But Englemere, with his connections throughout society, would probably not only know who had been named as trustees, but also be well enough acquainted with them to give an accurate assessment of how those men would view Davie's pretensions to the hand of a widowed duchess.

If Englemere should confirm that Davie could marry Faith without threatening her control over her sons, he could act. It wouldn't change the fact that, in today's England, marrying him would be seen by society as a big step down in the world. But as long as proposing to her wouldn't compromise her control over the sons who meant so much to her, he would feel free to finally reveal to her his deepest desire, and let her make the choice.

Did *she* think him the equal of Englemere and Witlow?

She certainly could have no doubt about the strength of his affection. He knew she felt at least a fondness for him. And she certainly desired him, he recalled with a deep sense of satisfaction.

But she'd have to feel a good deal more than just

'affection' to be willing to jeopardise her position in society.

Ask, and he faced the serious risk that she might turn him down.

Did he dare do so now, if Englemere cleared the way?

Or was it better to hang on to friendship, rather than attempt to take the relationship in a new direction, be refused, and lose everything?

For if he proposed, there would be no going back to simple 'friends'.

All, or nothing at all?

But he didn't have to answer that yet. First, he needed to track down Lord Englemere and discover whether he could, in good conscience, dare to move forward.

A finger-snap right in front of his nose brought him suddenly back to the present. He turned to the owner of those fingers, who was looking at him quizzically.

'So lost in contemplating our satisfying victory that you've forgotten where you are?' Ben asked. 'Or have the celebratory shouts left your throat too dry to speak? Let's refill your mug and take care of that!'

'No, don't,' he replied. After his spellbinding realisation, he was suddenly on fire to find Lord Englemere and discover whether he might hold the key to his future in his *own* hands. 'As Christopher reminded, we still have much to do—and the first step is getting the bill passed in the Lords. I'm going to hunt up Englemere and get his estimation on where we now stand.'

'Tonight?' Giles asked, giving him a puzzled glance. 'You don't think you could spare one evening to celebrate with the Hellions, before we move on to the next battle?'

'Englemere might be at Sir Edward's, if he didn't go back to Highgate Village.' He managed to manufacture a smile, which he hoped would deflect any curiosity over this sudden urgency. 'It shouldn't take long to stop by, and I imagine you will be celebrating all evening.'

'Can't promise not to drink all the ale before you get back,' Ben warned.

'Guess I'll have to take that risk,' he replied. 'I'll look for you here, later.'

'I may be off to Maggie before you get back, but I'll be looking forward to hearing what you learn from Englemere,' Giles said. But the assessing gaze he levelled on Davie told him his friend didn't completely believe his impromptu excuse for leaving.

If it all turned out well, he would explain the whole to Giles later. But with the outcome so uncertain, he didn't want to voice his hopes even to his closest friend. Giles would do anything to help him, he knew—but only Englemere, and Faith herself, could help with this.

Having to exercise all the willpower he possessed to stroll out at a leisurely pace, rather than in a tearing rush, Davie crossed the taproom and exited on to the street.

Once there, he jogged at double-time to the nearest hackney stand.

After the short transit from the Quill and Gavel near the Houses of Parliament to Sir Edward's town house in Moulton Street, Davie ran up the steps, filled with both excitement and trepidation. What happened in the next few minutes might well determine whether he would live with heartache for the rest of his life—or have at least a chance to build a future with the woman he'd loved for almost a decade.

Nothing, not even the satisfaction of passing the reform legislation over which he'd toiled for that decade, could compare to the euphoria engendered by that prospect. The very idea was so intoxicating, he hardly dared think it.

One step at a time. First he needed to determine whether proposing to Faith was possible.

The butler, knowing him to be a frequent guest, told him that the family was in their private parlour, but despite the lateness of the hour, he would notify his master that Davie had called.

'Is Lord Englemere with them, Shelborn?' Davie asked, his stomach churning with anticipation and dread.

'Yes, Lord Englemere will be spending the week, before he returns to Highgate. Political dinners, I gather,' Shelborn confided before bowing Davie into the formal salon and going off to inform his master of Davie's presence.

Too agitated to take the seat Shelborn had led him to, Davie paced the room. He was reasonably sure the butler would return with an invitation for him to join his mentor and Englemere, bringing closer the moment when he would discover whether his hopes could be realised or not.

A few minutes later, Shelborn returned to escort him to the private family parlour on the floor above. Anxiety and anticipation speeding his steps, Davie entered to find Sir Edward, his wife Lady Greaves, and Lord Englemere playing cards.

'Welcome, Davie!' Sir Edward said. 'Will you join us in a hand? Or are you too energised after your victory in the Commons today to sit still that long?'

'It was energising,' Davie affirmed. 'So much so, that I indeed find myself eager to move on to the next step. With that in mind, I stopped by on the hope that you would be here, Lord Englemere, and I might claim a few minutes of your time to get your estimation of the situation in the Lords, now that the chamber has learned of the bill's passage by the Commons.'

'If you gentlemen are going to talk politics, I shall go check on the children,' Lady Greaves said with a smile. 'There is no such thing as "a few minutes", once you start on that!'

'Please, don't let me break up your game,' Davie protested. 'If you don't mind chatting, my lord, I'm happy to wait on your convenience.'

'Considering how wretched my hand is, I'm willing to end the game now, before these gentlemen complete their most unchivalrous rout of me,' Lady Greaves said, tossing down her cards. 'Ned, dear, I'll see you when you come up later. Englemere, I wish you a goodnight, and will see you at breakfast tomorrow.'

With that, Lady Greaves rose, gave her husband a kiss and Davie a shake of the hand before walking out.

'Would my assessment be of any value, or would you rather be closeted with Englemere?' Sir Edward asked.

'No, please stay,' Davie said. Before Englemere could begin to answer his query, he interrupted to confess, 'With apologies, I didn't really seek you out to talk about politics. My urgency concerns a much more personal matter.'

'If it's more personal to you than the politics you've lived and breathed these last ten years, it must be important indeed,' Sir Edward said with a smile.

'It is,' Davie affirmed. 'Will you withhold any comment until I've told you the whole, no matter how…presumptuous you may think me? At that point, I will be most grateful for your candid opinions.'

After exchanging a puzzled look with Sir Edward, Englemere said, 'Agreed. So, tell us the whole.'

'I'm sure it doesn't come as any surprise to either

of you that I developed a great admiration for Faith—the Duchess of Ashedon—that first summer I served as your secretary, Sir Edward. Over the years, my affection and admiration have remained undiminished, nor have I subsequently met any woman I consider her equal. As you may know, after the Duke's death, we…rekindled the friendship we formed all those years ago. A renewed association with her has only strengthened the feelings I've held for so long. To the point that, I feel I must dare trying to move the relationship beyond mere friendship.'

Sir Edward and Englemere exchanged another glance. 'You mean, you want to *marry* her?' Englemere asked.

Relieved that the Marquess hadn't immediately shown him the door for his effrontery, Davie said, 'Yes, I would like to propose to her.'

'Do you believe she returns your affection?' Sir Edward asked.

'I know she cares about me. Whether she cares enough to marry me, I won't know until I ask. Although she cannot be unaware of my feelings, up to now, I have been very careful not to say anything that might hint I desire more than friendship. I'm now prepared to risk revealing my heart. However, I would not ask her to consider a marriage the trustees of her children would find so ill judged they would question her fitness to raise her sons, and decide to remove the boys from her care. What I'd like to learn from both of you, is how you feel the trustees would react, were she to marry me.'

He held up a hand, forestalling any comment. 'I'm not so naïve that I don't realise society would be shocked, even outraged, by such a marriage. But after years of work in Parliament, I believe I now occupy a position of sufficient authority and prestige that the trustees would find nothing objectionable in my *character*. Still, no amount of Parliamentary good works will turn me into a peer. I'm willing to let Faith decide whether or not she cares enough for me to face possible exile from society. But do you think my Parliamentary position good enough to satisfy the trustees?'

After a few minutes of shocked silence, during which Davie could hear his own heartbeat thudding in his ears, Sir Edward said slowly, 'You cannot doubt that we both esteem you personally, Davie.'

'I don't doubt that. But you both came to know me through rather…unusual circumstances, and our long association colours your opinion of my worth. Are you acquainted with the Duke of Ashedon's trustees? Enough to predict *their* assessment of my worth?'

'Having no inkling that his demise was imminent—' Englemere grimaced, doubtless remembering the tawdry circumstances of the accident '—Ashedon did not arrange for trustees before his death. At the time the estate was settled, Chancery appointed three men to serve in that role—his cousin, the Marquess of Trent, one of his maternal uncles, the Earl of Sandborn, and the family solicitor, Mr Campbell.'

'Sandborn?' Davie echoed, his anxiety ratcheting down a notch.

Englemere smiled. 'Yes, Sandborn, one of your staunchest supporters in the Lords. There would certainly be no objection to your suit from that direction, or from the solicitor. Trent, however, is as starched-up as they come, and might well have reservations about the duchess's remarriage to a commoner.'

'Must the trustees be unanimous in their approval?' Sir Edward asked.

'I don't know,' Englemere admitted. 'I have no expertise in matters of guardianship. However, Sandborn would offer strong support, and I'd be willing to put in a good word as well.'

'As would I,' Sir Edward said.

'So,' Davie began, trying to rein in his eagerness, 'you think I could try my luck, without any harmful repercussions from the trustees, if she should accept my suit?'

After exchanging glances, the two men nodded. 'We do,' Englemere said.

Hope, buried so long and so deeply, rushed out in a flood of excitement that had him leaping to his feet with a whoop of joy. 'Thank you!' he cried, shaking Sir Edward's and Englemere's hands in turn. 'She may send me away with my ears ringing for my presumption in asking for her, but at least now, I can dare to do so.'

'Hardly presumptuous, Davie,' Sir Edward said with a laugh. 'You're a landowner and a highly respected member of Parliament—not a factory labourer living in a garret, or some womanising fortune-hunter.'

'I don't care about her fortune at all—let it be tied up in her sons,' Davie said. 'My income doesn't compare to a duke's, but I can support her comfortably enough.'

'Far more important to me than you supporting her,' Englemere said quietly, 'is that you will *love* her. Something that bastard Ashedon never did. After all the misery he caused her, she deserves some happiness. If she believes she will find it with you, you'll both have my blessing, and Sarah's.'

'Mine and Joanna's, too,' Sir Edward said. 'We've grieved for her over the years, and would love to see her happy at last. *Both* of you happy at last,' he amended.

'Don't worry about the trustees,' Englemere said. 'If necessary, Ned and I will bring them around.'

Such a rush of joy and enthusiasm filled him, he

might be one of those Montgolfier hot-air balloons, released from the tethers binding it to earth to soar up, up, up into the sweet, pure air.

'Thank you both,' he said, shaking their hands again. He knew he was grinning like a village idiot, but he couldn't help it. He could barely restrain himself from turning cartwheels across the parlour rug.

'You're not going to try your luck at once, are you?' Sir Edward said as they walked him to the door.

'I would like to—but it's probably too late,' Davie said, trying to throttle back the compulsion to seek her out at once. 'I don't want to ride out to Brookhollow Lodge and wake them all up in the middle of the night. That is, I assume Faith and the boys are with Lady Englemere?'

The Marquess shook his head. 'Not that I know of. Were they supposed to be?'

This wasn't the time to reveal the machinations of the despicable Lord Randall—and Faith might well wish them never to be revealed. 'She mentioned she would like to take the boys out for a longer visit some time soon. I haven't seen her for several days, and thought she might have already left London.'

'As far as I know, they are still in town,' Englemere replied. 'But although the trip from here to Berkeley Square is short, it would probably be better not to invade that house at this late hour, either.'

'If you're going a-wooing, better to send a note and flowers ahead, with a request that she designate a convenient time to call on her,' Sir Edward said. 'Give you a chance to work out a pretty speech, too, so you don't just blurt out a proposal. Ladies do like pretty words.'

'Faith likes honest ones. Say what's in your heart—that will be enough,' Englemere advised.

'Good luck, Davie,' Sir Edward said. 'I hope Faith does accept you. She couldn't choose a finer man. Whatever you do, you do with your whole heart and soul.'

'If she does me the honour of becoming my wife, she'll have both in her keeping for the rest of my life,' Davie affirmed. Nearly bursting with hope, pride, urgency and impatience, he bowed to them both and strode out of the room.

## *Chapter Sixteen*

**W**ell aware that he was too agitated to return to the Quill and Gavel without the other Hellions immediately demanding to know what was wrong, Davie took himself back to his rooms at Albany. Sleep being equally impossible, he passed the rest of the night alternately pacing and rehearsing his proposal to Faith.

'Work out a pretty speech,' Sir Edward had advised. Though Davie had thought out carefully what he wanted to tell her, he suspected that, driven by the love he'd finally allowed to escape the shackles with which he normally confined it, once he gazed upon her face and knew that his whole lifetime's happiness would depend on how she answered him, he would probably forget every word.

So calamitous was the possibility of her refusing him, he almost decided not to visit her at all—yet. Should he indulge in the delight of her presence—as a friend—a few more times before he risked everything on the possibility of her accepting him?

But if she did, why delay that joy and live in an agony of uncertainty any longer than he must? If she were going to refuse him, better to know straight away, and start figuring out how he would salvage the shattered remnants of a life that stretched in a frighteningly long void ahead of him, if he contemplated a future without her.

How had he progressed so quickly, he marvelled, from feeling blessed just to share a few outings with her before she was caught up in her life again, to knowing that the rest of his life would be blighted if she wouldn't share hers with him?

Whenever that drastic transition had occurred, it was far too late to try to retreat into the safety of friendship.

That being the case, better to learn at once what his future held.

Sir Edward had also advised sending a note with flowers, asking her to set a time for their meeting. Probably advice as valuable as his prompting Davie to prepare a speech, but he was no more able to follow it. Waiting the whole of the night had been interminable enough; as soon as it was polite to make a morning call, he would go. If Faith accepted him, he'd deluge her with flowers after.

Some time after dawn, he bathed and shaved, wishing he'd allowed the nattily dressed Christopher to persuade him into ordering a new jacket and trousers the last time his friend had dragged him along on a visit to his tailor. Dressing with care, he went out for a breakfast of steak and ale, of which he ate only a few mouthfuls. Sipping at the ale, he checked his pocket watch every fifteen minutes until, finally, it was late enough to be permissible to call on a society lady.

His heart pounding so hard he felt light-headed, he left the inn and took a hackney to Berkeley Place. Hoping he would find Faith without encountering her dragon of a mother-in-law, he'd trotted up the front steps before he noticed the knocker was off the door.

Surprised and puzzled, he made his way around to the mews and crossed the back garden to the kitchen, where his vigorous knocking finally roused an elderly servant. After reprimanding Davie for pulling her away from the task of putting the house under holland covers, she sourly informed him that the Dowager, the duchess and her sons had departed London two days ago for their country estate in Derbyshire.

After he pressed several coins into the old woman's hand, which sweetened her manner considerably, she was prompted to add that while the Dowager had decided all sudden-like that she must go to Ashedon Court, the young duchess had said she welcomed the chance to let her boys spend some time in the country. Asked her opinion of how long the family would remain away, the woman replied that the duchess had said, with Parliament set to adjourn soon, they probably wouldn't return to London until the following spring.

Thanking the woman as he dropped one more coin into her hand, Davie walked thoughtfully back to the news. From the sound of it, the Dowager must have discovered her son was missing—and suspected he might have fled into the country. Unskilled at subterfuge, Faith would probably not have tried to persuade her mother-in-law there was no urgency in determining her brother-in-law's whereabouts, but simply acquiesced to the Dowager's plans and accompanied her to Ashedon Court. If Lord Randall should suddenly return to London, Faith would be as safe from him, buried in Derbyshire, as she would be staying with her sister Sarah in Highgate. Besides, she'd several times mentioned how much she missed being in the country.

Still, he'd begun to wonder, with a touch of panic, why Faith had not let him know she'd left town, when he recalled having told her he would be fully occupied over the next critical few weeks, pushing for passage of the Reform Bill. She probably thought she would have time to send him a note from Ashedon Court, explaining her change in plans, before he could discover her absence.

He was tempted to follow her immediately, to make sure there was no more alarming explanation for her silence…but there was the matter of the pending vote in the Lords. Driven as he was to speak with her and discover his fate, he couldn't dismiss the duty to see to its fruition the work to which he'd devoted the last ten years of his life.

He was hardly the only member of the Commons who'd be pushing for the Lords to pass the bill, he argued with himself. Surely others could keep the pressure on for the week or so it would take him to take care of *his* pressing business in Derbyshire.

He could go to the Quill and Gavel, and hope to find his fellow Hellions at a strategy session before their usual afternoon meeting in the committee room. Ask their opinion on how long it would take for the Bill to come to a vote in the Lords, and if they thought he'd have enough time to go to Derbyshire and return before the vote was taken, he would do so.

His course of action decided, he set off for the hackney stand.

To Davie's relief, he did in fact discover the Hellions in the private parlour they often bespoke when they were working outside the committee rooms. However, as he should have expected after his precipitous departure the previous evening, before he could get a word out, Ben rounded on him.

'Good thing I didn't save you any ale! Was Englemere so loquacious you couldn't get away, or did you forget you'd promised to return and give us his assessment?'

So preoccupied was he with his own personal quest, it took him a telling few seconds to refocus his mind and pick up the thread of that discussion. By the time he had, three speculative gazes were fixed on him.

'Unless discussion of the Reform Bill wasn't what set you running off,' Christopher said before he could answer.

'Isn't it time you trusted us enough to let us know what's really going on?' Giles asked quietly.

Well and truly caught, Davie blew out a frustrated breath. But Giles was right. Though there was nothing, besides advice, with which his friends could help him on this, on a matter of such importance to him, he ought to tell them what was happening.

'Very well,' he acquiesced, taking a chair. 'Get me some ale, and I'll explain.'

In a few succinct sentences, he related the quick progression of his renewed relationship with Faith, from unexpected meeting, to offering assistance, to the desire he had increasing difficulty controlling, to his epiphany last night, after which he'd sought out Englemere to determine if he could ask for her hand and still remain the man of honour and integrity he took pride in being.

His summary complete, he braced himself for derision. 'If you wish to make some crack about "pursuing the Unattainable", now is the moment.'

'It doesn't sound as if she is "unattainable" any longer,' Ben said quietly. 'And I'd hope you'd give us more credit than to assume we would mock your efforts, now that the relationship has turned from an impossible dream to a courtship that may actually win you a bride.'

'Englemere and Sir Edward did affirm the trustees could have no objections, I trust,' Giles said.

'They believed two of them would not. The third, a stickler for rank, would require some persuasion, but they thought they could win him over,' Davie confirmed.

'They should remind the stickler that Prime Ministers are often ennobled,' Giles said with a smile. 'You may end up with a title higher than his.'

'No, he'd turn it down,' Ben said. 'We're focused on abolishing the importance of titles, after all, not collecting them. Except for you, of course, Giles. You can't help being born a viscount who is destined to become an earl.'

'Thank you for excusing me,' Giles said drily. 'There's nothing wrong with titles, as long as men are judged and promoted for their own efforts, not merely because of an accident of birth.'

'So, when are you going to try your luck?' Christopher asked. 'Though she'd be a fool to turn you down.'

'After suffering through a decade of marriage to Ashedon?' Ben inserted. 'If she has any sense at all, she ought to jump at the chance to wed a man who'd actually mean his vows to love, honour and "keep himself only unto her".'

'I hope she will—if she loves me enough. That's the unknown, of course. Until I spoke with Englemere and Sir Edward last night, I didn't feel I could hint at wanting anything more than friendship.' Davie made a wry grimace. 'She's fond of me, I know, and friendship might be all she's interested in.'

'Then she *is* a fool,' Christopher said.

'Not necessarily,' Davie countered. 'She's a duchess, remember. Marrying a commoner would outrage a large part of the society in which she's moved all her life, and probably close many doors to her. That's a lot to ask.'

'If she loves you, I don't think that will matter,' Giles said.

'I hope not. I expect I shall find out soon. Which is what I came to ask you—'

'If you wanted our permission to address her, you have it,' Ben interrupted, a twinkle in his eye.

With an exasperated glance, Davie continued, 'I wanted to ask you how long you think it will be before the Bill will come up for a vote in the Lords. Faith isn't in London at present; I learned just this morning that she and the family have gone to Ashedon Court, in Derbyshire, and don't plan to return until next spring. I'd like to follow her to Ashedon immediately, if you think I'd have time to travel there and back before the Bill comes up for a vote.'

'You want to leave London?' Ben asked incredulously. 'With the most important vote of the last four hundred years about to happen? When we need every penetrating wit and every persuasive voice to convince the members of the Lords that the bill must and should be passed *now*?'

'I appreciate your desire to lay your proposal before the lady with all speed,' Giles said, frowning. 'But truly, Davie, there couldn't be a worse time for you to be away. It may be longer than a week before the vote is taken, but returning in time for that is less important than the work that needs to be done by all of us now, to ensure that we get the proper result once the votes *are* counted.'

'Here, here,' Christopher said.

Their advice was hardly unexpected, but Davie found himself resisting it. He'd given all of himself for years to the fight to create a better nation. Couldn't he be allowed a few *days* to pursue something of such compelling personal importance?

For several moments, none of them spoke, the only sound the tick of the mantel clock and the muffled voices from the taproom beyond. Finally, Ben broke the silence.

'No one knows better than you how important the next two or three weeks will be. If you still feel you must go to Derbyshire anyway, then go. I think I speak for all the Hellions in saying you'd travel with our best wishes and our blessing.'

Surprised it was the rake Ben, who'd never remained with the same lady more than a few weeks, rather than the faithful married Giles, who understood the strength of his compulsion, Davie nonetheless felt validated and humbled by their trust.

And he also knew, despite their approval, that he'd found his answer.

More than anything in the world, he wanted to make Faith his wife. But he could no more square with his conscience abandoning his duty to his country to pursue a personal matter, than he could have pressed Faith to become his wife, if doing so would have put her at risk of losing her sons.

'Thank you all for the vote of confidence,' he said at last. 'But…I guess I'll stay. We've waited ten years to alter the fate of the nation; I suppose I can wait another few weeks to find out my own.'

Giles reached out to shake his hand. 'Thank you. We all appreciate the sacrifice you're making.'

'It's only a few weeks' delay, Davie,' Ben said with a grin. 'Who, in that short time, could appear out of nowhere to carry your lady off from an estate in *Derbyshire*?'

'There had better be no one,' he retorted, exceedingly glad he'd made sure Lord Randall was tucked away in Calais.

But despite their high hopes and best efforts, it was an angry and frustrated group of Hellions who reassembled in the private room of the Quill and Gavel two weeks later, the day after the Reform Bill was voted down by the House of Lords.

'I still can't believe it!' Ben cried, banging his fist on the table. 'All that effort spent persuading a majority of the peers to pass the bill now, lest they incite the violence of a populace that so overwhelmingly supports it, and then this!'

'Even the most intransigent had agreed to abstain, if they couldn't in good conscience vote for it,' Christopher said.

'Only to have the clergy bring out their members in such numbers, the Lords Spiritual were able to outvote the Lords Temporal, and defeat it,' Davie said disgustedly. 'I stayed in London, talking to peers for days on end, for *this*? I should have left for Derbyshire two weeks ago.'

'The clerics back at Oxford called us "hell-bent" for daring to propose eliminating their seats in the House of Lords,' Ben said. 'Mark my words, if they haven't stirred up a devil's brew of trouble themselves, by opposing this.'

'I hope you're wrong about that, Ben,' Christopher said, looking weary. 'Where do we go from here?'

'I've heard there will be a call for a vote of confidence in Grey's government,' Davie said. 'He'll win it, and then advise the king to prorogue Parliament. All he's pushed for these last few years is getting that bill passed, and since it can't be re-introduced in the same session, he'll want to call a new one.'

'That will give you enough time to travel to Derbyshire and back,' Ben said. 'At least something positive will happen from proroguing the session.'

'Yes, we'll wish you luck—' Stopping in mid-sentence, Giles smoothed the front page of the newspaper he'd just opened. 'Hell and the devil, Ben, I'd hoped you were wrong, too. But it appears you weren't.'

'What do you mean?' Christopher asked. 'What's happened?'

The other three crowded around as Giles swiftly scanned the paper. 'News of the defeat of the Reform Bill must have spread through the countryside. According to the *Morning Post*, there have been riots in Derby, Nottingham, Dorset Leicestershire, and Somerset. The palaces of the Lord Mayor and the Bishop of Bristol were destroyed, the Bristol jail broken into and prisoners freed. Rioters even set fire to Nottingham Castle and Wollaton Hall, Lord Middleton's home.'

'Wollaton Hall!' Ben repeated, turning to Davie. 'Isn't Ashedon Court near there, outside Derby?'

Shock iced his veins, followed by the burn of anger. 'It is,' Davie affirmed grimly. 'Excuse me, gentlemen. I'm leaving for Ashedon immediately.'

Grabbing up his coat, Davie barely heard his friends' offers of encouragement and assistance as he rushed out, ticking off in his head the tasks he must complete in order to leave for Derbyshire. Hovering at the edge of his mind was the horrifying vision of Faith, his lovely, innocent Faith, menaced by crowds of angry men who didn't know the warmth and charity of the lady, but only that she lived in a house bearing a ducal coronet.

If she were harmed, he couldn't be responsible for what he might do.

## *Chapter Seventeen*

Two days later, Faith sat on a bank of the stream that divided the Home Wood at Ashedon Court, the skirts of her oldest gown tucked under her, watching as her boys fished. Sunlight spangled the trees drowsing in the afternoon breeze with a gold that brightened leaves just beginning to turn to their autumnal hues of red and yellow.

Edward, become quite proficient after nearly a month of practice, baited a hook for Colin, even the younger boy now expert in detaching his catch from the line. Looking on fondly, she thought how much more like a normal, happy eight-year-old her eldest had become, after three weeks out of the city and away from the influence of the tutor who'd been trying to turn him into a miniature of his arrogant, self-absorbed father.

To her guilty delight, Faith wasn't having to counter the Dowager's influence, either. Several days after their arrival in Derbyshire, the letter she'd penned in a disguised hand in London was delivered, informing her mother-in-law that a 'concerned friend' had seen Lord Randall board a packet for Calais. Alternately relieved to know her son was well and alarmed that he had departed to the peril of foreign shores, the Dowager had dithered over whether she would follow her son to offer succour, remain at Ashedon Court in the hope that he would join them there, or return to London. Finally choosing London as the most likely place Lord Randall would try to contact her—and no more a lover of country life than her son—she'd immediately begun preparations to return to the metropolis.

She'd harangued Faith about accompanying her to resume the duties required of a duchess in London society. To which Faith had sweetly responded that she had a higher duty to remain with her son at Ashedon Court, so the young Duke might become better acquainted with the land and responsibilities that were now his.

The Dowager hadn't been happy, but she'd recognised a winning trump card when she saw it. Left with no more ammunition to attack Faith's determination to remain with the children, she left in a huff, accompanied by an entourage with enough grooms, outriders and footmen to satisfy even their former tutor's concept of the consequence due a duchess.

As the clomp of hoofbeats and jingle of harness faded as the Dowager's coach disappeared down the Long Drive, for the first time since her marriage, Faith had felt entirely free.

Since that morning two weeks ago, she'd let herself drift through the days like thistledown blown on the wind. Rising early to take a bruising morning ride; sharing breakfast with the boys in the nursery; teaching them lessons that continued outside, as she identified trees and plants, fish, frogs and insects. Often, as they had today, they brought along a picnic lunch and fishing rods, ending the tutoring walk by throwing some hooks in the stream or, in Colin's case, climbing the nearby trees.

They'd also, during their rambles, stopped by the nearer cottages on the estate, introducing the tenants to the new little Duke—and overhearing several muttered comments about how the occupants wouldn't have recognised the old one, seldom as he came to the estate. The assessment troubled her; Wellingford hadn't been nearly so vast a property, but she'd grown up knowing all the families who worked the land, and she wasn't even the heir. She vowed that, before he saw London again, Edward would be able to say the same about his tenants.

During her rides, she'd got to know the grooms, and engaged a younger one with a sharp eye and a friendly manner to begin teaching the boys, to their great delight. Just last night, she'd penned the last notes to the prospective tutors recommended by Englemere, inviting each of the top three candidates to visit at Ashedon Court for a personal interview.

Back in the countryside she loved, for the first time in ten years free to manage her own time where her actions were not dictated, observed, or criticised by anyone else, she could almost feel herself growing stronger, more relaxed, and confident. The ability to read, think and act solely according to her own inclinations was setting her firmly back on the path to the person she'd once been, the path on which Davie had started her the night he'd rescued her in that Mayfair lane.

Ah, Davie. The only problem she hadn't resolved was what to do about Davie.

She'd penned him a note the night of their arrival at Ashedon, explaining her sudden change of plans, and received a brief one from him in return, approving her actions and wishing her a happy sojourn in the country.

He'd added that, once the Parliamentary session came to an end, he might pay her a visit at Ashedon.

The prospect filled her with excitement—and flung her into an agony of indecision. Here, in the open countryside, there were scores of forest bowers, shepherd huts, shady glens where there were no armies of servants, tradesmen or gossips with prying eyes to observe or report. Even the mansion at Ashedon Court was vast enough, nearly all its several dozen chambers unoccupied, that a midnight tryst in a guest bedroom could take place with almost no chance of discovery.

If he did visit, should she hold fast to her promise not to try to seduce him again? Could she? She might feel stronger and more resilient than she had in a decade, the continual disparagement that had taken such a toll on her sense of confidence and self-worth gradually fading into unpleasant memory, but she still couldn't do without Davie's friendship and support. If she lost that, trying to entice him into her bed, she wasn't sure how she would go on.

But she also wasn't sure how she could resist attempting seduction, when she wanted him so badly, wanted so much to experience the loving embrace of a man who truly cared for her—and sensed that, if she pushed just a bit harder, she might shatter the iron will restraining him and catapult him into responding.

The very idea sent a wave of arousal and excitement through her. Oh, how vividly she could envision it: his mouth on hers, his large, gentle hands tugging loose the hooks, undoing pins, freeing her from her garments so she stood naked before him. His mouth at her breasts, his hands parting her, caressing her; his lips back against hers, his tongue stroking hers as he entered her, thrusting that magnificent, rigid member deep inside again and again until she shattered, the incomparable pleasure of it carrying him over the brink with her…

She wouldn't hold him very long, of course. He would tire of her, as men did of the women who pleasured them, and move on. Would it be worth it to have him for that little space, knowing she could not have him for ever?

Was it worth risking, knowing that if she pushed them into becoming lovers, it was unlikely she'd be able to hang on to his friendship afterwards?

And so, round and round the two possibilities rolled in her head, as they had since the moment she'd had enough peace and time to think about them. Deny herself the pleasure she wanted so badly, the pleasure she knew he could give her? Or seize it, and risk losing the friendship so essential to her well-being?

Colin's cry of delight as he captured another fish brought her back to the present. With a regretful sigh, she let go the dreams of lying in Davie's arms, which, sadly, were likely to remain only dreams for a very long time. At least now, she had the joy of being with her boys, their days together structured just as she wanted them.

'Put that fish in the basket, too,' she called, rising to shake out her skirts. 'We should start back.'

Laughing at the chorus of protests, she said, 'Sorry, boys! We'll fish again tomorrow, if the weather is good, but remember, we planned to stop by the widow Banks's cottage on our way back. Matthew, will you carry the basket we brought for her?'

Subsiding with sighs, the boys dutifully gathered their gear, and after carefully adding their latest catch to the other three trout today's expedition had won them, they set off.

'Why does Mrs Banks need us to bring her bread and soup?' Colin asked, skipping along beside his brother.

'Because she'd old, and sick, looby,' Edward replied.

'Why doesn't her maid or cook help her?' Matthew asked.

'As a farmer's widow, she doesn't have a maid or a cook,' Faith explained. 'Usually, there would be children to help—'

'Like Mr Smith said, when he told us about having lots of chores on the farm when he was growing up?' Matthew interrupted.

'Yes, exactly.' How like Davie, to explain so vividly Matthew still recalled his remarks. How wonderful it would be, if he were here to share all this with them!

Pushing that unattainable desire out of mind, she said, 'Yes. But apparently all of Mrs Banks's children left to work in Manchester. One of Edward's most important tasks as owner of Ashedon is to know which of the tenants are old, or sick, or in need, and take care of them.'

'And I will, Mama.' Straightening to his full height, Edward reached out to Matthew. 'Let me carry the basket.'

'What can I take, then?' Matthew asked, reluctantly giving up his charge.

'Why don't we give her our fish?' Colin piped up. 'Fish is good to eat, isn't it, Mama?'

'That would be very fine,' Faith said, warmed by her son's spontaneous generosity. 'We'll see if she has anyone to cook it for her.'

'Can you cook fish, Mama?' Matthew asked. 'I know you can climb trees.'

Her thoughts flashed back to several impromptu barbecues with her brother Colten, fresh fish grilled over open fires they'd put together beside the banks of the trout stream at Wellingford. 'It's been a long time, but I suppose I still know how. Very well, we'll cook a fish for Mrs Banks, if she feels up to eating it.'

'If it was jam tarts, I might not give one away, but she can have one of my fish,' Colin confided, setting Faith to chuckling.

A short walk later, they reached the Banks cottage. The fields beyond it were fallow, the widow obviously not feeling up to working the land for some time. The cottage itself also looked neglected, Faith noted. She must remind the estate manager that it required fresh roofing thatch and a thorough inspection of the soundness of the timbers in the windows and framing.

Nodding to Edward, she let him knock at the door. 'Mrs Banks, may we come in? We've brought some things for you,' he called.

But instead of the frail widow, the door opened to reveal a husky, broad-shouldered young man, dressed in the rough clothes of a labourer.

'Who are you, and what do you want with my gran?' he asked, scowling at them.

'It's all right, son,' they heard the widow's weak voice from within. 'It's the Duchess and her sons. Please, Dickon, let them in.'

The man didn't move aside. Looking Faith up and down contemptuously, he said, 'Come to play Lady Bountiful, have ye, after paying no heed to nobody for years? Too late for that now, I reckon. As for you, little lordling, your grip over this land won't last much longer.'

Knowing her husband's lack of involvement in the estate, the man probably had a right to his grievance. But furious at his tone and manner, Faith looked him in the eye, saying coldly, 'Mrs Banks is ill, and we have food and provisions. Would you deny them to her?'

After a moment, the man looked away. Moving aside reluctantly he said, 'I s'pose you can bring them in.'

Head held high, Faith ushered her boys past Dickon, Colin, his eyes wide, clinging to her skirts. Ignoring the man who followed them in, as if he expected they would do his grandmother some harm, she walked over to the pallet on which the old woman lay and took her hand. 'How are you today, Mrs Banks? We've brought some bread and soup. And the boys caught you some trout, if you'd care for one.'

'And how do you expect her to eat it?' Dickon asked. 'She ain't got no cook to fix it for her, Your High-and-Mightiness.'

Faith looked back over her shoulder. 'She might once have had children who would care for her. But since apparently they don't any longer, I can cook it.' She looked back down at the old woman. 'If you fancy it now, Mrs Banks.'

The old lady smiled. 'A taste of fresh trout? Ah, Your Grace, can't say when I last had that!'

'You shall have it today, then. Boys, would you go outside and find some wood? There isn't any by the hearth.'

Ignoring the woman's grandson, who was now loitering uncertainly beside the woman's pallet, Faith walked the few steps to the hearth, hunting among the meagre supplies for a pan in which to cook the trout, and hoping she would remember how to gut and prepare it. She'd spent years being disparaged by a duke; the last thing she wanted was to have this arrogant commoner laughing at her ineptness at frying fish.

A few minutes later, sticks and branches in hand, the

boys hurried back in. 'Mama, there's so much smoke in the sky!' Matthew cried.

'Smoke?' she repeated, frowning. 'Where?'

'Coming from the direction of Ashedon Court,' Edward answered.

Putting down the pan, she followed the boys back outside. As they'd described, there was indeed a large pillar of dark smoke rising in the distance, from the place where the ducal palace stood.

Alarm fluttered in her chest. Sticking her head back inside the door, she called, 'I'm sorry, Mrs Banks, but there appears to be a problem back at Ashedon Court. I'll just leave the bread and soup, and come back later to prepare the fish.'

'You go on, then, Your Grace,' Mrs Banks said.

'Come on, boys, at the double-quick,' she said, breaking into a trot herself.

Only to have Dickon follow and stop her with a hand to the shoulder. 'You oughtn't go back, ma'am! Take the boys and head for the village. There's only trouble back there.'

For a moment, Faith stared at him incredulously. 'Not go back? That's my son's house afire! With a score of servants working inside, we must make sure everyone has got out safely, and organise a party to fight it.'

Shrugging off his hand, she made a scooting motion at the boys and picked up her pace, consumed with worry. The heart of Ashedon Court was an Elizabethan Great Hall, whose ancient hornbeam timbers would ignite like paper in a bake oven. Fortunately, the flanking wings were of brick and the roof slate, which would slow a blaze. But where had it started—?

'You don't understand,' Dickon cried, trotting after

them. 'This fire—it weren't no accident. It were set, deliberate.'

Astonished, she stopped to face him. 'Set? Why?'

'Lords like your husband saw fit not to pass the Reform Bill. We aimed to show 'em we'll not bow to their refusal no more.'

'Were the servants warned first?' she demanded. 'It wasn't their fault the Bill didn't pass.'

He looked away, not meeting her gaze. 'Dunno.'

Furious, she turned back towards Ashedon Court. 'A right fine victory it will be for your lot, if the under-butler gets trapped in the wine cellar when the roof falls in, or some maid in the attics! We'll go to the village and leave the house to you, but not until I know everyone's safely out.'

Dickon trotting by her side, Faith and the boys ran for Ashedon Court, the volume of smoke increasing as they neared.

As they burst out of the cover of the Home Wood and ran up the Long Drive, Faith was relieved to see the fire appeared to be in the stable block, not in the main house. By the time they reached the turn where the drive split, one trail leading to the stables, one to the house, she halted, panting. She was about to continue to the stables to check that all the horses had been led out when she realised that a crowd of men had gathered in the court-yard before the manor house, their angry shouts just discernible in the distance.

They must have spotted her, for several broke away and headed down the drive towards her. While Dickon beside her swore, Faith drew in a trembling breath and gathered her boys behind her.

This must be what Davie had meant, when he said Parliament *must* pass the Reform Bill. She'd just never imagined the repercussions of failure would touch her, and her boys, here.

Suddenly, she heard the sound of galloping hooves approaching on the Long Drive behind them. Ranging her sons behind her to face this new threat, she braced herself, wishing a bit hysterically that she had her riding crop, or even one of the sticks the boys had gathered for the fire, with which to defend them.

Her heart racing so hard she could scarcely breathe, Faith clenched her teeth and waited as the horseman reached them and vaulted from the saddle.

'Lord have mercy, are you all right, Faith?' he cried.

Faith gazed up, astonished. 'Davie?'

## *Chapter Eighteen*

Relief at finding her unharmed making his knees weak, all Davie wanted was to throw Faith on the back of his saddle and carry her to the safety of the village. But he couldn't take her and the three boys, and he knew she'd never leave without them.

Noting the stream of men now approaching them, he calculated the distance to the stables, and realised he couldn't get them there and harness a vehicle to take them away before the crowd reached them.

'Who are you?' he barked to the labourer who hovered at her side. If the man were part of the mob, keeping her here until the others could arrive, he could at least dispatch that threat.

'Banks,' the man answered. 'She were helping my gran. Don't think the two of us can hold 'em off, but we can slow 'em down.'

'We won't just slow them—we'll stop them,' Davie replied. Setting free his nervous, rearing gelding, who was more likely to trample them in his smoke-induced anxiety than provide a means of escape, he told Faith, 'The village knows what's happening, and the fire engine is on its way. Is there anyone you can trust at the stables?'

'Yes. Abrams, the groom who is teaching the boys to ride. He'll help us, I'm certain.'

'Take the boys and go at once. Tell him to ready a gig or a farm wagon, whatever he can put a horse to the quickest, and drive you to the village.' When she hesitated, he said, 'I know you are worried about the servants at the main house. But your first concern must be the safety of your sons.'

Her face clouded, she nodded quickly and gathered the boys. 'Come along, my dears. I'm afraid we'll just be in the way here.'

'Will you come with us, Mr S-Smith?' Matthew asked, his voice breaking.

Fury coursed through Davie anew, that Faith's home and perhaps safety had been put at risk, that her precious sons had been frightened.

'I'll come to you in the village afterwards.'

'Sh-shouldn't I stay, Mama?' Edward said, his words at odds with the anxiety on his face. 'This is my land, you've been telling me, and I'm responsible for the safety of its people.'

While Faith's eyes filled with tears, Davie said, 'You can delegate that task to me today, Ashedon. If you will allow me the privilege.'

The boy gave him a short nod. 'I—I will.'

The faint sound of jingling harness had Davie looking over his shoulder. To his relief, an open farm cart approached from the stables, pulled by two shying horses the driver was struggling to control.

'Abrams!' Faith cried, spotting the vehicle. 'It's all right,' she told Davie. 'He's the groom I told you about.'

'Here, Your Grace,' the man said, pulling up the team. 'Climb up with the youngsters, and I'll get you safely into the village.'

Without waiting for Faith to reply, Davie lifted her to the bench, while Dickon quickly assisted with the children.

'Take her to the inn. I'll come later.'

'No!' Faith cried. 'Just to the edge of the drive. If things…get out of hand, we'll continue, I promise. But I'll not leave Ashedon Court's people to the mercy of these rowdies unless I absolutely must.'

While Davie would prefer to countermand her, the mob was on foot, and as long as the cart kept its distance, the groom would be able to get her safely away, if necessary, before they could catch up.

He hoped it wouldn't be necessary. Much as he'd like to break a few heads, it would be much better if he could defuse this situation before it got any more out of hand, resulting in far too many angry farmhands being hung or transported.

'Very well. But make sure it's a safe distance,' he told the groom.

'It will be, I promise,' the man said, and set the vehicle in motion.

Watching until the wagon halted a good distance away at the curve of the drive, Davie turned back towards the manor house.

The first members of the crowd were almost on him.

Seeing his imposing size—and no doubt the furious determination on face—the first three halted, wisely hesitant to take him on by themselves. Spying a large boulder set decoratively at the juncture where the drive branched towards the stables or the house, Davie trotted over and scrambled up on it, until he stood a half-a-man's height taller than the men gathering below.

Knowing the importance of projecting authority and

confidence, he simply stood, holding the men below by the power of his presence, not attempting to speak until the majority had arrived from the courtyard. He had an orator's voice, born for addressing a crowd, and as they assembled below him, he drew on every bit of it.

'Men, you have a just grievance, and good cause for disappointment. But this is not the way to express it, or to bring to reality the goals we all share.'

'*We* share?' one of them shouted. 'We seen you with the Duchess!'

'Aye, you're just one of their lackeys!' cried another. 'A pet canary, singing for them in the Lords!'

'We aim to show 'em we won't put up with them tunes no more!'

'Why don't we pull him off his perch?' the first man shouted.

As several of the men moved forward, Davie braced himself, ready to play Big John to their Robin Hood at the river. But to his surprise, Banks put up his hands, warding them off.

'What, you turned traitor?' the first man snarled. 'And you tole us you was jest goin' to check on your old granny.'

'I did! But I don't hold with threatening women and boys. Besides, the Duchess was taking care of my sick gran.'

'It's not the Duchess or her children with whom you have a quarrel,' Davie said. 'You want your outrage to be heard, but continue in this way, and all you'll hear is the snap of the rope at the end of a hangman's noose. You're local men, aren't you?'

'Aye, most of 'em,' Dickon said.

'Which means you could be identified, arrested, tried, and hanged or transported. That will not aid your cause, nor keep your families clothed and fed, until we pass the legislation we all want.'

'What would the likes of *you* know about it?' one of the men jeered.

'A great deal. I'm David Tanner Smith, a Member of Parliament for Hazelwick, and I've been working towards the passage of a reform bill for ten years. I know you are all impatient that progress has been so slow. But it does continue, and the bill will pass. From there, we'll move on to address the next great issue, opening the vote to all. But only if we do not give those who oppose us reason to brand us as hooligans, intent only on destroying property and the social order.'

While there were mutterings about how the social order ought to be destroyed, the fire in the crowd had been banked. Already a few, doubtless having second thoughts about the wisdom of attacking a ducal property, were drifting off.

'How do you mean to get the bill passed, when all of them that killed it still sit in the Lords?' one of the instigators demanded.

'Because they may not be the only ones sitting,' Davie said. 'If it seems likely the Lords will vote down the bill in the next session, Grey will pressure the king to create new peers, enough to flood the Lords with supporters who will get the bill passed.'

At that moment, a horseman appeared at the corner of the drive, galloping past the farm wagon carrying Faith and the boys, and charging up the rise towards them. As the rider drew closer, Davie recognised him as Walter Downing, the Member of Parliament for the local district.

His arrival created a flutter in the crowd, some stirring as they identified their Parliamentary representative, a few more guiltily slipping away.

'Men, what's going on here?' he demanded as he reined in.

'Letting our displeasure be known,' one of the leaders returned with a surly look.

'Surely you don't mean to jeopardise all our progress by doing something foolhardy!'

'Is it true, what that man's telling us?' the leader asked, jerking his thumb at Davie. 'That Grey and the King will make sure the bill passes in the next session?'

'That man?' Downing said, belatedly looking up. 'Why, it's Mr Smith! I don't know what brought you here, but if you've kept these fellows from rash action, I thank you!' Turning back to the leader, he said, 'Henries, Mr Smith is one of the leaders of the Reform cause. Whatever he predicted, you can count on it!' Looking towards the column of smoke coming from the direction of the stables, he frowned. 'But what have you done here?'

Just then, the crowd's attention was deflected to the farm cart now driving back towards them, saving Henries from an answer. To Davie's displeasure, as he wasn't convinced the danger had been completely defused yet, Faith herself handled the ribbons.

'Your Grace!' Mr Downing cried as she brought the cart to a halt before them. With an aggravated glance towards Henries, he said, 'I hope the…disturbance today hasn't alarmed you.'

'An unfortunate…accident at the stables, I'm afraid,' she answered. 'But Abrams tells me all the horses were got out safely, and the fire engine from the village is on its way. I expect these men heard of it, and came to help. If you gentlemen could hurry on and man some buckets while we await the fire engine? Much of the building is stone, so I hope we can salvage the main part.'

'Off with you, men,' Downing said, waving them towards the stables. Most took to their heels immediately, apparently eager to put the incident behind them.

'So you are not inclined to summon the magistrate and…press charges against anyone?' Downing asked.

Faith turned a long, hard glance on the several ringleaders. 'Not at this time. I hope they're now convinced there is a better way to move forward.'

'Magnanimous of you,' Downing said. 'Henries, Markham, and you others, why don't you thank the Duchess, and go help the bucket brigade?'

After a chorus of mumbled 'Thankee, ma'am', the men set off, even the recalcitrant Henries finally offering Faith a grudging nod. As he strolled away, they heard the bells of the fire wagon in the distance.

Downing looked up to Faith and tipped his hat. 'Thank you, Your Grace, for a forbearance and understanding that, frankly, would not have been forthcoming from your late husband. I must admit, as I rode out, I feared the day would end with half the local farmhands headed for gaol and a hanging.'

As Davie clambered down from the rock and strode over to stand by the farm wagon, Mr Downing came over to shake his hand. 'Thank you, too, sir. I've heard the tales from Derby and Bristol and even as near as Wollaton. We don't need that here, or we'll never get that blasted bill passed!'

They all turned as the fire wagon appeared at the corner of the drive and laboured up the rise towards them. 'Now that the brigade is arriving, Mr Downing, why don't you encourage most of the men to return home?' Faith said. 'Abrams, take the wagon back, please. I'll walk to the house with the boys, and come back to the stables after I check on the staff.'

'Very good, Your Grace,' Downing replied. 'Thank you again.'

As the MP set off, Faith turned to the man who'd helped Davie hold off the crowd. 'Mr Banks, a special thanks to you, for coming to our aide. Your granny raised a responsible young man.'

'Man enough to admit when I been wrong. Thank *you* for looking after Gran. I'll see what I can do at the stables.' After doffing his cap to Faith, Banks waved down the fire wagon, hopped aboard and rode along as it passed them and headed towards the stables.

'Let me accompany you to the house,' Davie said, helping Faith and the boys down from the wagon. 'Just in case any recalcitrants are lingering in the vicinity.'

'Thank you, Mr Smith, the boys and I would appreciate that.'

Though he was finally able to draw an easy breath, Davie wouldn't be completely satisfied until he'd verified that the house was safe. Anger still stirred in his blood at the thought that those ruffians had threatened her and her boys—but how brave and magnificent she'd been, facing down that crowd!

'How did you happen to come to Ashedon today, Mr Smith?' Faith asked as he fell in beside them, arms held stiffly at his sides to resist the urge to sweep her into an embrace, just to feel the steady, normal beat of her heart against his chest.

'We read in the papers about the disturbances in the countryside after the defeat of the bill. When Wollaton was mentioned, I knew I had to come check on you. So you must excuse my dirt.' He motioned to his mud-splattered attire. 'I rode straight through.'

'From London?' She looked back at him, startled. 'You must be starving, as well as exhausted! We'll find something for you in the kitchen—assuming that mob didn't ransack the place.'

'If they did, you may have to reconsider not pressing charges. We need a new England, but not one built out of coercion and law-breaking,' Davie said grimly. 'I haven't worked the last ten years of my life for that.'

A few minutes later, they arrived at the main house and skirted the front to go to the kitchen wing. Rapping at the door, which unaccountably appeared locked, they were admitted by the butler bearing a fireplace poker and the cook brandishing a rolling pin, while several maids wept in the background.

'Your Grace! Thank the Lord! You are unharmed, I hope?' the butler asked.

'We are all well,' Faith replied. 'What of you in the house? Is everyone safe? Goodness, what a smell of smoke!'

'Oh, ma'am, I thought they would murder us!' one of the maids wailed.

'They first sought admission at the front door, which I locked after refusing them. They tried to force their way in here, but Mrs Pierce and I were able to prevent them. They did manage to set fire to part of the roof—'

'Trying to burn us alive!' the maid wailed again.

'But I sent the footmen up. They were able to put it out before it spread from the kitchen wing, but I fear it may take a long time to air the smoke from the rooms.'

'Thank you, Knoles, and Mrs Pierce, for your bravery and resourcefulness! Despite the turmoil, might there be something in the larder for Mr Smith? A close friend of the family, he read about the disturbances in the newspaper, and has ridden straight through from London to offer us assistance.'

'Of course, Your Grace, I can manage something,' Cook said. 'Susie, Mary, stop your snivelling and give me a hand.'

'Mr Smith, you were the one standing on the rock, addressing the crowd?' the butler asked. 'I could see you from the upper windows.' When Davie nodded, the butler said, 'We owe you a great debt. The crowd might have decided to rush the doors, or tried harder to set this building afire, had you not deflected them. Whatever you told them must have been very persuasive!'

'Dismay at their rash actions had begun to set in by then, and common sense to reassert itself. Mr Downing's calming presence finished the matter,' Davie said. 'I would appreciate a quick bite, Mrs Pierce, and then I'm off for the stables. I'll send the fire brigade down to check the roof, once they have the damage there contained.' Turning to Faith, he said, 'Why don't you take the boys up to the nursery, out of all the commotion?'

'Can I go to the stables with you?' Matthew asked. 'I like commotion!'

'Later,' Faith intervened. 'We don't want to distract the men from their work.'

'The housekeeper is making a survey of the main and bedchamber wings now, Your Grace,' the butler said. 'To see how far the smoke spread, and determine what needs to be repaired.'

'Very good, Knoles. I'll take the boys out of harm's way. Mr Smith, thank you again for your intervention. One hopes the crowd would have come to their senses before inflicting any more…damage, but I shall always credit you with making sure of that.'

Her eyes telling him she'd like to say—and do—

more, she simply pressed his hand. A sudden tremor running through him at the thought of what an angry crowd might have done to her, Davie felt that reassuring touch all the way to his bones.

'We'll talk later, Mr Smith,' she promised as she gathered her sons. 'Upstairs with you, now, boys! I bet Mrs Pierce will find something nice for your tea, as well as Mr Smith's!'

'So I shall, Your Grace,' the cook said as Faith ushered the children out. 'Mr Smith, Knoles will show you to the morning room. I'll have something sent up in a trice.'

'Just a quick nibble in the servants' hall will do for me, if that won't disturb your work,' Davie said, watching Faith walk out. *Why did it always seem as if the light in the room dimmed, once she'd left it?* 'I'd like to get down to the stables as soon as possible. By the time I get back, the housekeeper should have her report ready, and we can help the Duchess decide which repairs are needed first.'

Mrs Pierce nodding her agreement, he followed the butler to the servants' hall. Not until they'd sorted out the uncertainties left in the wake of today's disturbance, and he assured himself that Faith and her sons were truly safe, could he think about broaching the question he'd been wanting to ask her for the last three weeks.

# *Chapter Nineteen*

After an afternoon spent assessing damage and penning quick letters to Giles and Lord Englemere detailing the situation, Davie arrived back at the main house to find Faith had already dined and was about to tuck her sons in for the night. Invited to accompany her to give them the latest news, for, she said, their conversation all afternoon had concerned him and the extraordinary events of the day, he gladly followed in her wake as she took the stairs up to the nursery.

Acutely conscious of her lovely form beside him, torn between impatience to get her alone and uncertainty over whether he should wait a while longer before delivering his proposal, or try his luck at once, he followed her up.

The boys' exclamations of delight at seeing him were gratifying, if counter-productive to their mother's desire to settle them to sleep. 'I'm glad to see you, too, boys, but I shouldn't have come to bid you goodnight, if I'd thought I would keep you from your bedtime. It's been a long day, for you and your mama, and you all need to rest.'

'All the horses are safe, aren't they?' Matthew asked, as the boys subsided against their pillows.

'And the dogs?' Colin added.

'Yes. All the livestock are unharmed. Much of the stable wing will need rebuilding, but we found space in barns on the neighbouring farms to house the dogs and horses while the work is done.'

'Can we continue our riding lessons?' Matthew asked.

'I imagine you can, but that will be up to your mama.'

'You were very brave, Mr Smith, staying there to face the crowd,' Edward said.

'It's easier to be brave when you know you are right, and that by standing firm, you can protect people.'

'I was scared!' Matthew admitted. 'Maybe when I grow as big as you, I won't be.'

'I'll bet you won't be,' Davie replied with a chuckle.

'Mama, why did you tell that man the crowd came to help us, when they came to burn the stables?' Edward asked.

'Sometimes people get so angry, they do things they regret. The penalties under law for destroying property and threatening people are very harsh,' Faith explained. 'Having them arrested would hurt their families. I wanted to give them the chance to reconsider their behaviour, and do better in future.'

'Why *were* they so angry?' Matthew asked.

'Laws have changed, and many people lost the right to use common land to grow vegetables or keep a cow or chickens. That's made it hard for them to feed their families. They wanted to elect officials who could change that, and a few days ago, the new law that might helped do that was voted down. They felt they had lost something precious, and been betrayed in the bargain.'

'You mean like someone wanted to take away all their jam tarts, and leave them only a fish?' Colin said.

Faith smiled. 'Worse than that. Take all the jam tarts, all the fish, and leave them hungry.'

'I'd be mad, too,' Colin decided.

'So you see, they weren't angry at you, just disappointed that they'd not received the help they expected. They acted hastily, without thinking first, as we all do sometimes,' Davie said.

'So...we'll be safe here, tonight?' Matthew asked.

'I would never let anything happen to you or your mama,' Davie promised.

With a little sigh, Colin snuggled into his pillow. 'I think I can sleep now.'

'Good,' Faith said, kissing him on the forehead. 'Tomorrow will be better.'

'Can we go fishing again?' Matthew's drowsy voice asked.

'Perhaps. I'll have to talk with the staff. We might have to tend the dogs while they start the rebuilding on the stables.'

'Building!' Matt's sleepy eyes opened wider. 'Can I use a hammer?'

'Very possibly. But now, you must sleep.'

'Thank you for helping us today, Mr Smith,' Edward said. 'I was happy to let you protect Ashedon Court for me.'

'And I was privileged to do it,' Davie replied solemnly.

'Goodnight, boys,' Faith said.

'Goodnight, Mama. Goodnight, Mr Smith,' they chorused.

Together they tiptoed out the nursery door and walked down the long hall. 'How about a brandy?' Faith asked. 'I might even join you in one.'

'An excellent idea. If you will guide me to the library. Otherwise, I may wander all night without finding the way.'

Chuckling, she led him down the hallway, across a landing that overlooked the Great Hall, down a staircase into another wing. The odour of smoke increased notably as they proceeded.

Wrinkling her nose, she said, 'Thank heavens the smoke penetrated only as far as the central block. I don't think we could sleep, if the smell were as strong in the bedchamber wing.'

'I'm just glad they didn't succeed in setting fire to the whole place.'

'True,' she agreed, walking into the library and pouring him a brandy from the decanter on the sideboard, then pouring one for herself.

'You were serious,' he said, raising his eyebrows.

'Indeed,' she retorted. 'There's something about watching your stables burn down, your house being torched and your children menaced, that creates quite a thirst.'

Some of his earlier anxiety for her safety recurred, sending a shudder through him. 'Thank the Lord it didn't go any further.'

She nodded. 'Thank Him—and you. When you jumped down from your horse this afternoon, I was never so glad to see anyone in my life! Just having you nearby makes me feel safer.'

He bit his tongue on the urge to propose here and now. Instinct warned that, with things just returning to a semblance of normalcy after a day of chaos, it wasn't the moment to suggest she disrupt her whole life again. 'I hope I can always keep you safe,' was all he allowed himself. 'In fact, let me urge you to accompany me back to your sister at Highgate Village. I don't believe there will be more trouble, but I wouldn't like to risk it. You'll need the stable rebuilt and a complete airing of the main house before it's truly habitable again; you could have that visit with your sister while the work is underway. By the time it's complete, we should be close to finally passing the Reform Bill, ending any further threat for good.'

After sitting thoughtfully for a moment, she nodded in agreement. 'It would be better to move the boys from any possible danger, and no one could enjoy living in this smoke. Large as this manse is, it will take for ever to fully air it out.'

'Hire as many as you can from the village to help. They'll be glad of the wages, which will also sweeten the mood of the surrounding area.'

'Another good suggestion.' Taking one last sip of brandy, she set down the glass. 'Suddenly I'm weary. Will you walk with me back to the bedchamber wing? I wouldn't want you to get lost and end up sleeping on a trestle in the Great Hall.'

Now that they were alone, in the intimate camaraderie of candlelight and darkness, the desire always simmering beneath the surface intensified. The mere mention of 'bedchamber' made his member leap in anticipation. Having her escort him to his chamber was probably a very bad idea.

Before he could answer, she continued. 'I have to admit, I still feel a shiver down my spine, every time I turn my back.' She shook her head. 'I'm as bad as Colin! But I've never experienced such…naked animosity. It was…unsettling. How magnificently you handled the crowd, though!'

'Nothing like a little reminder of the gallows to make men reconsider their rashness,' he said wryly, finishing his own brandy.

While she blew out the candles on the sideboard, he picked up a brace, then escorted her from the darkened room. Shadows danced along her face as he walked her down the hallways, the battle between desire and good sense intensifying with each step.

He was barely able to breathe by the time she halted in front of a door. 'This chamber is mine,' she said, her voice as unsteady as his heartbeat. 'Would you go inside with me, and make sure no rioters lurk in the corners?'

His mind immediately played with the words of her request, bringing up images of another sort of penetration. His mouth too dry for speech, he merely nodded before opening the door and walking in, Faith trailing behind him. After making a circuit with the candelabra, shedding light across a sitting area, the hearth, a dressing table…and then back to a wide, four-poster bed, he set the candelabra on the bedside table and made himself walk back to the open door.

Halting there, he had to swallow twice before he could get any words out. 'Goodnight, Faith. Sleep well.'

She stepped over, closed the door and turned to face him. 'Oh, Davie,' she whispered. 'You don't really mean to leave me all alone tonight, do you?'

He *ought* to, but desire seemed to have snuffed out reason as completely as Faith had extinguished the candles in the library. He simply stood, unable to make himself quit the room, every bit of will engaged in keeping himself from picking her up and carrying her to the bed.

'Don't go,' she whispered again. Reaching up to cup his face in her hands, she leaned up and kissed him.

And, as always, he was lost.

In the time it took him to register the touch of her mouth against his, her kiss turned from tentative to frantic and demanding. Anxiety relieved, passion long denied—whatever it was, it drove him as powerfully as it did her. Opening to her, he scoured her tongue with his own.

She clung to him with one arm, trying with her other hand to raise her skirts high enough to wrap her legs around his. Still kissing her, their mouths locked, he picked her up and carried her to the bed. Perched on the edge, she yanked at his neckcloth, unravelling the knot and pulling the length free, jerking the neckline of his shirt open until she could slide her hands up and under, the imprint of her fingers sizzling against his bare skin.

As he leaned her against the pillows, driving his tongue into her, she pulled his hands to her breasts, gasping into his mouth as he rubbed his thumbs across nipples so rigid, he could feel their hardness through the layers of chemise and gown. She sought his hardness, too, trying to grasp and stroke the erection straining against his trouser front, fumbling for the buttons.

Knowing he'd never last if she touched him there, wanting her satisfaction to be complete and overwhelming, he pushed her hands away. Apparently misunderstanding his intent, she began tugging up her skirts.

But he was a large man. Not knowing how long since she'd last been loved—not wanting to know—and intent on giving her pleasure unmarred by discomfort, he helped her pull up the skirts, bunching them around her hips until the pale skin of her thighs gleaned in the candlelight. But instead of uncovering himself to straddle her, as she urged, he caressed his fingers up her legs, over her knees, across the bare skin of her thighs, over the softness of her stomach.

She cried out, thrusting her hips against his hand. And so he moved his fingers lower, stroking across her cleft, where she was hot, and wet, and oh so ready. Bending to kiss her again, his gentle fingers massaged and caressed, back and forth across that tender ridge in time to the thrusts of their tongues, until a few seconds later, she reached her peak and cried out, going rigid in his arms.

He let her sag back against the pillows, laying his cheek against her head while they both gasped for breath. But before he could move away and ease himself on to the pillows beside her, she thrust her hips against his hand again.

'More, my darling?' he whispered, giving her a tender kiss.

'More, please,' she whispered.

Quite ready to continue, he trailed his fingers from her centre down one bare thigh, up the other and back. Bending to kiss her again, he slid one slick finger into her warm depths. He felt the tremor within her as she gasped and angled her hips to invite him further. Stroking deeper, he inserted another finger, then another, stretching her, filling her, sliding in and out until, her hands clutching his shoulders, she shattered again.

This was bliss, he thought, gathering her against him, kissing her damp forehead, exulting at the response he'd drawn from her. But he shouldn't be surprised that his tree-climbing, crowd-confronting, tender-hearted Faith was as passionate as she was fiercely loving.

While he reclined in a euphoria of pleasant, if unsatisfied, satisfaction, she stirred against him. 'Ah, Davie, that was wonderful,' she murmured. 'But I want to feel you inside me. All of you. Now. Please.'

As she spoke, she worked open the buttons of his trouser flap, freeing the straining erection. Stroking him, she said, 'I think you want that, too.'

Her hand still on him, she lowered herself against

the pillows and urged him down over her. So close to breaking under the stimulation of her touch, he knew he couldn't hold back much longer, he gasped, 'No, not like that!' Gently removing her hand, he rolled to his back and held out his arms to her. 'I'd crush you, sweetheart. Ride me instead.'

'Willingly.'

And not only was she willing, wicked wench that she was, she retained enough of the presence of mind he was fast losing to be able to tease, straddling him and running a finger along his swollen length before guiding him home. Even then, she eased herself down on him gently, inviting possession one slow bit at a time, until he was nearly mad from restraining the wild motion his body craved.

But once she'd fully sheathed him, ah, then, she too abandoned any pretence of patience, moving with him in hard, frantic thrusts that soon had them both spinning into the abyss together.

Some time later, Davie drifted awake, floating happily in the grip of the most splendid dream he'd ever had—making love to Faith, falling asleep with her cradled in his arms, awakening to the warmth of her beside him, her soft breathing the only sound in a chamber gilded by flickering candlelight.

In the moment he realised the experience was real, not just the most vivid dream he'd ever had, a sense of awe and wonder suffused him.

He must convince Faith to marry him. Having tasted such magnificent joy, how could he go back to the dull greyness of a life without her?

Then she stirred and smiled up at him. "Oh, Davie, I've never been so happy.

'Nor have I, my darling,' he said, smiling back.

'Well, that is, I could be a *little* happier. If we dispensed with all these annoying garments.'

He grinned. 'Happy to oblige, my angel. Shall I blow out the candles first?'

'No, don't.' Her merry eyes grew serious. 'I want to see you. All of you. Oh, how often I've dreamed of it! I want to see every bit.'

Everything within him stirred and tightened at her request. 'Only if I can see all of you in return.'

To his delight, despite her boldness earlier, a shy blush coloured her cheeks. 'If that would please you.'

'How often I've imagined it,' he echoed her response, that prospect the ultimate fulfilment of all his many dreams.

'Then imagine no more.'

She eased from the bed and offered him the laces at her back. Swiftly he undid them, helped her out of her bodice, then her skirt. When she turned, the outline of her breasts clear under thin linen of the chemise, he had to halt long enough to kiss them, his member stirring as he cupped each full, heavy round. He had to stop again after he'd pulled off her chemise to suckle the soft pink nipples into rigid points, before caressing his way down her legs as he stripped off stockings and garters.

When she stood before him, fully naked, he could only stare, mesmerised. 'You're even more lovely than I imagined.'

'My turn,' she said, her voice trembling. Distracted by her nakedness, he was scarcely aware of shrugging off his jacket and vest, kicking off the already-unbuttoned breeches, peeling down his hose, until a draught of wind that rattled the shutters sent a cold breath of air to prickle his skin.

All he cared about was her molten gaze, fixed on him. 'What a wonder you are,' she whispered, running her fingers over the breadth of his shoulders, his chest, down arms and thighs whose muscles tensed at her touch. 'So big, so powerful. Such pleasure you give me.' Before he could guess her intent, she bent and kissed his erection.

Dizzied by the intensity of his response, he clutched at her shoulders to steady himself. Before the pleasure of it made him lose his balance entirely, she pulled him over to the bed, driving him mad again as she suckled and caressed. Knowing he was nearing the peak, he moved away from her, breaking contact.

Ignoring his body's protest, he slid to his knees before her. 'I want to taste satisfaction on you,' he whispered. The sloe-eyed seduction of her gaze spurring him on, gently he parted her legs and plied with his tongue the tender areas his fingers and shaft had pleasured, until she was pressing against him, sobbing for release.

She motioned him back on to the bed, pulling him up, pushing him back against the pillows, sheathing him to the hilt in one swift thrust. There was no pretence of teasing this time, just urgent, relentless movement that drove them both to completion.

Sated, dazzled, Davie subsided against the pillows. Exhausted after the anxiety of the day and his long hours of riding, he tucked Faith against his chest, blew out the candles, pulled the blankets over them, and fell immediately into the most contented sleep of his life.

## *Chapter Twenty*

Smiling drowsily, Faith snuggled into the warm, solid shape beside her. She couldn't remember, she thought with a sense of awe, ever feeling so safe and cherished, so completely happy and at peace. So *satisfied*.

And then she remembered. Davie, making love to her tenderly, completely, thoroughly. Davie, here in her bed.

Wasn't he? Suddenly terrified it was only a dream, she sat up abruptly, panic draining away to leave only delight when she saw he was, indeed, still lying on the pillow beside her, arms crossed behind his head. A beam of morning light illumined his face and the blue, blue eyes watching her, full of tenderness and the same sense of wonder she felt.

She leaned down to kiss him, sure in the whole history of the world, there had never been a sweeter, more beautiful awakening. 'You *are* still here,' she said as she released him.

'I am.' He reached up to trace the line of her jaw with one finger. 'Where I've wanted to be for so long. Where I never want to leave.'

She caught his finger and kissed it, then slipped it into her mouth and suckled it, drawing a groan from him and sparking a delicious flutter in her nether regions. Which, though oh-so-satisfied, seemed to indicate they were quite ready to begin the activities of the night all over again.

She took his hand and cupped around her bare breast. 'Last night was…magnificent. Amazing. I never dreamed such pleasure existed.'

He stroked her breast, drawing his hand up to caress the already rigid nipple. 'All for you.'

She whimpered, leaning into his stroking fingers. 'Now I understand why men and women have affairs.'

He stopped abruptly, his smile fading, and drew himself up against the pillows. Pulling her into his arms, he said, 'I don't want to have an affair with you, Faith.'

Alarmed by that blunt statement, she pushed away so she might watch his expression. 'You don't? How can you say that? You couldn't be so cruel as to dismiss me after only one night! Surely you care more for me than that!'

'That's just it. I don't want one night—I want *every* night. I want you in my life, in my arms, in my bed, from now until the day I die. I love you, Faith, totally and completely. I have, I think, almost from the moment we met. Won't you marry me, my darling?'

Shock washed the drowsy sensuality clean away. 'Marry you?' she gasped. 'But I had no idea—'

'Surely you had *some* idea. True, I never spelled out what I really wanted for us. At first, I didn't think I had the right. But the night the Reform Bill passed, I realised in the new England we wish to create, if I truly believe I am the equal of any man, I should act like it. In fact, with Lord Randall, and with the crowd today, I've been of *more* use to you than I would have been, had I been born a peer. The rioters would have ignored—or attacked—a nobleman, leaving you in danger.'

She shook her head wonderingly. 'I can't think of another man who could have accomplished what you did.'

'The only reason I hesitated to press my suit was my concern over the boys. Before I came to Derbyshire, I talked with Englemere and Sir Edward, to ask their opinions about how your children's trustees might react, should you marry me. They felt certain they would not disapprove—at least, not enough to remove your sons from your care. It only remains to determine if *you* believe I am your equal, and if so, to decide if you love me enough to suffer the other consequences.'

'Other consequences?' she echoed, still too shocked to really take in what he was saying.

'The titters from those who believe you've married far beneath you. Cuts direct from people who cross you off their guest list. Your own mother-in-law might refuse to receive you any longer.'

She laughed. 'I would rather call that a "blessing"! You should know more than anyone how little I would miss anything about society. But…marriage?'

Suddenly, she saw not Davie's dear face but Edward's, the night he proposed. How ardent he'd seemed, how completely intent on convincing her that he wanted her and only her, to be his wife and bear his children, his alone for the rest of his life.

How long had that ardour lasted? How much was it her fault that it had not?

'Unless you believe I'm not…good enough,' his voice recalled her.

'*You* not good enough?' she said incredulously, looking back at him. 'How can you even think that?'

Her avowal earned a fierce hug and an even more ardent kiss. 'Then you'll accept my hand?' he said as he released her.

Much as she hated to disappoint him, warning bells were sounding in her head like the voice of Cassandra predicting doom.

'I…oh, I don't know! You know I care about you. But…you've wanted me a long time. Loved me a long time. I…I fear you have created a vastly over-rosy image of me, as some sort of paragon, something I could never live up to. I'm not very special, really. I don't embroider, or sing, or play, or make clever, witty conversation. I fear I would end up…disappointing you, and I couldn't bear that.'

Fortunately, since she found herself perilously near tears, he did not laugh at her, or make some dismissive remark. Instead, he took her hands and looked straight into her eyes. 'You are special to *me*. A shining star who brightens the life of everyone around her. Who else would climb a tree, just to make her son smile? Or stand before an angry crowd who threatened her sons, and yet show mercy? A woman scorned and belittled by society, by the family that should have cherished her, who reacted with calm resignation rather than hate and vindictiveness. I've felt that way about you since the first day we met. My heart rejoices every time I see your smile, or hear your laughter. I expect some day, our world will have created machines to embroider, or play music, or even to sing to us. But I don't think there will ever be as beautiful a spirit as yours, or one whose sensitivity and compassion make my heart rejoice every time I see her.'

Davie—dear, dependable, compassionate Davie—hers to cherish for the rest of her life? Sensual, passionate Davie, the most magnificent lover she'd ever known?

It seemed…unbelievable that he would want to marry her. Despite what he vowed, could she really believe she could keep him in love with her for ever?

Accepting his hand meant that he would *be* in her life for ever—whether or not he still loved her. Unlike Edward, Davie would be faithful, kind and courteous, even if his affections towards her cooled.

She'd almost not survived becoming the wife Ashedon barely tolerated and regarded with contempt. She knew she could not survive becoming the object of Davie's faint disdain and polite disinterest.

The distress and turmoil of her emotions must have been painted on her face, for with a sigh, Davie let her go. 'I can't do more than promise my love. You have to believe it. Believe in us. If you can't, there's no point going any further. I won't be your lover, Faith. I will only be your husband.'

She fought to keep the tears back. The last thing she wanted was to drive him away. But did she dare ask him to stay?

While she wrestled with a response, he said, 'Don't marry me because you know I love you—only if you need and love me, and can't imagine being happy in a life that doesn't include me. Clearly, I've shocked you, and rather than press for an answer now—and force one I may not like—don't tell me anything, yet. Think about it carefully. If you decide your answer must be "no", I will accept that, and never importune you again. You'll have my respect and admiration for the rest of my life.'

'But not your friendship?' she asked, fearing she knew the answer.

His smile now was strained. 'That would be too... hard.'

With that, he rose from the bed and walked around, collecting and donning clothing scattered in haste during the night. Torn between accepting his suit at once and drawing him back to her bed, and letting him go so she might think about this when her heart wasn't pounding so hard with fear and distress, her head hurt, she simply watched. The urgency of making the right decision made her feel almost physically ill.

When he'd finished dressing, he came back to the bed. Looking at her face, he sighed. 'Dearest Faith, the last thing I wanted was to upset you. Take all the time you need. I'll be waiting. I've always been waiting for you.'

This time, she couldn't keep back the tears. 'W-won't you kiss me goodbye?'

He gave her a wry smile. 'I'll kiss you "hello", and much more, when—if—you accept my suit.'

'Will I see you again?'

'Like this?' He swept his hand to encompass the room. 'Not unless you agree to become my wife. Before I leave, I'll have a word with the estate manager, letting him know you'll want to have workmen from the village come in to assist with repairs to the stables and the main house, if you'd like.'

She nodded, feeling at the moment entirely unequal to making any decisions at all. 'Yes, that would be helpful.'

'Very well. I'll be at the Bow and Snare, in the village. Send me a note when you and the boys are ready to depart, and I'll ride over to escort you.'

'What shall I tell the boys, when they ask why you've gone?' she asked, grasping at one last straw to keep him here.

'Tell them I'm making arrangements to escort them to their cousins, for more riding, fishing, and tree climbing. They'll be delighted at the prospect. As I imagine you will, to spend some time with your sister. Goodbye, my darling Faith.' With that, he turned and walked out the door.

She sagged back against the pillows, still shocked and

stunned. Should she scramble into her clothes, ready to guide him out if he got lost in the maze that was Ashedon Court?

But, no, competent Davie would have no trouble in daylight, navigating his way out. And he'd likely be long gone by the time she could summon her maid and hurry into her clothes.

Maybe instead, she'd replay in her mind the glorious night he'd given her—and not think about the paralysing decision he'd left her with.

But she didn't have to decide right away, she told herself, trying to unseat the leaden weight that pressed at her chest every time she thought of having to make that decision. She'd have time with Sarah, unhurried time to think over Davie's unexpected proposal.

There was no question she cared for him—perhaps more than she'd ever let herself realise, until he revealed his desire to build a life with her. But did she dare accept him—and believe in a happiness which had never in her life been anything but fleeting?

A few days later, Faith sat in the sunny morning room at Brookhollow Lodge in Highgate Village, awaiting the arrival of her sister Sarah for breakfast and the private chat she'd been in desperate need of since Davie's surprising proposal—had it only been four days ago?

Despite the bustle of preparing the boys for the trip to her sister's, giving final instructions to the servants at Ashedon Court, and consulting with the chief workmen and the steward who would be overseeing the repairs, and then the long journey, taken in short stages so as not to tire the boys, the urgent question of how she should respond to his proposal was seldom far from her mind.

He'd not made the choice any easier, falling back, as

he'd promised, into the role of helpful friend, freezing out any attempt she made to take his hand, forestalling any chance to snuggle close on the carriage seat by riding beside the vehicle all the way. At the inns where they'd broken the journey, he'd arranged for rooms and meals with calm efficiency, while skirting her efforts to manoeuvre him alone in a hallway or stable yard to claim a swift, reassuring kiss.

Was he trying to show her what it would be like, were she to refuse him and allow them to dwindle into fond, but distant friends? Or was he giving her a glimpse into what life would be if she accepted him, and after a year or two or five, he finally realised she was only a modestly accomplished, ordinary woman, and fell out of love with her?

Would she end up, ultimately, more wretched with him than without him?

All she knew was the polite distance he'd maintained between them on the trip to Brookhollow had driven her mad with regret, longing, frustrated desire, and uncertainty.

Take all the time you need, he'd said. But she must decide, soon. She couldn't exist with this decision weighing so heavily on her, she could hardly breathe.

She ought to make the decision on her own. She hadn't consulted anyone about personal matters for years—hadn't had anyone to consult. Until she'd found Davie again—but he couldn't help her now.

The last time she and Sarah had discussed something this important to her future, she'd blithely dismissed her elder sister's plea that she wait before rushing into marriage with the Duke. This time, she intended to listen closely to the advice of the wise older sister who knew them both so well—even though the final choice would have to be hers alone.

Sarah's arrival interrupted her tortured thoughts. 'Sorry I'm late—another minor crisis in the kitchen.' She came over to give Faith a kiss before pouring herself some coffee. 'Did the boys settle in well last night?'

'Yes, although they are so excited about spending time with their cousins, I'm betting they scarcely slept a wink.'

Sarah turned a penetrating glance on her. 'Nor did you, by the looks of it. What is troubling you? I wouldn't be surprised if you're suffering bad dreams, after the scare you had at Ashedon Court! Please God, such uprisings will soon be behind us.'

'It was frightening, I'll admit. Though Davie did a wonderful job, settling down the rioters and restoring order.'

'I can't tell you how anxious we were after we heard about Wollaton! Englemere was just setting out for Ashedon when we got Davie's note that you were all safe and well. We'll never be able to thank him enough for taking such swift action.'

After choking down the one sip of coffee she could manage without having it rise back up her throat, Faith traced a nervous finger on the polished mahogany table. 'That wasn't all the action he took. Before we left for Brookhollow, he…he asked me to marry him.'

Her eyes widening, Sarah set down her cup. 'He proposed to you! Though, when I consider it, I shouldn't be surprised. One would have to be blind not to have noticed how much he's cared for you, as far back as that first summer with Ned and Joanna. And when he escorted you here recently…well, one could torch kindling with the heat evident between you. He might not be what the world would consider a good match, but one couldn't hope to find a man of finer character.'

'He's the most excellent man I've ever met.' *Which made the idea of living without him even more devastating to contemplate.*

Sarah leaned closer, studying Faith. 'You didn't tell me how you answered him. From the distress on your face, I take it you haven't yet decided. I know there would be those who'd claim you'd be failing in your duties to young Ashedon and the estate to remarry so soon, but there are trustees and stewards to oversee all that. Certainly, accepting Davie would mean a huge loss of consequence, but I don't think the prestige of being a duchess ever mattered to you. I know how he feels about you. The only thing that does matter is how you feel about *him*. You certainly seemed lighter, happier, more at ease than I'd seen you in years when you came here with him. Does he make you happy?'

'Oh, yes! I feel more like myself with him—the self-confident, assured, happy self I used to be—than at any time since the early days of my marriage. It isn't that.'

'Do you love him?'

Faith nodded slowly. 'I…I think I do. How could one help loving a man who is so strong, principled and compassionate? Not just with me—with everyone, from the poorest crofter to the indigent factory worker. I'm so in awe of all he's accomplished, and admire so much all he wants to do for this country.'

'And you love the way he kisses you,' Sarah added with a naughty twinkle.

Faith felt herself blushing, glad her sister hadn't guessed how far beyond a kiss they'd already gone. 'Yes. That, too.'

'Than why do you hesitate?'

'He's so…wonderfully attentive, and caring, and ardent. So convinced he wants me for his wife, to love and cherish the rest of his life. Just like Ashedon was, during our courtship and the early days of our marriage. I believed with all my heart that our love would last for ever.'

'But it didn't,' Sarah said gently.

'No,' Faith replied, that small word inadequate to express the depth of devastation her marriage had become.

'The difference, you see—what Englemere and I suspected and what time proved—was that Ashedon never really loved you. Oh, he made a good show of it, I'll grant you. Flattered and indulged all his life, he was brought up to believe only what he wanted was important, with no thought given to the feelings or needs of anyone else. He wanted a convenient, pliable wife—that she adored him, he took as his due. So he played the part that would gain him what he wanted. Do you believe Davie is only playing a part?'

'No. I think he truly loves me, and I know he would never humiliate me as Ashedon did. But loving him, giving myself to him…and having him eventually grow distant, as Ashedon did, while remaining faithful and kind, as his character would compel him to, would be even worse than Ashedon's treachery.'

Wanting Sarah to understand, she made herself continue. 'In my heart, I'd known for a long time, years maybe, that Ashedon no longer cared about me, if he ever had. Then, a few months after Colin's birth, I caught him as he was going out for the evening and asked if I could go with him, or if he might consider remaining at home, so we might spend the evening together. "Why would I want to spend an evening here?" he said. "You've no wit, no conversation, to balance against your appalling country manners. Now that you've done your duty and provided me with sons…well, the charms of an *ingénue* are highly overrated." It wasn't just his words, cruel as they were—it was the *look* on his face…'

Nausea rose in her throat and her stomach twisted as she remembered it. 'Disgust, contempt, disdain. As if an insect had crawled upon his plate.'

Sarah reached over to take her hand. 'Oh, Faith! I'm so sorry.'

'I thought I should die, sitting there as he left me. Just…stop breathing, and fade into nothingness. But the nursery maid came running in, saying Colin was crying to be fed, so I got up, and walked out, and went on. Oh, Sarah, if Davie ever looked at me like that, I *would* die.'

'But you know he loves you! Why would he ever be so unkind?'

'The entire time he's known me, I've been the "unattainable ideal". The golden girl, destined to marry to a duke, mistress of a great house, descendant of an ancient line—someone far above him. What will he do when he's around me long enough to realise I'm just… ordinary?'

'Davie has never been impressed by the pomp and circumstance of aristocracy—quite the opposite! He's called to what he sees in *you*, Faith. The sweet and loving spirit we all cherished as you were growing up. But it isn't his love you must believe in, it's yourself. I hate that Ashedon destroyed your confidence in your own worthiness. Davie believes in the joyous, confident person you can become again. But you're not going to be happy anywhere, or with anyone, unless *you* believe in it.'

A knock at the door interrupted them, a kitchen maid curtsying to relay the latest event in the continuing crisis below stairs. Rising, Sarah pressed Faith's hand. 'I'm sorry, I must go. Trust in him, and yourself, Faith.'

Faith shook her head. 'I was so wrong before! Do I have the courage to risk it?'

'All life is a risk.' Sarah leaned over to kiss her forehead. 'Don't let Ashedon punish you a second time, the doubt he instilled keeping you from seizing what could make you happy. If you truly believe Davie *would* make you happy.'

She certainly endured enough years of misery, Faith thought as she watched her sister walk out. But if she took a leap of faith with Davie, would she be claiming that elusive happiness—or only grabbing more misery with both hands?

Restless, unable to eat a bite, her head throbbing, Faith threw down her napkin and exited the room after her sister. She headed for the garden, hoping to walk out some of her anxiety without encountering anyone with whom she'd have to attempt the unlikely job of masking it.

Trust in Davie's love? Trust in herself? How could she embrace such a choice with confidence? No one could predict the future; there were a thousand things that could and probably would happen to erode the bond between them, creating annoyance, dissension or distrust.

Could she imagine anything that would destroy her love and admiration for Davie? Even if he were to cease the wonderfully tender actions towards her that so boosted her confidence, the caring and compassionate man he was would still command her love and admiration. She could with utter confidence predict he would never act towards anyone with selfish disregard for their welfare, or sacrifice others to achieve his own ambitions.

Look how he'd tried to protect even the men who'd tried to burn Ashedon Court from the consequences of their rash actions. He could have ridden in with the magistrate at his heels, ready to send them all to jail and a harsh punishment.

No, she could not imagine losing her love for him. As for his *loving* her…the mere memory of his touch set the banked fires of her desires flaming.

Did she think him so naïve, so self-deceiving, that he did not believe as completely in whatever it was he saw in her?

All life is a risk, Sarah had said. Where had she misplaced the reckless confidence she'd possessed as a girl?

After the heartbreak of Ashedon, she'd retreated deep within herself, going through the motions of life, giving herself only to her boys. If she sent Davie away, she could retreat back into that world of shadows and that safe half-existence. Protected from pain. Protected from joy.

Or reach out with both hands to embrace it.

Wouldn't it be worth claiming a few months or years of joy, even if she eventually lost it—than never experience it at all?

Yes, it would, she decided. She would never be the sort of clever, accomplished woman she felt could fascinate a man for a lifetime. But she could summon up enough courage to claim this man, for now. For however long she could hold him.

Maybe, God willing, for ever.

Finally decided, she pivoted around and headed back to the house. She didn't want to waste another moment.

An hour later, her children confined to Sarah's care, with the admonition that, with luck, she wouldn't be returning to Brookhollow for several days, Faith mounted her borrowed horse and set off for London. Calm now after the raging storm of her uncertainty, her only anxiety was finding Davie—and making sure her initial refusal hadn't made *him* change his mind.

The journey to London accomplished much more speedily on horseback, at Sarah's suggestion, Faith looked in first at the committee rooms in Parliament, then went to check at the Quill and Gavel. Finding neither him nor any of the Hellions at either place, she stopped to see Maggie—who, after asking what was wrong, accepted Faith's plea that she not enquire further, and gave her the address she requested of Davie's rooms at Albany. Leaving with an assurance that, once all was settled, Maggie would be the first to know, Faith set out again.

Lamplighters were illumining the encroaching darkness when Faith, having left her horse at a nearby livery, at last entered the courtyard at Albany. Boldly talking her way past the porter with a claim of needing to consult Mr Smith at once on a matter of great personal urgency—quite an accurate assessment, actually—she paced down the hallway.

Standing before his door, knowing he was within and that her whole future hinged on what happened in the next few minutes, she hesitated. Trying to banish the anxiety that made her dizzy, she told herself to focus instead on the wonder that was Davie, and how glorious it would be to be held in his arms again.

With a firm knock, she walked in.

Wondering why the porter hadn't announced the visitor who had just entered, Davie looked up from his newspaper, ready to toss a disparaging remark at Ben or Christopher or Giles. He had to blink twice to make sure he wasn't dreaming, when instead, Faith's lovely form filled his vision.

Jumping to his feet, he went over to meet her. 'Faith, what are you doing here? Why didn't you send me a note, I would have—'

Seizing his shoulders, she cut off his protest by pulling him down for a fiery kiss that made him forget, for a moment, that she'd just risked her reputation by paying a forbidden call on a bachelor establishment. When they finally broke the kiss, he had to struggle to make his mind focus on anything beyond his body's urging that he carry her into his bedroom.

'I trust this means you've decided to accept my proposal?' he asked, sure—*almost* sure—but greedy to hear her say the words aloud.

'Yes, I'll marry you. I'm only sorry I made you wait so long for my answer.'

Wild exultation was running through his veins, feeding the barely banked fires of desire. 'Thank you, God,' he whispered, gathering her against his chest, the very idea that she was agreeing to marry him so spectacularly wonderful he couldn't quite get his mind around it. For long moments, he simply held her, imprinting into his brain the marvellous feel of her in his arms, the even more marvellous news that he would be able to keep her there.

The reality of the situation finally penetrating both desire and delight, he gently pushed her away. 'But you mustn't stay here! We must smuggle you back out, my foolish angel, and hope no one but the porter ever learns of your visit.'

'I don't care a fig for my reputation, and I don't want to go. I want to stay here, with you, tonight. Oh, make love to me again, all night, Davie! Let me feel down to my bones how right we are together, how right we will always be!'

'Do you trust that, now?'

She shook her head a little, tears glimmering on her lashes. 'I don't know. Maybe. All I do know is you make me happy, and for however long it lasts, I love you and I don't want to live without you.'

'It will be for ever, my darling. I'll send you to Maggie's—in the morning,' he added before she could protest, 'I'm not saint enough to turn you away tonight—and get a special licence, so we may be married immediately. But first, I'll do this. Wait here.'

'Couldn't you show me in the bedchamber?' she asked, giving him a pout.

'Once we get there, I intend for your attention to be totally occupied by other things,' he promised.

She grinned. 'I like the sound of that. Very well, get whatever it is you wish—but quickly.'

Davie hastened into his chamber, to a small box he kept on the table beside his bed. Carefully lifting out the ten-year-old article within, he carried it out to the sitting room.

'Hold out your hand.'

When, still looking mystified, Faith complied, Davie tied around her finger a small length of twine, soft and fragile now with age. 'Remember the night, just before you left for London, when I tied that on your finger, promising I would be your friend for ever?'

'You kept it all these years?' she marvelled.

'In words, I promised friendship, but in my heart, I vowed to love you for ever. I didn't think I'd ever be able to do anything about it, but I kept this as a memento to that love—and the chance that some day, it might come true. If I could keep this all those years with so little hope, how can you doubt that I'll love you even more passionately when you're my wife? I'll give you another ring, with gold and diamonds and whatever you wish, but nothing else could demonstrate how long and faithfully I've loved you. Or underscore my promise to love you to the future and back. But let's make it official.'

Going down on one knee, he took the hand with the twine ring and said, 'Will you marry me, Faith Wellingford Evers? To have and to hold from this day forth, for ever?'

She leaned down to kiss him. 'I will. And I'm ready to begin that marriage of minds and bodies right this minute.'

'Whatever you desire, my love.' With that, he snuffed out the candle, picked her up, and carried her to his chamber.

\* \* \* \* \*

# JOIN US ON SOCIAL MEDIA!

Stay up to date with our latest releases, author news and gossip, special offers and discounts, and all the behind-the-scenes action from Mills & Boon...

 millsandboon

 millsandboonuk

 millsandboon

*It might just be true love...*

# MILLS & BOON

## THE HEART OF ROMANCE

---

## A ROMANCE FOR EVERY KIND OF READER

---

**MODERN**

Prepare to be swept off your feet by sophisticated, sexy and seductive heroes, in some of the world's most glamourous and romantic locations, where power and passion collide.
**8 stories per month.**

**HISTORICAL**

Escape with historical heroes from time gone by. Whether your passion is for wicked Regency Rakes, muscled Vikings or rugged Highlanders, awaken the romance of the past.
**6 stories per month.**

**MEDICAL**

Set your pulse racing with dedicated, delectable doctors in the high-pressure world of medicine, where emotions run high and passion, comfort and love are the best medicine.
**6 stories per month.**

*True Love*

Celebrate true love with tender stories of heartfelt romance, from the rush of falling in love to the joy a new baby can bring, and a focus on the emotional heart of a relationship.
**8 stories per month.**

*Desire*

Indulge in secrets and scandal, intense drama and plenty of sizzl hot action with powerful and passionate heroes who have it all: wealth, status, good looks…everything but the right woman.
**6 stories per month.**

**HEROES**

Experience all the excitement of a gripping thriller, with an inter romance at its heart. Resourceful, true-to-life women and strong, fearless men face danger and desire - a killer combination!
**8 stories per month.**

**DARE**

Sensual love stories featuring smart, sassy heroines you'd want as best friend, and compelling intense heroes who are worthy of the
**4 stories per month.**

To see which titles are coming soon, please visit

## millsandboon.co.uk/nextmonth